4 Books in 1!

4 Books in 1!

Coco Simon

Simon Spotlight
New York   London   Toronto   Sydney   New Delhi

This book is a work of fiction. Any references to historical events, real people, or real places are used fictitiously. Other names, characters, places, and events are products of the author's imagination, and any resemblance to actual events or places or persons, living or dead, is entirely coincidental.

SIMON SPOTLIGHT
An imprint of Simon & Schuster Children's Publishing Division
1230 Avenue of the Americas, New York, New York 10020
This Simon Spotlight edition July 2022
Copyright © 2019, 2020 by Simon & Schuster, Inc.
All rights reserved, including the right of reproduction in whole or in part in any form.
SIMON SPOTLIGHT and colophon are registered trademarks of Simon & Schuster, Inc.
Hole in the Middle, *So Jelly!*, and *Family Recipe* text by Valerie Dobrow
A Donut for Your Thoughts text by Samantha Thornhill
For information about special discounts for bulk purchases, please contact Simon & Schuster Special Sales at 1-866-506-1949 or business@simonandschuster.com.
The text of this book was set in Bembo Std.
Manufactured in the United States of America 0522 FFG
10 9 8 7 6 5 4 3 2 1
ISBN 978-1-6659-1842-8
ISBN 978-1-5344-6027-0 (*Hole in the Middle* ebook)
ISBN 978-1-5344-6030-0 (*So Jelly!* ebook)
ISBN 978-1-5344-6540-4 (*Family Recipe* ebook)
ISBN 978-1-5344-7374-4 (*A Donut for Your Thoughts* ebook)
These titles were previously published individually in hardcover and paperback by Simon Spotlight.

#1
Hole in the Middle
7

#2
So Jelly!
143

#3
Family Recipe
287

#4
A Donut for Your Thoughts
441

Hole in the Middle

Chapter One
Donuts Are My Life

My grandmother started Donut Dreams, a little counter in my family's restaurant that sells her now-famous homemade donuts, when my dad was about my age. The name was inspired by my grandmother's dream to save enough money from the business to send him to any college he wanted, even if it was far away from our small town.

It worked. Well, it kind of worked. I mean, my grandmother's donuts are pretty legendary. Her counter is so successful that instead of only selling donuts in the morning, the shop is now open all day. Her donuts have even won all sorts of awards, and there are rumors that there's a cooking show on TV that might come film a segment about how she started Donut Dreams from virtually nothing.

My grandmother, whom I call Nans—short for Nana—raised enough money to send my dad to college out of state all the way in Chicago. But then he came back. I've heard Nans was happy about that, but I'm not because it means I'm stuck here in this small town.

So now it's my turn to come up with my own "donut dreams," because I am dreaming about going to college in a big, glamorous city somewhere far, far away. Dad jokes that if I do go to Chicago, I have to come back like he did.

No way, I thought to myself. Nobody ever moves here, and nobody ever seems to move away, either. It's just the same old, same old, every year: the Fall Fling, the Halloween Hoot Fair, Thanksgiving, Snowflake Festival, New Year's, Valentine's Day and the Sweetheart Ball . . . I mean, we know what's coming.

Everyone makes a big deal about the first day of school, but it's not like you're with new kids or anything. There's one elementary school, one middle school, and one high school.

Our grandparents used to go to a regional school,

which meant they were with kids from other towns in high school. But the school was about forty-five minutes away, and getting there and back was a big pain, so they eventually decided to keep everyone at the high school here. It's a big old building where my dad went to school, and his brother and my aunt, and just about everyone else's parents.

Some kids do go away for college. My BFF Casey's sister, Gabby, is one of them. She keeps telling Casey that she should go to the same college so they can live together while Gabby goes to medical school, which is her dream. It's a cool idea, but what's the point of moving away from everything if you just end up moving in with your sister?

Maybe it's that I don't have a sister, I have a brother, and living with him is messy. I mean that literally. Skylar is ten. He spits globs of toothpaste in the sink, his clothes are all over his room, and he drinks milk directly from the carton, which makes Nans shriek.

My grandparents basically live with us now, which is a whole long story. Well, the short story is that my mother died two years ago. After Mom died, everyone was a mess, so Nans and Grandpa ended up helping out a lot. Their house is only a short drive down the street from us, so it makes sense they're around all the time.

Even their dog comes over now, which is good because I love him, but weird because Mom would never let us get a pet. I still feel like she's going to come walking in the door one day and be really mad that there's a dog running around with muddy paws.

My mother was an artist. She was an art teacher in the middle school where I'm starting this year, which will be kind of weird.

There's a big mural that all her students painted on one wall of the school after she died. The last time I was in the school was when they had a ceremony and put a plaque next to it with her name on it. Now I'll see it every day.

It's not like I don't think about her every day anyway. Her studio is still set up downstairs. It's a small room off the kitchen with great light. For a while none of us went in there, or we'd just kind of tiptoe in and see if we could still smell her.

Lately we use it more. I like to go in and sit in her favorite chair and read. It's a cozy chair with lots of pillows you can kind of sink into, and I like to think it's her giving me a hug. Dad uses her big worktable

Hole in the Middle

to do paperwork. The only people who don't go in are Nans and Grandpa. Dad grumbles that it's the one room in the house that Nans hasn't invaded.

Sometimes I catch Nans in the doorway, though, just looking at Mom's paintings on the walls. Mom liked to paint pictures of us and flowers. One wall is covered in black-and-white sketches of us and the other is this really cool, colorful collection of painted flowers with some close up, some far away, and some in vases. I could stare at them for hours.

I remember there used to be fresh flowers all over the house. Mom even had little vases with flowers in the bathrooms, which was a little crazy, especially since Skylar always knocked them over and there would be puddles of water everywhere.

Sometimes when I had a bad day she'd make a special little arrangement for me and put it next to my bed. When she was sick, I used to go out to her garden and cut them and make little bouquets for her. I'd put them on her night table, just like she did for me. Nans always makes sure there are flowers on the kitchen table, but it's not really the same.

Grandpa and Nans own a restaurant called the Park View Table. Locals call it the Park for short.

DONUT DREAMS

They don't get any points for originality, because the restaurant is literally across from a park, so it has a park view. But it seems to be the place in town where everyone ends up.

On the weekends everyone stops by in the mornings, either to pick up donuts and coffee or for these giant pancakes that everyone loves. Lunch is busy during the week, with everyone on their lunch breaks and some older people who meet there regularly, and dinnertime is the slowest. I know all this because I basically grew up there.

Nans comes up with the menus and the specials, and she's always trying out new recipes with the chef. Or on us. Luckily, Nans is a great cook, but some of her "creative" dishes are a little too kooky to eat.

Nans still makes a lot of the donuts, but Dad does too, especially the creative ones. Donut Dreams used to have just the usual sugar or jelly-filled or chocolate, which were all delicious, but Dad started making PB&J donuts and banana crème donuts.

At first people laughed, but then they started to try them. Word of mouth made the donuts popular, and for a little while, people were confused because they didn't realize Donut Dreams was a counter inside

Hole in the Middle

the Park. They instead kept looking for a donut shop.

My uncle Charlie gives my dad a hard time sometimes, teasing him that he's the "big-city boy with the fancy ideas." Uncle Charlie loves my dad, and my dad loves him, but I sometimes wonder if Uncle Charlie and Aunt Melissa are a little mad that Dad got to go away to school and they went to the state school nearby.

My dad runs Donut Dreams. Uncle Charlie does all the ordering for food and napkins and everything you need in a restaurant, and Aunt Melissa is the accountant who manages all the financial stuff, like the payroll and paying all the bills. So between my dad, his brother, and his sister, and the cousins working at the restaurant, it's a lot of family, all the time.

My brother, Skylar, and I are the youngest of seven cousins. I like having cousins, but some of them think they can tell me what to do, and that's five extra people bossing me around.

"There's room for everyone in the Park!" Grandpa likes to say when he sees us all running around, but honestly, sometimes the Park feels pretty crowded.

That's the thing: in a small town, I always feel like there are too many people. Maybe it's just that there are too many people I know, or who know me.

Right after Mom died I couldn't go anywhere without someone coming up to me and putting an arm around me or patting me on the head. People were nice, don't get me wrong, but everyone knows everything in a small town. Sometimes I feel like I can't breathe.

Mom grew up outside of Chicago, and that's where my other grandmother, her mother, still lives. I call her Mimi. We go there every Thanksgiving, which I love. I remember asking her once when we were at the supermarket why there were so many people she didn't know. She laughed and explained that she lived in a big town, where most people don't know each other.

It fascinated me that she could walk into the supermarket and no one there would know where she had just been, or that she bought a store-bought cake and was going to tell everyone she baked it. No one was peering into her cart and asking what she was making for lunch, or how the tomatoes tasted last week. Nans always wonders if Mimi is lonely, since she lives by herself, but it sounds nice to me.

Everyone in our family pitches in, but I officially

Hole in the Middle

start working at Donut Dreams next week for a full shift every day, which is kind of nice. I'll work for Dad. He bought me a T-shirt that says THE DREAM TEAM that I can wear when I'm behind the counter.

We have a couple of really small tables near the counter that are separate from the restaurant, so people can sit down and eat their donuts or have coffee. I'll have to clean those and make sure that the floor around them is swept too.

Uncle Charlie computerized the ordering systems last year, so all I'll have to do is just swipe what someone orders and it'll total it for me, keep track of the inventory, and even tell me how much change to give, which is good because Grandpa is a real stickler about that.

"A hundred pennies add up to a dollar!" he always yells when he finds random pennies on the floor or left on a table.

Dad will help me set up what we're calling my "Dream Account," which is a bank account where I'll deposit my paycheck. I figure if I can save really well for six years, I can have a good portion to put toward my dream college.

So we're going to the bank. And of course my

friend Lucy's mom works there. Because you can't go anywhere in this town without knowing someone.

"Well, hi, honey," she said. "Are you getting your own savings account? I'll bet you're saving all that summer money for new clothes!"

"Nope," said Dad. "This is college money."

"Oh, I see," she said, smiling. "In that case, let's make this official." She started typing information into the computer. "Okay. I have your address because I know it. . . ." She tapped the keyboard some more.

See what I mean? Everyone knows who I am and where I live. I wonder if people at the bank know how much money we have too.

After a few minutes, it was all set up. Afterward Dad showed me how to make a deposit and gave me my own bank card too.

I was so excited, not only because I had my own bank account, which felt very grown-up, but because the Dream Account was now crossed off my list, which meant I was that much closer to making my dream come true. I was almost hopping up and down in my seat in the car.

"You really want to get out of here, don't you?" asked Dad, and when he said it, it wasn't in his usual joking way. He sounded a little worried, and I immediately felt bad. It wasn't as if I just wanted to get away from Dad.

"You know," he said thoughtfully, "I get it."

"You do?" I asked.

"Yeah," he said. "I was the same way. I was itchy. I wanted to go see the big wide world."

We both stared ahead of us.

"I don't want to go to get away from you and Skylar," I said.

Dad nodded.

"But think of Wetsy Betsy."

Dad looked confused. "Who is Wetsy Betsy?"

"Wetsy Betsy is Elizabeth Ellis. In kindergarten she had an accident and wet her pants. And even now, like, seven years later, kids still call her Wetsy Betsy. It's like once you're known as something here, you can't shake it. You can't . . ." I trailed off.

"You can't reinvent yourself, you mean?" asked Dad.

"Exactly!" I said. "You are who you are and you can't ever change." I could tell Dad's mind was spinning.

"So who are you?" he asked after a few more minutes.

DONUT DREAMS

"What?" I asked.

"Who are you?" Dad asked. "If Elizabeth Ellis is Wetsy Betsy, then who are you?"

I took a deep breath. "I'm the girl whose mother died. I sometimes hear kids whisper about it when I walk by."

I saw Dad grimace. I looked out the window so I wouldn't have to watch him. We stayed quiet the rest of the way home.

We pulled up into our driveway and Dad turned off the car, but he didn't get out.

"I understand, honey. I really do. I understand dreaming. I understand getting away, starting fresh, starting over. But wherever you go, you take yourself with you, just remember that. You can start a new chapter and change things around, but sometimes you can't just rewrite the entire book," he said.

I thought about that. I didn't quite believe what he was saying, though. In school they were always nagging us about rewriting things.

"But you escaped," I said. "And then you just came back!"

"Well, you escape prison. I didn't see this place as a prison," Dad said. "But Nans as a warden, that's . . ."

Hole in the Middle

He started laughing. "Seriously, though, I left because I wanted an adventure. I wanted to meet new people and see if I could make it in a place where everyone didn't care about me and where I was truly on my own. I never had any plans to come back, but that's how it worked out."

"So why did you move back here?" I asked.

"Because of Mom," said Dad. "She loved this place. I brought her here to meet everyone and she didn't want to leave."

"But Mimi didn't want her to move here," I said, trying to piece together what happened.

I had always thought it was Dad who wanted to move back home. Mom and Dad met in college. She lived at school like Dad did, but Mimi was close by, so she could drive over for dinner. Mom and Dad hung out at Mimi's house a lot while they were in college.

"Noooo," Dad said slowly. "Mimi wasn't too thrilled about Mom's plan. She didn't really understand why Mom would want to move out here, so far from her family, and especially where there weren't a lot of opportunities for artists."

"So she changed her mind?" I asked.

I never remembered Mimi saying anything bad

about where we lived, but Dad would always tease her, saying, "So it worked out okay, didn't it, Marla?"

She came to visit twice a year and always seemed to have a good time. "It's a beautiful place to live," she would say, smiling.

"Well," said Dad. "It took Mimi a while to change her mind. But she saw how happy Mom was and how much everyone here loved Mom, so she was happy that Mom was happy. That's the thing about parents. They really just want their kids to be happy, even if they don't understand why they do things. If you decide to move away from here, I'll miss you every day, but if that's what you want to do and that's what makes you happy, then I will be there with the moving truck."

"So if I tell you I want to move to Chicago for college, you'll be okay with that?" I asked.

"If you promise to come home and visit me a lot," said Dad, grinning.

"Deal!" I said.

"I love you," said Dad.

"I love you back," I said.

"Okay, kiddo, let's go in for dinner. Nans goes mad when we're late."

Hole in the Middle

"Dad, isn't it correct to say that Nans gets angry? Because, like, animals go mad but people get angry."

"In that definition, Lindsay, I think that is an entirely correct way to categorize your grandmother when you are late for dinner. She gets mad!"

I giggled and opened the car door.

"Ready, set, run to the warden!" said Dad, and we raced up to the house, bursting with laughter.

Chapter Two
First Day of Work

The plan was that I'd start working at Donut Dreams two weeks before school started. That way I'd get into my regular routine and not have to adjust to a job at the Park and a new school at the same time. For the school year, I'll work after school two days a week and one day on the weekends.

But since much of the waitstaff take vacations at the end of the summer, it was all hands on deck, according to Grandpa, and the whole family was taking full-day shifts at the restaurant.

Mornings were always way complicated because things start early in the restaurant business. Even if the Park didn't open until six thirty in the morning, that meant everyone, including the cooks, the busboys, and the waitresses, got there by five o'clock to start prepping the food, brewing coffee, sorting the daily bread deliveries, and making sure the ovens were on.

Since we own Donut Dreams, everyone just assumes that we eat donuts at every meal, and that they're stacked everywhere in our house. But we actually eat like everyone else, and Nans only lets us have donuts on the weekends, just like Mom did.

So Monday morning I put on my Dream Team T-shirt and got downstairs early. Nans already had my fruit and juice at my place at the table. Since she got up early to make the donuts, by the time Skylar and I got up, she joked that she should be making lunch. Dad had to be at the restaurant early in the morning, so after Mom died, Nans was the one who came back home from the restaurant to stay with us when Dad had to leave.

Nans was making me scrambled eggs and I was surprised to see Skylar, still in his pj's, eating his cereal.

"What are you doing up?" I asked. "It's not like you have to go to work today."

"Nans woke me up," he whined. "We have to drive you to work. So even if I don't have to go to work, I still have to get up."

DONUT DREAMS

"You can get in the car in your pajamas!" Nans said, exasperated. "I just can't leave you here alone while I run Lindsay to work!"

Skylar rolled his eyes. "Well, can I at least get a donut while we're there?"

Nans sighed. "Sure," she said with a grin. "On Saturday."

It probably seems weird to eat breakfast before you go to work in a restaurant, but working in a restaurant is hard, and you don't get a lot of breaks. It's not like you can stuff snacks in your apron pockets either. You're on your feet the whole time and running around, and you can barely sip a drink, let alone eat. During slow times the staff will grab a plate in the kitchen, but as soon as you have a customer you have to put it down, so no one ever has a leisurely burger or anything.

Nans jingled her keys, and Skylar sighed loudly and pushed back his chair. I took one last look in the mirror before we left, and then Nans drove down the curvy road toward the restaurant.

I could ride my bike to work, especially in nice weather, but Mom would never, ever let us ride on Park Street. She said people went too fast around the curves.

Hole in the Middle

It's kind of weird that even though Mom died, some of her rules are still here, and nobody has tried to get rid of them. At first we did things like staying up really late because everyone was so distracted, and nobody seemed to notice. Plus, there were, like, hundreds of people at the house and stopping in at all hours.

But one night at dinner, Dad said, "Okay, life as we know it is going to be very different, but there are ground rules that stay the same."

After that we had bedtimes and regular meals and all the old rules seemed to kick back in.

When we pulled up to the restaurant, it was six fifteen. You could tell Nans was torn, because she wanted to go in and check things out and get a few things done in the office, but Sky was scowling.

Nans glanced in the back seat. "Sky, do you want to go say hi to your dad?"

But before he could answer, Dad came bounding out of the restaurant. "A fine family morning!" he bellowed, smiling at me. "Look at this wonderful employee on her first day at Donut Dreams!"

He actually looked really proud, and I kind of blushed a little.

DONUT DREAMS

"She's going to be spectacular, as always!" said Nans, smiling.

"And I get to see my boy!" said Dad, reaching in to give Sky a squeeze.

"I had to get up early," Skylar whined.

"Good practice for when school starts!" said Dad. "And since you made the very big effort of getting into the car, I have a little treat for you." He handed Skylar a bag.

"Donuts!" screamed Skylar, and Dad laughed.

"First-day-of-work exception," Dad said. "Don't get too used to it!" He gave Skylar a kiss on the head and added, "Have fun at camp!"

Then he turned to me and opened the car door. "And you, my dear, are mine for the day. Let's get to work!"

My cousin Kelsey was also working behind the counter at Dreams, and she gave me a quick wave when I came in.

Kelsey and my other four cousins all work at the Park and Dreams. Kelsey is only older than me by a month and a half, but she always tells people I'm her younger cousin.

"You know what to do?" asked Kelsey.

Hole in the Middle

I nodded and slipped behind the counter with her and put on an apron. Dad was talking to the manager of the restaurant about something, so I turned around and stared at the rows of donuts, making sure they were all lined up and that the shelves were clean.

When Mom was alive I went home right after school, but after she died, Dad would pick Skylar and me up and bring us to the restaurant so we could be near him. We'd hang out at a table and do our homework or color for a few hours before Nans would take us home for dinner. I had watched the counter at Dreams for a few years, so now I knew exactly what had to be done.

If you look around, a restaurant is kind of a fascinating place. It's usually busy—if it's a good restaurant, that is—and there are people sitting and talking about stuff, and if you pay attention, you can learn a lot. And most people don't stop talking when someone comes over to the table. So even if I helped clear a table or dropped off a glass of water, I could really get an earful. That's what I loved most, picking up little pieces about people that you wouldn't normally know.

Grandpa loves to go around and talk to everyone,

and he stops and chats with the regulars, especially the ones at the counter in the morning. He knows everything that was going on in town, but he never spills it to any of us, which drove Mom crazy.

"Oh, come on," she'd say. "I know they were probably talking about it at the Park. What's the dirt?"

And he would just smile and shake his head and say, "I just pour the coffee. What do I know?"

But Grandpa never misses a beat, so you have to be on your toes. I once saw him correct people for not properly wiping down a table, or not setting it right, or sloshing a glass of water when they put it down.

I know that he likes things tidy, which is hard when you sell donuts, because some of them have sprinkles or are crumbly. So when you lift them off the tray, you get crumbs everywhere—on the shelf, on the floor, and sometimes on the counter.

At Dreams there's a lot of wiping and sweeping, because if Grandpa sees sprinkles all over the glass counter, he won't be pleased. He'll say, "Is that counter eating those sprinkles?" So the first thing I did was wipe down the counter, which was already clean.

"Ugh," whispered Kelsey, "it's the East twins."

The East twins were running up to the case and

putting their fingers all over the glass front. The two boys were adorable, but every time they came in, they made a huge mess.

"Hi, Mrs. East," said Kelsey. "What can we get you today?"

Mrs. East always looked like she'd just run through a windstorm. There were always papers coming out of her bag, and her clothes were usually wrinkled or stained.

But she was really nice, and after Mom died she made us a lot of dinners and brought them over. She even came over with a picnic lunch one day for me and Sky and took us to the park.

"Oh, let me get the boys settled here," she said, lifting them into chairs. "Jason, please stop hitting your brother!"

"That one, that one!" the boys started yelling, waving their little hands at the donuts.

"Boys!" said Mrs. East. "Use your manners! And Christopher, stop screaming!"

The boys scrambled off their chairs and ran back to the counter. Luckily, there was no one else waiting, because it took them a full ten minutes to choose their donuts.

DONUT DREAMS

I had one hand over the chocolate iced one when Christopher yelled, "No, no, no, not that one!" and I had to move my hand around the shelf until it was hovering over the "right" one.

"Thank you," said Mrs. East. "You girls are amazingly patient! And I'm more frazzled today than usual. We just got back from vacation with my mom, and even though we love them, moms can be such a pain sometimes. Right, girls?"

She looked up as she was handing us the money for the donuts and froze. Her eyes went wide as she looked at me, remembering, and then her hand flew over her mouth.

Kelsey shifted from foot to foot nervously.

This happens a lot. People will say things and then be really scared that they said the wrong thing in front of you. Before Mom died, even when she was sick, all of a sudden everyone was really careful about what they said around me. For a month after Mom died, my friends wouldn't even talk about their moms in front of me.

I talked to Aunt Melissa about it, because she was who I went to for a lot of stuff these days.

"Honey, people are trying to be considerate. But

sometimes you have to help them, too," Aunt Melissa told me.

Poor Mrs. East looked a little like she might cry. Kelsey looked at me expectantly.

"Yeah, you should hear Kelsey complain about Aunt Melissa," I joked.

Kelsey opened the cash drawer and smiled. "Yeah, but she's got nothing on Nans, and you basically live with Nans."

We laughed, but Mrs. East still stood there, silent. I could tell she still felt awful.

"That'll be five fifty, please," said Kelsey, and Mrs. East suddenly looked down and realized she still had the donut money in her hand.

"Oh thank you, honey," she said.

She took the donuts to the boys, who shoved them into their mouths in five seconds flat. Then she walked back over and grabbed some extra napkins.

"Sometimes you take things for granted," she said to me, I guess as an apology. "How was your summer, Lindsay? You excited for your first day at Bellgrove Middle School? Oh and the big Fall Fling is soon, right? Did you do any dress shopping this summer?"

Fall Fling is, I guess, a big deal. It's the fall dance at

the middle school, and everybody goes. I think they go because there's not much else to do, but kids start talking about it around the Fourth of July.

My BFF, Casey, had already started looking online for a dress, and she's been poking me to go shopping. The thing is that shopping for school is a little weird these days. Usually Aunt Melissa takes me and Kelsey to the mall that's an hour and a half away and we stock up, or we just order stuff online.

"I'm not ready to start thinking about school," I said. "It's still summer!"

"You're right!" laughed Mrs. East. "You enjoy every last drop of summer!"

Then she went over to try to wipe the boys' faces, which were covered in donut icing. It was also in their hair.

"So did you pick out a dress yet?" I asked Kelsey.

"Not yet," she said. "I found a few online that Mom said she'd order so I can try them on. Here, I'll show you."

She grabbed her phone from behind the counter, which was a big no-no. Grandpa did not let anyone have a phone when they were "on the floor," which meant out in the open in the restaurant.

Hole in the Middle

"You have to pay full attention!" he'd say.

I hated this rule, because if there was some downtime, it could get really boring.

Dad came over then. "Are you girls doing okay?" he asked, eyeing the mess the Easts were making.

"Yep," said Kelsey. "We've got it, Uncle Mike." She slipped her phone into her back pocket.

"Kelsey, you know the rule," said Dad. "And if Grandpa catches you, it won't be pretty."

"I asked to see her dress," I said, trying to cover for her.

"What dress?" asked Dad.

"The dress she might wear for Fall Fling."

Dad looked confused.

"Fall Fling is a big deal, Mike," said Aunt Melissa, who had come up behind him.

"Oh, so I guess . . . well . . . we'll have to get Lindsay a dress?" he said, and he sounded so scared we all laughed.

But I had kind of wondered about it. I mean, Aunt Melissa usually took me shopping for school clothes, but no one had mentioned dress shopping. There was one store in town that had some fancy stuff, and that's where Casey's mom would probably take her.

"It's covered, Mike," said Aunt Melissa. "You're a great brother, but I would never count on you to pick out a dress."

Dad looked relieved.

"So you bought me one?" I asked, confused.

"Nope," said Aunt Melissa. "Your grandma Mimi did. Actually, she bought ten."

"Mimi?" I asked. "*Ten* dresses?"

"Yes," said Aunt Melissa. "There's some store near her that specializes in this kind of thing. I think she originally bought a dozen, but I told her that was crazy, so she narrowed it down to ten."

"Ten?" yelped Dad.

"Well, she's only going to keep one," said Aunt Melissa. "Unless you can wear more than one dress at a time. Can you, Linds?" she asked, teasing.

"So wait," Dad said. "Lindsay's grandma picked out her dresses? Can't Lindsay pick out her own clothes?"

Aunt Melissa laughed. "Your grandmother has wonderful taste," she said to me. "But there's a lot to choose from, don't worry. We will make sure you love whatever you end up wearing. Plus, she's insisted on bringing them when she comes, so she'll—" She stopped midsentence. "Oops."

Hole in the Middle

"When is she coming?" I asked.

"Melissa!" said Dad. Then he sighed. "Okay, Mimi is coming for a surprise visit. Or at least it was supposed to be a surprise. She wanted to be here for you guys on the first day of school."

That was a little weird.

"Well, you know, it's a big deal, especially because you're starting middle school. She wanted to be here," said Dad.

"We're going to have a little dress party," said Aunt Melissa. "Kelsey, Molly, Jenna, and I are coming, and Nans, of course. Plus Aunt Sabrina and Lily. And we thought we'd invite Casey, too."

Aunt Sabrina is married to Uncle Charlie, and she's my cousins Lily and Rich's mom.

"I'm not invited?" asked Dad.

"Definitely not," said Aunt Melissa. "We already have too many opinions with that crew."

"My little girl is going to a dance," said Dad, and he got a little teary.

"Is anyone working today or should we all have a cup of tea?" asked Grandpa, whispering loudly behind us.

"It's okay, Dad," said Aunt Melissa. "We just had

DONUT DREAMS

a five-minute family huddle about scheduling." She winked at us.

"Yep," said Dad, taking her cue. "And here's Lindsay reporting for her first day at Donut Dreams."

Grandpa beamed. "There's always room for family in the Park!" he bellowed. "Now get back to work, everyone!"

After we cleaned up from the East twins, which required sweeping and mopping the floor and cleaning the table and chairs they'd sat in, it was a little slow.

The lunchtime crew was getting busy on the other side of the restaurant, and I saw my cousins: Jenna, Kelsey's older sister, and Lily in their waitress uniforms, serving table after table.

Jenna, Lily, and Lily's older brother, Rich, were the only ones allowed to wait on tables, because they were old enough. Molly, Kelsey's other sister, was a runner, which meant she filled the glasses at the tables, brought extra ketchup or hot sauce if someone asked for it, and replaced a napkin if someone dropped it on the floor—stuff like that. Then Kelsey and I were on the Dream Team. One day Skylar would probably work here too.

Hole in the Middle

We got a little busier after lunch, when people would buy a donut to go. Kelsey and I had a good rhythm together, with one of us putting the donuts in a bag and the other one ringing up the customers and keeping the line moving. (We knew some of the regulars' orders already.)

Principal Clarke, who was the principal of the middle school where I'd be going, smiled at me as she came up in line.

"Well, I think you'll be joining us soon, Lindsay," she said.

"Yes, ma'am," I said. "Looking forward to it!"

"Oh, I can't wait to have you. It's going to be a great year!" She watched as Kelsey packed her dozen donuts. "I'm headed over for a meeting now and thought I'd sweeten up some of the teachers!"

"Well, donuts usually do the trick!" I said.

I wondered about the teachers. Some of them were friends of Mom's. But even if you know someone, they can act totally different when they're in front of a classroom.

After Principal Clarke left, Kelsey whispered, "The sweetest donut in the world won't sweeten Mrs. Gable up."

I giggled because she was right.

Mrs. Gable taught at the middle school and also happened to be my next-door neighbor. She was what Nans called "a prune." She was always complaining about things and was never really friendly.

Dad always shoveled her walk and helped rake her leaves anyway, which I thought was nice, since she was always yelling over the fence that Sky and I were making too much noise in the backyard.

Eventually, we slowed down again. We had to run an inventory report, which showed how many donuts and which kinds we'd sold, so that we could plan better and not run out. But since Uncle Charlie made the system automatic, we did that in about a minute.

Kelsey and I leaned on the counter. "Are you nervous about middle school?" she asked. "Because it's different."

"Not really," I said. "How different can it be?"

"You wouldn't think that much, but it is," said Kelsey. "At least that's what Jenna tells me."

I raised an eyebrow.

Jenna always acts like she knows everything, and Kelsey and her sister Molly always believe everything she says. Since Jenna is already in high school, they act like she's the queen. Jenna's always been supersweet to me and I love her, but sometimes her know-it-all attitude can get a little irritating.

"So according to Jenna, how is it different?" I asked.

"Well," said Kelsey, "for one thing there's more homework. And you move around from class to class a lot more."

I expected those things. I mean, last year Mrs. Graves told us every single day, "You'll see next year in middle school . . . the teachers won't tolerate anything less than your best. And there will be a lot more work!"

And moving around from class to class? It might be nice to get a bigger change of scenery. I still wasn't worried.

"So what kind of dresses do you think Mimi picked out?" asked Kelsey.

"Don't know," I said, starting to wonder myself. "There are lots more stores near where she lives, so she probably has a range, right?"

Kelsey shrugged. "Well, there's definitely more there than there are here. I mean, there's only one dress store in town. So you're lucky, because your dress will probably be really different from everyone else's."

"Yeah," I said, perking up. "That's true, and pretty cool."

Dad came over just then and whispered, "Elbows off the counters, girls, and look alive . . . or Grandpa will eat you alive!"

We giggled and stood up straight.

The main restaurant always had customers, but Donut Dreams definitely had busy times and not very busy times. We swept the floor again and moved the donuts around on the shelf, but there wasn't a whole lot to do.

I felt bad because my other cousins were running around the restaurant. It wasn't East boys' level of crazy, but my friend Hannah's three year-old brother, Tristan, could be a handful, and he kept dropping his silverware on the floor. Molly would have to scoot over, pick it up, and bring him a new fork or spoon.

Mrs. Wood was always really nice, but even she was getting tired of Tristan's behavior.

"For goodness' sake!" she yelped. "No more forks! That's it!"

Molly froze, a new fork in hand.

"Molly, honey, you can leave that with me, and

Hole in the Middle

when Tristan starts behaving, he can have his fork," Mrs. Wood said.

Molly put the fork on the napkin, as Grandpa taught us to do, and skittered away. She shot us a look across the room and rolled her eyes.

I wasn't really sure why Molly was a runner and Kelsey and I were "on the counter," but that's the way it was set up.

Maybe because Molly is technically a little older than us, even though we're all in the same grade at school. Molly was adopted, and right when she came home with Aunt Melissa and Uncle Chris, they found out they were having a baby, and that was Kelsey.

But even though Molly is ten months older, a fact she likes to point out a lot, Kelsey and Molly are pretty much the same age. Grandpa used to call them the "almost twins" until last year, when Molly threw a fit about it.

"That one has sass," Nans said, when Molly exploded at Grandpa.

"She has spunk, and we love her for it," said Aunt Melissa. "And she's right. The girls aren't twins."

Molly's spunk might be the other reason that she wasn't working behind a counter. I could totally see her saying to the East twins, "Just pick a donut already!"

Plus, Molly has a lot of energy, and she doesn't mind running around.

Donut Dreams closed at six o'clock every day. Nans said you couldn't really keep donuts fresh past that point, and not a lot of people eat donuts at night, which is a strange but true fact. It got really, really slow in the afternoon, so I took my break.

When I came back to the counter, I worried a little bit because in our family we always talk about "business" and whether "business is slow" or "business is good." Busy was always good, slow was not.

Jenna dropped off a tray full of food to the Woods' table, then came over to us.

"How are you doing, girls?" she asked. "Can you spare a cinnamon donut? I'm starving."

Kelsey reached into the case and put a cinnamon donut on a napkin.

"Oh, that was such hard work," said Jenna. "You sure you guys can handle this job?"

"Maybe," I said.

Jenna laughed. "You can definitely handle it. My sister Kelsey is not a fan of working."

Hole in the Middle

"Well, it's the end of summer," Kelsey whined. "Everyone else is at the lake today!"

"They've been at the lake all summer!" said Jenna. "How is today any different?" She had a point.

"Because it's like the last stretch of summer that we should hold on to before we go back to school."

Jenna gave her a look.

"Trust me, Kelsey," she said. "You aren't missing anything."

Jenna and I agreed on life here. Jenna was always bored and always planning.

"That one's got her eye on the door," Nans always said, and Aunt Melissa would sigh.

"She has big dreams. But she'll come back," she would reply. "They always do. Just wait and see."

But with Jenna I wasn't so sure. She was constantly talking about moving to Los Angeles, where the weather was beautiful all year. Jenna studied really hard and was always talking about her grades and whether they were good enough to get into a good college.

Jenna took the donut into the kitchen to eat. That was another rule here: no eating on the floor.

I know, it's crazy, right? I mean, we make and serve

food but can't eat in front of the customers. You'd think they'd want us to advertise that the food is so delicious we eat it ourselves. But on the other hand, I guess it wouldn't be good for a customer to ask us a question and us to answer with a mouthful of donut.

"Is Mom taking you home after work?" she asked Kelsey.

"I think so," said Kelsey. "But we have to wait for Molly's shift to end too. That's another hour."

"Well, maybe Uncle Mike can drop you off," said Jenna. "I think Lily is driving me, or maybe Rich."

Lily and Rich were both older, and both of them had their driver's licenses. Rich was the oldest cousin, and Skylar was the youngest. Nans joked that her two grandsons bookended the girls in between.

At big family dinners, I always felt a little sorry for Rich because he was definitely outnumbered, but Sky loved him and followed him everywhere.

Finally it was closing time, which meant we had to clear the shelves, clean the counters, empty the trash, and close out the register. Grandpa didn't like us to close out until actual closing time, because he said it turned away customers if they thought they needed to rush before you went home.

Hole in the Middle

So Kelsey and I watched until the clock said six o'clock on the dot, and then we sprang into close-mode. We made a good team and played Rock-Paper-Scissors to see who had trash duty, which was the worst.

You had to empty the trash, throw the bag into the Dumpster in the back, then lug the trash can into the parking lot and hose it down. Even though there should have been just napkins and cups, there was always something really gross in the trash can. One time I had to scrape out gum, and it was awful.

"Great job today, girls!" said Dad as we signed out.

Everyone who worked at the Park recorded when they started working and when they stopped. Aunt Melissa was a stickler for records, and she was always complaining that someone didn't log out.

"Ready to do it again tomorrow?" asked Grandpa.

Kelsey sighed. "Ugh."

"Hey, young lady," said Grandpa. "You should consider yourself lucky to have a job!"

"Grandpa, I am!" she said, pouting. "But it's the last few days before school starts!"

"And then what happens?" Grandpa teased. "The big bad school monster comes out?"

Kelsey laughed. "Grandpa! We will have homework and we have to sit in school all day and not do fun things like swim in the lake and stay up late!"

"Oh, my poor, poor granddaughter," said Grandpa. "Are you allergic to work? Because if you are, we may need to kick you out of the family!"

"Dad!" said Aunt Melissa. "You can never kick anyone out of this family!"

"Especially not me!" said Kelsey.

She was right. Kelsey was always Grandpa's favorite. It wasn't like he didn't love all of us, but there was something about Kelsey that allowed her to act in a way that would have made Grandpa very prickly with the rest of us.

Nans said that it was because Kelsey was named after Grandpa's mother Katherine, and that Kelsey was very much like her.

"I'm taking the girls home," said Dad. "Melissa is waiting for Molly to finish her shift. I'll be back soon."

Kelsey and I followed him out to the car. We had been inside for most of the day, so the sun felt especially hot and bright. We blinked as we walked.

"Melissa said I could drop you at the lake if you wanted, Kels," said Dad.

Hole in the Middle

"I can't go like this!" Kelsey said. "I'm in my work clothes."

"But it's just the lake," Dad said.

"Uncle Mike, you can't go to the lake in work clothes," said Kelsey. "Besides, everyone is probably headed home now anyway."

Dad shrugged. Our town isn't that big, but it's kind of spread out in parts, so there are a bunch of us who live five minutes away and then there are people like Kelsey, who live on the other side of the lake.

Some people have boats and just row or drive across the lake instead of taking a car. There have been a lot of stories about kids taking boats out at night, and Dad has already hammered it into our heads that it's too dangerous to do that.

At Kelsey's house, Uncle Chris opened the door when he heard the car pull up and waved to us.

"See you tomorrow," I said to Kelsey as she opened the car door, and she sighed.

It was still pretty sticky and hot. I guess a lot of people were on vacation, because the town seemed quiet, which was kind of nice.

"So how was your first day?" asked Dad as we drove away from Kelsey's house.

"Pretty good," I said. "A little slow."

"Yeah," said Dad. "Time of year. You'll see, it will speed up. That's when the days go a lot faster."

Dad and I drove in the quiet. It was nice having this time with just him, without Skylar or Nans or Grandpa or a million other family members. I actually didn't mind the slow pace of the day. I hoped things didn't speed up too quickly.

Chapter Three
My BFF Is Back!

I didn't have to worry about things going quickly, because even though the next day was kind of slow at Donut Dreams, it had a nice rhythm.

Kelsey and I were pretty good about splitting the "ick" stuff, as we called it, like hosing down the mat behind the counter or making sure the chairs were clean underneath (you wouldn't believe). I liked chatting with the customers, and I knew almost everyone who came in.

After a flurry of morning customers, I had a second to sip some water. I was itching to check my phone because I knew my best friend, Casey, was coming home today, and I couldn't wait to see her.

But even though my phone was in my apron

pocket, Grandpa had been especially vigilant this morning, and I didn't want him to catch me using it.

Grandpa has been telling every customer that he now has six out of seven grandchildren working at the restaurant.

"One more and it's a full house!" he'll say.

I cannot imagine Sky working . . . at all. He'd probably complain the entire time and try to eat all the donuts.

On the one hand, it is nice to work with my family because we help each other out. One day, while here after school, Lily dropped a huge tray she was carrying, and it made such a loud crashing sound that everyone stopped talking and stared at her.

In a flash Molly, Jenna, and Rich ran over to help her, and they got everything up off the ground in record time.

Another time crazy Mr. Brown, who is known to have a temper, yelled at Jenna for not toasting his bread well enough, and Grandpa walked over and said, "Hey, Ed, are you yelling at one of my favorite granddaughters over a tuna sandwich?" and calmed him down right away.

Family always has your back, and while Grandpa

can be tough, he is also pretty protective of us.

I was busy wiping down the counter when I heard someone scream, "I'M BAAAAAACK!" That could only be one person: Casey, my best friend in the entire world! We've been friends since we were born, because we were born exactly one day apart and were in the hospital together.

She has gone to sleepaway camp for the past few summers, which generally makes me miserable because I miss her so much. At her camp you can't have computers or phones, so she can't e-mail me, let alone text me, and I hate not being able to talk to her. Casey sometimes sends postcards, but it's not the same thing.

I spun around and Casey charged at me, hugging me over the counter.

"So how much did you miss me?" she asked.

"A lot!" I said.

"I need to know everything that I missed this summer!" she said.

I blinked. "Seriously? You missed nothing, Casey. You know that!"

"Really?" she asked. "I was hoping something exciting might have happened."

DONUT DREAMS

"Um . . . no," I said.

"Well, you got a job!" she said, grinning. "Spin around and let me see your uniform."

I spun around, pointing to the DREAM TEAM on the back of the shirt.

"Nice, nice," she said.

"Casey!" Kelsey squealed, coming back from the kitchen.

She was so happy to see Casey, she almost dropped the tray she was carrying.

"I have returned!" said Casey dramatically.

"Wow, you look different," said Kelsey.

I looked at Casey. She did look different.

First of all, she was wearing a little makeup, which was surprising because I knew her mom hadn't let her wear any before the summer. She also seemed to be a few inches taller.

She was wearing shorts and a T-shirt, but she looked . . . well, more put together or something, not like she just threw clothes on, which I knew for a fact was what she usually did. And they were usually clothes she had stashed under her bed. She had on a cute pair of sandals, and her toes were painted purple with glitter. Her hair, which was usually in a ponytail, was down and bouncy and curled like she'd just had it styled.

"Did you just get your hair cut?" I asked.

"No, but I used a blow-dryer," she said.

"You used a blow-dryer in August?" I asked.

Normally, I only blow-dried my hair when it was freezing cold and Nans was yelling that I couldn't possibly go outside with wet hair or it would freeze on my head.

"I have been dying for those sandals!" said Kelsey. "But Mom won't let me get them. Did your feet grow too or can I borrow them?"

"Kelsey, are you taking the shoes off poor Casey as soon as she returns to our fine town?" asked Dad, who was grinning.

He loved Casey and came out from the kitchen to say hello the minute he heard her voice. "Hey, Case. Did you have any big summer adventures?"

"I did!" said Casey very seriously. "I had some monumental softball games."

Then she burst out laughing. "It was great. I had a lot of fun, and it was nice to get away."

I'll bet, I thought.

I had asked Dad if I could go to summer camp,

but he wasn't too into the idea. I made a note to myself to start bugging him about it early for next summer. Maybe he'd change his mind next year.

Casey's phone buzzed, and she looked at it with a giant smile on her face. I had never seen her smile like that before.

"Who's bugging you besides me?" I asked.

"Oh, just someone I met at camp," she said. "His name is Matt."

Matt?

"You have a boyfriend?" Kelsey yelped.

"He's not really my . . . ," said Casey. "Well, he's kind of . . . I don't know. Summer's over, and he lives far away, so . . ."

My head was spinning a little. We barely spoke to boys. I mean, we spoke to them, but we had never looked at our boy *friends* as potential boyfriend material.

"You came home from camp with a boyfriend?" Dad asked. "Well, that's it. Lindsay is never, ever going to camp now!" He laughed.

"Daaaad," I said, crossing my arms.

"Who has a boyfriend?" asked Lily, whizzing by.

"Oh, Casey!"

Hole in the Middle

She gave Casey a squeeze and winked. "Well, I'd say that sounds like you had a good summer!"

"I did!" said Casey, and then her mom came in.

"Hey, I said you could run in, honey," Mrs. Peters said, exasperated.

Then she saw me. "Oh, Linds, I've missed you!"

"You missed Lindsay more than you missed me!" said Casey, all huffy.

"Well, she doesn't give me as hard a time as you do," said Mrs. Peters, embracing me in a big hug.

Mrs. Peters takes Casey to camp and then goes to visit her mother, Casey's grandma, for the summer. Casey's grandma moved to Arizona so she could be warm all year, which drives Mrs. Peters crazy because they don't get to see her a lot.

"How is Granny?" I asked.

"Good, good," said Mrs. Peters. "She sends her love and said we should all come see her when it snows, because she'll be at the pool!"

"Ooh, that could be fun," Casey said, her mind already whirling.

"Casey, the dog is going nuts in the car," said Mrs. Peters. "We were on our way back home, but you know we *had* to stop and see Lindsay first!"

"Well, I am the main attraction of the town," I said, grinning.

"Of course you are," Casey said. "Okay, I'll come over later."

"Casey, you just got home, and Dad and I would like to have dinner together as a family!" said Mrs. Peters.

"Okay," said Casey. "After dinner, then!"

"Can I have you for twenty-four hours?" asked Mrs. Peters. "Seriously, Casey. You and Lindsay have plenty of time to catch up."

"Fine!" said Casey. "At least I can text now. I'll TTYL, Linds!"

I gave her another quick hug, and she was halfway out the door before she whipped back around.

"Oh my gosh, I missed the donuts almost as much as you! We need four, please!"

I smiled, because I knew that she liked cinnamon, Gabby liked old-fashioned, and Mr. and Mrs. Peters liked powdered jelly. I carefully put them in the bag.

"Those are on the house!" Dad called. "Welcome back, Casey. We missed you!"

"Thank you," said Casey. "I promise I'll eat them all, even the ones for my parents!"

Hole in the Middle

Dad laughed, and Casey and her mom rushed out.

I was so glad to have my BFF home. I missed having Casey as my go-to, because she just always knew what I was thinking or how I felt about things, and I didn't need to explain everything to her. She just got me.

On the other hand, Casey seemed different. I mean, a boyfriend was a big deal. Who was this guy Matt?

Maybe Jenna was right. Maybe middle school *was* going to be different.

Chapter Four
Early Dismissal

At eleven o'clock the next Monday morning, Dad sauntered up to the counter and asked if I wanted the rest of the day off.

"Really?" I asked, surprised.

"Yep," said Dad. "We leave at noon."

"Wait," I said. "Leave for where? To do what?"

"Special surprise!" Dad called over his shoulder.

"No fair!" said Kelsey. "I get stuck here and you get a day off?"

I didn't know what to say, because it actually didn't sound very fair.

"You can leave too," said Rich, who was walking over wearing a Dream Team tee. "I'm covering the counter from noon to six."

Hole in the Middle

"Yes!" Kelsey yelled, and pumped her fist. "Lake bound!"

The next hour actually sped up because we were crowded, and I felt bad about turning over the counter to Rich. I guess more people were coming back from vacation because the Park, Donut Dreams, and even the town itself was busier.

My next customers were Mrs. Ellis and her daughter Elizabeth, aka Wetsy Betsy. I mean, it's terrible that we're friends and I still think of her as Wetsy Betsy, but I can't get it out of my head.

It's not like anyone really calls her Wetsy Betsy, except for Mitchell Stewart, who is kind of a bully anyway. "Hey, Wetsy!" he'll say when he sees her. She just ignores him, but I'm sure it bothers her.

"Hi, Lindsay!" Elizabeth said.

I smiled back at her. "Hey, Elizabeth."

"How has your summer been, Lindsay?" asked Mrs. Ellis. "Did you enjoy the rec classes as much as Elizabeth did?"

Elizabeth and I—along with most of the kids—went to the camp that the town ran for a few hours every morning. We hung out at rec because we both liked the art classes, and Elizabeth was really good at ceramics. She helped me work the wheel so I could make a bowl for Nans.

"It was pretty good," I said. "I wish summer was twice as long, though!"

"I do too!" Mrs. Ellis said. She worked at the high school, so she had most of the summer off too.

The thing I've learned about working in a restaurant is that people generally want to talk to you. I guess it's polite? They can't just say, "Give me that donut," so they say, "Oh, it's so hot out that I decided to treat myself to a donut and cool iced tea to wash it down. Isn't it just so hot?" So I end up talking about the weather a lot.

"Pretty soon it will be Fall Fling, and I can't believe you girls are starting up with all that soon!" said Mrs. Ellis.

Ugh, Fall Fling again.

When you live in a town where nothing ever happens, little things are a big deal. But I wasn't sure what she meant by "starting up with all that." Starting up with what? Getting dressed up? We did that already on holidays and for family things. Last year was Nans and Grandpa's fortieth anniversary, and we all had to get really dressed up. Dad even wore a suit.

Hole in the Middle

"Enjoy the last of summer, dear!" Mrs. Ellis said.

Elizabeth waved. "See you at the lake!" she said.

Here's the thing: everyone goes to the lake. But nothing really happens at the lake. We all take our towels and phones and some of us bring books, and everyone sits around talking to each other. If it's really hot, we'll jump in, and some kids play volleyball in the water, but mostly it's a lot of just hanging out. On a beautiful day it's really nice, but it also gets pretty boring by the end of the summer, with all of us running out of conversation and just staring out into the lake.

The lake was a big deal this year because it was the first year that me and my friends were allowed to go without an adult. There were lifeguards there, but the lifeguards were mostly the older brothers and sisters of my friends.

Everyone is always so intent on being there, though. It's like buying tickets to a show, but there's nothing on the stage, you know? Everyone just ends up watching each other, even though we've all been staring at each other for years.

I guess there's one thing that has changed. When we used to go with an adult, we'd sit with them. Kids hung out with their families. Since we're going with friends now, we're all arranged in slightly different circles. All the middle school kids sit together with the high school kids mostly at one end of the lake.

Without Casey this summer, I mostly sat with Kelsey and her BFF, Sophia. Sometimes Molly would hang out with us too. I guess it is weird that Molly and Kelsey have totally separate friends, since they are sisters and in the same grade, but they are so different that it makes sense.

Kelsey likes to think she's friends with everybody, and that everyone likes her. She always cares about what people think, and she is obsessed with being in on everything.

I still remember the fit she threw in third grade when she wasn't invited to Anna's birthday party. It turns out she was; Anna had just accidentally dropped Kelsey's invitation on her way to school.

Molly is much more of a free spirit. She could not care less what people think about her, and pretty much always says what's on her mind, which does tend to get her in trouble. Nans says she has absolutely no filter from her brain to her mouth. But Molly is also a lot of fun, and she's the first one to organize a kayak race across the lake or a s'mores contest to see who can build the biggest one.

She's really good with little kids, too, so they're always running over to her at the lake. Molly says that when she's old enough she's going to babysit instead of working at the Park, but Aunt Melissa says, "Molly, family first. If we need you, we need to know you'll be there."

There are only twenty-five girls in my grade, so the truth is, even if we split ourselves up, we are all kind of forced to hang out together. There are a ton of cousins and one set of twins, so there are also a lot of people related to each other. My point is, you can't really get away from anyone. Sure, I'm going to avoid some of the meaner girls, but at some point I'm going to be in class or on a team with them.

"Okay, Rich," said Dad. "You got this?"

"I got it," said Rich, eyeing the door because a bunch of his friends from the soccer team had come in and were swarming the counter.

"Hiiiiiii, Lindsay!" called Mason R.

There were three Masons on Rich's team, so they went by Mason R., Mason L., and Mason B.

Mason R. leaned over the counter. "Hey, can you

give me a dozen donuts even if I only pay for a half dozen?" He smiled.

I smiled back. "Nope," I said.

Mason R. laughed.

Rich's friends always tried to get us to give them free donuts. Uncle Charlie brought them to every game, and each of those guys ate about four. Uncle Charlie joked that the soccer team would eat us out of business.

"Get out of here, Linds," said Rich, "before they try to get you to sell them the whole case at half price."

Dad was waiting for me off to the side of the counter. "Okay, Pops," he said to Grandpa. "We're off. I'll see you later tonight!"

Grandpa gave me a quick hug. "Are you sure your grandma Mimi's plane is on time?" he asked, looking at his phone.

I looked at Dad. "Mimi's plane?"

"Pops!" Dad yelled.

I giggled. I guess Grandpa had just ruined some sort of surprise!

Chapter Five
Grandma Mimi

"What?" said Grandpa. "She already knows her grandma Mimi is coming!"

I laughed. "Well, I didn't know she was coming *today*!" I said.

"For goodness' sake," said Dad, throwing up his hands. "No one in this family can keep a secret!"

Grandpa looked around. "Well, no one told me this was still a secret. They just told me her whole trip was a secret but Melissa spilled!"

Dad shook his head. "Okay, Lindsay," he said. "I thought it would be nice to pick up Grandma Mimi from the airport, so we have a ways to go. Let's get out of here before Grandpa and the family also tell you what I'm getting you for your birthday and every other secret we still have." Then he laughed. It was hard to stay mad at Grandpa for long.

The airport is about two and a half hours away, in St. Louis. Sometimes Dad takes us to St. Louis for a weekend, which is a lot of fun. It's so crazy different there, with so much more to do. It's weird that you can get in a car, drive, and end up someplace that's so different from where you started.

"I figure we'll get there in time to pick up Grandma Mimi," Dad said, heading out to the highway. "Then we'll have an early dinner and head back."

"We're having dinner in the city?" I said, realizing I still had my Donut Dreams T-shirt on with a pair of shorts.

Dad usually wore a nice button-down shirt to work with pants and nice shoes, so he always looked a little dressed up to me. And Mimi was always, always dressed up. No matter where she was, she always had lipstick on and some kind of jewelry. I tried to picture Mimi on the plane like a lot of other grandmas, wearing sweatpants and a sweatshirt, but I just couldn't do it.

"Mimi wants to take you on a little surprise excursion in St. Louis," said Dad. "And Uncle Charlie wants me to meet with one of our vendors for the restaurant, so I'll leave you guys to it. Then I'll pick you both up for dinner. Okay?"

"Sounds great!" I said.

Some people might think it's strange that I am looking forward to hanging out with my grandma, but I love being with Mimi. It was the rest of the family that sometimes annoyed me.

Dad is always on time for everything, so of course we got to the airport a little early. I watched people lugging bags or rolling suitcases, and I wondered where they'd been or what adventure they were heading off to.

"What's one place that you've never been that you'd like to see?" I asked Dad.

Dad and I did this a lot, asking things like, *If you could eat only one thing for twenty-four hours, what food would you choose?*

"Hmm," Dad said. "Well, Europe was wonderful, but if it has to be someplace I've never been, I think I'd love to go to Japan."

I nodded. I always forget Dad had traveled a lot with Mom, before she got sick.

Mom lived in France for a year during college,

and when Dad went to visit her, they traveled all over Europe.

"But you know I'm not a big traveler," said Dad. "I like being home. It's fun to see other countries, but I miss home when I'm away."

"Did Mom miss home when she was living in France?" I asked.

"Well, she definitely missed her family and her friends," said Dad. "And me!" He laughed. "But I think she liked learning how people lived in different cities. To some extent she had to learn how people lived in our town too."

I thought about that. "You mean like how we pronounce certain words?"

"Well, that, yes," said Dad. "But also that everyone eats dinner early or that people think it's rude if you don't say hello when you see them out and about, that kind of thing. When she first moved here, she could not get used to the fact that people would just walk in the front door without knocking first. For about six months, she screamed when anyone came into the house."

I laughed. "Well, to be fair, people only walk in if you've invited them over or are expecting them.

Hole in the Middle

It's not like we just randomly walk into each other's houses!"

"Of course not!" said Dad. "But even then. One time when Casey's mom came over, she startled Mom so much that Mom dropped an entire platter of meatballs and spaghetti she was making for dinner. There was red sauce everywhere . . . even on the ceiling."

I cracked up. "Wow, that sounds like a mess!"

"It was," said Dad. "There was sauce in her hair and dripping from above. And we all laughed at her, and she did not like that one bit!"

I giggled. I was used to seeing Mom covered in paint but not sauce.

Then I spotted Mimi striding toward us. She was hard to miss. Mimi doesn't exactly look like a grandma, or at least not like what most of my friends' grandmas look like.

She wears bright red lipstick that's always perfect—it never smudges, even when she eats (and I've watched her!). She is always what she calls "smartly dressed," which means she's usually in pants, with a nice top and a jacket and heels.

I've never seen her wear jeans, and the only time

she wears sneakers is when she goes for a run, which she does every day. Dad sometimes teases Mimi about wearing sweats, but we all know she doesn't own one sweatshirt.

Today Mimi had on these cool sunglasses and a scarf wrapped around her neck, I guess because she was cold on the plane. Her feet, as always, made a *click, click, click* sound with her shoes.

"Baby girl!" Mimi cried out, and grabbed me for a big hug.

She smelled like flowers. She took off her sunglasses and propped them on top of her head.

"Let me take a good look at you. Oh, you are even more beautiful than ever, and . . ." She looked at Dad. "She's the spitting image of Amy, isn't she?"

Dad smiled. "Well, she's Lindsay, so she looks like Lindsay to me," he said.

"Oh, you know what I mean!" said Mimi. "Lindsay, you look more and more like your beautiful mother each time I see you."

She looked at me for a minute longer. I wondered if she was imagining me as Mom, or Mom with my head. Or Mom's head on me.

"Good to see you, Mike!" Mimi said then, giving

Hole in the Middle

Dad a long hug. "You seem to be faring well."

"I am!" said Dad.

"You know I would have been happy to drive out to you," said Mimi.

"Don't be silly," said Dad as we walked toward the exit of the terminal. "Happy to give you some company on the trip. And we like our city trips, don't we, Linds?" He winked. "It's good practice for when Lindsay leaves us and moves to the big town!"

"Oh?" said Mimi. "There's so much to catch up on! Lindsay, I want to hear everything you're up to! And how is my sweetie Skylar? Did you leave him at home? I was hoping he'd join us!"

Dad grabbed Mimi's bag and we piled into the car. "Well, I didn't think he'd last while you went out," he said as he started up the car engine. "Unless you take him shopping for video games."

"Well, I'm happy to shop for Sky, too," said Mimi, "but all he wears are those terrible athletic clothes. He looks like he's going to the gym all the time!"

"Marla, that's what all the boys wear," said Dad.

Mimi shook her head. "I bought him some button-down shirts," she said. "And a few pairs of pants."

DONUT DREAMS

Dad rolled his eyes and smiled at me in the rearview mirror.

"Where are we going today?" I asked Mimi. "Dad said it's a surprise."

Mimi nodded and smiled. "Oh, it is," she said. "It definitely is."

Chapter Six
A Day at the Museum

Mimi typed an address into her phone, and we were off to the St. Louis Art Museum. Before I knew it, Mimi was ready to march me into the museum, but not without first touching up her makeup and hair in the car.

"Oh, I'm such a mess from traveling!" she said.

I tried not to giggle as I looked at Dad, because not one hair on Mimi's head was out of place.

Dad pulled up in front of the museum and let us out.

"Have fun," he shouted as we waved goodbye.

At the entrance, Mimi asked a man at the information desk for "a docent named Ellen Colbert."

The man picked up the phone and made a call.

"She'll be right down," he said.

DONUT DREAMS

I turned to Mimi. "Docent?" I asked.

Mimi smiled. "A docent is a museum guide."

A few minutes later a woman came to the desk and said, "Marla?"

"Yes!" said Grandma. "But you can call me Mimi! And are you Ellen?"

Ellen nodded. "I am! Jenny told me you were coming with your granddaughter."

I admired Ellen's black suit and silky white blouse. She wore black patent-leather pumps, and tiny little diamond stud earrings twinkled in her ears. She looked dressed up, yet she still managed to appear comfortable at the same time. Not an easy look to pull off.

Mimi shook Ellen's hand.

"This is my beautiful granddaughter Lindsay," she said, tucking my hair behind my ear. "Look at that gorgeous face!"

"Mimi!" I said, and I could feel my face getting hot.

Ellen laughed. "Oh, that's what grandmas do!"

She led us into the museum and started pointing out all the different paintings.

It was incredible. Even though Mom was an artist, I had never been to an art museum before.

Hole in the Middle

Ellen smiled at me. "We have something here your grandmother has been eager to show you," she said. "She's been calling me nearly every day, asking, 'Is it still on? We didn't miss it, did we?'"

I looked up at Mimi questioningly. She didn't say anything.

Ellen laughed. "I think it's time to tell her, Mimi!"

Mimi nodded and took me by the hand.

"There's a special exhibit here this month," she said. "I'm just so glad I was able to get you here in time before it ended."

Then we walked down a hallway and there was a sign that read, THE ST. LOUIS ART MUSEUM IS PROUD TO HONOR CLAUDE MONET. EXHIBITION ON LOAN FROM THE NATIONAL GALLERY OF ART, WASHINGTON, DC. There was a security guard at the entrance who smiled and nodded at us as we walked in.

I gasped. Monet was my mom's absolute favorite artist. When I walked into the exhibition, I felt like I was dreaming.

"I'm sure your mom must have talked about Monet to you," Mimi said, smiling.

"Oh, you know, just . . . all the time," I said. "I know he painted by observing and using his own thoughts and emotions in his art, instead of drawing things exactly as they were in real life. Is that right?"

Ellen was nodding. She was also smiling from ear to ear.

"Very good! Yes, it's called impressionism, Lindsay," she said.

I walked over to one painting that caught my eye. It was called *Palazzo da Mula, Venice*. It was wonderful. I felt as if I could dip my hand into the cool blue water.

"Mom always talked about Monet and the way he painted water," I said.

Mimi tapped me on the shoulder. "Let me show you one of your mom's favorites," she said.

It was called *Woman with a Parasol—Madame Monet and Her Son*. It was a woman walking through a field of flowers, holding a parasol, with a little boy walking close to her.

As I looked at it, I took a deep breath.

"It's so . . . soothing, isn't it?" I said. "The puffy white clouds, the way her scarf is gently blowing in the breeze . . . I love how everything is so soft, and a little blurry." I gave a little happy sigh. "I could look at this for hours."

Hole in the Middle

"You know, when Monet was alive, his work was criticized," Ellen said.

"Why?" I said. "How could someone not like this?" I pointed to the painting.

"Some critics said Monet's work was blurry not by choice, but because his eyesight was failing," Ellen explained. She shook her head. "They just wanted to criticize his work, instead of seeing the beauty behind it." She sighed. "Monet is one of my favorites too."

"Which goes to show you should do whatever you want when it comes to art," Mimi said. "Paint how you love to paint, write what you love to write, sing what you want to sing!"

She turned to me. "The point is, you're never going to make everybody happy, Lindsay, so it's important that you make *you* happy."

I nodded. "Thanks, Mimi."

Of course all this made me think of my mom. She always painted what made her happy. I pictured her sitting by her easel, softly humming as she mixed colors from her palette.

I remembered one time when she had just finished a painting; I caught her looking at the final product, her head tilted slightly to one side, with a small, satisfied smile on her face. "I can never get it exactly the way I see it in my mind, Linds," she told me. "But this one is close."

Monet painted a lot of water lilies, but there were other paintings I found equally wonderful. Fishing boats, sailboats, cathedrals: they were all beautiful to me.

After I made sure I had looked at every single one, Mimi called Dad to come pick us up, and told him we were going to make a quick stop at the gift shop first. Mimi bought me an art book all about Monet's paintings. It was pretty expensive.

We met up with Dad and got into the car, and the minute he saw the bag from the gift shop, Dad immediately whipped out his wallet, thinking I had asked Mimi to buy the pricey art book for me.

But Mimi waved her hand, shooing him away, saying it was a gift and her treat.

After some protest, Dad eventually put his wallet away. "But I'm paying for dinner," he said. "No arguments. It's not up for discussion."

Mimi nodded seriously. "Yes. Food I'll let you pay for," she said. And we all laughed.

Dad and Mimi and I stopped at a restaurant Dad

wanted to try for dinner, and he went to talk to the manager while Mimi and I settled into a booth.

"I worked up an appetite," said Mimi.

I realized I was pretty hungry too. I looked at the menu, which was huge, and everything sounded good.

"Okay," said Dad, sliding into the other side of the table. "There are a few things I'd like to try, so let me know if there's anything that catches your eye. Otherwise I'll order for everyone."

"That makes it easy," said Mimi, and she slapped her menu shut and slid it to Dad.

Dad ordered enough food for about ten people.

"Uh, Mike, it's just the three of us, right?" asked Mimi.

"It's market research!" said Dad.

It was strange to be in a restaurant that wasn't the Park. I noticed how busy the staff was, and, because it was a big restaurant, they really had to move fast to get from the kitchen to the tables.

It was also weird to be out to dinner and not see one person we knew. I wondered if you could spend a whole day in a city without seeing anyone you had ever met before. You would be totally anonymous.

I wondered if that was good or bad. You could pretty much do what you wanted to do, but then again, if you didn't show up somewhere, would anyone know? What if you needed help and didn't know anyone to ask? What if you just wanted to see a friendly face but all you saw were strangers?

It was also a little weird being someplace with just Mimi and Dad. After Mom died, it seemed like three of us (me, Skylar, Dad), went everywhere together.

When we were a family of four, I didn't really notice when Mom was out or Skylar was off doing something. And since Dad worked a lot, there were a lot of times it was just Skylar, me, and Mom.

Now I'm always aware of where Dad and Skylar are, and it's like I'm constantly looking around for Sky if he's not with us. If I moved to the city, it would just be Dad and Sky back home.

For some reason that thought made my throat feel a little funny. Maybe without the two of them, I would be lonely.

Dad must have read my mind, because he said, "Ah, it's strange not to have Skylar here, but Mimi, you should consider this your last meal with no whining while you're visiting."

Hole in the Middle

Mimi laughed. "Oh, Sky is a good kid," she said. "I can't wait to see him. But today is about Lindsay! Tell me about middle school. Are you excited?"

Here we go again, I thought.

"Not really," I said. "It's a new school but the same kids, so not much is different."

"Oh!" said Mimi, surprised. "Your mom spoke so highly about the school, though. It has wonderful programs, especially for art. And some of her friends still teach there, right?"

I nodded.

"Well, Carla teaches there," Dad said. "You remember her, right, Mimi? And Laurie is still the assistant principal."

"Laurie is Casey's mom," I said.

"Of course!" said Mimi. "I remembered that. It will be a little weird for Casey then, right?"

I remembered talking about it with Casey before she left for camp, when she was packing up her stuff and there were clothes thrown all over her room. I knew she was not too happy to have her mom at school with her.

"I mean, I'll see her every day, all day!" she said, flopping on her bed. Then she sat up. "Oh, I'm sorry," she said. "I'll bet you'd do anything to see your mom every day."

I was quiet for a second, which I can only do with Casey. Usually I'd just quickly say, "Oh, it's okay" to get the awkward moment over.

But Casey understood. She tilted her head and waited for me to think it through.

I thought about how I'd feel if Mom was my principal. She'd always know if I got in trouble, if there was a test, if I was talking to someone or not.

"No, I get it," I said. "I mean, yes, of course I'd do anything to have my mom back. But if she was here and things were normal, I would not be too happy having her watch me all day."

Casey sighed. "That's why Gabby liked high school so much. She got rid of Mom on an hourly basis!"

"But it's not just you," I said. "Jessica Walsh's mom is a teacher there, and Jake Todd's dad is a science teacher. Claire's mom works in the lunchroom, and Richie Miller's mom works in the office. Almost every teacher or staff person there has a kid who goes through that school at some point. . . ."

"True," said Casey. "It's totally worse for Claire. I

mean, her mom is probably not going to let her eat only french fries for lunch." She giggled.

"I know!" I said.

"'Claire, you come back here and get milk and some fruit!'" Casey imitated in a high voice.

"'And you sit with those nice kids over there!'" I imitated in a high voice too.

We collapsed into giggles on the floor.

"Well, thank you for showing me that someone always has it worse," said Casey.

"It is my duty as your friend to always make you feel better!" I said.

She smiled. "It's going to be a long summer without you, Miss L.!" she said.

"Don't worry," I said, laughing. "You're in for an even longer year with me when you get back."

"Ugh!" said Casey, and then she hopped up. "Okay I can only take three books, so help me decide here!"

We spent the next hour debating the books Casey had on her shelf until her mom peeked in and said, "Ladies, I can assume you're having a good time, but need I remind you that someone named Casey has to be packed and ready to go in the morning? The very early morning?"

DONUT DREAMS

Then we got down to business, with me calling out the things that were on Casey's packing list and Casey folding them up and stuffing them into a giant duffel bag.

That day seemed like a long time ago now, especially with the first day of school right around the corner. Maybe everyone was right. Maybe middle school would be different. Maybe everyone was worried about it for different reasons. Maybe I should be worried about it.

On the car ride home I looked out the window at the lights of the city as they disappeared behind us. As much as I loved the city tonight, I was glad to be going home, where Sky and Nans and Grandpa were waiting for us and where I knew tomorrow morning I'd have a text from Casey.

Chapter Seven
Middle School Musings

Sure enough, the next morning there was a text from Casey, asking me what time I would be home from work. I texted her back, put on my Donut Dreams shirt, and went downstairs, where Nans and Mimi were already having coffee.

"Ready for work?" asked Nans, putting a plate of scrambled eggs in front of me. "Mimi is going to wait until Prince Sky wakes up, so I can drive you to the Park and get some things done in the office."

"Thanks," I said.

I looked from Nans to Mimi and smiled at them as I ate. It was nice having both grandmas here at the same time.

"Okay, all done! Reporting for duty," I said,

finishing up my breakfast. Mimi reached over to clear my plate.

"I can do it," I said. I didn't want Mimi to do any extra work for me.

"Oh, you get to work, honey. I'll clean up," said Mimi.

Nans raised an eyebrow but didn't say anything.

She would always say, "I am not a waitress in my own home!" whenever one of us didn't clear our plate and scrape it off before we put it in the dishwasher.

"Should I pack a snack in case you get hungry?" asked Mimi, opening the fridge.

"Uh, Mimi," I said. "I'm going to work in a restaurant. Where there is, um, a lot of food."

She spun around. "Oh, right," she said. Then she laughed. "That would be like bringing books to a library!"

"Kind of," I said.

Mimi was not the type of person to ever sit down. After dinner Nans and Grandpa would sit and talk while they had coffee or tea. When we were at Mimi's house in Chicago for Thanksgiving, she would jump up and clear the table and start cleaning the kitchen. I never saw her sit around, really. She always had projects, as she called them, or "tidying up" around the house. There was never anything out of place at Mimi's house, so she must spend a lot of time tidying.

"Well, have a good day, Lindsay," said Mimi. "I know you'll do a great job!" She gave me a kiss, and I followed Nans out the door.

When we got into the car, I said, "Nans, Mimi tried to send food to a restaurant!"

"Well," said Nans. "She means well. She doesn't know how to help when she comes, so you can't really blame her. Plus, walking into the house is hard for her, Linds. She misses your mother so much."

"Why would she miss her more at our house than at her house?" I asked, puzzled.

"Well," said Nans. "Your mom really made that house your family's home. Her stamp is all over it, from the garden in the back to her studio, to the mural she painted in Skylar's room. It's hard to be there and not think she's going to come around the corner."

"You know she's not going to come around the corner!" I said a little loudly, and Nans glanced at me.

"Well, I think Mimi does too," she said slowly. "But maybe part of her hopes that when she comes to visit, your mom will be there, just like she used to be."

For a while I thought Mom would reappear. Every day I'd wake up and think, *Maybe that was just a nightmare*, and she would be downstairs making me French toast. But after a few months, I stopped thinking that.

"Do you think she likes coming here?" I asked.

"Your grandma? Oh, very much," said Nans. "She just loves seeing you and Skylar and spending time with you. Right after your mom died, she thought about moving here because she missed you so much."

"She did?" I asked, surprised.

"Yes," said Nans. "But she was still working then, and her life was really in Chicago. So she made a promise to herself to visit as often as she could."

Just then a car pulled out in front of us really slowly, and Nans tapped the brakes.

"Holy moly!" she said. Then she peered over the steering wheel. "Is that your cousin Lily?" she asked.

I looked at the car. "Probably," I said.

"I am going to have a serious talk with her and with Charlie," Nans said. "She can't possibly think it's okay to drive like that!"

Lily was a really bad driver. Grandpa made her

park in the back of the restaurant, away from any customers, because in the first few months after she got her license, she hit two parked cars.

She didn't drive fast and she was a really nervous driver. She said she didn't like driving near any other cars, but of course, that was often unavoidable. Usually Uncle Charlie drove with her.

Nans went on and on about Lily's driving until we got to the Park.

"Lily!" she said, rolling down the window as we pulled in. "Young lady, we are going to talk about your driving!"

Lily sighed, and I gave her a look as if to say *sorry*, but I also took it as an opportunity to hurry in.

Every morning Grandpa sits at the podium right before we open and watches everyone come to work. He knows who gets there on time and who slides in. He notices if you are trying to eat a bagel while you're setting up or if your uniform isn't clean.

"Hello, lovely Lindsay!" he boomed, and I gave him a hug before I tied my apron.

Then I got out the glass cleaner and started polishing the case, even though it was already gleaming. I saw Grandpa glance over and smile.

Kelsey came streaking in a few minutes after me. "Grandpa the Great!" she said, saluting him. "Reporting for duty!"

Grandpa smiled and gave her a wink.

Kelsey went to put her bag in a locker in the back and then came bounding back.

"Okay, I want to hear all about your trip," she said.

"I'll show you," I said, noticing that Nans and Grandpa were going over the specials for the day.

I slipped Kelsey my phone. She flipped through the pictures of the art, her eyes getting bigger and bigger.

"This is so cool, Lindsay! I can't believe you got to see all this. I'm totally asking Mom if she can take me to this place."

"It was kind of fun," I said. "Ellen, the woman who worked as a guide at the museum, showed me some really amazing things."

Kelsey nodded.

"Kelsey . . . alert!" I hissed, and she shoved the phone in a drawer.

Dad and Grandpa were headed over. "Okay, guys, we have a special order today," said Dad. "The track team ordered three dozen donuts for the first track practice of the season." He handed me a piece of paper. "Can you pack up the boxes with everything they ordered? Someone will run them over at eight."

Grandpa looked over my shoulder at the order. "Looks like we're going to need some refilling of the shelves, Jane," he called to Nans.

Nans looked over and nodded, then headed back to the kitchen. Kelsey and I smiled . . . fresh donuts out of the fryer are the most delicious thing ever. I knew I'd have to elbow her to get back to the kitchen to "pick up the refills" and snag a freshly made donut.

Everyone was setting up their stations, and by six thirty we were ready to go, with the first customers coming in at 6:31. The regular breakfast customers have been coming for years.

Mrs. Selling was walking slowly, using a cane, and Rich offered her his arm to lean on. "Mrs. Selling, can I help you to your usual table?" he asked.

Mrs. Selling smiled at him.

"Coop, your grandson is just a gem," she said to Grandpa.

Our family's last name is Cooper, but everyone calls Grandpa Coop.

"Well, he learned from the best!" Grandpa said.

"The crew is all here!" Mrs. Selling said, looking around. "You're a lucky man!"

"I am," said Grandpa. "I am!"

Then he grabbed a coffeepot to start pouring everyone's morning cup.

Grandpa knew how everyone liked their coffee: with milk, with sugar, or with nothing added. The regulars didn't even have to ask him; they just sat down and he came over with their cup and saucer.

Suddenly we heard a crash, and everyone turned around to stare. Dropping things in restaurants is always the worst, especially if it's crowded. Everyone just stops and I imagine you must feel like you want to sink into the floor.

Usually what goes down is either silverware, which makes a loud racket, or worse, a dish or glass, which shatters. If there's food on a plate, it makes a huge mess. This time it was a tray, and of course, it was Lily who had dropped it.

I love my cousin, but Lily is a bit clumsy. Uncle Charlie always jokes that to have Lily work as a waitress means ordering an extra set of dishes, because she breaks so many.

Rich and Molly rushed over to help, and I heard

Hole in the Middle

Grandpa sigh as he strode over with a broom.

"Poor Lily," whispered Kelsey.

"I know," I whispered back. "So embarrassing!"

Lily is really pretty and smart. She has long, wavy dark hair and bright red lips, even without lipstick, and everyone always tells her that she looks like Snow White. Someone passing through town told her she could be a model if she wanted to, in New York. But Lily really wants to be a nurse like her mom, my aunt Sabrina.

"So what outfit are you wearing for the first day of school?" Kelsey asked.

"I don't know," I said. "I haven't really thought about it. Plus, it will still be hot."

Kelsey tilted her head. "Then can I borrow one? I want to wear something new!"

"Sure," I said. "But I just don't get dressing up for the first day. We'll probably see everyone the day before school starts. So why would you dress up the next day, just to see the same people at school?"

Kelsey paused. "Well, I don't know. I guess it's like Thanksgiving or a holiday. I mean, you see your family all the time, but for certain things you just dress up."

"Yeah," I said. "That makes sense."

Kelsey looked at her watch. "This is going to be such a long day. I almost wish school had started already!"

We packed up all the donuts for the order and stacked the boxes into bags.

"All set?" asked Dad, glancing in.

"Yep," I said. "Ready to go."

"Okay, I need someone to run these over to the high school," Dad said, looking around.

"I'll go!" said Lily.

Uncle Charlie, Dad, and Aunt Melissa all said, "No!" at the same time, and Lily stomped off, looking hurt.

"Jenna!" Uncle Charlie called. "Delivery!" He tossed her his keys. "And hide the keys from your cousin!"

Nans came out of the kitchen.

"What did you say to Lily to upset her?" she asked Uncle Charlie.

Kelsey and I saw our opening. She grinned at me and nodded, and I skittered into the kitchen to grab the fresh donuts from the rack.

Lily was sitting on a stool in the corner, her lip quivering.

Hole in the Middle

"Are you okay?" I asked.

She sighed. "I don't think I am cut out for waitressing," she said, shaking her head.

Nans strode back in.

"Lily," she said, "we're going to put you up front at the host station today. Do you have your regular clothes instead of your uniform?"

"Well, I have clothes to change into for after work," said Lily, grabbing a skirt and a top out of her locker and holding them up. She showed us a pretty pink top and a black skirt.

"That'll do," said Nans. "Change and then up front you go!"

Lily didn't need to be asked twice. Rich subbed in as a waiter, and Lily managed the podium up front.

She was really friendly and so chatty that people didn't even mind waiting for a table during the lunch rush. Plus, she knew exactly where everyone liked to sit. She even helped Mr. and Mrs. Block load their son Preston into his high chair.

"He never goes in without a fight!" Mrs. Block said. "You have the magic touch!"

"There's a place at the Park for everyone," said Grandpa, giving Lily a hug on her way back to the podium. "We just needed to find the right one."

Then he spun around at me and squinted. "Lindsay Cooper, you have powdered sugar on your nose, young lady!"

I looked at Kelsey, and she started laughing. "You got caught, Linds!"

"Eating the profits!" said Grandpa, pretending to yell. He acted as if he was mad at us, but he was just kidding.

※ ※ ※ ※ ※

Dad dropped me off at Casey's house after my shift ended. We had a few days left before school started. Casey's mom was at school, helping to get everything ready.

"She's in a crazed place," said Casey. "Back to school is always nuts in my house. Dad is busy too, with everyone's back-to-school visits."

Casey's dad is a doctor, and he takes care of just about everyone in town. My aunt Sabrina is a nurse in his office. She met Casey's dad when they both worked in the same hospital, and she invited him and his wife to a birthday party she was having for Uncle Charlie. That was how Casey's parents met.

Hole in the Middle

Aunt Sabrina likes to say, "It's a good thing they came to my party!"

Casey led me up to her room, which is generally pretty neat, unless you open her closet or look under her bed. I looked around, and either I hadn't noticed it last week or she just put it up, but there was a picture of a boy on the bulletin board above her desk.

Usually she just had pictures of the two of us goofing around, and there were a couple cute family photos from when she was little.

But the boy photo was a new addition.

"Who's that?" I asked.

"Oh . . . ," she said. "That's my friend Matt."

"Your friend?" I asked.

"Well, I guess . . . I don't know."

"Is he your boyfriend?"

"Mom won't let me have a boyfriend yet," Casey said. "We're just pals."

I nodded, but I was a little confused as to why she had his picture up. I decided to let it go for now.

"Kelsey keeps asking me what I'm wearing on the first day of school," I said.

"Why?" Casey said. "What's the big deal?"

"Exactly!" I said, relieved.

I feel like Casey is the one person who really sees things the same way I do.

"I'll probably wear these pants," said Casey, pulling a pair out of her closet. "They're light cotton, so they'll be okay even if it's still hot out. And that top . . . now where is it . . ." She was pulling things out from under her bed. "Oh, here it is!"

It looked like a regular outfit to me.

"Do you think middle school is going to be different?" I asked.

"Well, everyone says it is," she said. "It's a different building, and we walk around to our classes and have lockers, so in that way it will be different. And we get split up into different classes, so there's that."

"But I mean, *we* won't be different, right?"

"You and me?" she asked. "Like, am I going to change overnight?"

I laughed. "No, well . . . maybe? It's just that everyone is making such a big deal about it and I think it's just . . . school starting."

"Well, I guess there's only one way to find out," said Casey.

I nodded, and we heard the front door open.

"Casey?" Mrs. Peters called upstairs.

Hole in the Middle

"Up here with Lindsay!" Casey called down.

Mrs. Peters came upstairs. She looked tired.

"Well, we are set," she said. "School is ready for you. Now are you ready for school?"

Casey laughed. "No! I need more summer!"

"You know what?" said Mrs. Peters. "After today, so do I."

We followed her back downstairs and she made us a snack, just like she did when we were in first grade: sliced grapes, cheese on crackers, and what she calls banana boats, which are sliced bananas with peanut butter on top.

"Mom, how is middle school going to be different?" Casey asked, her mouth full of crackers.

"From your old school?" Mrs. Peters asked. "Well, it's a different building and a different schedule, moving around from class to class, and that takes some getting used to."

Casey looked at me. *Just as we'd thought.*

"But at this age kids are trying new things and changing, too. You might find your friends going off in new directions," Mrs. Peters said.

Casey and I thought about that for a moment.

"You mean like Brett Carr will suddenly start

playing soccer instead of being a piano genius?" I asked.

"Maybe," said Mrs. Peters. "That's why it's so exciting. You can really start figuring out who you are and what you like."

"What if we already know what we like?" asked Casey.

"Well, some kids do," said Mrs. Peters, "Brett is probably still going to be a piano genius. He's been playing since he was three. But it's always good to be open to new things too. You may not even be aware that you'd love being on the volleyball team until you try it."

I looked at Casey and giggled. She broke two fingers playing volleyball last summer, and she hates it.

"Okay, maybe volleyball is a bad example," said Mrs. Peters, laughing.

I guess I looked a little worried, because Mrs. Peters put her arm around me and said, "But whatever changes, I know you and Casey will always be friends."

"What? Of course we'll be friends always!" yelped Casey. She slid over and threw her arms around me. "Don't try on any new BFFs!"

Hole in the Middle

I laughed and hugged her back. "I won't. You are stuck with me!"

Later that night, I thought about what we'd talked about. I usually fell asleep really fast, but I was tossing and turning, thinking about what Mrs. Peters had said.

What would I decide to do that was different? What if I didn't want to try anything different? I tried to stop my mind from spinning so I could get to sleep.

Finally I decided that even if middle school was different, if Casey was around, it would all be okay. Plus, I had my dreams, and I knew those would never change. The next thing I knew, it was morning.

Chapter Eight
Dress Party or Pity Party?

Mimi had talked about a "dress party" for me since she'd arrived, and even though it made me feel a little squirmy, I figured it would be fun. I don't really like being the center of attention, but I would be with my family and friends. It wasn't like I'd be strutting down a runway.

"It's party day!" Mimi trilled as she came into my room in the morning. "So much fun awaits! But first, work!"

I groaned. A day off would be nice, but the plan was for me to go to work in the morning.

Kelsey beat me to the Donut Dreams counter and was bouncing up and down, she was so excited.

"Do you think your grandma will let me keep

one of the dresses that you don't like?" she asked.

"Uhhhh," I said, unsure.

"I mean if Mom pays for it!" said Kelsey. "Oh, I'm so excited I just can't wait. Aren't you so excited to see what she picked out?"

I started to answer, but Kelsey cut me off.

"I mean, what if you hate everything?" she asked, her eyes getting wide. "That would be a disaster!"

"Well, a flood or a tornado would be a disaster," I said. "Not liking a dress is not a disaster."

Kelsey rolled her eyes at me.

"Okay, okay," she said. "But, like, everyone is going to be staring at you and expecting you to just go crazy over one of them!"

"Kelsey, no one who knows me expects me to go crazy over a dress!" I said, starting to get exasperated. "It's just a dress, and Mimi thought it would be a fun thing because—"

"Because you don't have a mom to take you shopping," Kelsey said.

I stopped stacking the napkins on the counter. "What?" I asked, a little shocked.

Kelsey looked at me. "Well, I mean, that's why we're all making a big deal about it, right? Everyone's mom takes them for their Fall Fling dress, and they thought this would kind of make up for the fact that you can't do that. We're trying to fill in for your mom."

I felt like someone had punched me in the stomach. "Um, I have to go to the ladies' room." I said, and bolted, practically running across the restaurant.

I closed the door to the stall and took a deep breath. It hadn't even crossed my mind that this wasn't a dress party—it was a *pity* party. I felt my cheeks get hot, and I could feel tears welling up in my eyes. My hands were shaking too, and I crossed my arms over my chest to kind of hold myself together.

The door to the bathroom swung open.

"Lindsay?" It was Kelsey. "I'm sorry. I'm so sorry. I think that came out wrong."

I gulped. "It's okay," I said, but my voice was shaking and the tears were starting to come.

"Lindsay, can you come out? We both left the counter, and I'm afraid Grandpa is going to notice," Kelsey said.

She waited a second and I gulped again.

"I need . . . ," I said. "I need a second, okay? Can you cover for me?"

Hole in the Middle

"Of course," Kelsey said. I heard the door shut and then suddenly swing open again, and then she paused. "It's not because we feel sorry for you. It's because we want to help in case you're sad about things."

I nodded, but then realized Kelsey couldn't see me. I quickly wiped my eyes.

The door shut and I heard voices outside. A few minutes later Aunt Melissa came in.

"Lindsay?" she called. "Honey, are you okay?"

"I just have a stomachache," I said.

Aunt Melissa stood right outside the stall. "Sweetie, can you please come out?"

The bathroom door opened again and I heard Jenna and Lily whispering. Goodness, there was nowhere at the Park I could go and be alone!

Aunt Melissa tried again. "Honey, sometimes we all say that Kelsey has no filter, but in truth it affects the whole family. Sometimes things come out really awkwardly or wrong. I'd like to set the record straight."

"Is she all right?" It was Nans, squeezing in.

I sighed. "Please, please can I have a minute alone?" I sniffed. "I just . . . I just need a minute."

"The girl needs some alone time!" declared Jenna.

"Everybody out." They all filed out.

I just needed some air to think a little bit. But how was I going to walk out of the bathroom and look like everything was fine? Or leave my shift?

There was a knock on the door. Again.

"Lindsay, it's Daddy." Wow, he hadn't called himself Daddy in a long time.

"Um, this is awkward, because I can't actually come into the ladies' room, but I'd like to talk to you and not through the door."

I sighed. There was no way I could just slip back to work. I pushed open the door to the stall and looked at my puffy face in the mirror. I threw some cold water on it and patted it dry, which felt good.

When I came out of the bathroom, Nans, Jenna, Lily, and Aunt Melissa were all standing there with Dad, looking anxiously at me.

"This way," said Dad, taking my hand and leading me back through the kitchen.

He opened the back door and a breeze hit my face. Finally, I could breathe. Dad sat down and patted the step next to him. I sat there for a few minutes, just thinking. It was nice not to have to say anything.

"The thing about family," Dad finally said, "is that

they always mean well, but sometimes they don't say exactly the right things. I'm sorry you got upset."

"So are they having a dress party because they feel sorry for me?" I asked.

"No!" Dad almost yelled. "They are having a party because Mimi wants so badly to make shopping for this dress a special experience. She knows how much Mom would care about taking time to make sure you had a dress you loved, and she's trying really hard to make it a memorable thing for you."

"So why didn't Mimi just take me dress shopping?" I wailed.

Dad looked across to the trees at the end of the lot. "I think she's trying to make it a happy occasion. But in truth, it's a sad occasion for her. She feels terrible that Mom didn't get to experience this. And she feels even more terrible that you don't get to have Mom here. So her idea was to have a fun party to distract from the plain fact that everyone is missing Mom."

I was quiet for a few minutes, thinking about that. "So it's actually Mimi who feels sorry for me?"

"Well, not exactly," said Dad. "This isn't a pity party. And it's not even just about one person. It's about feeling bad that someone we love can't be here. Yes, we all feel bad about that. And we feel bad that you're missing Mom. But that's compassion. It's different from just feeling sorry for you. When you're in a family and someone is struggling or feeling bad, your family does everything they can to try to make it better. That's really what this party is about."

"Well, now I feel bad that I just made a scene," I said. "I'm really sorry."

"You didn't make a scene," said Dad. "If you want to do that, just drop a full tray at lunch like your cousin Lily."

I giggled. "Daaaad!"

"I know," said Dad. "It's not nice. And Lily is so kind, so it's especially not nice. But speaking of being nice, you should apologize to Kelsey."

"Why would I apologize to her?" I asked. "She made me feel awful!"

"She didn't mean to," said Dad. "You have to understand that no one has ever really dealt with something like this before in our family. There's no guidebook to say, 'When someone feels like this, you should do that.' People are trying and doing the best they can. Your cousin Kelsey did a lot of the organizing for the party, and she's the one who

Hole in the Middle

helped Mimi choose the dresses. She's been working on this for the past month. She really wants it to be a special day for you."

"She has?" I asked.

Dad nodded. "She managed to keep that a secret, which is a pretty big deal."

"Yeah," I said. "Especially in this family."

Dad laughed. "You're right. You can't hide anything in this family, that's for sure. Speaking of hiding, what do you say we get back to work before Grandpa sends out a search party for us?"

I sighed. It was nice just sitting outside.

Dad reached over and pushed my hair off my face. "You okay?"

I nodded and stood up.

When we went back inside, Nans looked up from where she was in the kitchen. I saw Dad nod to her and she nodded back. She didn't say anything, but she watched me walk to the floor. I passed Jenna, who blew me a kiss. Lily tugged on my apron bow as she passed by.

I looked at Grandpa, who was reading something at the podium. He wiggled his finger at me, and I thought he was going to give me the business for leaving the counter. Instead he gave me a giant hug.

"Remember how loved you are," he whispered. Then he went back to reading. "And now get back to work!" he said, without looking up.

Kelsey was reaching for a glazed donut when I got to the counter.

"Hi, Mrs. Lee," I said. "Kelsey is getting you a freshly made one up there!"

Kelsey held a donut, and I opened a paper bag for her to put it in before I rang it up.

"Oh, it's so nice that you girls get to work together," said Mrs. Lee.

"It really is," I said, looking at Kelsey.

Kelsey looked relieved. "Yep," she said. "Because you get to work with people who love you."

"Oh, aren't you girls just the sweetest?" Mrs. Lee said. "You are sweeter than the donuts!"

I giggled as she left. "Kelsey, we are sweeter than the donuts," I said.

"Hmm," said Kelsey. "Like, sweeter than the chocolate ones or the plain ones?"

"Oh, definitely the ones with sprinkles," I said, laughing.

"How about the crème-filled ones?" she asked.

"Yeah, those too," I said. "And absolutely the jelly-filled."

"Ugh, I hate the jelly-filled," Kelsey said. After a minute she asked, "So you aren't mad at me?"

"I'm not mad," I said.

I didn't want Kelsey to feel bad, but I guess she did, because she took out the garbage without even bargaining with me. She also wiped under the tables and chairs. We closed up the counter a little early to get ready for the dress party, and I was waiting for Dad to take me home when Casey appeared.

"Hey, what are you doing here?" I asked.

"Your chariot awaits, madam," said Casey. "We're taking you home." She waved to Jenna and Lily, who appeared with big bags of stuff.

"What's all that?" I asked.

"We are your glam squad," said Jenna. "I'm doing hair, Lily's doing makeup, and Casey is doing your nails."

"Really?" I asked.

"That way," said Lily, "you can see what you'll look like when you're all done up in the dress."

Jenna twirled her keys. "Let's go. I have orders from Kelsey to stay on schedule."

DONUT DREAMS

I looked over at Kelsey, who was rolling up the mat behind the counter. I ran over to her to help.

"Go!" she said, shooing me away.

I gave her a big hug. "Thank you!" I whispered into her ear.

I didn't know what else to say, but I guess it was enough, because she hugged me back and said, "This is going to be such a fun night!"

Then she pushed me toward Jenna and Lily, and Casey grabbed my hand.

"Operation Glam!" said Casey. "Reporting for duty! I hope the Glam Squad is ready, because this one is going to need a lot of work!"

"Casey!" I yelped. "That's not nice!"

She laughed. "I'm kidding, Linds. You're perfect just as you are. Now let's go, Cinderella. The ball is starting soon!"

Chapter Nine
Operation Glam!

"First, a shower," demanded Jenna when we got home. "We start from scratch here."

I wrapped myself in my bathrobe, wondering what else was ahead of me.

Mimi was downstairs setting up and had chased me out of the living room. I noticed that the dining room table was already stacked with plates and teacups. I peeked out the window and saw Dad and Nans unloading boxes of food from the car.

Dad was taking Skylar night fishing, and Sky was so excited he was running up and down the hall and nearly collided with me.

"Watch it!" I said.

He stopped. "Why are you taking a shower at the

end of the day? Are you going to bed early?"

"No," I said. "I'm getting ready to try on some fancy dresses for the Fall Fling."

Sky looked confused. "Well, I'm going fishing, so maybe Dad will let me take a bath in the river!"

"Eeeuuw," I said. "You will take a bath with a toad. That's disgusting!"

"That would be so cool!" Sky said, and ran down the stairs. "Dad! Dad! Lindsay said that maybe I can take a bath with a toad!"

"That's not . . . ," I started to yell after him, but then decided to let it go.

I took a quick shower, and washed and combed out my hair. I wrapped my towel around me and sat down on the bed.

Jenna and Lily both looked at me seriously as if they were about to perform surgery.

"Makeup first," said Lily, and she started dusting powder on my face.

"Not too much!" said Jenna. "Nans will not be happy."

Lily nodded. "She doesn't need much," she said, winking at me. "Because she's naturally pretty."

I blushed.

Hole in the Middle

Then Jenna took out a blow-dryer and a curling iron and was tugging at my hair for what seemed like forever. Casey was carefully putting bright pink polish on my toenails.

I heard the door opening and closing downstairs and started to get a little nervous. "So how many people are coming?" I asked.

"Well, the four of us," said Jenna, "and Casey's mom, Aunt Sabrina, my mom, Molly and Kelsey and Nans and your grandma Mimi."

"And Gabby!" said Casey.

"Right," said Jenna. "Gabby too!"

"Twelve of us?" I yelped.

"Yeah, it takes at least a dozen people to decide on one dress," said Lily, smirking.

Finally they all stepped away, looking at me. Lily reached over and pulled some hair behind one of my ears. Then she nodded at Jenna.

"Okay, go look," said Jenna.

I went over to the mirror. At first it didn't even look like me. Well, it looked like me, but more glamorous. My hair was shiny and wavy and it didn't even look like I had makeup on, just a little pink on my cheeks and lips.

I grinned. "I think I'm ready for my big modeling job!" I tossed my hair and struck a pose.

"We're coming down!" Jenna yelled down the stairs. I heard everybody cheer and applaud.

"We're ready!" Kelsey yelled back up.

Lily helped me into a button-up shirt so I wouldn't mess up my hair, and I pulled on a pair of jean shorts.

I followed Jenna, Lily, and Casey but stopped as I got halfway down the stairs.

The living room was set up like a giant dressing room. The sofa and chairs were pushed along the wall and someone had rolled up the rug. There was a rolling rack like you see in a big store, and it was filled with dresses. Next to the rack was a line of shoes, some of which I recognized as Kelsey's. A full-length mirror was propped up on the wall, and I saw Nans's sewing basket next to it.

There were balloons tied to the chairs, and flowers in bunches on the end tables. It definitely looked like a party.

"Well, come on down, Ms. Lindsay!" said Mimi. "Let the dress games begin!"

I stood next to Mimi, not sure what to do.

"Okay," said Kelsey. "Here are all the selections."

Hole in the Middle

She pointed to the rack. "You decide where you want to start. Then you try on all the dresses until we find the perfect one."

Everyone was looking at me and I felt a little shy.

Mimi pulled out a green dress. "I thought this would be so pretty," she said. She grabbed my hand. "But come look and pick one to start."

I took the one Mimi was holding. "This is nice," I said. It was dark green with light green ruffles on the skirt.

"Okay, that's the first one then!" said Kelsey. She pointed to the corner of the room, where someone had hung a bedsheet. "That is your dressing room!"

"And I am your official dresser!" said Molly. "Some of these dresses have a lot of buttons!"

I giggled and followed Molly to the corner and behind the sheet.

I pulled on the dress and Molly zipped it up. "It fits!" she yelled out.

"Good job on getting the sizing right!" Nans said to Mimi.

"Oh, I'm so glad," Mimi replied.

I looked at Molly. "Well, you have to come out of the dressing room so everyone can see!" she hissed at me.

I took a deep breath and shuffled out, and then Molly pushed me into the center of the room.

"Oh, you are just so lovely," sighed Mimi.

"That's beautiful, Lindsay," said Aunt Melissa.

"I love that color," said Mrs. Peters.

"You look like grass," said Skylar from the hall.

"Sky!" Nans scolded, and everyone started laughing.

"Okay, we're on our way out now and just came to say goodbye," said Dad, pulling Skylar. "Gone fishing! Lindsay, you look beautiful as always, but choose the dress that makes you happiest, okay?"

"And one that doesn't look like a soccer field!" called Skylar.

Everyone cracked up again, and Dad scooted Skylar out the back door.

"Well," I said. "Now all I see is grass."

"No grass dresses!" said Kelsey. "Next!"

Casey tugged at a purple dress. "This is nice!"

"Okay," I said, grabbing it.

Molly helped me get out of the soccer dress and into the purple one, which was a lot more complicated. It had a halter top that tied behind my neck and a zip on the side that was really tricky to pull up. Then there was a light purple sash that tied around the waist.

"What's taking so long?" demanded Kelsey.

"I'm going as fast as I can," Molly yelled back.

"Girls!" said Aunt Melissa.

Molly stood back and scrunched up her nose. "I don't love it," she said. "But go see for yourself."

The skirt swished when I walked out. I wasn't sure what to do, so I stood next to Mimi.

"Well, that's pretty too," she said. Then she steered me to the mirror.

The dress reminded me of something, but I couldn't put my finger on it.

Casey came over and put her hand on her hip, looking at me. "Uh, do you remember that doll you had that you used to tote around everywhere?"

I looked at her blankly.

"Cressida!" said Mrs. Peters.

"Cressida!" said Nans. "Oh my, I remember Cressida!"

"Yes!" I squealed. "She was my favorite doll. She came in a big poufy purple dress . . . oh." I peered in the mirror. "I look like Cressida!"

"You totally do!" laughed Casey.

We both collapsed into giggles.

"Next!" said Kelsey.

Mimi handed me a pink dress while Molly tugged the Cressida dress off me. The pink dress had a long pleated skirt and the body was really fitted. It had buttons that ran up the side.

When Molly was finished fastening the last in the long row of buttons, she tilted her head to the side. "This one has possibilities," she said.

I walked out and over to the mirror.

"Ohhhh," said Mimi. "Oh, that's so pretty. And I love the color."

Nans and Aunt Melissa nodded.

"Try these with it," said Aunt Sabrina, handing me a pair of silver sandals.

Nans, Mimi, Aunt Melissa, and Aunt Sabrina were all smiling, but Kelsey put her hands on her hips.

"It's really pretty," she said. "I love it. But somehow it just doesn't seem like *you*."

"Oh but I like it!" said Casey.

"I feel like there's something missing," said Kelsey.

"Um, guys, I'm right here," I said.

"Yes," said Mimi. "Let's ask Lindsay what she thinks. Lindsay?"

Hole in the Middle

"I like it," I said, watching myself in the mirror. "It's really pretty."

"Well, there are a lot of others," said Kelsey, pointing toward the rack. "You should buy something you love, not something you like."

I looked at the rack, and one dress caught my eye. "Well, I may as well try on a few more," I said.

I toted the one I chose into the dressing room. "Molly!" I called.

"I need a break!" said Molly. "I'm getting a snack! There's food set up in the dining room, people!"

Everyone laughed, and I heard people moving around to the dining room.

At first I felt a little hurt that everyone had abandoned me for some food, but then I thought, *Well, when I put this one on, I can make a grand entrance.*

Chapter Ten
True Blue

I pulled the next dress on myself and easily zipped it up. It felt light and flowy, like I could run around in it if I wanted to. I turned around to leave and I heard a gentle *swish, swish* from the bottom of the skirt, which made me happy for some reason. I felt like I had on a magical fairy dress, like I could float across the room without my feet touching the floor.

Everyone was in the dining room when I came out, so I walked over to the mirror to get a look before anyone else could see.

I stopped when I got close. There was a picture of Mom that we had on a table in the front hall. She was in a cornflower-blue dress, smiling at the camera, her head tilted back and her eyes crinkled up with laughter. It was taken when Mom and Dad were at a fancy party in Chicago, right before we found out Mom was sick.

I looked down and realized the dress I was wearing was the same purplish-blue color of her dress. It made my hair look darker and my lips look brighter. I looked a lot like Mom in that picture.

"Oh!" I heard a gasp behind me. It was Mimi, and her hand flew to her mouth.

Everyone rushed back into the living room and everyone, it seemed at once, said, "Ohhhhh!"

"That's it!" said Kelsey. "That's the magic dress!"

"Oh, Lindsay," said Mimi. "You look so beautiful."

I spun around. "I look like Mom."

Mimi looked startled. Then she smiled. "You do. You look exactly like her, and that color . . ."

"It's her favorite color," I said, remembering. "True blue."

"True blue," Mimi whispered, and I could see her eyes were filling up with tears.

The room was really quiet. Mimi came over and put her hand on my shoulder, looking at me in the mirror. I didn't know if she was looking at me or if she was seeing Mom.

DONUT DREAMS

True blue was a color Mom made up. She always said her favorite shade of blue was a little purple, a little white, and a little gray mixed together. She mixed it up on her paint palette and even kept some in a paint jar on her shelf. It was hard to find anywhere, but this dress was the closest to her shade of true blue I had ever seen outside of her paintings.

And suddenly, I missed her more than ever. My grandmothers were here and my aunts and cousins and BFF, but the one person who was missing was Mom, and I really, really wished she were here. I missed her all the time, but at this moment, wearing this dress, it hit me hard that she wasn't here. I started to cry, and I just couldn't stop.

Mimi hugged me tight, then Kelsey and Nans, and Aunt Melissa and Casey. There were so many arms around me that I didn't know whose hands or arms belonged to who. Soon we were a big pile of crying arms.

Finally it was Molly who yelled, "And break!"

We were all so startled we laughed. Casey handed out tissues, and everyone blew their noses.

Mimi cupped her hand under my chin. "You okay?" she asked.

Hole in the Middle

I nodded and smiled. "Mom would want me to wear this dress," I said. "It would make her so happy."

Tears streamed down Mimi's face, but she was smiling. "She would have picked this out herself," she said. "It's the perfect dress for you."

Nans knelt down next to me. "Someone hand me my sewing box."

Jenna passed it to her and Nans started pinning the dress up a little. Lily helped me put on a pair of sparkly sandals, and Jenna pulled my hair so it was half up, half down. I still looked like me, but with a dreamy dress.

"Done!" said Kelsey, satisfied.

Everyone clapped.

"Whoo-hoo Team Dress!" said Molly.

"And now we eat donuts!" said Casey.

Nans and Mimi helped me out of the dress and I slipped back into shorts and a shirt. I followed Nans into the kitchen to help with the donuts.

"Do you know why I love donuts, Lindsay?" she asked.

"Because they're delicious?" I answered, watching her roll out the big ball of dough.

"Well, yes," she said. "But see how I make them?

DONUT DREAMS

You use the dough cutter to cut out circles from the rolled-out dough."

I nodded as I watched her. I had seen her make donuts millions of times. She could probably make them in her sleep.

"Each donut is a circle," she said. "You drop the circles in the oil or the fryer and scoop them right out when they're done."

I watched as she tossed the circles of dough into bubbling-hot oil in the pan.

"The thing is," said Nans, "they have a hole in the middle, but they're surrounded by dough." We both watched as the dough bubbled.

"That hole," she began, "reminds me that sometimes there's a hole inside us. Sometimes it gets filled or sometimes we don't notice it as much, but it's always there."

She scooped out the puffed-up donuts with a slotted spoon and laid them on paper towels to drain.

"But there's always dough surrounding the hole." She put down the spoon. "Do you know what I'm trying to say?"

"Sort of," I said. "We all have a hole in us?"

Nans cocked her head. "Sometimes we do.

Hole in the Middle

Sometimes those holes close up and sometimes they get smaller, but they're always there. But no matter what, those holes are surrounded."

"So our family is a donut?" I asked.

Nans laughed. "Kind of. I like to think the donut is more of a symbol of our family. That even when there are holes that can never be filled, there's a lot of sweetness totally surrounding them to help them not get any bigger."

She looked at me like she wanted me to say something, but I wasn't sure what.

"Lindsay," she said, putting her hands on my shoulders and looking into my eyes. "You are surrounded by people who love you. I want you to always remember that."

I smiled. "I will."

"Hey, where are those donuts?" Molly yelled as she stormed into the kitchen.

Nans laughed. "Right here! Right here!"

I helped her pile them on a platter, and Molly carried them out to the table.

When I sat down in the living room, I couldn't help noticing Kelsey sneaking looks at a certain silvery gray dress. She kept walking by it and touching it.

"Why don't you try that on?" I asked.

She spun around. "Me? Oh, I couldn't. These are all for you to try on."

"Well, I already have my dress," I said.

"But it's your party," she said.

"If it's my party, then you have to do as I say," I teased.

"Well," she said, looking longingly at the dress. "This is really beautiful."

"Come on," I said, and pulled her toward the dressing room.

I helped put on the silver dress. It had lots of layers that made it shimmer when Kelsey moved. There were these see-through ruffles that went around the bodice and short sleeves that kind of looked like wings. I stood back.

"Kelsey, you look like a fairy princess," I said.

"Like for Halloween?" she asked.

"No, no, like a beautiful princess," I said. "Go look!" I pushed her out toward the mirror.

"Hey!" said Molly. "Kelsey, those dresses are for Lindsay!"

"Well, I already found mine," I said.

"So the rest are up for grabs?" asked Molly.

Hole in the Middle

"Girls, girls!" said Aunt Melissa. "These were chosen for Lindsay. This is her party. We will find your dresses later!"

"Well, if they like some of these, why not let them try them on?" asked Mimi. "We have so many. Plus, it will save me the trouble of returning all of them!"

Aunt Melissa looked at me. "Are you okay with this? These dresses were for you to choose from."

I nodded my head. "I made Kelsey try this one on. She loves it, and look how pretty she is in it!"

Everyone gathered around Kelsey. "It is beautiful on her," said Mimi.

"Well," said Aunt Melissa. "If you don't mind me just buying this from you, then we'll have two girls with dresses for the Fling."

"Two down!" cried Mimi. "And two to go. Casey and Molly, do you see anything you want to try?"

Casey looked at her mom.

"Go ahead," Mrs. Peters said. "If the dress store comes to you, why go to the dress store?"

Casey took the pink dress off the rack. "I know you didn't love this," she said. "But I do. Can I try it?"

I grabbed her hand and pulled her toward the dressing room. "We'll be right out!"

The dress had looked nice on me, but it looked amazing on Casey. Casey's mom pulled it up a little and smoothed down the skirt.

"Oh, I love that on you!" said Mrs. Peters.

"All right, Molly," I said. "Do you see anything you like?"

Molly smiled. "Well, I kind of like the soccer-field dress," she said.

We all started laughing. "So try it on!" said Mimi. "Don't let Sky be your fashion police!"

Molly came out in the dress. She stopped, did a spin, and put her hand on her hip.

"Dahling, I think this might be just fabulous!" she said, and we all laughed.

"You know, it really suits you," said Aunt Melissa, smiling.

"Let me fix your hair," said Jenna, pulling Molly's hair up off her neck.

The green dress looked nothing like a soccer field on Molly; it looked perfect.

"You all need to put on your dresses so we can take a picture!" said Lily.

So we all scrambled into our dresses as Nans scolded us to watch out for all the pins she'd put in them. I was in a blue dress, Casey in pink, Kelsey in silver, and Molly in green.

"It's a rainbow of pretty!" said Aunt Sabrina. "Get in close so I can fit the whole dress into the shot!"

We stood together, arms around each other, smiling.

"Everyone say, 'Fall Fling'!" said Aunt Sabrina.

"Fall Fling!" we all yelled, and held still for about a second.

"Dance party!" cried Jenna, and she put on some music.

We were dancing around while Nans and Mimi shouted at us to be careful with the dresses. But we didn't care. We all grabbed hands and danced, laughing and twirling.

Chapter Eleven
Post-Party Chat

Later that night, my dress was hanging on the back of my door and I could see the outline of it in the dark as I pulled up the covers in bed.

Sky had thrown a fit about going to sleep, and through the wall I could hear Dad reading to him to try to soothe him, even though it was late.

I wasn't supposed to have my phone in my room at night, but I had actually forgotten to leave it downstairs in the charging station, and I was too tired to go back down anyway. I grabbed it and flipped through the pictures Aunt Sabrina sent us from the party. We all looked happy and goofy, and I had to say those dresses looked pretty good on us.

My favorite picture showed me in the middle,

smiling and sort of spinning, with everyone around me in a circle, laughing.

I looked hard at that shot. I realized as I scrolled through that both my grandmothers were there, both my aunts, my BFF, and all my girl cousins. There was one person who was missing, of course, and that was Mom.

Dad knocked on my door. "From what I heard, it was a pretty good party," he whispered, coming in.

By the time Sky and Dad came home, the party had wrapped up and all the dresses had been packed up.

"Dad," I said, then stopped.

"Yes, honey?"

"I missed Mom tonight."

Dad sat on my bed. "I did too," he said. "But I heard your dress was her favorite color." He squinted at it in the dark.

"It's true blue," I said, smiling.

"Sometimes," said Dad, "I'm reminded of Mom in ways that make me feel like she's still here."

"Like a ghost?" I said, alarmed.

"No, no," Dad said. "Like in the way Sky laughs exactly like her, or the way your dress for the dance ended up being her favorite color."

DONUT DREAMS

"Nans says that we're like donuts," I blurted out.

"Hmm," said Dad.

"She says that we have holes in us, and I guess for me that hole is where I miss Mom."

"Oh, I see," said Dad.

"But that like a donut's shape, we're surrounded by people, in a tight circle, so that hole doesn't get any bigger."

"That's exactly right," said Dad. "You have so many people who love you. They may drive you nuts, but they love you. And you might not like that they surround you all the time, but they always have your best interests at heart."

I laid back on the pillow and yawned. Suddenly I felt really tired.

"Okay, young lady, it's time for bed." Dad reached over to switch off my night-table light when I noticed a little bouquet of flowers next to my stack of books.

"Hey!" I said, sitting back up.

There were violets and bluebells in a little vase.

"Oh," said Dad. "Sky found those today when we were fishing. We weren't sure where to put them when we brought them home, and Mimi thought maybe you would like them."

Hole in the Middle

I smiled. "They remind me of Mom," I said.

"They do," said Dad, smiling back. "True blue."

"She's still here, sort of," I said, yawning.

"She's always with us," said Dad quietly.

I flopped back onto my pillow. I couldn't keep my eyes open. I knew Dad was still sitting on my bed like he did when I was younger, waiting for me to fall asleep, but I was so tired I couldn't even say good night.

It was nice having him there, and knowing that Sky was asleep on the other side of the wall. Mimi and Nans and Grandpa were all in the house, all of us together, one big circle.

I pulled my blanket tighter, and as my eyelids fluttered, all I saw were shades of blue.

Chapter Twelve
A New Beginning

And just like that, before I knew it, it was the first day of middle school. It was still pretty warm, so I just put on a short-sleeved purple T-shirt that Mimi had bought for me, a silver bangle bracelet, and a new pair of jeans. I wanted to look nice and fresh, but I didn't want to get super dressed up or make too big a deal out of it.

"Well, don't you look beautiful!" Nans said, as I sat down at the kitchen table.

She plopped down a plate of homemade pancakes (my favorite) in front of me, and I saw she had made a smiley face with syrup.

I laughed. "Thanks, Nans," I said as I dug into the pancakes.

Hole in the Middle

She was still staring at me. "Yes," she said, nodding approvingly. "You look perfect. Lovely, but not overly done."

I smiled at her. "That's just what I was going for," I told her.

Then I added, "You remembered Mom used to make pancakes on the first day of school." Nans nodded.

"And she would always say the same thing to me," I said. "She used to tell me to have a great day, and to remember to always be my 'own special self.' It felt a little silly when she kept saying it as I got older, but by then it was sort of like a first-day-of-school tradition, and she had to say it. I made her say it."

I smiled at the memory, but then I was startled to look up and see Nans's eyes filling with tears.

Oh no! That was the last thing I wanted.

Luckily, just at that moment, Skylar came bounding into the kitchen.

"Oh boy, pancakes!" he yelled. "Awesome!"

Nans dried her eyes and put a plate in front of him. She tried to lighten the subject.

"What did your mom say to Skylar on the first day of school?" she asked.

DONUT DREAMS

I grinned. "Keep your mouth closed when you eat." Nans laughed.

※ ※ ※ ※ ※

When I walked through the doors of Bellgrove Middle School, I paused in front of the mural that my mom's students had made in her honor.

I had been worried that seeing it every day would make me sad, but I actually felt really happy when I saw it.

I noticed that some students had painted in bright, cheery colors, and others had sketched in charcoal. Parts of the mural showed wildflowers in bloom (which my mom would have loved), and another section showed a stormy sky, and then another section showed a rainbow.

Each student painted whatever they wanted and didn't worry about whether it blended in with the rest of the mural. The end result showed so many different personalities and styles that it was all the more beautiful.

I reached out and ran my hand gently across the colors. "Always be your own special self," I whispered. "Thanks, Mom."

Hole in the Middle

In that moment I could feel her presence. Even though I couldn't see her anymore, I knew she was always with me. And I would always have my family and friends to help me through rough times, and make the hole inside me a little smaller.

I took a deep breath and walked into my first class.

So Jelly!

Chapter One
I Don't Like Change

My friend Sophia was looking at me like I was crazy. "But you have a job!" she said. "That's so cool!"

I sighed and pushed my bangs off my face. They were really starting to annoy me, and I had to decide if I should just let them grow out or get them trimmed.

"Well, yes and no," I said. "Yes because it's cool to work at Donut Dreams, but no because it's hard work, and I'd rather be doing a lot of other things, like going out for pizza tomorrow with you."

I work at my family's restaurant, the Park View Table, after school Fridays and one day on the weekends. This week I'm working on Sunday.

Inside the Park there's a donut counter, Donut Dreams, that my grandmother started with her

DONUT DREAMS

homemade donuts, which are kind of legendary around here. I work at the Donut Dreams counter with my cousin Lindsay.

Pretty much the rest of the family, from my sisters to my mom to my grandparents and everyone in between, also works at the Park. It's definitely a family business, and everyone in the family is expected to help out at the restaurant. We are paid, of course, but it's not like there's some discussion about where you want to work.

When Grandpa and Nans, which is what we call our grandmother, think that you're ready, you get offered a job, and then they figure out the best place for each of us in the restaurant. Saying something like, *No thanks, I'd rather lifeguard at the pool than work in the restaurant,* isn't really an option. Or at least no one has really tried.

I don't mind working with my family, but it's hard when my free time is eaten up by work while my friends get to hang out and do things—like how Sophia, Michelle, and Riley were planning to go out for pizza after school the next day.

"Hey! Are you coming with us tomorrow?" asked Riley as she plunked herself down at the lunch table.

So Jelly

"She's working," said Sophia with her mouth full.

"What?" said Riley, and then without waiting for an answer, she called out, "Oh hey, Isabella, over here!" Sophia and I looked up to see Isabella walking toward us.

We live in a small town called Bellgrove, which is the kind of place where everyone knows everyone else and always has. People rarely move here, so we've been in school with the same kids since kindergarten.

Poor Elizabeth Ellis is still known as "Wetsy Betsy" because she peed her pants in kindergarten. That's awful, and maybe I'd feel differently if I were Elizabeth, but I think it's still pretty nice to hang out with kids you've always known. So now that we're in middle school, it's not like there are suddenly any new kids around, but it seems like the groups of friends are changing.

Sophia, Michelle, Riley, and I have been what my dad calls "four peas in a pod" since we were toddlers. We have other friends too, but everyone knows we've always been a crew.

But when school started, Riley was suddenly really into hanging out with Isabella, who seems to be joining us at lunch on the regular.

DONUT DREAMS

Whenever I complain about having more people around instead of it just being the four of us, my mom always replies, "When it comes to friends, additions are always okay, but subtractions are not."

So I'm trying to be okay with more friends, but sometimes I'd like to subtract Isabella and just make it Sophia, Michelle, Riley, and me, like it always has been.

Sophia wrinkled her brow a little bit when Isabella sat next to Riley. No one else noticed, but if you've known her for eleven years like I have, you'd have noticed.

Michelle uses a wheelchair, and she wheeled her way over to my side. "Scootch over," she said, and I made room for her.

"Hey, Isabella," Sophia said.

Isabella put her tray down and looked like she was going to cry.

"What's wrong?" Sophia asked.

"You guys, I totally think I am going to fail my coding class," Isabella said. "I just do not get it."

"Bella, it's only the second month of school!" said Riley. "You'll get the hang of it." I had never really heard anyone call Isabella "Bella" before.

So Jelly

"Yeah, chill out, Isabella," Michelle said. "Take a deep breath. It's going to be fine."

"Ugh," said Isabella. "It's just so hard and there's so much pressure. I mean, they all say that everything starts to matter in middle school if you want to go to college!" she complained.

"You still have a long way until college!" I said. "No need to worry about it now. Trust me, my sister Jenna is in high school. That's when the pressure really starts."

That wasn't entirely accurate. Jenna had been talking about college for a good seven years. Jenna is the oldest of my siblings (she's a junior in high school) and a little bossy. Actually she's *a lot* bossy.

She and Lindsay, and even my adopted sister Molly, who is a few months older than me, are always talking about going away to college. My parents are okay with this, but I can tell they don't want us to go too far. Jenna talks about how she wants to go to a school in California, which kind of scares me.

She is also always talking about "getting away" from our small town, like it's some bad place to be. She loves reading about big cities or seeing movies that take place in big cities. One year for her birthday, Jenna asked for a bunch of travel guidebooks to all the big cities in the world, even though she's only been to one of them: Chicago.

I don't understand why you'd ever want to leave Bellgrove. This town is home to me. I mean, sure, it would be nice to go somewhere sometimes without being totally recognized, but then again, seeing familiar people is kind of nice.

I like that the person who cuts my hair has been cutting it since I was a baby; that the librarian, Ms. Castro, has known me since even before I could read; and that every year we do the same things, like go apple picking at Green Hills Orchards in September before we get the same hot apple cider at Corner Stop.

I like living within a few minutes of just about every single person in my extended family. All those things to me are not just dull things we're stuck with—they're traditions and familiar people and they make me feel safe.

I know I'll have to go to college in another town because there isn't a college here, but the closest state university, where my mom and dad and aunt and uncle went to school, is about two hours away. Mom

So Jelly

keeps reassuring me that I can come home on the weekends if I want to.

When we have these conversations, Jenna just rolls her eyes and says, "Really, Kelsey? Stretch yourself! Open your eyes to new adventures! It's only two hours away!"

But to be honest, two hours away from *everything* I know sounds like plenty of an adventure for me.

"So," Sophia said, jolting me back to the table. "Are you going to try out for the field hockey team like we talked about?"

I nodded. "Yeah, it sounds fun, and Mom really wants me to do something active," I said.

Mom and Dad are always taking us on walks or bike rides, even when it's freezing cold outside. I wasn't too sure how I'd like playing competitively, but I love to be outside, especially in fall when the air turns crisp and smells so good.

"As long as I can still keep my hours working at the restaurant," I added.

"But your grandparents own the place where you work!" Riley said. "I'm guessing they can work with your schedule!"

"You'd think," I said, "but Grandpa is a stickler for

not giving us special consideration. We still have to clock in a certain amount of hours, unless our grades slip. School comes first."

"So if you fail a few tests, you can get out of work," snorted Isabella, or *Bella*.

"If I fail a few tests, I'd have a lot more to deal with than missing work," I retorted, kind of snapping at her. I don't know why, but Isabella gets under my skin sometimes.

"Well . . . ," said Riley. She paused, and Sophia and I looked up. "Bella and I were thinking about doing soccer instead of field hockey."

I caught Sophia's eyes, which looked as surprised as mine.

"That's great!" Michelle said. "So now I'll take photos of the soccer team as well as field hockey." Michelle takes awesome photos and dreams of being a professional photographer someday.

Riley bit her lip. "The thing is, I'm not sure I'm great at field hockey, and I know I'm a pretty good soccer player, so I want to try out for the team."

Isabella looked at her and smiled. I had a weird feeling they'd talked about this before. Sophia looked at me.

So Jelly

I shrugged. "Well, you should always do what makes you happy," I said. "Soph and I will be a team of two on the field hockey team."

Riley looked at me strangely. "Okay," she said. "I just don't want you guys to be disappointed that we all wouldn't be playing field hockey together. But you're right, you have each other on the field."

"Yep, we have each other," said Sophia.

It was quiet for a second, and then Michelle asked me, "So how is work going?"

I shrugged. "It's okay. A lot of the time I'd rather be somewhere else, but everyone in the family works there, so it's my turn to step up. Or at least that's what Grandpa said."

"Do you get to eat the extra donuts?" asked Isabella. "Because oh my goodness, I could eat, like, a dozen of those at a time."

"No," I said. "We donate the ones that haven't sold at the end of the day."

Sophia and I exchanged a smile, because everyone always asks me that question.

People think if you work at a donut shop you eat donuts all day, every day. In elementary school, Joshua Victor asked me if our house was made of donuts.

"Well, you've been known to show up with donuts," teased Riley, and I laughed.

I do try to bring donuts to my friends' houses when we have extra or when Mom brings them home.

"Work perk!" I said.

"Oh, I can almost taste those cider donuts," moaned Isabella. "Shoot, now all I want is a cider donut. It's definitely better than . . . whatever this lunch they're serving is."

"My favorites are the coffee-cake donuts," Michelle said. "And the chocolate ones with rainbow sprinkles. Or the plain glazed ones. Or . . ."

"We get it. You like donuts!" Riley said with a laugh.

Just then the bell rang. We gathered up our stuff and hustled out to our next class.

As we were going into the hall, Sophia grabbed my arm and hissed, "What is going on with Riley?"

I sighed and shrugged. "She *is* really good at soccer," I said.

"Well, Riley may be good at soccer, but she'd better be good at being our friend," said Sophia, and before I could respond, she shot off down the hall.

So Jelly

Isabella, Riley, and Michelle turned in a different direction, heading toward language arts, where they were in a class with my sister Molly. Before they went into their class, I caught Molly's eye as she walked by in the hallway.

It was obvious she could tell something was up. She was looking at me as if to ask, *What's going on?*

But I just said, "You'd better catch up to your potential new soccer teammates," and hurried off to my own class.

Middle school was different, that's for sure, and I don't think I like change.

Chapter Two
Sisterly Love

My dad is usually home after school. He teaches woodshop at the high school during the year, and in the summer he works for a construction company that his brother owns.

Molly and I dumped our stuff in the cubbies that he built us, kind of like lockers, near the back door and found him in the kitchen, making a snack.

You'd think that because Mom's family owns a restaurant she'd be a really good cook, but she totally is not. She jokes that's why she married Dad, because he can whip up anything and it's always delicious.

I sniffed. "Ooh, popcorn!"

"And hello to you too, honey," said Dad.

He was popping kernels in a deep pot on the

So Jelly

stove, and the kitchen smelled like a movie theater. He pushed a plate of sliced bananas and peanut butter toward us.

"Dad, where are the raisins on top?" Molly asked.

Dad used to call this snack "ants on a log," which we thought was hysterical. He slices the bananas lengthwise, smears on peanut butter, then scatters raisins on top. He used to tell us that they were ants crawling on a banana log. We thought it was funny, but it could also explain why I hate raisins . . . I mean, eww, eating ants! I always pick them off.

"We're out," said Dad. "It's still back-to-school season, and Mom and I have been so crazed and busy we haven't been able to get to the market."

"So, ant-less?" asked Molly.

"Yes, I'm afraid we are out of ants, Molls," said Dad. "So I am making it up to you with some popcorn."

"If we put these on top . . . ," said Molly, cocking her head and thinking.

"They could be clouds on a log," I said, taking a piece of hot popcorn.

"They could be fluffy sheep on a log," said Molly. "That makes more sense. Why would clouds be on a log?"

Dad grabbed the grocery list that Mom kept on the fridge door and wrote *raisins* on it.

"Okay, I'm still finishing up this summer job and I have to install the cabinets I built," he said. "So I'm going to head out until dinnertime."

This year Mom and Dad have been letting us stay in the house without them home, but only during the day. Dad is always here after school, though, which is nice, even if he's sometimes really annoying and asks a ton of questions about our day.

Today, though, Dad was in a hurry.

"Okay, dinner is in the slow cooker," he said, "so whatever you do, do not turn that thing off, or we'll all starve. Mom will be home by five thirty. We both have our phones at the ready, so just text or call if you need anything."

"Where's Jenna?" I asked.

"At work," said Dad. "Wait, is she at work? This new schedule . . . ," he muttered.

He scurried over to the bulletin board in the kitchen, where Mom keeps a monthly calendar and writes down who goes where on each day. Dad calls it the Command Center.

"Yep, yep, she went to work after she had a

student council meeting, and Mom will bring her home when her shift ends," said Dad.

"Dad, did you just lose track of a daughter?" teased Molly.

"No!" said Dad, but we all laughed.

Mom is crazy detail-oriented. Everything at home is organized beyond belief. Like the cans in our kitchen cabinets are basically alphabetized. Her socks are folded a certain way and arranged by color. Maybe it's because she's an accountant, and, as she says, accountants have to be precise about things because they work with numbers.

As the accountant for the restaurant, she makes sure that all the finances are up to date, like the staff gets paid, the bills are paid on time, and at the end of the month the restaurant isn't spending more money than it's making.

Uncle Charlie does all the ordering, everything from napkins to food to supplies like extra water glasses, because in a restaurant you are always breaking glasses. Uncle Mike runs Donut Dreams, where I work. Nans plans out the menus and figures out the daily specials, and makes her special donuts, and Grandpa . . . well, as Grandpa proudly tells everyone, he steers the ship and keeps it on course.

Everyone has their "own lane" as they all like to say, and they say that a lot to each other, as in "Hey, get out of my lane!" when they step on each other's toes. Everyone has a different role, but we all work together.

Dad builds things, so he has to be precise too, but in a really different way. When he's building something, he's all about measuring, and remeasuring, and cutting things accurately so everything fits together.

But when he isn't building something he isn't too precise, which drives Mom crazy. Once he went to pick me up at dance class . . . only I wasn't at dance class, I was waiting for him to pick me up at the library. He also once dropped off Molly for a playdate at the wrong house.

He's always messing up the laundry, too. Just last week Jenna was struggling and trying to get into a pair of jeans until she realized that they were mine; Dad had put them away in her closet instead.

"I have it together!" said Dad, a little indignantly.

"Okay," said Molly. "So you know you have to take me to soccer, right?"

"What?" said Dad, looking panicked.

So Jelly

"Practice starts at six," said Molly. "It's on the board!"

Dad went over to the bulletin board. "Oh ... yeah, there it is."

Just then our phones lit up with a text message from Mom.

> All good? Everyone home?

"It's like she senses when we need her," said Molly, laughing.

"She probably just wants to check in to see how school was," said Dad.

He texted back,

> All OK.

Molly added,

> Dad forgot soccer.

About two seconds later, Mom called Dad's phone. He picked up immediately and reassured her that everything was fine and that he would be home in time to get Molly to soccer, and that he would take me with him if she wasn't home from work yet.

He then left the house to finish his work, and the house was nice and quiet.

Not that my older sister Jenna or Dad or Mom are loud people, but you notice when they are around. I can always hear Mom puttering around the house, or Jenna playing music.

Sometimes I even hear Molly practicing with her soccer ball against a wall somewhere, stopping only when Mom or Dad yells, "Molly, cut it out!"

I wondered if our house would still be like this once Jenna left for college, when it would just be the four of us. It seems so weird that she wouldn't be here every day. The thing about having two sisters is that you get really used to having them around.

"Do you ever wonder what it will be like when Jenna moves out?" I asked Molly, who was sitting right next to me at the counter.

"What?" she asked, looking up from her phone.

"When Jenna goes to college," I said, a little annoyed that she wasn't listening. "When it's just the four of us instead of five, do you worry that it will be weird?"

So Jelly

Molly wrinkled her forehead. "I dunno," she said. "Like will we miss her?"

"Well, we'll miss her, sure," I said. "But I mean, what will dinner be like without her? What will the weekends be like?"

"Well, the weekends will be easier, because we don't have to worry about making noise and waking her up," said Molly, in her very matter-of-fact Molly way.

This was true. Jenna liked to sleep in on the weekends, and she was always barking at us to keep it down. Molly and I are early risers.

"But won't it be like one person is just missing?" I asked.

I knew Molly wasn't always into these kinds of conversations, so I was pushing it.

"Things change, Kelsey," Molly said in a tone that sounded like she was explaining it to a two-year-old.

"Oh, never mind," I said, and pushed away my chair. Molly was making me feel worse instead of better.

Sometimes getting people to talk in our family was impossible. My cousin Lindsay was the one I used to talk to about everything. We're just about the same age and grew up together, so in a lot of ways we are more like sisters than cousins.

But Lindsay's mom, my aunt Amy, died a couple years ago after being sick for a long time. If you talk to Lindsay, she doesn't burst into tears or anything, or at least not usually, but I'm always really careful when I talk to her now, especially if I'm talking about my family.

If, say, I complain about Mom, I'm worried that Lindsay is really thinking, *Oh, well, at least you still have your mom*. If I tried to talk to her about how weird it would be with Jenna gone, I'm afraid she would think, *Well, she's just going to college. She's coming back. But my mom isn't.*

Lindsay is actually really sweet, so I don't think she'd think those things on purpose, and she would never say them to me out loud, but there are things I just can't talk to her about anymore.

"You'd better get your homework started before Mom gets home," said Molly.

I looked over, annoyed, and I noticed that while I'd been sitting there thinking, she had already set up her laptop and was typing away.

Molly is only eight months older than I am, but

So Jelly

she acts like she is my much older sister. So between her and Jenna, I really feel ganged up on sometimes and like I am the baby of the family.

Jenna and Molly are a lot alike. They are both super organized and they belong to a million different clubs and are always thinking about their next project or what they'll be doing in ten years.

Dad calls me Kelsey Dreamer because I guess I daydream a lot, and I like to take my time doing things. I just don't feel that crazy rushing sense or the competitiveness that Jenna and Molly seem to have been born with.

I opened my laptop, logged in, and clicked over to the homework page and sighed. Ugh. There is *so* much homework in middle school. There was no way I'd finish before dinner, which I hated. I liked to be able to relax after dinner, and have what Dad calls downtime, when you kind of just do nothing.

I peeked over at Molly. "Do we have to read this whole chapter for history?" I asked.

"Yes," said Molly, her hands flying over the keyboard.

I opened the window and breathed in. "Ooh, someone is burning leaves," I said. I love that smell.

DONUT DREAMS

I positioned my chair so the breeze from outside tickled my face. It was a shame to spend such a beautiful afternoon inside doing homework.

Then I looked over at Molly again. "Did you finish reading it already?" I asked.

"Yeeesss," said Molly with a hint of annoyance, not looking up from her laptop.

"What is it about?" I asked.

"KELSEY!" Molly screamed so loud I jumped. "You have to do your own homework! I'm not going to do it for you!"

"I wasn't asking you to do my homework," I said crossly. "I was just curious."

"If you're curious, then open the book," said Molly, and she sounded exactly like Mom when she said it.

I sat there for a few more minutes, listening to the leaves crinkle in the wind. Dad was going to make us help rake them up on the weekend.

"Kelsey, I can help you if you get stuck, but you have to start and you have to try," said Molly.

"Okay," I said, eating some more popcorn. "This tastes so much better when Dad makes it on the stove than in the microwave," I said. "And it's fluffier."

So Jelly

Molly looked at me sideways. "Thanks for the review, Princess Popcorn," she said.

I snickered.

Molly looked over and giggled too. Then she grabbed a handful and chewed. "You're right," she said. "This does taste good."

She glanced over at me with a mischievous twinkle in her eye that I know well and said, "Sheep on a log! Well, what if those sheep *flew*?"

Then she hurled a fistful of popcorn at me.

"MOLLY!" I screamed, shaking popcorn from my hair but laughing.

I tossed some down the back of her shirt.

"Oh, it is *on*, Princess Popcorn!" she said, and showered me with half of what was in the bowl.

We were both throwing the popcorn and cracking up when we heard my mom say, loudly, "Girls, what on earth is going on in here?"

Jenna peered around her. "Are you maniacs having a popcorn fight?"

We both said, "No!" while popcorn fell from our hair, and we tried not to giggle.

Mom sighed and handed me the broom and Molly the dustpan. "I don't even want to know. And

DONUT DREAMS

I don't want to see anything either... please clean up this mess."

I started sweeping and Molly scooped up the piles, but we couldn't stop laughing.

"Sheep on a log!" Molly whispered, trying to stifle her laughter.

"What are sheep on a log?" asked Jenna.

"What happens when you don't have ants," I said, and Molly started to laugh even harder.

"What?" asked Jenna, but she started to laugh too.

Sometimes that happens when we're all together. We just start laughing and we can't stop, sometimes over something silly and sometimes over nothing at all.

Mom looked at the three of us cackling and threw up her hands. "I don't get it," she said. "But the sound of you three girls laughing is always the best."

Molly and I settled down and cleaned up and Jenna started to set the table. I felt another surge—this was so nice—the three of us together with our own secret kind of language.

Why would you ever want to leave it? I just wished it could stay this way forever.

Chapter Three
Morning Meeting Surprise

Every day at school we have the morning meeting in the cafeteria. All the classes gather there and we hang out until Principal Clarke stands up and reads any announcements or talks about upcoming events.

I headed over to the corner table where I always sat with Sophia, Michelle, and Riley, and I was surprised to see Isabella sitting there already.

"Good morning!" she said, smiling at me.

I looked around, thinking it was odd that she wasn't sitting with Olivia, whom she was normally always with.

"Hi!" I said, and dropped my backpack on the table.

Isabella was best friends with Olivia. They'd been

inseparable all summer long and they'd join us at the lake, usually with Hannah and Elizabeth, too. I hadn't really seen the two of them hanging out much since school started, though....

Casey and my cousin Lindsay sat across from us. Casey and Lindsay had been BFFs since they were babies. We're all still friends with each other, but we all have certain friends we're closer to than others. Or at least we used to.

"How was soccer?" I asked Isabella.

"Oh, Riley didn't tell you?" she said.

Again, I got this short-tempered feeling. It wasn't like she'd said anything bad or wrong, but it was just the fact that she said it that bothered me.

"No, that's why I'm asking you," I said.

"Oh," said Isabella, either not noticing I was annoyed or ignoring me. "She did really great. She was on a scrimmage team with Molly."

I wondered why Molly hadn't mentioned it.

Riley bounded in, chomping on a bagel, with Sophia in tow. Riley was a total talk-fest, while Sophia and I were usually quieter until we got going. We're both early risers but not naturally enthusiastic morning people.

So Jelly

"Hey, Bella Bella!" Riley chimed.

Sophia and I looked at each other, annoyed at her perkiness.

A minute or two later Hannah sat down with us, and so did Elizabeth. We all paused for a moment while Elizabeth unpacked her food. Her mom made her the most awesome sandwiches and salads.

Every time my grandfather would see Elizabeth at the restaurant, he would remind her to tell her mom there's always a job open for her as a chef if she wants one.

Elizabeth smiled at all of us as she took out her sandwich.

"Nothing very exotic this morning," she informed us. "Cream cheese on date nut bread."

"That's exotic to me," Michelle said. "I've never had cream cheese on anything but a bagel!"

"The crunchy nuts are good with the cream cheese," Elizabeth said.

We all chatted about our food for a few minutes when suddenly Hannah cleared her throat dramatically so we all turned to look at her.

"So, I'm running for student council," she said, whipping her phone out. "And in order to run, I need twenty-five signatures to get on the ballot."

"I'll sign," said Sophia, and took Hannah's phone. "Wait . . . you're running with Olivia?"

"Yeah!" said Hannah. "Olivia is my running mate. Our campaign slogan is 'Two Girls Can Get It Done!'"

"I didn't know you guys were that friendly," I said.

"What do you mean?" said Hannah. She waved her hand around. "We've all known each other since kindergarten!"

That was true. But when did Hannah even start talking to Olivia, let alone hanging out with her? We'd all hung out at the lake together this past summer, but I'd never noticed Hannah and Olivia being particularly buddy-buddy.

"You need a campaign plan," said Riley, signing after Sophia. "We should talk about it after school when we go for pizza."

"But Kelsey can't come," said Michelle. "She has to work."

They all looked at me.

"Sorry," I said, looking down at the phone and signing my name.

Part of me wasn't so mad that I had to work. I

So Jelly

wasn't sure about all this new student council stuff or hanging out with Olivia, Isabella, Hannah, and Elizabeth instead of just Sophia, Michelle, and Riley.

"Good morning, ladies and gentlemen," said Principal Clarke into the microphone.

The room settled down.

"Today we have to report that a lost gray sweatshirt was left in the STEAM lab. If it's yours, please come to the office during lunch."

"Oh that's mine!" yelled Jeff Simons, and everyone laughed.

"Okay, Jeff. You can pick it up later," said Principal Clarke. "Also, we have some exciting new programs this year. We've decided that we are going to elect class representatives for each grade, one student per grade.

"And this position will be different from student council. Our representatives will actually be representing their classes with the teachers and working on how to improve your school day. So think of your rep as your human suggestion box.

"The idea is that you can go to your rep with issues or concerns or questions, and your rep will bring them to a committee that some teachers and

I will be on to make decisions about your concerns.

"The rep should be someone who is a good listener, who can work with many groups of people, and who is enthusiastic about our time at Bellgrove Middle School. We have nominations that will go in the ballot box in the cafeteria.

"If you know of someone you think can best represent your class, please write down their name and submit it to us. The results will be announced next Friday."

There was a lot of conversation and murmuring. Lindsay and Casey nodded at each other and then looked at me.

"Our grade representative should be you, Kelsey," Casey said.

"ME?" I looked at them, stunned. "Why?"

"Well," said Lindsay, "you get along with everyone, and you're a pretty good student."

She cleared her throat, because she knew I'd had a lot of trouble with social studies last year.

"And you really do always know the right thing to say. Also, if it's supposed to be someone who loves BMS, well, anytime anyone says something bad about Bellgrove, you always say how wonderful it is. You

So Jelly

should be, like, the spokesperson for living here."

I knew that Lindsay, like Jenna, couldn't wait to get out of Bellgrove, so I wasn't quite sure if she was complimenting me or if she was shading me just a little bit.

Sophia put her arm around me. "You are the best representative for everything, Kels," she said.

"Absolutely!" said Riley. "I vote for Kelsey!"

I smiled.

You can always rely on your BFFs. Even when they try out for the soccer team.

Chapter Four
A Bad Day At Work

As far as jobs at the Park go, working at the Donut Dreams counter is one of the easiest, and I think that's why they gave it to Lindsay, then just paired me with her. It's not that everyone always just gives Lindsay a pass. I mean, she does have to work, but it's like everyone in our family tries to make things a lot easier for her if they can.

After Aunt Amy died, Mom sat us down and talked about how we'd need to be sensitive around Lindsay. And while I totally get that, I also wonder when we won't have to tiptoe around her anymore, and when things can finally go back to normal.

I was in a little bit of a sour mood when I arrived

So Jelly

at the Park, because I knew Sophia and Riley and Michelle were out for pizza and I had to work.

Michelle had texted me,

> Wish u were here!

She had also sent a selfie of her taking a huge bite out of the most amazing slice of pepperoni pizza I had ever seen. My mouth had watered just looking at it.

Guess I looked more grouchy than I thought, because when I walked in, tying my apron behind me, Grandpa boomed, "What's wrong? Aren't you glad to be at work today, my lovely Kelsey?"

He was standing at the front podium of the restaurant. A podium is kind of funny, when you think about it, because we have one at school. It's like a stand that they roll out when we have an assembly or a speaker, and the speaker stands behind it.

We have one at the restaurant, because that's where the host stands. The host greets everyone who comes in and asks how many people are in their party (which also makes me giggle, because how is going out for lunch a party?), and then shows them to their table.

DONUT DREAMS

My cousin Lily is the host a lot because she's really friendly and patient with people. She's also not the *best* waitress because she's a little clumsy, so they had to find another job for her.

I sighed. "Well, I'm coming to work on a beautiful day, Grandpa," I said.

"And?" he bellowed.

"And my friends all went out for pizza after school and I had to come to work," I said, frowning. I knew I sounded a little bratty, but I couldn't help it.

"Some people would be very glad to have a job, Ms. Kelsey," said Grandpa. "You are lucky to be able to start making money to save for college."

College. Again. Why was everyone so obsessed with college?

"And," he said, "that's why they call it work and not play. Just like homework. They don't call it 'homeplay,' do they?"

I shook my head.

"Now, try not to look so grumpy," said Grandpa. "Customers don't like buying a sweet donut from a grumpy server!"

I blew the bangs off my forehead. They were annoying me today too.

So Jelly

I forced a smile at Grandpa and walked over to the Donut Dreams counter, where Lindsay was already wiping down the glass case.

"Hi," I said unenthusiastically.

"Bad mood?" asked Lindsay.

"Yeah," I said, and then I regretted it.

I mean, what did I really have to be in a bad mood about in front of Lindsay? I still had my mom and dad and everyone was healthy.

I put my phone under the counter, as we had to do when we were working. Grandpa was a real stickler about that.

"How busy are we?" I asked Lindsay, who was making sure all the trays were filled and neat.

"Not too bad," she said. "I got here a little early and there were some high school kids, but not a huge crowd."

I leaned on the counter, which was another Grandpa "no-no." You were always supposed to look "alert and approachable," according to the rules. Grandpa had *a lot* of rules at the restaurant.

When you started working at the Park and at Donut Dreams, you got a little employee handbook with all the rules listed. Most of them were pretty obvious, like always wash your hands, which is reasonable if you are serving food (because eeeeuuw!), but some of them were a pain: no cell phones, no leaning, say hello to everyone you see, no eating in the dining area of the restaurant—only in the kitchen. Grandpa thought it looked sloppy to have the employees shoving food in their mouths or dropping crumbs all over the place.

Sometimes Lindsay and I snuck a donut under the counter if we were really slow. It is hard to be around them all day without wanting just a little bite, but usually by the end of my shifts, I never want to see or smell a donut again.

Mom came out of the back room, where her office was, and waved at me.

"Ah, I wanted to make sure Jenna dropped you off," she said.

"I'm here," I said.

Mom frowned. "Did you have a bad day?"

"No," I said, not really wanting to get into it.

Mom looked at me for a second, paused, then gave me a quick kiss on the head. Then she went over to Lindsay and gave her a quick kiss too.

"How was your day, honey?" she asked.

So Jelly

Lindsay smiled. "It was okay," she said, "but we have tons of homework over the weekend!"

"That's middle school for you," said Mom. "Hey, did Nans talk to you about starting piano lessons?"

Lindsay shook her head.

"Okay," said Mom. "Because your dad said you were interested, so I'm trying to find a teacher who can come to the house."

"Cool," said Lindsay. "Thanks, Aunt Melissa."

I wondered why Mom was busy trying to find a piano teacher for Lindsay.

Nans and Grandpa were always around, so they could help out. So that meant that Lindsay and her brother, Skylar, had three people looking after them, plus Mom. Jenna, Molly, and I only had Mom and Dad, and they were barely hanging on with how busy they were.

"Okay, girls, have a good shift," said Mom. "I've got to get back to work. Wait . . ." She turned around. "Did you girls have a snack after school?"

"Nans packed me some peanut butter crackers," said Lindsay.

Mom looked at me. "Did Dad give you anything?"

"Well, all we had were graham crackers, since no

one had time to go to the supermarket this week," I pouted.

Mom looked a little annoyed at my pout. "Well, luckily you work in a restaurant with a pretty extensive menu. What do you want?"

"Nothing," I said. "I'm not hungry."

I knew I was acting a little snotty and I didn't even really know why, but I still couldn't help myself.

Mom sighed and I could tell she was about to say something, but then she changed her mind.

"Okay, well, I'm here if you need me," she said, and then headed back to her office.

Lindsay and I wiped the shelves down in silence, then swept the floor behind the counter. Then we ran out of things to do, so we just tried to look busy.

The after-school crowd comes in various waves. Grandpa usually shuffles some people around and has one of the waitresses work the donut counter to serve some of the kids before Lindsay and I get there.

"I didn't know you wanted to take piano lessons," I finally said.

Lindsay shrugged. "Yeah, well, Dad keeps telling me I need more activities. And I don't really like any sports, so we figured music might be good. Hey,

So Jelly

speaking of sports, do you have field hockey tryouts tomorrow?"

"No tryouts yet," I said, "Practice starts tomorrow, and we scrimmage so they can watch everyone. Then they do the observations and decide who makes the team."

I heard the bell ring when the front door to the restaurant opened, and a pack of kids came swarming in and made a beeline for the Donut Dreams counter.

"Brace yourself," I said.

"Oh boy," said Lindsay. "Here come the East twins."

For the next half hour we were slammed, with kids whining, "That one . . . no, no, that one," as our hands hovered over exactly which donut they wanted.

Freddy Benson had a fit, claiming that his sister got a bigger donut than he did, even though they were exactly the same.

One mom came in with two little girls. They had enormous blue eyes and hair so blond it almost looked white. They looked like two tiny angels—sweet and innocent.

One of the girls asked me for a chocolate glazed donut, "with extra sprinkles, please." The second girl wanted a jelly donut. Their mom looked exhausted and just ordered a coffee.

I handed the first girl her chocolate donut, heaped with sprinkles.

She thanked me politely and then promptly smashed the donut into her sister's hair and face. "That's for losing my Barbie," she yelled.

Her sister screamed and then threw *her* donut at her sister, before anyone could stop her.

Grandpa was there immediately to help clean up.

"That's a waste of two delicious donuts, young ladies," he said to the girls.

He was trying to look stern, but I saw he was trying really hard not to laugh.

Their mom was mortified and kept apologizing.

Grandpa waved his hand as if to say, *Don't worry about it*, and then gave the mom an old-fashioned donut on the house.

Another mother was leaving the restaurant area when both of her kids (a boy and a girl) spotted the Donut Dreams counter and started chanting, "Donuts! Donuts! Dooo-nuts!"

The mom sighed heavily and said, "Donuts aren't really good for you."

So Jelly

"They are good for the soul," Lindsay said seriously.

"And for your tummy!" I said, laughing.

"You know what they say," Grandpa said, joining the conversation. "You can be sad before you eat a donut. And you can be sad after you eat a donut. But nobody is ever sad *while* they are eating a donut!"

The mom laughed and said to her children, "All right. Just this once!"

The kids whooped and cheered as they picked out their treats.

"Oh, they'll be back," Grandpa said with a smile.

Lindsay and I looked at each other after the line finally died down and said, "Whoa" at the same time.

I started sweeping up all the sprinkle crumbs on the floor, and she was wiping down the small tables and chairs that we have right next to the counter.

We almost had everything back to normal when Uncle Mike, Lindsay's dad, came over.

"Hey, girls," he said. "Listen, Skylar has an earache and I need to run him over to the doctor." He looked a little worried. "Nans is with him in the car out front but he doesn't want Nans to take him, so she'll come here and will step in if anything comes up for you."

"Poor Sky," said Lindsay.

DONUT DREAMS

Skylar can be an enormous pain, but he's also really cute. I flinched because I used to get earaches all the time and they were really painful.

Lindsay and I watched as Uncle Mike switched spots with Nans in the car outside, and Nans headed into the restaurant.

I almost said, *Poor kid probably just wants his mom*, which is what I want when I get sick, but I caught myself just in time.

"How are my girls?" asked Nans.

"Selling lots of donuts today!" said Lindsay.

"Excellent!" said Nans. She came over and gave me a little hug. "Always happy to see my girls hard at work."

She went over to talk to Grandpa, then headed into the kitchen.

At the end of the day's shift, we need to use the iPad and enter in all the sales. That automatically adds up how many donuts we sold and how much money we should have in the cash drawer. If the cash drawer doesn't match the receipts, there can be a big problem.

Then we pack up all the extra donuts. Every night Grandpa drops them off at the police station, the firehouse, and the senior center, so we divide

So Jelly

them into three boxes. If there aren't enough to fill three boxes, then Grandpa puts in some cake or pie so everyone still gets some goodies. As we packed up the boxes at the end of our shift, I started to relax a little bit from the week.

We have something called Family of Five Fridays. Every Friday all five of us are home for an early dinner together, and after dinner we all either watch a movie or play a game. We've been doing it ever since I can remember. Jenna tried to get out of it a few times to go out with her friends, but Mom and Dad put their foot down, and she stopped trying. Sometimes we can hang out with friends after school, but we can't miss dinner.

We were just about done with the boxes when Mom came over with her keys in her hand. "When you're done closing, just let Nans know," she said. "I'll be waiting outside."

"Is Nans taking me home?" asked Lindsay.

"Oh!" said Mom. "Didn't Mike tell you? You're coming home for dinner with us tonight. That way your dad can get Sky in bed and we can try to make sure you don't get sick too. We'll run you home after we're done with game night."

DONUT DREAMS

"Oh," said Lindsay, and she didn't seem sad exactly, just kind of uncertain.

So now Lindsay was barging in on Family of Five Friday. I knew it wasn't nice, but that made me even more crabby. Family of Five Fridays was about *our* family of five. It wasn't about "additional guests." Like I said, I don't deal well with change.

I sighed.

Why couldn't anything just stay the same?

Chapter Five
Not a Team Player

I got up early on Saturday like I usually do. Jenna is the only one in our family who sleeps in on weekends.

The rest of us are early risers, and when I got downstairs, Mom and Dad had already gone for their run and Molly was sitting at the table reading a book, dressed in her soccer outfit.

"Does anyone know I have field hockey today?" I asked, and Molly looked up.

"Is it on the board?" she asked.

I looked. "Yeah."

"Then they know. Or at least Mom does."

I sighed, poured myself a glass of orange juice, and sat down.

On Saturdays Mom doesn't have to be in the

office, so she and Dad go for their run, and then we have a big breakfast.

"Why were you in such a bad mood last night?" Molly asked.

"I wasn't," I lied.

"You were," said Molly matter-of-factly.

She turned the page of her book. Molly was always able to do more than one thing at a time.

"And honestly, I'm not sure you were too friendly to Lindsay," she added

"I don't think I was *un*friendly," I said.

I just kind of ignored Lindsay. Which you could say wasn't very friendly. I was just so mad to have her crash our Family Friday night.

"So what's up?" Molly asked.

I decided not to answer her and went upstairs to get dressed for field hockey. I had played last year, but it was basically just for fun. I wasn't sure what to expect with something more competitive.

I texted Sophia to see what she was wearing, then settled on shorts, a T-shirt, and a sweatshirt, since it was getting a little chilly this time of year. I put my hair in a ponytail and looked at my face in the mirror.

Jenna started wearing a little makeup in high

So Jelly

school, but Mom was really strict about what she could wear.

I noticed that some of the girls in my class were wearing makeup this year. It was weird: the day before school started, nobody was wearing any makeup when we were at the lake, and then the next day at school, a lot of girls just showed up with lip gloss and mascara and even, in the case of Marina Miles, blush.

I didn't think I could push it, and it was just field hockey practice, so I brushed my hair out, put on a little bit of the pink lip gloss Jenna had given me, and went downstairs.

"Are you wearing lip gloss to hockey practice?" asked Molly. My sister does not miss a thing.

"No," I said sarcastically. "My lips are naturally this shiny and pink."

She scowled at me.

Mom and Dad came through the side door, panting and laughing.

"I was not that slow today," said Dad.

Mom shook her head. "Your pace was off," she said. "It was like running with a turtle."

Everyone in my family was active, which was great, but they were also competitive. Mom and Dad

DONUT DREAMS

didn't just go on a weekly run together, they actually raced each other.

Molly was a little nuts about soccer and always played in the competitive league, and Jenna is one of the stars on the tennis team and is always talking about her form. She's a great player, but she can be a little annoying when she talks about tennis.

Me, well, I like sports and I like to play, but I don't always care who wins the game. So I wasn't really nervous about field hockey, just more curious about what it would be like.

Dad took a quick shower and drove me to the town field where everybody goes to practice.

"Do you want me to stay?" he asked as I opened the car door.

"You don't have to," I said. "But it ends at noon, so can you pick me up then?"

"I'll be here!" said Dad.

He waited until I trotted over to the field and then waved and drove off.

Sophia was waiting for me on the field, as planned. Hannah was already there talking to her, and I spotted Olivia walking toward them. I could also see Michelle already snapping tons of photos from the sidelines. It

So Jelly

was an all-middle-school team, so there were also a lot of older girls who were hanging out together.

Hannah waved to Olivia, and Olivia walked over to us.

"Hi," she said shyly. "Anyone else a little nervous?"

Hannah looked around. "Well, if it's just the four of us and they need representation from every class, it looks like we're in without even having to show them we know how to hold a stick!"

We all laughed.

"Oh, speaking of representation," said Olivia. "I nominated you, Kelsey, for the class representative."

"You did?" I said, surprised.

"Yeah, I asked Casey, and she said she and Lindsay were suggesting you to everyone because you're such a good listener. And Lindsay said you were really supportive, too."

"She's the best listener," said Sophia, flinging her arm around me. "I'd vote for her for anything!"

"Oh speaking of voting," I said. "Olivia, I hear you're running for student council with Hannah."

"Yes! Vote for us!" said Hannah, smiling.

"Well, the two of you have my vote too," I said.

"Thanks!" said Olivia. "That means a lot."

She said it really warmly, and I realized that maybe she was nice. Maybe it was just that I didn't know her well enough before.

"Hey, we should post pictures of our practice on our campaign page," suggested Hannah.

She took out her phone, and she and Olivia grinned for a selfie.

"I'll caption this, 'We're on the team and we are a team!'" Hannah said.

"Oh, that's good!" said Olivia. "But we're not on the team yet."

Coach Wickstead blew her whistle. "Okay, girls!" she shouted.

She called us over, then split us into teams of six so we could play three on three. Then she divided the field and assigned us our spot.

I was paired with two older girls, Amanda and Tracey. Amanda took charge and dropped the ball and we started to play.

I noticed that she grunted a lot and would mutter, "Pass, pass," or "Defense," either to herself or to one of us, I wasn't even sure. It was kind of annoying.

We took a water break and all sat on the side of the field. It was one of those perfect fall days where

So Jelly

it was warm and sunny but there was a little bit of a breeze.

Say what you will about being stuck in a small town, like Jenna and Lindsay do, but we were stuck in a beautiful town, that's for sure. The old oak trees around the field were thick and tall, and you could hear the brook behind them actually bubbling. There was blue sky forever. If you leaned back and looked up, it felt like you were inside a big, blue snow globe.

The whistle blew again and we finished our last scrimmage. Coach Wickstead had us log our stats at the end of the practice.

Amanda wrote ours down. "Don't worry," she said to me. "This is just the first practice."

I was surprised, because I hadn't really been worried. I mean, I hadn't scored, but I didn't think I'd played badly.

As we were walking to the parking lot, I told Sophia what Amanda had said.

"Oh, she's the star player," she said. "She lives and breathes field hockey. Don't mind her."

Dad was waiting by the car, watching my cousin Rich practice lacrosse on the field next to us. He waved to Rich, then turned to me.

"How'd it go, kiddo?" he asked.

"It was okay," I said. "Next practice is Monday."

"I didn't want to hover," said Dad, "or make you nervous."

"Why would I be nervous?" I asked. "It was just a practice! Plus, it was fun!"

"Well," said Dad. "You know the coaches are still watching to see where the strengths are and who might play each position. Plus, Jenna . . ."

"Oh, well, Jenna is kind of nuts about that stuff," I said.

"Yes, she is," said Dad. "But she's conditioned us!"

Jenna is insanely superstitious about who comes to her matches, where we sit, and even, one year, what Mom wears.

Jenna had won a really tough match one time when Mom was wearing a sweatshirt, and Jenna made Mom wear that same sweatshirt to every match she had for the rest of the season. By the last match we called it the "stinky sweatshirt," even though Mom swore she washed it after each wear. It's totally bonkers.

We drove over to Molly's soccer practice, and Dad and I sat on the bleachers, watching. Molly liked Dad to watch her practices and games, and they always talked about them afterward.

I spotted Riley and Isabella on the field. Riley was right; she was really good, and pretty confident on the field. She and Molly were passing the ball back and forth, smiling at each other and nodding.

Then she and Isabella passed the ball back and forth. Isabella wasn't as fast or as great with her foot skills, which for some reason made me just a little happy. Maybe she wouldn't make the team.

"Wow, I didn't know Riley was playing soccer instead of hockey with you," Dad said.

"Yeah," I said, and stopped. I didn't know if I felt like getting into it.

"So some of the peas in the pod split?" Dad asked, clearly wanting to know more.

"We didn't split," I said testily. "Riley just thinks she's better at soccer, that's all."

Dad looked at me closely but didn't push it. Instead he said, "I was just making a little joke. Split peas . . . get it?"

I groaned.

"Hiya!" Riley waved to us as the practice ended. "How was hockey?"

"It was okay," I said. "You looked good."

"Did I?" Riley asked, and grinned. "That's good to hear. Your sister is a real monster out there. I hope I can keep up with her."

"If I don't get home and eat lunch, I'm going to eat the car," said Molly.

"Let's go, girls," said Dad. "I can afford lunch, but I can't afford another car!"

Jenna was sitting at the kitchen table, scrolling through her phone, when we came inside.

"How was hockey?" she asked.

"Fine," I said. "It was a nice morning to be outside."

Jenna looked at me strangely. "Well, yes, but how did you do in the practice?"

"Okay, I guess," I said.

"How were the other girls?" asked Dad.

He was making himself more coffee as Molly made a peanut butter sandwich.

"They're good," I said.

"Last year they had really good offense but not such a great defensive line," said Molly. "Is Amanda playing this year?"

"Yes," I said. "She was on my scrimmage team."

So Jelly

"Oh wow," said Jenna, "so they paired you with the star. That's a good sign."

"A sign of what?" I asked.

"That you'll make the team," said Jenna, speaking slowly.

"Oh, I'll make the team," I said. "There are only four girls from my year trying out. They'll use us somehow."

"But you might not get to play," said Molly.

"Eh," I said. "I don't mind. I still get to play in the practices. Besides, the games might be too much pressure."

"Kelsey, are you sure you even want to be on the team?" asked Dad. "If you want to play and not compete, you can probably just play with some friends when you feel like it."

The three of them were looking at me like I didn't understand field hockey. I could feel my face get hot, and my hands balled up. I stood up and faced them.

"I understand that I'm not going to be the star of the team. I understand that I might not even make the first line. But I can still be part of a team and still have fun," I snapped.

I looked at Dad. "And that is why you and Mom

tell us to play in the first place. So if I got that wrong, and you want me to be stressed out and beating myself up and not enjoying a morning on the field getting a great workout with some girls, let me know," I added.

Molly's and Jenna's eyes popped open wide. Even Dad looked like he didn't know what to say.

I looked at them all like they were crazy, grabbed a glass of water, and marched upstairs.

Maybe they could all go away, I thought, *and just leave me here in peace.*

Chapter Six
The More the Merrier—Not!

Monday mornings are the worst. The *worst*. But Monday mornings in my mind actually start on Sunday night.

Sunday night in our house is "planning night," according to Mom. We go over everyone's schedule for the week, and then Mom and Dad make sure everyone is covered—that means anyone who needs a ride or needs to be picked up somewhere has a parent to meet them or bring them where they need to be. Mom puts everything on the board, and some weeks can get pretty insane with all the scribbles.

Mom was just about to write in next weekend's plans when Jenna said, "It's Fall Fest this weekend!"

"Wow, that happened fast," said Mom. "Time is

just flying by." She shook her head and wrote it on the board.

Fall Fest is a big deal in town. One Saturday every fall, there is a festival with a parade, music, and food. The Park is a big part of it, and Donut Dreams, of course, because who doesn't love an apple cider donut at a fall festival?

A lot of the businesses or even school groups, like the high school field hockey team, have booths that sell stuff or give away things like T-shirts or even mugs. Everyone wears school colors, which are red and white.

That night, after performances from a few of the school choruses and the high school marching band, there's a big bonfire at the lake. Everyone comes down with blankets, and families sit together with chocolatey s'mores and watch the fireworks that end the night.

Fall Fest is also a big deal for our family. Since everyone in our family is usually a little crazy working at Fall Fest, between the food that the Park provides and the donuts that Donut Dreams sells in the morning, we have a tradition called Family Fall Fest.

So Jelly

The night before, Dad fills in for Mom at the restaurant, helping to pack up food and equipment to move it to Main Street, which is where the parade and booths are.

Mom takes the three of us out for dinner—"just us girls," as we like to say—at one of our favorite restaurants, Louie Louie, which is a couple towns over. They have two things that we always get: fried ravioli and something called butter cake, which is this gooey vanilla cake that I could eat for days.

We actually get dressed up, even though the restaurant isn't too fancy, and it's a lot of fun. Even Molly wears a skirt or a dress.

"So next Friday is Family Fall Fest?" I asked excitedly.

"Seems that way," said Mom.

"Butter cake!" Molly yelled. "Yes! Oh, I can taste it already!"

"Fried ravioli!" cried Jenna.

"I want you to remember St. Louis fried ravioli the next time you think about going to school in California," teased Dad.

"I'll just have it when I come home, Dad!" said Jenna, laughing. "Besides, in California you can have strawberries all year round. Much healthier for you!"

"Yeah, but fried ravioli tastes better!" said Dad.

This perked me up. I loved Family Fall Fest, and I was excited because even if the week was a hard one—hello, math test—there was a really great weekend waiting for us.

"This year Lindsay is coming with us," said Mom.

She was acting as Dad's sous chef, chopping the veggies for the stir-fry he was making.

"To Fall Fest?" I asked, confused.

"No, to *Family* Fall Fest," said Mom without looking up. "I thought it would be nice to include her. The more the merrier."

"But Mom, it's supposed to be just US!" I wailed.

Mom looked up from the cutting board, surprised, and Dad turned around to look at me too.

I didn't mean to sound so angry about it, but a tradition was a tradition. It was pretty rare that the three sisters were together with just Mom, and besides, Family Fall Fest had always been that way.

"Well," said Mom slowly. "Lindsay is family. And Family Fall Fest is, well, about our family. I think she'd really appreciate being included."

"Well, if it's Family Fall Fest, then why not invite

So Jelly

Dad," I said testily. I knew it didn't sound very nice when I said it out loud, but I just couldn't help how angry I was.

"It's just girls," said Mom. "And Dad is helping Grandpa, Nans, Uncle Mike, and Uncle Charlie so they can prep for the next day." I could tell by her tone that she was quickly getting irritated and impatient with me.

"Kelsey, you have been such a brat all weekend," said Jenna. "What is going on?"

"I'm not a brat!" I yelled.

But even as I was saying it, deep down inside I knew I was.

"Girls!" said Dad. "Cease-fire!"

He and Mom exchanged glances, and I could tell that he had probably told her about how angry I got after being grilled about hockey practice.

"I've already invited her," said Mom in that kind of voice that means *this is done and we are not discussing it further.* "And she was so happy. Remember, Kelsey, that it's been a tough time for her, and family is all about being there for each other when times are tough."

"Well, it's been a tough year for me too!" I said,

and as Mom was opening her mouth, I added, "And no, I don't want to talk about it!"

I stomped up the stairs to my room, which thankfully was nice and quiet and, most importantly, away from my family.

In our house you can pretty much hear everyone from every room, and I could hear Mom and Dad murmuring about me and asking Molly what was going on at school.

A few minutes later there was a knock on my door, and, expecting it to be Mom or Dad telling me it was time for dinner, I said, "I'll be right there."

But Jenna poked her head in. "Hey, pip-squeak," she said, calling me a nickname that she hadn't used in a while.

She flopped down on the bed next to me and looked at my face. "Are you wearing lip gloss?"

I sighed. "Yeah."

"It looks nice," she said.

Then she ran out of the room and came back with what looked like a giant tube of lipstick.

"What's that?" I asked.

"A blush stick," she said. "Hold still."

She dotted the apples of my cheeks and rubbed

it in, then sat back and smiled. "Oh, that looks good. Go look."

I looked in the mirror on the back of my door. It looked like I had just gone for a brisk walk, and even though it wasn't obvious, I looked happier and a little glowy. But I did not feel glowy inside.

"Sometimes," said Jenna, "even when you don't feel great, you have to put on a happy face, and soon enough the rest of you follows."

"Huh?" I asked.

"Look, middle school is hard," said Jenna. "I get that. Your friends are changing and it seems like everything is happening all at once. But sometimes you just have to go with change and see where it takes you. It could be really good."

"So I should pretend to be happy all the time and just wear makeup to mask the grumpiness?" I asked.

"Not at all!" said Jenna. "That's not what I'm saying. You can be mad and sad and disappointed. But just saying no to trying something different and sitting out the chance to change isn't great either. You never know what new things could be exciting or open up new doors."

I moaned. "You sound like Mom," I complained.

"New opportunities! Well, what if I like the old opportunities?"

"I think you're missing the point," said Jenna. "Just be open. Just because Lindsay is coming with us to dinner doesn't mean that Family Fall Fest can't be great. It just means that while we're having one of our favorite nights, we're including someone who is family and who very much wants to be there with us. That's what family does, Kelsey."

I knew she was right, but she could be right and I could still be angry at the same time. I let those two things float around in my brain for a little bit.

"Dinner in five," said Jenna, and hopped up from the bed.

"Jenna?" I asked. "Will you miss us?"

"When?" she said.

"When you go to college in California. Will you miss us as much as we'll miss you?"

"Okay," said Jenna. "First of all, we still have a year and a half before I'm going anywhere. Second, I don't know for sure that I'm going to school in California. I have to be accepted first. And third of all," she said, holding up three fingers, "are you serious? I will miss you guys like crazy! I'll be thinking of the four of you and probably be lonely that it's just me on my own!"

"So why don't you just stay close?" I asked.

"I might," said Jenna. "But I also think it's kind of cool to see what I can do on my own. I'll always have my family, and it doesn't matter to me if they're five minutes or five hours away. I know they're there."

I thought about that. It mattered to me. I'd much rather be five minutes away from my family.

Jenna gave me a hug. "No matter where I am, I'm always your sister," she said. "Your big sister. Your big, bossy sister who will always tell you what to do, even when you're fifty!"

I giggled just as Molly appeared in the doorway. "What's so funny?" she said.

"Me when I'm fifty," I said.

"Huh?" said Molly. "Uh . . . okay. Dad sent me up to tell you it's dinnertime. It's the Sunday Special too. Shrimp."

Ugh, I hate shrimp.

See, sometimes Monday morning starts early.

Chapter Seven
Just Another Manic Monday

Principal Clarke was trying to get everyone's attention for the morning meeting. "It's a big week in Bellgrove!" she said. "Settle down and tune in, because there is a lot going on!"

I was sitting with our new crew, which was Isabella, Olivia, Hannah, Riley, Michelle, and Sophia. We filled out a whole table sitting together. *Addition is better than subtraction,* I heard Mom say in my head. I guess she should know; she is an accountant.

"First of all, the student council elections are coming up," said Principal Clarke. "This week you'll see those campaigns start with posters in the halls. Next week we'll hear from the candidates in prepared statements, and then we'll have a Q and A session,

So Jelly

when you can ask them questions. Then we'll have the election. It's an exciting time at Bellgrove Middle School!"

I looked over at Hannah and Olivia. Olivia was biting her nails. I guess running for office could be stressful. There's no way I would ever want to sit in front of the entire school and answer questions. Ugh.

"Next," said the principal, "as many of you know, we have Fall Fest this weekend."

The room erupted in cheers.

She smiled. "I know, it's a great weekend. We have many opportunities to volunteer, so check the sign-up board in the back of the cafeteria if you'd like to help out. Even if you just come to the event, be sure to show your school spirit and wear your red and white colors!"

Sophia nudged me. "Can I borrow your red cardigan?" she asked. "The one with the pattern on it?"

I nodded.

The rest of the day was, well, it was a Monday. Somehow I smooshed my turkey sandwich that Dad packed me for lunch and the soup sloshed out from my thermos, soaking the brownie he'd put in there because we always got a special treat on Mondays.

DONUT DREAMS

I slammed my locker on my finger and was late to French class because I forgot my book and had to run back for it.

And because it was Family Fall Fest on Friday, we'd switched my day working at Donut Dreams to Monday for this week.

I trudged into the Park, and sure enough, Grandpa was waiting at the podium.

"Okay, this cranky face is getting to be familiar," he said. "And I don't like it."

I couldn't tell if he was teasing me or reprimanding me, so I tried to make my face look as happy as I could.

"It's been a Monday, Grandpa," I said.

"Mondays are rough," he said, nodding.

I don't know why, but just then I kind of flung myself at him and buried my head in his arm.

He gave me a big hug and patted my back. "Is this more than a miserable Monday?" he asked, concerned. "Everything okay, sweetie?"

My grandpa was what most people described as "a force," but he could also be a really big softy, especially with his grandchildren.

I took a big breath and lifted up my head. "Yeah," I said. "It's okay. Middle school is hard."

So Jelly

"Ahhh," he said. "Change is hard. Why do you think I just sit at this podium every day?" He chuckled and looked up as Mom was rounding the corner. "Melissa, your daughter says middle school is hard."

"What happened at school today?" asked Mom with a worried look.

"Nothing," I said.

Mom and Grandpa looked at each other, and Grandpa shrugged. "Well, something happened to your mom today," he said. "Big news!" He beamed.

Mom laughed. "Well, I don't know if it's big news, Dad. But they asked me to come speak at a conference in St. Louis about small businesses."

"It *is* big news!" said Grandpa. "Of all the people in that big city, they asked our Melissa! That's because she's so smart and such a good businessperson. She keeps this place humming!"

"Oh, just Melissa keeps this place running, huh, Dad?" teased Uncle Charlie as he put down his clipboard and came over to join us.

"When is the conference?" I asked, curious.

Mom never really went away on business trips, but once in a while she, Uncle Charlie, and Uncle Mike would go to a convention.

"It's in a few weeks, actually," said Mom. "Which means I need to put together a presentation pretty fast."

Uncle Mike came over then. "Is this a staff meeting?" he asked. "Or a family convention over here? Because I have donuts to sell and Fall Fest to plan. What does everyone think about red frosted donuts this year, so we're in with the school color theme?"

"Red donuts sound gross, Mike," Mom said. "Plus, they might not look too appetizing."

"Well, maybe more pink?" said Uncle Charlie. "Or you could just have jelly donuts. Those are red on the inside. And we're all red on the inside for Fall Fest!"

I laughed. "I'm reporting for duty," I said, saluting them and walking over to the donut counter.

Lindsay was there, as usual, before me. It should seem weird that she would beat me to work, since we both got out of school at the same time, but I took the bus home with Molly and then Dad or Jenna drove me over.

Lindsay was picked up at school by Nans, who brought her to the Park. I felt a little twinge just then because I got to go home, where Dad was always waiting for me.

After Lindsay's mom died, she came to the

restaurant with her dad after school. She and Skylar used to sit in a booth and do their homework until someone could take them home.

I remembered just then that Aunt Amy made these really great pies in the fall, and I wondered if Lindsay missed going home to her mom, in a kitchen that smelled like fresh apple pie.

Lindsay was helping Mrs. Ellis pack up a box of donuts to take to the soccer team.

"Hi, Mrs. Ellis," I said. "Mind if we put one in there for Molly?"

"Oh, this is for everyone on the team!" she said. "Or everyone trying out. Gosh, I hope they all make it. They are all such terrific girls."

I popped in a chocolate-glazed donut, which I knew was Molly's favorite. Then I threw in an old-fashioned donut, because I knew that was Riley's favorite. I didn't know what Isabella's favorite was.

"Okay, we have two of each kind," said Lindsay. "So hopefully no fights over who gets what!"

"Thanks, girls," said Mrs. Ellis.

After Mrs. Ellis there was a steady stream of customers picking up treats for after school or after practice.

DONUT DREAMS

"Welcome to Donut Dreams," I said, spinning around, ready to help the next customer.

I looked up and Ms. Castro, the town librarian, was smiling at me. "Hello, dear!" she said. "I was hoping you'd be here!"

"I'm usually here on Fridays and Sundays," I said. "But we had to change the schedule this week due to Fall Fest."

"Well, I haven't seen much of you since school started," she said. "I know the start of the year can be stressful, and I'm hoping you still have some time to stop by."

"You usually have trouble keeping me away!" I said. "I've been a little busy, but I've been meaning to come in. I heard about a book by P. J. Night that I really want to read."

"Oh, I know just the one you are talking about!" said Ms. Castro. "I'll put it on the reserve shelf for you!"

"Thank you!" I said.

I had been telling Ms. Castro that I wanted to do her job ever since I was really little and Dad would take me there for the story-time hour.

Dad and Mom would smile when I said I wanted to be the Bellgrove librarian and say, *We'll see. You can*

So Jelly

be anything, so let's see what you really love. But I loved books and I loved to read. And I loved that library. I didn't see why I would have to look any further.

I packed up Ms. Castro's order and we finally had a break.

"Hi, there," Lindsay said. "Whew, that was a rush."

"Yeah," I said. "I guess busy is better than not."

"True," she said.

Then I remembered I had field hockey after work today. "This is such a long Monday," I moaned.

"Since when is there a short Monday?" asked Lindsay. "I'm starving. Nans forgot to pack me a snack. Want a donut?"

I shook my head no. "It's slow now. Go ahead and just sneak it," I said. "I'll be lookout."

Lindsay looked around, then pinched a jelly donut from the case. She bit into it.

"Mmm, these are so good," she said. "Want a bite?"

I nodded and leaned over, but when I bit into the donut, I must have hit a pocket of jelly, because it spurted out and a big blob landed on my nose.

"Ugh!" I said.

You never knew what was going to hit you in the face on a Monday.

Chapter Eight
I'm a Lot Like Dad

My Monday continued at field hockey practice. It was a really nice evening and after the day I'd had, I didn't mind having a chance to run with the fall air filling my lungs.

But every time I started to relax, Amanda would yell, "Pass, pass, pass," or "Downfield, faster!" She was barking orders at me and it really annoyed me.

Coach Wickstead called us over. "Okay, girls, I've seen some tremendous talent and some good hustle. This year we're going to have a starting team and what I'm calling the supporting team. If you're on the starting team, that means you start all games. The supporting team will sub in and rotate as I feel is right for each game."

So Jelly

Naturally, Amanda made the starting team. So did Sophia! Isabella, Olivia, and I were part of the supporting team, which was okay with me.

I gave Sophia a big hug. "Hey, A-lister!" I said.

"Are you disappointed?" she asked.

"I'm kind of relieved," I said. "I like the game, but I'm not sure I like the pressure."

"I get that," said Sophia. "And we still get to practice together! But that one makes me nervous."

She motioned toward Amanda.

Amanda came over. "Congratulations, Sophia," she said. "Kelsey, you're a good player. You gave me a run for my money during some of those drills!"

I was surprised, but I couldn't help smiling. I gave Amanda a run for her money?

That night at dinner Mom told us about the conference she'd been asked to present at. It was all about how small businesses managed their finances and grew.

To be honest, it sounded a little boring, but it was still pretty cool to have a mom who spoke at conferences.

Dad raised his glass and said, "Let's all toast your awesome mother!"

DONUT DREAMS

Then he marked the weekend she'd be away on the calendar to "make it official."

For some of the trips Mom or Dad made to St. Louis, we took turns going with them. Molly had gone with Dad over the summer when he went for a certification course. Jenna went with Mom a few weeks ago for back-to-school shopping. So this meant it was my turn.

"Hey, I'm supposed to go with you to the city next!" I said. "Just the two of us."

"Well," said Mom, "I need to check the school calendar and see if it will work. Plus, this time I'm not just attending a conference. I have to speak there, so it might be different. But yes, you are up in the batting order."

I was excited. A trip with Mom would be lots of fun, and I couldn't even remember the last time it was just me with Mom. She'd be all mine. I was almost hopping up and down in my chair just thinking about it.

"How was everyone's day?" asked Dad. "Besides Big Shot Mom's?"

"Everyone is getting ready for Fall Fest," Jenna said. "The tennis team has a booth where we'll be

So Jelly

doing face painting. It's going to be a lot of fun."

"The soccer team is working at the balloon booth. But no one knows how to make balloon animals," said Molly.

"Did you hear Mike's latest plan?" asked Mom. "He wants to do red donuts. Or at least jelly donuts, because they're red inside."

"Red donuts don't sound too great," said Dad, making a face.

"What about red velvet? Red velvet donuts could be very tasty," Mom said.

"Oh. Okay, I didn't think of that," Dad said. "I'm building a new stand for the Park this year that has a red awning. It's going to look fantastic."

"The field hockey team is helping the Park," I said.

"Ooh, that's great!" said Mom. "We could use the help."

"Yep, that was my idea," I said. "We can help serve."

"So when will they announce the final team?" asked Dad.

"Oh, they already did!" I said. "I made the supporting team, but not the starting team."

Everyone looked up.

"Good job, Kels!" said Jenna.

"Way to go!" said Molly.

"Why didn't you tell us?" asked Mom.

"It's not really a big deal," I said. "As I predicted, because there were only four girls from my grade, we all made it. I'm not playing on the A team, but it's okay. I still get to practice, and maybe next year I'll start."

Dad nodded. "That's right. You can play and have fun and see if you want to play more competitively next year."

"Do you think Riley will make the soccer team?" I asked Molly.

Molly nodded. "She's really good. I'm not sure about Isabella, though. She hasn't played as much."

Ha ha, I thought, then stopped myself because I wasn't sure exactly why I wouldn't want Isabella to make the team. I wondered how Riley would feel playing alone.

Later that night I was finishing homework and Dad came into my room, holding a piece of paper.

"Hi, Kelsey," he said. "So I have the hockey schedule, and I marked the games I think I can make."

"Oh," I said. "Dad, I don't think I'll even be playing."

"Well, that's okay," he said. "You're still part of the team, right?"

"Yeah," I said. "And it turns out I like being part of a team. It's fun. But I don't love the pressure of game day. I get too stressed out."

"That's how I was!" said Dad.

"You were?" I asked, surprised.

"Yep. When I played soccer, I loved the game, but I hated game day. I was always too nervous that I'd do something stupid and everyone would be there watching me."

"So what did you do?" I asked.

"Well, I realized it really was about being a good teammate and just playing my best," said Dad. "Winning or losing didn't change the game for me, and that was always my mantra."

"That sounds fun," I said. "And not complicated. Like just show up and have fun and don't worry about standings or playoffs or stats."

"Exactly," said Dad. "Even when people around you are getting a little crazy or excited, you just need to remember to listen to your own voice and stay centered. Even if someone is yelling that you made a dumb play, you just act like you have a colander in your brain."

"A colander in my brain?" I asked.

"Yes," said Dad. "A colander, like the kind we use when we drain the pasta water in the sink. But a colander in your brain means that you hear the good stuff and the positive stuff and you drain out all the bad stuff."

"Well, sometimes it's important to hear bad stuff," I said, thinking about how Mom would tell us that we had to be called out on our bad behavior so we'd recognize it.

"Of course," said Dad. "Constructive criticism is great and it can be very useful. But I'm talking about how nuts people can get in the heat of a game. That kind of stuff you just need to let go."

I nodded. I sort of understood.

"You know, Kelsey, if you don't want to play at all you don't have to, but once the season starts, you need to commit. So as of tomorrow you're in or out."

"I know," I said. I also knew that Dad was giving me a way out. I could just come home after school and not play on the team and not even have to worry about Amanda. Was that what I wanted?

All of a sudden, I was really tired.

"You know what I think you need?" asked Dad. "A good night's sleep."

So Jelly

"Yeah," I said, yawning. "And you know what else I really need? I really need Monday to be over."

I hoped that when I went to bed later, I wouldn't just lie there thinking about everything. Tonight, more than anything, I needed a deep, dreamless sleep. And a fresh start in the morning.

Chapter Nine
Team Spirit At Last

Olivia was waving to me at the lunch table, and I groaned a little inside because I really just wanted to hang with Sophia, Michelle, and Riley so I could talk to them about my hockey doubts.

"Addition is better than subtraction," I repeated to myself.

"Hello, teammate!" Olivia chirped.

"Hi, B squad teammate!" I said.

She laughed. "Go B team, go B team! Hey, here's another B-lister!" she said as Hannah sat next to Olivia, setting her tray down carefully so she didn't spill her chili.

"Hey, I can live with B-list hockey, but I hope I'll be in A-list student council," Hannah said. "We have so much work to do. I also have a lot of ideas."

"Can I help?" asked Isabella, as she sat down and spread out her lunch.

"Sure!" said Olivia. "But I thought you thought it was a dumb idea to run for student council."

Hmm, I thought. *So maybe that's why Olivia and Isabella weren't BFFs anymore. Because Olivia decided to run for student council with Hannah?*

"I didn't say it was a dumb idea," said Isabella. "I said I wasn't as interested in it. And that's okay. We can do different things and still be friends. Plus, I said I'd help you with your campaign."

"Well, it hurt my feelings," said Olivia.

"Olivia, I'm just not a student council person," said Isabella. "I don't have the patience to listen to people, and getting up in front of the school and speaking . . . ugh."

I was surprised. Isabella was an outgoing person. "I get that," I said.

"Right?" said Isabella, turning to me. "Can you imagine getting up at that podium?" She shivered.

"It's not a big deal," said Olivia. "We've known all these people for years!"

"It's totes a big deal," said Isabella. "Trust me."

"Okay," said Olivia. "Then if you don't mind and you still want to, I need help. We need a whole strategy and a plan for what we want the council to act on in the next year."

Isabella took out her phone. "Of course I want to help. That's what friends do. I've got my list maker here. Let's start."

Sophia sat down. "The line in the cafeteria is so long and so slow that now I have about three seconds to eat lunch!" she said.

"Well, there's one," said Olivia. "Make the cafeteria more efficient."

"Or give students a longer lunch period," said Michelle as she wheeled over next to me.

"Oh, that's a good one," said Olivia.

Sophia turned to me. "You can work with student council when you become our class representative," she said.

"I'm not even sure what the class rep does," I said.

"You heard Principal Clarke," said Isabella. "You represent us and talk through what our concerns are so that the council and teachers have some input. And the people who are in charge of making decisions will hear our voices and keep us informed about what's going on. This way, if we request something, and if we can't have it, hopefully we won't just hear a flat no. We will hear the reason behind it. We'll be able to keep our fellow classmates informed about everything going on."

"But that's not me," I said. "I have no idea how most people feel about things."

"But you are sensitive and a good listener," said Michelle. "You always see the best in things. And you really get people. You know just what they need."

I wondered who she was talking about, because that sure didn't seem like me lately. Lately I felt grouchy and selfish.

"Not so sure about that, Michelle," I said. I looked around. "Hey, where's Riley?"

Nobody knew, which was odd.

"Maybe she decided to study in the library," said Isabella. "We have a coding test next period."

We all hurried to finish our lunch.

"Write that down," said Sophia to Olivia. "Stop rushing us through the day. I don't deal well with rushing!"

Olivia nodded. "I can try, but I can't invent more hours in the day. That's a little beyond me!"

DONUT DREAMS

We laughed as the bell rang.

"And that's a wrap!" said Isabella.

"Ugh!" said Sophia, shoving a mini burrito in her mouth. "I'm definitely going to get a stomachache."

As I was headed out, I saw Riley in the hall, and she didn't look great.

"What's wrong?" I asked.

"Get a pass and meet me in the bathroom!" she whispered.

So I asked for a restroom pass and met her there. "What's up?" I asked, checking the stalls to see if anyone else was in there.

"I don't want to play in the soccer scrimmage today," said Riley.

"What? Why?"

"Because I'm scared," said Riley. "It's super competitive. Your sister and the other girls have been playing for a while, and it's my first year. What if I make a stupid play, or fall on my face?"

"You won't!" I said.

Riley looked at me.

"Okay, even if you do, what's the worst that can happen?" I asked.

"People will laugh?" said Riley.

So Jelly

"Well, then they aren't good teammates," I said. "Look, you made the team! That means you're a good player!"

"If I mess up everyone will wonder why I made the team," she said.

"Or they'll just think you had a rough day on the field, but that you tried, which is the most important thing," I said.

"What if I lose the game for the whole team?" she asked.

"One person can never lose a game for a team. It takes a whole team to win or lose a game," I replied.

Riley stared at me for a moment. "Okay, since when did you become Tammy Teammate and what have you done with Kelsey?" she asked.

"Well, I'm trying to help you," I said. "Besides, you just need to block everyone out during the game. You are a good player and you love the game. Just keep thinking about that and don't listen to the voice that says you can't do it."

"Thanks," said Riley. "And I'm glad you aren't mad at me."

"Why would I be mad at you?" I said.

"I thought you'd just be mad that I didn't play

hockey with you and Soph because we do almost everything together," she said.

"I'm disappointed we can't all play together," I said. "But I want you to do what you love and what you're good at. And we don't always have to do everything together to stay friends."

Huh, I thought. *That's kind of like what Isabella said to Olivia.* And it made a lot of sense.

"We are still friends, right?" Riley said.

"What?" I said. "Of course!"

"Well, I figured you and Sophia were so mad that I kind of got kicked out of the peas in a pod club. I like Isabella a lot, but it's not the same as the four of us."

"You can't get kicked out of this club," I said firmly.

"We probably are going to get kicked out of class if we don't get back there," said Riley.

She splashed some water on her face.

"Better?" I asked.

She nodded. "Thanks, Kels," she said. "You always know exactly what to say to make me feel better."

"That's what friends are for!" I said as I pushed open the bathroom door.

"Even when they throw up from nerves on the soccer field?" she said.

So Jelly

"Even then," I said. "But try not to do that. You'll be the Wetsy Betsy of the soccer team."

"Oh no," said Riley, stifling a laugh. "I'll be Ralphing Riley! I'll be known forever as the girl who spewed her lunch on the goal line!"

We were both laughing hard as we scurried back to class, but my conversation with Riley got me thinking.

I hadn't wet my pants in school or thrown up on a field. I likely wouldn't be the star of the hockey team. So what would I be known as?

Chapter Ten
Everything's Going Wrong

That afternoon Sophia and I decided to go along with Dad to Molly and Riley's soccer game for support.

"Do me a favor," I said to Molly. "Look out for Riley, because she's really nervous."

"Well, that's normal. I still get nervous before games," said Molly.

I was surprised. "You do?"

"Sure," said Molly. "What if I make a stupid play in front of everyone?"

"That's what she's worried about!" I said.

Sophia and I sat on the bleachers with Dad and cheered on the team. They were really good, especially Riley. She was running up and down the field super fast.

So Jelly

"It's like watching lightning!" Dad said.

The team won, and I was really happy watching Riley jump up and down at the end of the game. Sophia and I ran down for hugs.

"See, no Ralphing Riley!" I said.

"Thank goodness!" said Riley. "Molly really helped me out. She's a good teammate."

I smiled and reminded myself to thank Molly for that later.

"You can make it up to me by watching me sit on the bench during our hockey game!" I suggested.

Sophia rolled her eyes. "Just because you don't start doesn't mean you won't play!" she said.

"Oh, I hope I don't play!" I laughed. "I don't need that stress!"

But the next day it was me on the field for another scrimmage game, and I looked up to see Dad and Molly in the stands with Riley. I felt embarrassed because they really were watching me just sit there.

The game was a tough one, and I was cheering on Sophia, who was defending against a really aggressive player from the other team. I flinched a few times, but she hung in there.

The sun was sinking and it was getting a little

chilly, especially since I was only warming the bench and not myself.

There were only a few minutes left in the game when Coach Wickstead blew her whistle for a time-out. "Okay, the front line is tired. Time to start subbing in, girls."

I wasn't really paying attention, which was probably why I missed that she called my name.

"Are you sure?" I asked, as she motioned to me.

"You're up, Kelsey," she said. "Let's see what you can do."

I felt sick to my stomach.

Sophia was playing next to me, and she jogged over. "Okay, Kelsey. You can do this. Play like we're not playing a game. Play like we're just out here on the field, having a good time. Ignore everything else."

I nodded. I remembered what Dad told me. *A colander in your brain means that you hear the good stuff and the positive stuff and you drain out all the bad stuff.*

Colander, I thought. *Use a colander.*

The ball dropped and off we went. I took Sophia's advice and decided to just pretend we were practicing. I used Dad's advice and blocked out the other girls.

I'm actually holding my own, I thought.

So Jelly

I vaguely heard Dad yelling, "Go, Kelsey, go!" and Riley yelling, "You got it, Kelsey!" but I just tried to shut everything out.

In the huddle, Amanda said, "You're doing great, Kelsey. I'm going to pass to Sophia, and she'll pass to Tracey, who'll pass the ball back to me, and then I'll pass to you. I need you to be close to the crease to get the ball in. Okay?"

"Okay," I said.

It felt like the whole play was in slow motion. Amanda set the play up as she said. She passed to Sophia, who passed to Tracey, who was running fast up the field. Amanda ran into place and passed the ball to me.

It was a clear shot and I was concentrating on not missing. I pivoted and *thwack*, hit the ball. I watched it arc and hit the post . . . and bounce out.

I stood there for a second, stunned. It was a shot I had made a million times before.

In the second I paused, the other team scooped up the ball and trampled down toward their goal. I heard them yelling in victory as I stood there, alone, near our goalkeeper.

I had just lost the game.

I felt like I couldn't move. I saw Dad stand up and look at me, while Molly covered her eyes with her hands.

It was Sophia who came jogging back up the field and put her arm around me.

"Great shot!" she said. "It was a great shot and you got it up the field."

We walked back to the bench, my head hanging low. I didn't want to talk to anyone.

"Good game, girls," Coach Wickstead was saying. "Nice hustle out there and great teamwork. Good to see you on the field, Kelsey. Next time we're going to have you play longer."

Longer? Was she crazy? How would that help?

Everyone gathered their things, and I took my backpack and walked toward Dad.

"Great game!" he said cheerily, and I gave him a sour look.

"You can't make every shot you take!" said Molly encouragingly. "You looked good out there!"

Riley gave me a hug and whispered, "You did good and you didn't throw up!"

"Can we just go home?" I asked.

On the way home I got a text from Michelle.

So Jelly

> Hey u! Sorry I missed the game today. How was field hockey?

I sighed. I really wasn't in the mood to rehash the game right now. I texted back,

> It was OK, TTYL.

At home we had a quick dinner and we all settled in for homework. I don't know how Jenna plays music while she does homework; I need total quiet.

I was startled when there was a knock at my door. Mom poked her head in.

"I had an idea," she said. "This conference I'm speaking at happens to be during fall break, so you have that Friday off school. What if I take you and Lindsay to St. Louis with me, and we can make it a little fun weekend trip?"

Suddenly I was furious. I didn't know if it was the tough week or I was more sore about the game than I'd thought, but I just sputtered, "Lindsay?"

"Yessss," said Mom slowly, walking into my room. "I thought it would be nice to include her. She might like a special trip out of town."

I crossed my arms over my chest. "Mom, you know who else would like a special trip out of town? With her mother? Just with her mother? Because her sisters each got a turn going by themselves and didn't have to share a parent?" I was kind of yelling.

"You don't think it would be nice to include Lindsay?" asked Mom, raising her voice just a little.

"It probably would!" I was actually yelling now. "But I don't want to! This is *my* trip. You are *my* mother. And it's *my* turn!"

"Okay, let's take a breath here," said Dad, who came into the room.

"I don't want to take a breath!" I said. "I'm so sick of tiptoeing around Lindsay! I'm sorry she's had a tough time. But my mother is here and I shouldn't have to give up my trip with my mother just because my mother isn't dead!"

Mom drew in her breath sharply. "Kelsey Jane Lakes!" she yelled.

From the other room, I heard Molly say to Jenna, "I can't believe she just said that."

For some reason that made me even madder. I felt like my two sisters were teaming up against me! Mom and Dad were also looking at me like they

So Jelly

didn't know who I was or what to say to me.

"Time-out here," said Dad. "Kelsey, I don't think you meant what just came out. I know you didn't. But we're all a little worked up here, so let's take a breath and calm down before we say anything else we might regret."

Mom and Dad shut the door behind them.

I threw myself down on my bed. I don't know why I was so moody and so angry lately. It was just that so much was happening and so much was changing, and nobody seemed to understand what I was feeling. I didn't even know what I was feeling half the time.

All I wanted to do was make everything go back to the way it was.

I opened up my notebook and tried to do some math homework, but it was hard to concentrate. After a while I just pushed the book away and stretched out on my bed, staring up at the ceiling.

Then I got up and put my pajamas on. I wanted to go to bed early and forget this horrible day ever happened.

About an hour later Dad knocked on my door. "How about some cookies and milk?" he asked.

I nodded and followed him down to the kitchen.

DONUT DREAMS

I saw the light was on in Mom's office, so I guessed she was working on her presentation.

Dad had made chocolate chip cookies, which were my favorite. They were still warm from the oven, and I washed the first few bites down with some cold milk. I was still annoyed, but the warm cookies were helping.

"Doesn't get any better than that, does it?" Dad said, grinning.

I swallowed and waited. I was sure I was going to get a speech or something.

"We can see that things are a little topsy-turvy this year," said Dad. "You have a lot going on."

I waited.

"Your friends are all trying new things, like different sports or student council."

I guessed Molly had told them about Hannah and Olivia.

"And I get that getting into the groove at work is difficult as well. And we expect a lot of you between school and holding down a job, when not many of your other friends work."

I nodded.

"If school and Donut Dreams are too much, we

So Jelly

can dial back the number of days you work," said Dad. "Maybe two days is just too much right now."

I shrugged.

"Now as for your cousin Lindsay," he said.

I stared down at my lap. I knew I wasn't being kind about Lindsay.

"I know you and Lindsay are close," Dad said. "And I know you care about her. You really looked out for her when her mom first passed away a couple years ago. And I know that can sometimes feel like a burden."

"It's not a burden," I said.

"No, it is," said Dad. "It's still a burden even if you're happy to do it. It means that you're shouldering caring for someone else, and doing that takes up a lot of energy."

"I'm different," I blurted out.

Dad was about to say something, then stopped. "Different how?"

"I'm not competitive. I like living in this small town. I don't want to go away to college. I don't want to run for student council. And I don't want to share Mom with anyone more than Jenna and Molly, because sharing her with them is already too much.

And I don't know why everyone wants me to be the class representative."

Whoa. That all just came out.

"Okay," said Dad, and I could see that this was maybe more than he thought he'd get into. He rubbed his head.

"First of all, there's nothing wrong with not being competitive. And you're right, your personality is way different from your sisters', and that's okay. As for not moving away, well, your mother and I grew up here, so no arguments on that front." He thought for a second.

"And about sharing Mom, well, we know that's a lot to ask. You're right about that. You, Jenna, and Molly all need your mother. And she tries really hard to make sure you all get what you need from her. But right now Lindsay needs her too. You may not think that's fair, but sometimes what's needed outweighs fair. Yes, the family is worried about Lindsay, and about Sky. But I can tell you that after your performance the past week, we're all pretty worried about you, too."

Good, I thought.

"You've always been the happy-go-lucky one," Dad said. "But this past week you've been sad and

So Jelly

moody, sometimes for no reason. Or at least no reason that's obvious to the rest of us."

He paused as if he was waiting for me to say something. But I didn't feel like discussing the bad mood I'd been in all week.

"So is Lindsay coming to St. Louis?" I asked.

"I'm not sure," said Dad. "Mom and I need to talk about it."

"Okay," I said. "Can I go back upstairs now?"

Dad gave a big sigh, like he was relieved. "Sure. Actually, that's a good idea. Why don't we all get a good night's sleep and talk about it when we're fresh tomorrow?"

As I went back upstairs, I passed Mom's office. I heard her clicking away at her keyboard and I stopped for a second, hoping she would open the door, but she didn't.

I felt guilty about yelling at her and guilty that I had a mother I fought with.

I went up the stairs and saw Jenna's door was open. Jenna and I have always been super close. Mom and Dad loved to tell me the story of when they brought me home from the hospital and Jenna yelled, "MY baby! MY Kelsey!" and told everybody I was *her* baby, and she would try to hold me and feed me any chance she could get.

Jenna was in bed with her laptop, doing homework, and I crawled in next to her. When I was really little, I would scoot across the hall and get into bed with Jenna when I was scared.

Tonight, Jenna didn't even blink. She pulled up the covers around me without saying a word and I snuggled in. I could smell her shampoo on her pillow, which always reminded me of roses.

If I closed my eyes, maybe the week would be over faster, and we could all just start again.

Chapter Eleven
A Good Talk

Luckily, the rest of the week was kind of quiet. Mom and Dad didn't mention St. Louis, and I knew well enough not to bring it up.

On Thursday, I had another hockey game, and I was a little nervous about being thrown in. After some really nice fall weather it had been warm again, and the late afternoon sun felt like it was burning me as I sat on the hot metal bleacher.

I noticed that Dad had shown up at my game again. He never waved at me or anything, but I saw him sitting there with his hands crossed over his long legs. Most of the parents were on their phones or chatting, but he was always sitting off a little bit, just watching.

It was nice to know that even for that short period of time, I had his full attention.

Sure enough, Coach Wickstead blew her whistle and called, "Kelsey, let's go. You're in!"

I took a deep breath, smiled at the thumbs-up from Sophia, who was coming off the field for a break, and ran to my spot.

I took my cues from Amanda and Tracey, and I ran down the field with the ball. I passed to Tracey, who broke free and scored. We all cheered, and I was happy as I ran off the field.

Somehow when I jumped up to play I'd lost my water bottle, and I had to go search for it under the bench. When I came back, Dad had made his way down the stands and was talking to Coach Wickstead.

Coach had gone to school with my uncle Mike and had known Dad for a long time too. They were talking about the game when I came trotting up.

"Nice playing today, Kelsey," Coach said.

"Thank you," I said. "I think those six minutes were really important!" Then I laughed.

"Hey, six minutes can win or lose a game," said Coach. "Every player adds something."

I tried hard not to laugh again, because I didn't

So Jelly

think I was anywhere close to being an anchor for the team.

"You know why I love watching her play?" Coach asked Dad.

"Because she's good!" Dad said, and I could tell from his voice that he really meant it.

"Well, yes, she is," said Coach. She looked at me. "I love watching you play because I can tell you love it. I love watching a player smile as she races across the grass with her hair flying out and the wind behind her. It does my coach and my player heart good."

I was surprised.

"We have a lot of talent on the team," Coach continued, "and each player really brings something unique. Some bring skill, some bring a competitive spirit, some are just workhorses. But you, Kelsey, you are rare." She tilted her head at me. "You remind everyone on that field that this is fun, that this can be exhilarating. Any good team needs that."

Dad was smiling really widely. "I always tell her that it's not about winning or losing," he said.

"It isn't!" said Coach. "It's about the joy of the game. And you definitely show us how that works."

I looked at her to see if she was buttering me up

or something. I mean, it sounded like something Dad or Mom would say to me to make me feel better, but a coach?

"Kelsey, you remind me of me when I used to play for fun," said Coach. "I know you don't love competing, but I think if we can get you more comfortable, then you can play longer and longer and the competition of the game won't faze you. By next year I'll have you playing full halves. And you'll still be loving the game. That's my goal for you."

"Well," I said. "I guess I can work on that."

"We can work on your skills," said Coach. "But I don't want you to work the fun out of your game. I want you to enjoy it. I want you relaxed. I want you to always have a blast. Does that make sense?"

I nodded. It did. "But isn't it *also* about winning the game?"

Coach laughed. "Well, if we were selling tickets in a big stadium and I had to win all the time, maybe I'd feel differently. But I'm more interested in showing a great team how wonderful this sport can be."

Dad reached over and put his arm around me.

"You're doing right by this one, Chris," Coach Wickstead said.

So Jelly

"Don't I know it!" Dad said. "Now we have to do right by her history teacher by getting her homework done!"

We waved to Coach as we headed off the field.

Dad and I were quiet, walking to the car, and we drove in silence. But before we got back through town, Dad pulled into the Frosty Freeze parking lot.

"What are you doing?" I asked.

He looked a little guilty. "You had a good game. It's just a little celebration that's not a donut!"

"You don't have to ask me twice," I said, and shot out of the car.

We walked up to the window and I ordered a King Frosty, which was a big milkshake with tons of ice cream, whipped cream, and butterscotch syrup.

"If I eat this whole thing, I'm probably not going to do too well on dinner," I said.

"Well, it's Mom's turn to make dinner tonight," said Dad. "So . . ."

"Dad!" I said, but I laughed. Mom was a terrible cook.

Dad ordered a King Frosty with chocolate sauce, and we headed toward the picnic tables to slurp them down.

"We have to hide the evidence and get rid of the cups before we get in the car," Dad said.

I was slurping away when Dad said, "So, like I said the other night, we're a little worried about you, Kelsey."

"I remember you said you were worried the other night," I said. "But why?"

"Because usually you don't let things bother you. You live by your own rules at your own pace. Mom and I have always marveled about that. You don't need to go off to a big city to prove anything; you'll be just as happy moving twenty feet away. You know yourself, and you're confident. And that's special."

Huh. Here I'd been thinking that was just boring, not special.

"But lately you seem the opposite of happy. I don't know if it's a phase or an adjustment or if there's something going on, but I want to remind you we are here to talk and help."

I took a big slurp and thought about it. I wanted to talk to Dad, but even I wasn't too sure why things were bothering me so much.

"I don't do too well with change," I said slowly.

Dad nodded and waited for me to go on.

"Sometimes I have all these feelings that come at

So Jelly

once, and I don't know where they're coming from or why I feel them. And when that happens, I just want everything to go back to the way it was."

"I get that," said Dad. "In a lot of ways Mom and I always want the three of you to be really little again, when a lollipop could solve any drama and make everything better. It was easier."

"Are you trying to tell me this is hard for everyone involved?" I said, kind of teasing him.

"Yes!" said Dad. "Because sometimes I don't know what I'm doing and I'm just making it up as I go."

"Dad!" I yelped. "You're the dad! You're supposed to know exactly what to say and what to do!"

"Doesn't work that way," said Dad. "There's no manual. Mom and I figure it out as we go. Sometimes we don't get it right. We should have seen that Mom spending a lot of time with Lindsay could make you feel a little neglected."

I looked down. "I feel bad about that," I said, using my toe to dig in the sand under the table.

"Well, we'd like you to see that Lindsay needs all of us. But it's also a really natural way to feel, and we get that, too. Mom feels terrible."

"She does?"

"Yep, she feels like she's letting you all down by spreading herself too thin."

Poor Mom. I knew she was trying. Now I felt extra bad.

"So it's okay that I feel bad about Lindsay and want to help her but still feel mad that she gets Mom's attention when I need it too?"

"Of course!" said Dad. "That's totally normal. We just should have seen it coming and been able to help work through that stuff."

"So how do we make this better?"

"I haven't read that far in the manual yet," said Dad, smiling. "But don't worry, I'm getting to that chapter next."

I laughed and chucked the cup in the trash.

Dad stood up and made a hoop shot into the can.

"Nice!" I said, and we jumped back into the car.

We hadn't solved anything, but I felt so much better. It was amazing what a good game, a good shake, a good talk, and a great dad could do.

Chapter Twelve
Clearing the Air

Poor Principal Clarke could barely get us to settle down for announcements on Friday. Everyone was buzzing about Fall Fest.

"Attention! Attention!" she kept saying.

Finally, she nodded to Mr. Schmitt, the lacrosse coach, who blew his whistle so loudly that everyone covered their ears, but it did the trick.

"I know we're all excited about Fall Fest," Principal Clarke said, "but we have a whole day of school to get through before the weekend kicks in!"

She surveyed the room. "Okay, now a quick announcement before we start the day. I have the results of our class representative election. Well, it wasn't really an election, it was more of a nomination.

DONUT DREAMS

The students who received the most nominations for each class will serve as class rep for one year. Now, for our sixth-grade students, the rep will be Kelsey Lakes."

Sophia, Riley, and Michelle were hugging me, and everyone at my table was yelling, "Whoo-hoo," so loudly that I didn't even hear the names of the reps for the other classes.

"If the reps I just announced can meet me during their lunch periods today, we can talk more about these exciting new responsibilities."

The bell rang and everyone flooded out into the hall, talking and laughing.

Lindsay gave me a hug. "Ms. Rep!" she said.

"I knew you'd win!" Michelle said.

Molly pulled on my ponytail. "Hey, sis, you won't forget about the little people who know all your family secrets now that you're an elected official, right? You'd better be nice to me."

It was exciting, but I had no idea what I had just gotten myself into. Or more specifically, what my class had just got me into . . .

I knocked on Principal Clarke's door at lunch, and she called, "Come in."

So Jelly

I peeked my head in and she said, "Oh, Kelsey, welcome! Come on in!"

She moved over some piles of papers on her desk and motioned for me to sit down. "Did you bring your lunch? Oh good, we can eat together."

I unscrewed my thermos and wondered if it was okay to eat ravioli in front of my principal.

She brought over a thermos of soup and sat down and started talking, so I just decided to shovel in my lunch while I had the chance.

"I'm so excited for you to be in this position, Kelsey," she said. "And I can't say I'm surprised that your classmates nominated you, as I think you're the perfect person for this job."

"Um, exactly what is this job?" I asked.

I was panicking a little at the word "job." I already had a job, and one was quite enough, but two? Ugh.

"Well, it's mostly about being the person who students can come to with their issues or concerns. This is a new position, so we're just feeling it out right now, but our hope is that one day per month we'd be able to set you up in an office or at a desk," she said. "Your classmates can come talk to you about things like changing the lunch menu or getting more involved with the volunteer safety team in town, that kind of thing."

I nodded. "Maybe there could also be an e-mail address for this role, so if someone doesn't want to wait, they can always contact me," I said.

"Oh, that's a great idea!" Principal Clarke beamed at me. "I knew you'd be good at this!"

"Okay, but . . . ," I said. "Well, what am I supposed to do with these issues?"

I panicked a little more. Was I supposed to solve these problems? I could barely solve my own problems!

"You'd bring them to a monthly committee meeting we'd have with all three of the class reps, me, and a few teachers who have volunteered to help. We'll talk through what's possible, like maybe offering a more diverse lunch menu, and what's not, like the suggestion I think you'll get to shorten the school day!"

"Okay," I said. "So it's basically a listening position?"

"Exactly," said Principal Clarke. "I think students feel better when they know there's an ear listening to them. Most people do. You aren't expected to solve any issues and you won't be making major changes, but you'll be a sympathetic voice and you'll be able to help them voice their concerns to us. I truly believe that a lot of frustration comes when people think they aren't being heard."

The bell rang.

"Oh my, these lunch periods do go by quickly, don't they?" Principal Clarke said as she gulped her soup.

"My friends and I were just talking about that!" I said. "Students really need more time to eat!"

"So do teachers and principals!" said Principal Clarke. "Great point. Let's put that on the list! Can't wait to get started!"

As I walked to my next class, I thought about my new job. I would have to listen to my classmates' concerns and suggestions, and then Principal Clarke would listen to me and the other class reps. Then Principal Clarke and the other teachers would try to figure something out.

First, Dad didn't know how to figure out how to solve my issues. Now Principal Clarke admitted she wasn't sure how to solve whatever might come up.

One thing was for sure: I was surrounded by

adults who really needed to start giving me answers.

※ ※ ※ ※ ※

On Friday afternoon Jenna, Molly, and I were squeezing each other in and out of the bathroom as we showered and dried our hair.

The doorbell rang and I knew it was probably Lindsay.

"Can you get the door?" Jenna yelled.

I went downstairs because I was the only one who was dressed. I was wearing a pink-and-gray minidress and short gray boots.

Jenna was doing our hair and helping us pick out outfits, and she was arguing with Molly about whether pink and orange actually went together.

Lindsay was standing on the front step, and I waved to Nans backing out of the driveway.

"Welcome to chaos," I said. "The fashion team is upstairs."

Lindsay followed me into Jenna's room, where it looked like she had every outfit she owned on the floor.

"Hey, Linds," said Jenna. "Do you need a fashion consult or are you all set?"

So Jelly

"Uh," said Lindsay, looking down. "You tell me?"

Jenna took a moment to take in Lindsay's outfit. "You look great," Jenna said, and she really did.

Lindsay had her shiny hair in waves and she had on this really cute blue denim dress that tied at the waist, and boots.

"Did your grandmother get that for you?" Jenna asked.

"Uh-huh," said Lindsay.

Her mom's mom lived in Chicago and was always sending her these great outfits that she'd found.

I was a little jealous because the shopping is not great out here. Everyone always dresses the same because everyone ends up at the same stores, or ordering online, which is kind of annoying.

Lindsay turned to me and smiled shyly. "You look nice, Kels," she said.

I just nodded and sort of grunted at her. I still wasn't exactly thrilled that she was coming with us.

Lindsay seemed to pick up on my grumpy attitude. "You okay?" she said.

"I'm fine," I lied. "Just looking for my gray bag," which was practically right in front of me. "Oh, here it is."

DONUT DREAMS

I grabbed it and walked away from Lindsay as quickly as I could. I glanced back for a moment and saw her watching me with a puzzled look on her face.

"Are you girls ready?" Mom called from down the hall.

She was running late because things at the Park were always crazy the day before Fall Fest. The Park provides almost all the food, so there's a ton of setup and prep work. When she called us, she already sounded a little frazzled.

"Mom, you're going to shower, aren't you?" Jenna asked. She looked worried.

"Yes," said Mom. "Don't worry, I won't embarrass you, Jenna!"

Mom can get ready faster than anyone I know. Sometimes when she and Dad go out we time her, and she can take a shower, get dressed, and do her hair and makeup in twelve minutes flat.

"I don't have extra time, so I get used to doing things fast!" she says.

Since Jenna knew Mom would be ready soon, she hustled into an outfit and gave up arguing with Molly, whom I thought looked really cute in an orange dress with a pink jean jacket over it.

So Jelly

Within fifteen minutes, we were all in the car and headed to Louie Louie. Mom had the radio on and we were all singing along. I kept looking at Lindsay to see if she felt out of place, but she seemed like she was happy to be there.

Mrs. Selden has been the owner of Louie Louie forever, and she gave us all hugs when she saw us. "Now, let's see how beautiful everyone is getting. Oh my, you girls all look so glamorous as you get older. But your mother just keeps getting younger and younger." She and Mom laughed at that one.

Mrs. Selden always sends over extra bread and appetizers and extra desserts when we're there, and even before the waiter took our order, there was this really good cheese bread and riplets, which are these spicy crunchy fries, on the table.

Mom also ordered us sparkling water so that we'd "have something proper to toast with."

"To my best and most favorite girls in the world," she said, holding up her glass. "Who get more beautiful and whom I love more and more every day."

We all smiled and drank and I wondered if it was weird for Lindsay. I mean, Mom is *our* mom. Naturally she loves the three of us more than Lindsay, right?

DONUT DREAMS

Does Lindsay think that our mom loves her equally? I thought about this for a little while. Then the fried ravioli came and we all dived in.

Molly was telling a hilarious story about how someone stepped in doggie doo at the soccer game, which Mom kept saying was not appropriate dinner conversation, so Molly would stop. Then three seconds later she'd say, "So you want to know how it ends, right?" and she would tell a little more.

"Oh, I feel badly for the crew at the Park," said Mom, checking her phone under the table. "They really still have a ton to do to get ready for tomorrow."

"But this is our Family Fest!" I said.

"I know, I know, Kelsey," said Mom. "But here we are living it up, and poor Uncle Mike and Uncle Charlie are getting two hundred fifty donuts packed up for tomorrow! It doesn't feel right."

We finished dinner, and as we were all in a gooey-butter-cake coma, Molly said, "Hey, I have an idea. Let's stop by the Park and help out."

We all looked at each other.

"Well, is anyone tired?" asked Molly.

We all shook our heads.

"Let's do better than that," said Mom, with a

So Jelly

mischievous look in her eye. "Let's bring them dinner!"

"We're going to bring dinner to a restaurant?" asked Jenna.

"Yeah!" said Mom. "They won't have to cook it, so they'll be thrilled! Don't you know that's the secret of restaurants everywhere? Cook for people and they're happy!"

We ordered a ton of stuff off the menu to go. While we were waiting, Jenna said, "Okay, one last toast to the girls!" and raised her glass.

"I'm glad to be one of the girls tonight!" said Lindsay, raising her glass too.

I glanced over at her, and she was beaming from ear to ear. I realized that this was the happiest I'd seen Lindsay in a really long time. All of us were smiling and having fun and it didn't matter one bit that we had an extra person with us. Why did I ever get so upset about it? Family was family.

I raised my glass and said, "And one more . . ."

Everyone looked at me.

"Always additions," I said, looking at Lindsay and smiling. "They're better than subtractions. I'm really happy you're here with us, Lindsay."

"Cheers!" said Mom, and she gave me a little

DONUT DREAMS

wink. "More is always better. Always listen to the accountant when it comes to numbers."

"Or in this case, the accountant's daughter!" I said.

Mrs. Selden packed the food into to-go bags, and we piled into the car and headed back to Bellgrove.

We drove up to the Park and could see all the lights on and a lot of people walking around inside. Mom used her key and threw open the front door.

"The party is here!" yelled Molly.

Nans and Grandpa came out of the kitchen, and Uncle Mike, Uncle Charlie, and Dad all looked up. Then they saw that one of the things we'd brought was fried ravioli, and everyone grabbed plates and dug in.

"You're all dressed up!" said Nans. "Don't start packing things and moving things!"

"We can change!" said Jenna, and Mom ran us home and we all grabbed jeans and T-shirts.

When we returned we each took a job, either sorting and packing donuts or folding the menus that we were giving out with every purchase. There was something really fun about working on a project together, and everyone was playing music and singing as we worked an assembly line.

Finally we loaded everything into Uncle Charlie's

So Jelly

pickup truck and we were set. We drove home exhausted but excited.

It had been our second Family Fall Fest of the night, and I couldn't decide which one I liked better.

※ ※ ※ ※ ※

Fall Fest starts off with a parade, and every year it's usually the sports booster club, the veterans' association, the town officials, and the dance squad who make their way down Main Street.

Since the sports booster club covers every sport that's played, it means every kid shows up in his or her uniform to march as well. The kids toss candy to the spectators lining the street. Everyone ends up at the festival part, which has different food stations, and booths that are sponsored by all the clubs and businesses in town. It's like a giant street fair.

We needed extra help during Fall Fest, so some of the field hockey team and the soccer team were helping at the Park's booth, which looked incredible thanks to Dad's frame and awning. The front of the booth actually looked like a real building, and it really stood out. Isabella, Hannah, and Sophia were behind the counter with me for my shift, and it was fun to

DONUT DREAMS

work with my friends, except Isabella kept eating the donuts.

"Isabella!" I said. "You'd never last at Donut Dreams!"

"I know," she groaned. "But they are soooo good. Every time I have a bad day, my mom comes home with one of them for me!"

Olivia and Michelle came by for a visit and, of course, to have a donut.

"Donuts make you smile," said Sophia seriously.

"Maybe that should be our new slogan," I joked.

"Let's not talk about slogans," groaned Hannah. "We're still working on ours for the election. So far 'Two Girls Can Get It Done!' is still the most popular. But today I don't want to think about the election. Today I just want to have fun!"

"Okay, but just one suggestion," I said. "How about something like 'You Talk, We Listen'?"

"Hey," said Hannah. "That's good!"

"I love it!" said Olivia.

"Well, everyone appreciates it when someone listens, right? That's why Principal Clarke said they created the class reps. So everyone gets a chance to be heard."

So Jelly

"It's true," said Hannah. "That's really why I'm so interested in student council."

"It is?" said Olivia. "I thought it was that you just wanted to be in charge and make decisions."

"What?" said Hannah. "No, Isabella and I really share the same idea that we should be representing our class and helping to influence things that can make school a better experience for everyone."

Olivia looked like she was stewing for a second. "Well, sure . . . ," she said. "I knew Isabella felt that way. . . ."

Hannah gave her a strange look. "Sometimes you just have to let people know you're open to hearing them, and they'll tell you how they feel."

Olivia didn't say anything, and Sophia and I raised our eyebrows at each other.

We were selling jelly donuts and apple cider. "Come get your true red spirit!" we called as people lined up. The shift went by fast, and after we worked, we were able to walk around.

I waved to Principal Clarke, who was my new buddy, and went over to the town library's booth, where I took one of Ms. Castro's recommended reading lists. Some of the new titles looked so good, and I made a promise to myself to stop at the library soon.

At dusk we all made our way to the lake and spread out blankets. Sophia and Riley and I squeezed onto one, and Olivia and Isabella plunked onto another right next to us. Hannah and Elizabeth sat down on the other side, and Michelle wheeled herself next to me in her chair. I saw Lindsay sitting a few rows over, with Casey.

Lindsay looked up and rushed over to me, giving me a hug. "Are you mad that I'm not sitting with you?" she asked.

"Why would I be mad?" I said.

"Well, we're family," she said.

"True," I said, "but I'm not sitting with Molly or Jenna, and they're family."

"Yeah," said Lindsay. "I'm just always worried people will get upset. I mean, everyone has been so nice to me since Mom died, and sometimes I just want to be treated normally, not like I'm special or anything."

"We don't treat you specially," I lied.

"Well, usually you don't," said Lindsay. "And I appreciate that. I know you probably didn't want me around during your Family Fall Fest with your mom

So Jelly

and sisters. I probably wouldn't have wanted me there either. But the thing is, I was glad that you thought it was okay to just be you and not treat me like I might break into a million pieces. It's hard to walk around and not want to snap my fingers at people and say, 'Act normal!'"

I blinked in surprise.

"Whew," she said. "I did not count on saying all that! But you're a good listener, and I guess mostly I just need someone to hear me."

I gave her a hug and said, "I am always here to listen to you. Now go back to your real BFF. I mean, if we're keeping it real, this blanket is full."

She laughed and said, "Meanie!" as she skipped back over to Casey.

I lay back and looked at the stars. It was a clear night, and it looked like the night sky had a million little glittering freckles. I thought about the last few weeks and how Dad and Jenna had listened to me, and about how my family always looked out for each other.

Maybe Principal Clarke was right. Maybe you didn't have to solve anything, you just needed to listen. And if it was as easy as that, maybe I was finally starting to figure this stuff out.

Chapter Thirteen
Family Is Everything

Mom and Dad and I had a talk after Fall Fest, and Mom told me that it was my turn to go to St. Louis, but they were also putting Lindsay in the rotation, and she would get the opportunity to go next.

I thought that sounded fair, and I knew that Lindsay would probably appreciate the time alone with Mom too.

"It was your mom's idea," Dad told me.

Mom and Dad looked at me, and I smiled. "Dad, you are a really good listener, but Mom is really good at solutions."

They both laughed.

Since Mom was speaking at the conference on the following Friday, she decided she would pick me

So Jelly

up right from school on Thursday, so we could drive to St. Louis that afternoon.

After her presentation we'd drive home in time for Family Friday dinner. I would finally have Mom all to myself.

I had my bag packed Thursday morning before I left for school, and I was so excited I could barely get through the day.

☼ ☼ ☼ ☼ ☼

Before I knew it, it was time for Mom and me to hit the road. We dropped off Molly and Mom gave Dad a kiss goodbye.

"Knock those city folks dead, honey," he said, and Mom hopped back into the car.

Soon we were on the highway and on our way.

"Ugh, this drive," Mom groaned. "This is how we drove back and forth to school when I was in college. I always hated this drive and I still do."

"Why?" I asked, looking around.

The trees were finally changing color, and the side of the road looked like a yellow and orange rainbow.

"It's so boring!" said Mom. "I would count the water towers to see how far away I was. We are four water towers away from State. Unless they built some more lately..."

"I think it's relaxing to take a long drive," I said, settling back in my seat. "Are you nervous about your speech?"

"A little," said Mom. "I don't mind speaking in front of people, especially about what I know so well, but I get a little nervous that someone will tell me I'm wrong or I don't know what I'm talking about."

"But you do know what you're talking about! That's why they want you to speak as an expert!"

"I don't know everything, honey. I know what I know about our business. So I'm an expert on the Park, but outside that ... I'm not so sure."

The Park was pretty successful, I guess. It had been around for fifty years. The food was always good and the people who worked there were always welcoming. I couldn't imagine it not being there.

"So if you didn't work at the Park, where would you work?" I asked, curious.

"Oh," said Mom. "Well, after college I was offered a lot of jobs in business."

"Like what?" I asked.

"Like in accounting offices in St. Louis, at an

So Jelly

investment firm in Chicago, and at a bank in New York. They were exciting job offers."

"Chicago? New York?!" I asked. "Really?"

"Yep," said Mom. "And I interviewed at all of them. I thought about each one.... Some were really good opportunities. It wasn't an easy decision."

"And?"

"And?" asked Mom. "Well, clearly I chose to come home and work for Grandpa and Nans at the Park."

"Why?" I asked, thinking about Mom living in Chicago or St. Louis. I couldn't even imagine her in New York.

"Well," said Mom, "you and I are a lot alike. I thought about what those jobs could offer me, and some of them were really interesting, big career paths. But in the end, I felt like I was happiest, and could be happiest, in Bellgrove. I wanted to come home."

"Did you regret it?" I asked, looking at her.

I never knew Mom even thought about living anywhere else. I was trying to think of her working for an investment firm, wearing a fancy suit and carrying a briefcase.

"Nope," said Mom. "Not a bit. Sometimes I wonder about choosing a different path. I mean, that's natural, but this is definitely where I want to be, and I'm lucky enough to be doing something I like very much with the people I love the most."

"Well, I'm glad at least you didn't go to California," I said. "Or New York or Chicago, for that matter."

Mom laughed. "No, I'm not a California girl. We'll have to see if Jenna is. Maybe she is and maybe she'll be back. I would not be unhappy if the three of you stayed in Bellgrove, but you each have to find the place that makes you happy."

We made it to St. Louis in time for dinner, but Mom wanted to check into the hotel first. We've stayed in hotels before for vacations, but we don't stay in them too often, and I'm always excited when we open the door and I get to see our temporary home. I checked out the fluffy beds and the view, then unwrapped the little soaps they give you in the bathroom.

Mom and I settled on a restaurant that was close to the hotel, so we walked over.

It was weird to be out to dinner with just Mom. First of all, when your family owns a restaurant, you don't eat in restaurants a lot. At home we mostly went out for tacos or sushi or pizza or Chinese food, since

So Jelly

the Park didn't serve any of those types of food. Louie Louie was our special restaurant, but we only went there once or twice a year.

Mom ordered me something called a Shirley Temple, which tasted like ginger ale with cherry juice mixed in it and a cherry on top. It was delicious, and I felt very fancy and city-like.

"What are you thinking?" asked Mom, as I put my chin in my hand.

"I'm trying to remember the last time it was just you and me, without Molly or Jenna or Dad or anyone else," I said.

"When was it?" asked Mom.

"When I had strep throat over the summer and you took me to see Dr. Miller."

"Oh!" said Mom. She sighed. "That's not good. I wish I could do a better job of spending more time with each of you individually. You girls really need that."

I nodded.

"Well, now you have my full attention," she said. "So shoot. What do you want to talk about?"

"I don't know!" I said.

"Well, I want to know how middle school is," said

Mom. "Like, really want to know. Not just 'it's good.' I want to know how you feel about it. Give me some real feedback."

"Oh!" I said. "Well . . . it's actually okay. I mean, there have been some bumps. I'm friends with more people, I guess, which is good, and now I'm on the hockey team, which I like more than I thought I would. Plus, I'm the class representative, which I guess is pretty cool since people had to vote for me."

"It's very cool!" said Mom. "That's quite the vote of confidence from your peers!"

"I guess the best way to say it is that I'm finding my way," I said.

"That's exactly what you're supposed to be doing," said Mom. "No one knows their way directly. They don't call it middle school for nothing! You're in the middle of a lot of change and a lot of decisions. It takes some winding paths and some detours before you get on a road you feel is the right one. Just keep yourself open to people who want to help and are here to listen. You have to let them in."

I thought about that. So not knowing everything was okay. Not having solutions was okay.

"It's a lot, right?" said Mom. "But I don't worry

So Jelly

about you figuring out the right path. Just remember how kind you are. That's the key to everything. That kindness will always win out, and I know you'll stay true to yourself."

"You mean I won't be mean to my poor cousin?" I asked.

"Well, I hope you aren't mean to *anyone*," Mom said. "Jealousy is a real feeling. It's completely natural and totally understandable. Rather than squish it down, though, if you talk about it, you might feel better."

"So I'm supposed to say, 'Hey, Lindsay, I'm kind of jealous that everyone is looking out for you'?" I asked.

"Noooo," said Mom. "Well, maybe, if you said it a little more sensitively. And if you can't talk about it, then sometimes it's okay to just let that feeling be for a bit. Let's just say life is kind of like a jelly donut. Now the jelly is a sweet and delicious surprise when you bite into it, right?"

I nodded.

"But you don't always see it in there; it can be a surprise. And sometimes, if you bite it the wrong way, it spurts out all over you."

DONUT DREAMS

"Yeah, that happened the other day at work," I said. I shuddered a little as I remembered.

"Okay, I'm not going to ask why you were eating donuts at work," Mom said, giving me a look. "Sometimes life throws us a little. It's okay to be thrown and be uncertain and be a little squishy like jelly. Take your time. Listen to yourself. Eventually it will be okay. Jelly can be sticky, but it's rarely the end of the world."

We were talking so much that before I knew it, dessert was in front of us.

"Oh my goodness," said Mom. "This is the second time we're having butter cake in two weeks. This is not the healthiest eating we've done!"

"Oh, Mom," I said, with a mouthful of cake. "We sell donuts every day!"

"You got me on that one, kiddo," she said, and she stuck her fork in her cake.

※ ※ ※ ※ ※

The next morning I heard Mom blow-drying her hair after her shower, which she rarely did.

I got up and opened the curtains to let in the light.

So Jelly

Mom peeked out of the bathroom. "Oh, did I wake you?" she asked.

"No," I said. "I just woke up."

Mom wanted to get coffee and rehearse her presentation one more time before the conference, so I got dressed too. The plan was that I'd go with Mom and sit in the back of the meeting room (quietly, I'd promised!).

After Mom's meeting was over, we'd be able to go out and see the city a little bit before we headed back.

"Whoa . . . Mom!" I exclaimed as she came out of the bathroom.

Mom spun around so I could see her outfit from every angle, and I hardly recognized her. On most days she wore a button-up shirt, a blazer, and jeans to work, and depending on the season, either ballet flats or boots. She always looked cute, but definitely casual.

Today she was wearing a really nice black suit with a fancy patterned silk blouse under it, and black patent leather high heels. She had a really pretty necklace on that I hadn't seen her wear before, her hair was blown out, and she had on makeup. She looked amazing!

"I can polish myself up for the city!" Mom laughed.

DONUT DREAMS

"Wow. Let me take a picture!" I snapped her photo and sent it to my sisters.

> Check it out! Our cool, stylish mom is ready to fire up her speech!

In two seconds Molly texted back,

> Whoa. Are you sure that's our mother?

It would be another hour at least before Jenna even saw it.

Mom and I made our way to the meeting site, which was a big glass office building. I helped her set up her laptop and crawled under the table to plug in the cord, and she clicked through her presentation to make sure everything was reading on the big screen.

I looked at the rows of chairs and wondered if they'd all be filled, and within an hour, they were. Since I was all the way in the back, I could see how many people were in the audience. I hoped Mom wasn't too nervous.

If she was, you'd never know, because after she

was introduced, she strutted out like a pro and walked through the presentation. I couldn't follow everything she was talking about—lots of gobbledygook about profit and margins—but she spoke loudly and clearly and was even funny. At the end everyone applauded, but no one clapped louder than I did. After Mom's speech she had to stay and talk to a few people.

I stood a little off to the side and at one point Mom called me over and said, "This is my daughter Kelsey." And everyone made a fuss over me, told me I was pretty and how much I looked like my mom. It was a little embarrassing, but nice, too.

When everyone left, she said, "Okay, let's make a run for it!" and we ran back to the hotel, where she changed back to the mom I knew in less than five minutes.

"Ugh, I hate high heels!" she said, throwing them back into her suitcase.

"Do we have time to walk around a little?" I asked.

"We do!" said Mom. "Let's see the town."

We went wandering up and down the streets, popping in and out of all these cute clothing stores and a few antique stores. We found a shirt for Jenna, and a phone case that was just perfect for Molly. It was made out of soccer ball material. I saw a really pretty lavender scarf at this very sleek new boutique and picked it up.

"Do you like that?" asked Mom.

"Yes, but not for me," I said. "You know who would like this? Lindsay."

Mom nodded. "It would look great with her dark hair. And that's very sweet of you to think of her too."

We put all the bags into the car and Mom said, "Ready to say sayonara to St. Louis?"

"Yep," I said. "St. Louis is great, but take me home to good old Bellgrove!"

"Your wish is my GPS command!" said Mom, and she punched in HOME in the car system and off we went.

Mom had been right; it was a pretty boring ride, and I guess I was tired, because the next thing I knew, I woke up in our driveway.

"We're home!" I called as we stepped into the house.

"We missed you!" called Dad from the kitchen.

I sniffed. "Ooh, lasagna!" I said.

"No, my name is Dad, not lasagna," joked Dad, giving me a hug. "And yes, I made a giant lasagna to welcome you home."

So Jelly

"How'd it go?" he asked Mom, pulling her in for a kiss.

"She killed it," I said. "Mom is pretty impressive."

Dad laughed. "Yes, I know."

Mom peered in the oven. "Chris, how big is that lasagna? It's enough to feed an army!"

"You know who likes lasagna?" I asked, not even pausing. "Lindsay. And Uncle Mike and Skylar. If we have extra, should we invite them for dinner?"

Mom smiled. "Well, if you tell my brother there's lasagna, he'll be here in about three seconds."

I texted Lindsay,

> R u guys hungry? It's lasagna night! Come on over!

and sure enough, she immediately texted back,

> We're on our way!

I set the table for three more and thought, *Always additions.* I looked out the front window just as Uncle Mike pulled up to the house. I smiled and opened the door, eager to let my family in.

Family Recipe

Chapter One
Family and Friends

I threw down my bag, then picked it up again and stuffed it into the cubbies that Dad had built us by the back door.

My sister Kelsey yelped, "Heeeeyyyy!" behind me when the door slammed before she got inside.

"Too slow!" I said, and walked into the kitchen, kicking off my shoes.

"Too messy!" said Dad, pointing to my shoes. "In the cubby, please."

"Molly slammed the door on me," Kelsey whined behind me.

"Welcome home, girls!" said Dad. "It's nice to see you, too!"

Dad had made us a platter of cheese and crackers

and set it out on the kitchen counter. Kelsey and I dove for it hungrily.

"Did you eat lunch?" Dad said.

"Yeah," I said, stuffing a cracker and cheese in my mouth. "But that was, like, three hours ago."

"I miss snack time at school," said Kelsey.

"Kelsey, we haven't had snack time at school since kindergarten!" I said.

"Well, they should have it in middle school," said Kelsey. "Everyone would be less cranky in the afternoon." She gave me an accusing look as she ate a cube of cheese.

"I'm not cranky," I said after I swallowed another mouthful of cheese and crackers. "I'm hungry."

"Okay," said Dad. "Eat your snack then let's see. . . ." He walked over to the bulletin board in the kitchen, where Mom kept all the calendars and schedules. "Today is Tuesday. Molly, you have soccer at four thirty."

"Yep," I said, picking out two crackers and a bit of cheese before making myself a mini sandwich. "I know."

"So that means homework needs to get started pronto," said Dad.

Family Recipe

"Yep," I said again while devouring my mini sandwich. "I know."

"Kelsey, I need you to help Mom with dinner when she gets home from work," said Dad, still examining the bulletin board. "Wait, wait, you have hockey. Now how is this going to work . . . ?"

"Dad," said Kelsey, finishing off the last of the good crackers. "Mom went over it this morning. Jenna is driving me to hockey and you are taking Molly to soccer."

"Right!" said Dad, smacking his head. "I thought Jenna was working today, but she's just tutoring after school."

I went back to my cubby and took out my laptop and my French book.

"What are you doing?" asked Kelsey.

"Starting my homework," I said, setting up at the table.

"Now?" asked Kelsey suspiciously.

"I have soccer in an hour and a half," I said. "And hours of homework tonight, which is totally insane."

"You could start it when you get home from soccer," Kelsey said.

I rolled my eyes.

Kelsey is not entirely organized. My dad says Kelsey likes her downtime, but in reality, she just doesn't like to do homework.

It's not that I like doing homework, but I honestly don't mind when it's interesting. The drill stuff, like my French homework, is really annoying, so I like to just bang it out when I get home and get it over with.

Kelsey would be whining about her Spanish homework at nine o'clock tonight.

"Kelsey, why don't you take a page from Molly and get started too?" asked Dad.

She sighed dramatically.

Dad sighed dramatically back at her.

"How are we even related?" I grumbled, and grabbed another cube of cheese.

"You have Mom's systematic approach," said Dad. "It's good that at least half the family has it."

I laughed. "More than half," I said.

Mom and I are organized, and Jenna is too. Dad says that he and Kelsey, on the other hand, are "dreamers."

"Okay, now Mom and dinner," said Dad, looking a little worried. "I was going to prep some veggies so she can make an egg dish, but . . ."

Family Recipe

"Mom and eggs," I reminded him, "are generally not a good pair."

"Definitely not," said Kelsey. "Remember when she tried to hard-boil them?"

Both of us started giggling.

Even though Mom's family owns a restaurant, she cannot cook to save her life. She tried to hard-boil eggs to make egg salad once, and we still don't know what she did, but all the eggs started exploding. It was a huge mess. I'm pretty sure there's still some egg stuck on the ceiling over the stove.

My theory is that Mom senses us, especially when we talk about her. Just at that moment, the phone rang, and sure enough, it was her.

Kelsey spoke to her first, going on and on about how ridiculous it was that she had so much homework.

I knew exactly what Mom was saying to her without even hearing it. *If you stopped complaining and just did the homework, you'd be halfway done by now.*

Mom and I are a lot alike in that way. I have no time for drama or complaining.

Kelsey handed me the phone.

"Hi, honey," said Mom. "How was your day?"

"Fine," I said.

"Fine?" asked Mom, and I could tell she was wrinkling her face up.

"Yeah," I said. "You know it takes a few weeks to get into the swing of things with a new school year."

"That's true," said Mom. "Do you have a lot of homework?"

"While Kelsey was complaining, I got half of it done," I said, smirking as Kelsey stuck her tongue out at me.

Mom laughed. "You're just like me, kiddo!"

After I was done talking to Mom, I handed the phone to Dad.

He talked to her for a few minutes and then said excitedly, "Hey, girls, Grandpa made his famous chili at the restaurant today! Mom's bringing it home!"

"Dinner!" Kelsey yelled, punching the air.

"Yeah!" I yelled too.

Grandpa's chili was super delicious, so I was already looking forward to it even though my stomach was full of cheese and crackers. But I'd be hungry again after running around during soccer practice.

Dad smiled and nodded. He hung up and said, "Dinner is saved."

Family Recipe

I knocked off most of my homework pretty quickly after that and went upstairs to get ready for soccer.

I started playing soccer when I was in kindergarten, and I've loved it ever since. I love how fast the game is, but I also love that there's a strategy. It looks like a crowd of people is just running around after a ball, but in reality, you have to have a plan to get the ball down the field. Everyone on the team has a specific role for moving the ball around.

I heard my older sister Jenna burst in the front door downstairs, because Jenna doesn't do anything quietly.

"I'm hooome!" she called.

"Start the parade!" Dad says like he always does.

Jenna is in high school, and she can drive, which she thinks makes her a lot cooler than she is, but she actually is pretty cool.

She is also kind of intense. Mom says that Jenna is a "demon on the court" in tennis, which makes sense because Jenna is really competitive.

"Molly, ten-minute warning!" Dad called upstairs. "Soccer starts in twenty, and it takes ten to get there!"

I threw my hair in a ponytail and headed

downstairs. I didn't love having practice after school because I was already tired. We had it in the mornings the week before school started, which was better, even though I had to streak myself beforehand with tons of sunscreen, making my eyes all stingy when I sweated.

"Hi, Molls," said Jenna, slamming the fridge. "Dad, what do we have for a snack? I'm starving."

Dad pushed the cheese and cracker plate toward her, and Jenna scowled.

"They ate all the good crackers!"

"There are bad crackers?" Dad said. "Huh. I didn't realize we could divide crackers into good and bad. That's good to know."

"Dad, you know what I mean!" Jenna fumed and opened the cabinet to rummage through it. She opened a box and stuffed a few crackers into her mouth.

"Eat some cheese and fruit with those," said Dad. "That's the healthy part."

"Dad, I'm old enough to drive a car," said Jenna. "I know what healthy food is!"

Dad sighed and gave Jenna a hug. "You may be driving, but I will always see you as the adorable

Family Recipe

toddler who called herself Wenna because she couldn't say her *Js* yet."

I burst out laughing as Jenna rolled her eyes at him. Dad is so sentimental sometimes that we call him Mr. Goo.

"And *you*," said Dad dramatically, hugging me hard. "You were my baby who refused to say Dada or Daddy. That's the first word most kids say! But not you. It was Mama, Mama, Mama. Then Wenna. Then dog . . ."

I was laughing because I knew the rest. "Then 'kit cat' for Henry the cat," I said.

"Yes!" said Dad. "Kit cat, *then* Daddy. Finally! You nearly killed me!"

I smiled. We actually have a video of me sitting on Dad's lap right before I touched his nose and said "Daddy" for the first time. He was so happy he looked like he was going to cry.

"Sorry about that," I said, then hoisted my soccer bag over my shoulder.

"Okay. My child who now loves me has soccer," Dad said to Jenna. "Kelsey is . . . where is Kelsey? Kelsey?" he bellowed upstairs. "Are you on the phone before you finished your homework?"

"Probably," said Jenna, smirking.

Kelsey came downstairs looking guilty. "I had to ask Lindsay what the assignment was," she said.

"Kelsey . . . ," Dad warned.

"Fine, I'll start my homework."

"Great!" said Dad. "Jenna will take you to hockey while I take Molly to soccer. Okay, kiddo," he said to me, and we headed out to the car.

Even though I've been sitting in the front for a long time now, it still feels weird to ride next to Dad in the front seat.

"You excited about the game this weekend?" Dad asked.

"Yeah," I said, "but the first game of the season is always hard. There are some different girls playing this year."

"That's expected," Dad said. "That's why you have practice, to get to know each other's strengths and rhythms."

"Yeah," I said, and rested my head against the window.

One of the good things about Dad is that he understands that even though I like to talk, I also like to be quiet at times. Jenna talks nonstop and Kelsey is either talking or texting, and we can all be a little noisy, but sometimes I like to zone out, especially when I'm getting ready for soccer. It kind of clears my head so I can focus. Mom used to joke that I had an on/off switch and nothing in between.

Dad pulled into the lot at the soccer field and we got out of the car.

I guess it's kind of weird that Dad still comes to my practices now that I'm in middle school. I noticed the other day that most kids get dropped off, but Dad sits in the bleachers, watching. He's not one of those parents who yells from the sidelines, which I am very thankful for, but he definitely pays attention.

"Okay," he said, taking his coffee mug. "I'll be in the stands if you need me, honey. Have a great practice!"

I waved and trotted off to the sidelines.

My BFF, Madeline, was on my team. And this year, Riley and Isabella were playing with us too, which was both good and weird. Good because I liked them both, but weird because Riley was better friends with Kelsey than me.

Coach Wendy had us out on the field before I could think about it too much. We warmed up and did some drills, and then she had us count off for a few three-on-three scrimmages. I liked those because if you have a full team on the field, you aren't always on the ball. When it's just the three of you, it can be much more intense.

Madeline was on my squad. We've been best friends since preschool, and we've been playing together forever, so I know almost without thinking which way she's going on the field or when she'll decide to take a shot.

We were passing the ball back and forth pretty well when Riley said, "Hey, guys, I'm on your side," which startled me a little.

I nodded and passed to her, and she tripped over the ball. Her face got red, and she said, "Sorry," and looked down at the ground.

Riley is a good player, but when she thinks people are watching or there's a clutch moment, she sometimes just whiffs on the ball.

"It's okay," I said. "Let's work you in better."

I nodded toward Madeline and she nodded back.

"Play forward," I said to Madeline.

I passed the ball up the field to her, and she made a really nice kick to Riley, who sank it in the goal.

Family Recipe

"Now that's it!" called Coach Wendy happily. "That's it, that's it, girls! I saw what you did there. Worked each other in and figured out how to play together. Great job!"

Riley took a bow, and I laughed. I looked up at Dad, who gave me a thumbs-up and a grin.

We played for another thirty minutes before Coach Wendy blew the whistle.

"Girls," she said. "This weekend is our first game. I don't care if we win."

Everyone looked at each other.

"I care that you play well as a team," Coach Wendy explained. "We have a long season and plenty of games to win, but let's do this as a team, okay?"

We all nodded.

"Now give me a G!"

"G!" we all yelled.

"What's that for?"

"Go!" we yelled.

"G is for?" she said, smiling.

"Great!" we yelled.

"G is for?"

"Goal!" we yelled. "Go! Great! Goal!"

I wondered if I was the only one to realize that

the cheer didn't exactly make sense, but it sure got us all riled up.

Once I sank into the seat in the car, I realized how tired I was. "Oof," I said. "That knocked me out."

"Well, you did a heck of a lot of running," said Dad.

"Speaking of running, did you get a chance to run today?" I asked him.

Usually he went in the morning, but once school started, it was harder for him to get out in time.

"Nah, I missed today," Dad said, wincing. "And I definitely feel it."

"There's a track around the soccer field," I said, thinking about it. "When you bring me to practice, you can just do some laps instead of sitting in the bleachers."

"What, you don't like your old dad sitting around watching you?" he joked.

"Dad," I said, already knowing where this was going. "I like having you at practice. I want you to be at practice. But I also know how much you like to run."

Dad smiled. "Ah, okay. I thought you were trying to nicely tell me you were too old to have your dad

Family Recipe

with you! I thought maybe I embarrassed you."

"I know," I said, and rolled my eyes. "Mr. Goo, you are very sensitive!"

Dad laughed. "You know what Mr. Goo who is sensitive wants?"

"What?" I asked as we turned onto our street.

"Some chili!" he said. He pointed to our car, which was in front of us.

"Then step on it, sir," I said. "Because if we don't get home soon, the rest of the family is going to eat it all! Follow that chili!"

"Give me a *C*!" said Dad.

"*C*!" I said.

"Wait, we don't have time to spell out chili," said Dad. "How about just 'go'?"

"You know, maybe we should say, 'Give me a *G*' for Grandpa," I said, picking up my bag. "Go, Grandpa, for saving us from Mom's dinner!"

Dad cracked up and said, "Let's keep that cheer between us."

Chapter Two
The Assignment

Every morning in school, we meet in the cafeteria until the morning meeting, which is usually a bunch of announcements, is over. Then we go off to our first class.

Soccer the day before must have wiped me out more than I thought, because I was feeling kind of hazy. I bumped into my cousin Lindsay as I headed toward my first-period class, which was history.

"Are you still asleep?" she joked. "You usually get up so early!"

"I know!" I said. "I'm wiped out from school and soccer."

"Are you working after school?" she asked.

I nodded. "Yep. I have a shift today."

Family Recipe

Our grandparents own a restaurant in town called the Park View Table. They run the whole thing, and it's seriously a family operation.

Mom works there in the accounting office. Uncle Mike, who is my mom's brother and Lindsay's dad, runs Donut Dreams, the donut counter in the restaurant. Mom's other brother, Uncle Charlie is in charge of all the inventory and orders.

Jenna and my other cousins Rich and Lily also have shifts at the Park after school and on weekends. This year, Lindsay, Kelsey, and I started working at the Park too.

Lindsay and Kelsey manage the Donut Dreams counter, while I'm a runner, which means you "run the floor." So if my sister Jenna, who is a waitress, serves someone a hamburger and they ask for ketchup with it, I would be the one who runs to get the ketchup and brings it to the table. I also bring more napkins and refill customers' water glasses, that kind of thing.

It's not very glamorous, but to be honest, there's nothing really glamorous about working at a restaurant. It's a lot of hard work.

"Me too," Lindsay said. "Ugh, being a runner seems like a very un-fun job."

"Nah," I said. "I don't mind it. Actually, your job at the counter seems worse. If there are no donut customers, it must be *sooo* boring!"

"But when it's slow, we can just stand around and hang out!" said Lindsay. "I guess Grandpa and Nans gave us the right jobs."

We slid into our seats. Lindsay's seat was in front of me, while Eric Sellers had the seat behind me.

Ms. Blueski was our history teacher and she was new, which was a little odd, since we don't get a whole lot of new people who move to our town.

She had just finished her student teaching, and we were her first class of kids, which Eric decided to take advantage of. He was usually pretty annoying, but he's been even more obnoxious lately. I knew he was just testing Ms. Blueski.

"Can I go to the bathroom?" Eric asked.

I turned to see him waving his hand. I had just seen him come out of the restroom before class, so I knew he was trying to get out for a few minutes to waste some class time.

"I am sure you *can* go to the bathroom, Eric," said Ms. Blueski, and the whole class giggled. "But you *may* go to the bathroom after I get to a break in the lesson. You just came from morning meeting and you had a break between classes."

Eric looked mad and wiggled around in his seat uncontrollably. "But I really have to go!" he said.

Ms. Blueski looked at him. "Do you think you're going to wet your pants?" she asked. "Because if so, then please do go now."

The class was howling with laughter. "Look out! Eric is going to wet his pants!" called out Adam Linzer, who was sitting on my right side.

Harry Watson scooted his chair away. "Hey, don't get me wet too!" he called.

Eric turned red.

"Eric, why don't you go now?" said Ms. Blueski. "We will get started so the rest of the class doesn't have to wait for you, but I can wait to talk about the assignment until you get back."

Eric hurried outside.

"Run, Eric!" yelled Adam. "Before you have an accident!"

"Okay, okay," said Ms. Blueski. "Let's settle down."

Three minutes later, Eric came back in. He must have just been standing in the hall.

"All right," said Ms. Blueski. "Now this is a history

class. History is important because we learn about the future from things that happened in the past. It gives us an understanding about the world and a context for how we live now. You may think history has to do with wars or things that happened a very long time ago, but history can be more recent, too. And it can be personal. Every one of you, for instance, has a history."

We all thought about that for a second. Most people in this class were born in Bellgrove, Missouri. We've spent our whole lives here, and most of us could recite our own history, which was kind of boring.

"Our first assignment is going to explore the History of You," said Ms. Blueski. "And to start off that exercise, we're going to do a family tree. I have one up here as an example on the whiteboard.

"You'll need to fill in as much of the tree as possible with parents, grandparents, aunts, uncles, and cousins, going as far back and as far out as you can. To get you started, I have some blank trees that I'm passing around."

I took a sheet and turned to pass one to Eric.

"We're going to start off with the basics you know," said Ms. Blueski. "This week's assignment is to talk to your family to see how much of the tree you can fill in with the spots I provided. I think when you do this, you'll find out all sorts of interesting things about your relatives that you may not know as you gather as much information as you can."

Everyone looked down at their sheet. It seemed kind of straightforward. I put down my name first, then Jenna's and Kelsey's.

Eric leaned forward and said into my ear, "Is that your real tree?"

"What?" I said.

"Since, you know, you're adopted," Eric said.

"Oh my goodness!" I said. "I had no idea!"

Adam laughed. Lindsay turned around and said, "So are you writing your family history or Molly's family history, Eric?"

"I'm just saying that she might write her mom down on her tree, but that's not her real mom," said Eric.

I felt my heart start to beat fast.

Everyone I grew up with knew I was adopted. I mean, I don't look at all like my family. My skin is a different color, my hair is kind of different, and my eyes and nose look different too. But nobody outside my family and close friends really talked about it. It was just a fact: "Molly is adopted."

Sometimes people said or did weird things, like the time I went to my friend Ava Baker's house for dinner, and Mrs. Baker made me wonton soup. I guess she thought that because I was born in South Korea, I would like it, but I didn't. And wonton soup is Chinese, not Korean.

Mom said that one of the things about being adopted is that you might have to educate people like Mrs. Baker.

I didn't feel like educating Eric just then.

"Have you ever met your mom?" asked Eric. "I mean, your *real* mom."

"I've seen her real mom," said Lindsay. "She is actually my aunt Melissa. Aunt Melissa is pretty real."

I looked at her gratefully.

"Well, yeah, I mean she's Molly's mom, but if she does her history on a tree, there's got to be her other family," said Eric. "Like she has a mom and a mother."

My other family? My stomach was flip-flopping around.

"She has one family," Lindsay said firmly. "Although maybe you have another family. Maybe

Family Recipe

your real mother is a monster ghoul, because only a monster ghoul could produce such a jerk."

"His mom can be really strict," Adam said, laughing again.

"Hey, back off my mother!" said Eric.

"Is there a problem over there?" asked Ms. Blueski.

"We're gathering information," Adam told her. "About Eric's monster mom."

The class laughed.

Then the bell rang, and I was never so happy to be able to run out of a class.

Chapter Three
Dad Is My Real Dad

I went to French class, and then lunch. Dad packed our lunch every day, so I didn't have to waste time in line. I flopped down at the table with Madeline.

"Bad day?" Madeline asked.

"Yeah," I said, sighing.

"What happened?" Madeline asked.

"Eric Sellers can really be a giant jerk," I said.

"Can be?" Madeline said. "You mean he is. Anyway, what did he do?"

"He's just a jerk," I said. "I don't even want to talk about it."

"So who is going to help me with this coding assignment?" moaned Madeline.

I shrugged. Today I had enough problems of my

own to solve. I didn't really have time for Madeline's.

After lunch I passed Lindsay in the hall on my way to phys ed.

"Hey!" she said, grabbing my arm. "Are you okay?"

"Eric is just a jerk, that's all," I said. "I'm good."

"He sure is," Lindsay said, nodding. "Don't let him get to you."

"He didn't," I said. I smiled to reassure her, but as I headed toward the locker room, I knew I was lying.

Luckily, in phys ed we just had to run on the track. Sometimes I run with Mom and Dad on the weekends, when they do shorter distances.

The thing I love about running is that I can just let my mind go. And when I'm running for myself, not, say, as part of a relay team, I only have to think about my pace, my legs moving, and my arms pumping. I don't have to worry about anyone else but me in my own lane.

Today we were doing sprints. As soon as I heard the whistle I tore down the track as fast as I could. The wind blew my hair around and felt good hitting my face. I wasn't really paying attention until I saw Dad standing at the fence.

DONUT DREAMS

He was leaning on it, talking to Mr. Walsh, who was the phys ed teacher. Dad is a carpenter and teaches woodshop at the high school down the street. Mr. Walsh and Dad do a running club together, so sometimes Dad comes down to the track to do a few laps with Mr. Walsh after school.

"I'm not spying!" said Dad as I jogged over.

"He's not!" laughed Mr. Walsh. "I asked him to come down with the forms for the race we're doing next month."

"But," said Dad, "I saw this speeding bullet coming down the track and thought, 'Whooooa!'"

"And he said, 'Hey, that's my girl!'" said Mr. Walsh.

"It sure is!" said Dad, beaming.

I blushed a little. "Okay, Dad. I have one more class left. Do you want to come watch me during English lit, too?"

"I love English lit," said Dad, teasing, "but I left the car at school so Jenna can drive to work, and I'm going to run home now."

I noticed just then that he had changed from his work outfit into his running shorts and T-shirt.

He hoisted his backpack on. "Got all my stuff in here!"

Family Recipe

Mr. Walsh blew the whistle. "Okay, crew, bring it on in!"

He gave Dad a high five and said, "Run tall, Chris!"

"Bye, Dad!" I called, then followed Mr. Walsh over to the bench. I watched as Dad ran off.

Dad had what Mom called a long gait, which in running means that you have a wide step or stride. He could take about three strides running and be half a block away from me. But no matter how fast Dad went, his body always seemed really calm and relaxed. It looked like the only thing moving was his legs.

Seeing Dad made me feel better. I mean, he was my *real* dad, no matter what Eric Sellers said.

Chapter Four
Family, Work, and Perfect Pie

After school I waited on the front steps with Kelsey and Lindsay. Nans was picking us up to take us to the Park for our shifts.

Grandpa was always in a better mood when a lot of family members are working shifts in the restaurant together. If there was a shift where no family members were available, he hired local college students to help out but he wasn't happy about it. He loved having family around all the time.

Nans was pretty short and drove this really big white car. You could barely see her head above the steering wheel, so it almost looked like the car was driving itself.

Kelsey opened the car door and called out, "Hiya,

Family Recipe

Nans. Here's the crew reporting for duty!" She jumped in the front seat next to Nans while Lindsay and I sat in the back.

"My girls!" said Nans. "I'm so glad to have such a lovely group of girls as my granddaughters!

※ ※ ※ ※ ※

When we got to the Park, we changed in the workroom, which was just a little room off the kitchen with lockers and benches and a full length mirror on the wall. There was a rack of uniforms hanging in the corner.

I had to wear a Park collared shirt and a long apron and black pants. Lindsay and Kelsey wore aprons too, but they could wear jeans and Donut Dreams T-shirts, which made me a little jealous.

I went to the mirror to pull my hair back off my face in a wide headband, and I saw Mom come in behind me.

"Hi, girls!" she said, hugging Lindsay and Kelsey. She came over and kissed the top of my head. "Everyone have good days?"

We all nodded. Lindsay looked over at me for a second, but I didn't want to catch her eye.

"Put your hair in a pony, pumpkin," said Mom. "Rules are rules."

I sighed. "Grandpa and his rules," I said.

"Actually, that's not Grandpa's rule. That's a health and safety rule for all places that serve food. I mean, you wouldn't want someone's hair in your food. Oh, that'd be really . . ."

"Totally disgusting," I said, and pulled my hair into a pony, but I kept the headband on too.

We all walked out. I passed Uncle Mike and Uncle Charlie, who were having a meeting with a salesperson at the counter. They waved, and I saw Uncle Mike go give Lindsay a hug hello.

Sometimes I feel bad that I have a mom and a dad, while Lindsay just has her dad. I mean, she has all of us, too, but her mom died a couple years ago. She once told me that it was hardest after school, because that was the time of day when she most realized her mom was really gone.

After she told me, I told Mom. I felt bad about telling Mom something Lindsay had shared only with me, but Mom's been helping Lindsay a lot since her mom passed.

When I told her, Mom got really teary but said

she was glad she knew. "We look out for each other in this family," she said. "So you need to tell me when someone is sad or upset so we can all help. That's what a family does."

Then she talked to Uncle Mike and to Nans, and now, even if Uncle Mike is there, Mom always makes sure either she or Nans is there after school for Lindsay too.

It's not the same, but it's still reminds her there are other people who love her. Mom is really good about figuring out how to make stuff better.

I walked out of the workroom, tying my apron behind me. Jenna was doing setup, which meant she was checking tables before the dinner rush, making sure there were silverware and napkins at each place setting.

"Hey, little sister," she said. "Can you make sure all the salt and pepper are good to go?"

I nodded and headed over to the station where we kept pitchers, condiments, and all the stuff you'd need to go with your meal. I made sure all the salt and pepper shakers were full, which was another one of Grandpa's pet peeves.

"Half a shaker of salt?" he'd say if he spied one

on the table. "Customers are going to think they will only get a half a hamburger, too!"

My older cousin Rich was waiting tables with Jenna, and he came over and pulled my headband.

"Gold star from Grandpa!" he said, teasing. "Hair off your face and a ponytail! But before you get that star, let's check. Maybe you left out a grain of salt in that shaker."

"Well then, that one is going to your table!" I said, laughing.

He grinned and grabbed the salt shaker and put it on his tray.

There was only one table that had a customer. What was weird was that in just a short time I'd started to know who the regular customers were.

Mrs. Rose, who was a nurse, was always here early. She was still in her scrubs. She was here every day around this time because she stopped after her shift at the hospital.

She was only in her late thirties but sometimes she could look older because she always seemed so exhausted. She was really sweet though.

Jenna nodded to me, so I headed over to Mrs. Rose's table with a pot of coffee.

Family Recipe

"Can I fill you up, Mrs. Rose?" I asked.

"Oh yes, sweetie," she said. "I need another cup so I have energy to get to my dog-walking group. Otherwise those puppies will run all over me!"

"I didn't know you did a dog-walking group!" I said excitedly.

"It's for the rescue group I volunteer for," said Mrs. Rose. "We take dogs that don't have homes and care for them until they can be adopted. This way they don't have to stay in shelters. I meet up with the other rescue workers once a week for a dog walk, and we celebrate if a dog is no longer there and has been placed with a family."

"Wait, you can see a dog one week on a walk and the next week the dog is just gone?" I asked, shocked.

Nans is always telling me I have no filter, and I just say what I think without, as she says, *processing it*.

"Well, a rescue home is never meant to be permanent. Sometimes the dogs are with us for a week, sometimes a few months, until we find the right home for them."

I thought about that for a second. "So you might take care of a cute little puppy but then someone else gets to keep it?"

"Yes," said Mrs. Rose. "Sometimes I get attached to the animals, and I miss them when they're gone. Some dogs just make you want to keep them forever. But part of what brings me a lot of happiness is seeing the best, loving homes these animals find for the long term."

I nodded, but I guess I looked a little skeptical.

I saw Grandpa wander over, another pot of coffee in his hand.

"Oh look, Mrs. Rose," he said. "You can tell this is one of my granddaughters, because she's quick on the refill, just like her old granddad!"

Grandpa put his arm around me and grinned. I couldn't tell whether he was checking out my headband.

"You just love having your grandchildren here, don't you?" said Mrs. Rose, smiling.

"Of course I do!" said Grandpa. "I get to see all my grandchildren, and I get to boss them around, like telling them to get over to their station and fill up all those ketchup bottles!"

We all laughed.

I knew Grandpa wasn't totally joking about me getting over to refill the ketchup. He ran a tight ship at the Park, and he was everywhere and saw everything. He liked that I was friendly with the customers, but he also didn't like us to dawdle.

Sometimes I got caught up in conversation with someone and he'd beeline it over to me.

I would say, "Well, Grandpa, I didn't want to be rude," and he would say, "I know, sweetie, but you have to know how to cut off a conversation. They didn't invite you to sit down with them and eat!"

I secretly thought Grandpa and Nans were also worried I would upset someone because I did have that tendency to speak without thinking. It's not like I made people mad a lot, but I did get a lot of eye rolls, with people saying, "Molly, you can't just say that!"

I looked across the restaurant and saw Kelsey wiping down the donut counter. Lindsay was ringing up a kid I recognized from high school and laughing.

The donut counter, Donut Dreams, had a different rhythm than the diner most days. People came in for donuts early in the morning, and then there were two after-school rushes, one after middle school and one after elementary school let out.

Then there was a lull, because not a lot of people

eat donuts before dinner, although in my opinion that would not be a bad habit.

Our shifts were usually from four o'clock to six thirty. If we were really busy, we'd stay until seven. You could feel the restaurant start to change after five o'clock, when the regulars and then families would come in for dinner. It got busier and noisier and people moved faster.

Mom had been trying to convince Grandpa to add a take-out option so people could pick up dinner and eat it at home, but Grandpa wasn't too sure about that.

"Why would you eat food out of a bag?" he would ask. "Here you sit down, someone brings you dinner, and cleans up after you!"

He did have a point.

A few minutes before five o'clock, Nans gave the signal and the waitstaff headed toward the kitchen for a quick meeting.

"Hello, everyone," Nans said. "Let's quickly go over the specials for tonight."

I loved this part, because Nans liked everyone to taste the specials so they'd know what they were describing if anyone had questions.

Family Recipe

Tonight, for instance, the special was stuffed peppers with orzo. Nans sliced a few for us so everyone could have a piece.

The peppers were grilled and soft and filled with orzo, which is pasta shaped like rice, and some onions. It was delicious, and I was glad I tried it, because if I had to describe it, I would be able to say that uncooked peppers are crunchy, but once you grill them they are soft and a little sweeter, just like onions.

The other special was a dessert, Nans's famous apple pie. Nans passed out pieces of that too, and she winked as she gave me a really big one.

I smiled because she knew her apple pie was one of my all-time faves.

"Do you need to double-check that you still like this?" Nans asked me.

"I think I do, Nans," I said.

"Since you're the apple pie enthusiast, you're on apple peeling duty," she said.

As everyone else filed out, she put me to work at the counter. She spooned a little bit of the filling into a dish and gave me a spoon.

"I know you just ate a piece of the pie, Molly," she said, "but I want you to taste the filling separately to make sure it's just right. What do you think?"

"Nans, your apple pie is perfect. Like, it just can't get any better. But I wonder if there's a way for us to make apple pie donuts," I said.

"But we have apple cider donuts that everyone loves," said Nans. "I can't make enough of them sometimes."

"I know," I said. "But apple pie donuts would be different, because they would have a filling. Like cream donuts, but instead of cream, the inside could be apple pie filling."

Nans smiled. "Thank you for saying my pie is perfect," she said. "But even perfection can sometimes get better. And let's see what we can come up with for the donuts. While I'm making more perfect pies, it's time for you to hit the floor."

Chapter Five
Curious Kids on My Shift

I gave Nans a quick kiss, then headed out. Kelsey and Lindsay were already getting ready to close the Donut Dreams counter, which annoyed me a little bit because they were almost done with their shift. After they did cleanup and mopped the floor, they'd head to a booth to hang out or eat until my shift was over, and then Mom would drive the three of us home.

"Molls, can you drop the check off at Mrs. Rose's table?" Jenna asked, whisking by me and handing me the paper receipt. "Then I'm gonna need your kid skills with the Sherers." Jenna indicated a table with a mom and three boys, all of whom were crying.

"Oh, boy," I said as Jenna headed over to them.

I love kids, and I'm usually really good with them.

DONUT DREAMS

This summer I ran a babysitting group at the lake, which was fun. The parents would drop the kids off with me, but stay on the beach in case I needed help.

I could usually manage four or five at once. I would play games with them or we'd read a book. Sometimes I brought some art projects, but it turned out that anything that involved glue while you were dealing with kids in sand was a very bad and very messy idea.

"Can I get you anything else, Mrs. Rose?" I asked.

Grandpa had taught us to ask that before we gave them the check. "If you just hand them the bill for the meal, the customer will think they can't order anything else. What if they're still hungry? I can't have customers leaving here still hungry!" he had said.

"No, I'm all set," said Mrs. Rose, looking at her watch.

I placed the check on the table. "Please pay up front," I said, exactly like I was taught. "And have fun with the pups tonight!"

"I certainly will," she said. "Are you a dog person, Molly?"

"Yes!" I said, a little loudly, and Mrs. Rose laughed.

"Would you like a dog?" she asked. "Because we

have so many dogs who need loving homes."

"I would just love a dog," I said longingly. "But the problem is Mom and Dad. They think that three kids is enough work, and one dog plus three kids is too much."

"Well," said Mrs. Rose, chuckling, "they have a good point there. Maybe when you're a little older and things settle down, they'll change their minds."

"I hope so," I said, but I wasn't convinced.

"I have to show you the most adorable puppy that came into our group. She's just precious." Mrs. Rose rummaged through her bag and fished out her phone. Then she fumbled for her glasses.

I shifted from foot to foot as I saw Grandpa looking at me and shaking his head from side to side. He gestured toward the table with Mrs. Sherer and her three kids.

Jenna looked a little frazzled. The kids had thrown all the silverware on the floor.

"Here we go," said Mrs. Rose, tapping at her phone. She held it up and I moved in.

"Oh!" I said, and grabbed the phone from her. "Oh my gosh, that has to be the sweetest, cutest, best puppy ever."

DONUT DREAMS

I couldn't stop staring at the screen. I wanted to jump inside the phone and grab the dog and run off with her.

She was a tiny puppy with fluffy white fur that almost covered her eyes. She looked like a mini fur ball with two pointy little ears sticking out.

Just then Jenna peered over my shoulder. "Oh, Mrs. Rose," she said. "That's trouble. My sister has wanted a dog forever, and that's a cute one!"

"I know!" said Mrs. Rose. "And this one is just so sweet. And a little sassy, too. She has a way of telling you exactly what she wants."

"Sounds like someone I know," said Jenna, smirking at me. "But right now there's no way Mom will say yes. I do, though, need a little assistance with table fifteen," she said, nudging me.

I sighed and handed the phone back to Mrs. Rose. "Well, keep showing me pictures of that pup," I said. "Maybe one day. But right now I have some fork fishing to do!"

I scooted over to table fifteen, where the Sherers were, and picked up four forks and four spoons. Mrs. Sherer had four knives in front of her.

"Thank you, sweetie," she said. "Here, I can give

you three knives. If we leave them, the kids will try to use them as swords."

I smiled slightly. "Well that's creative," I said.

"Yeah," she said. "They can be quite innovative. Can we get a basket of bread? There was one, but . . ."

"I see it," I said, dropping to one knee. "It must have fallen on the floor."

Mrs. Sherer sighed. "Sorry," she said, looking embarrassed.

"Not a problem," I said. "I'll be right back."

I went to the kitchen to pick up a new bread basket. I sniffed. The kitchen smelled like apple pie.

Grandpa was helping load a tray for Jenna. "Did those Sherer kids go through an entire basket of bread?" he asked.

"No, they dropped an entire basket of bread on the floor," I said.

"Okay, get them another one quick," he said.

I ran back out with the bread, and as I passed Rich, he said, "Hey, can I get refills of water on table ten, please?"

I nodded, dropped off the bread, and grabbed the pitcher.

Table ten was Mr. and Mrs. Grasso, who owned

DONUT DREAMS

a bookstore in town called the Book Nook, which I loved.

"Molly!" said Mrs. Grasso. "How lovely to see you. I hope you have time to read between school and work!"

"And soccer," said Mr. Grasso. "I heard you've been tearing up the field!"

I laughed. "Now who told you that?"

"You know your grandfather. We get all the grandchildren updates!" he said.

"Yes, pretty regularly," laughed Mrs. Grasso.

"I need help on eight," whispered Rich as he speed-walked by with a huge tray, heading for the Sherers' table, and I nodded.

"Go, go," said Mr. Grasso. "It's busy tonight!"

"Yep," I said. "Just how I like it!"

I filled their glasses, then hurried over to help Rich unload the tray, setting the plates at each place in the center of the place mat, like Grandpa instructed. You're supposed to turn the plate when you put it on the table so the entree faces the customer, but to be honest, I don't even know what that means.

I looked at the plate of spaghetti and meatballs. Was it upside down? Was there a top to a plate of

Family Recipe

spaghetti and meatballs? It seemed like a question my math teacher would ask.

The kid was kind of looking at me as I worked it out, so I said, "That spaghetti looks so good. Hope you enjoy it!"

He smiled and dug in. I don't think he cared if it was upside down.

"Fifteen," Jenna hissed as she walked by carrying two plates.

I trotted over to table fifteen, where the Sherer kids had balled up napkins and were throwing them at each other.

"Hey," I said. "Anyone want to have a coloring contest?"

They all looked up. I dug into my apron pocket and took out some packets of crayons that I had loaded up on during setup.

"You can actually use your place mat as a piece of paper," I said, giving each of the Sherer kids a packet of crayons.

I had ripped the packet open for them first, because there's nothing worse than handing a kid a package of something they can't open. I learned that the hard way this summer when I handed out

Popsicles that were each sealed in plastic bags.

"Now," I said. "Each of you draw your favorite dessert from the menu. We have ice cream, chocolate chip cookies, or pie tonight." I hoped I was right about the cookies. We usually had three options for dessert on the kids' menu. "Draw which one is your favorite, and if you eat your dinner, you may be able to order what you drew."

I looked over at Mrs. Sherer a little nervously. "Right?" I asked. Some parents were really strict about how many treats their kids had.

"It's a treat to go out to dinner," said Mrs. Sherer. "Or it's supposed to be. So, yes, if you eat your healthy dinner, you can each get a treat."

"YAY!" The kids all started cheering loudly, and everyone in the restaurant looked over.

"Okay, okay," I said. "But let's keep it down a little. Otherwise we'll have to give everyone in the restaurant cookies!"

Just then Jenna shot out of the kitchen, holding a tray on her shoulder. I wanted to try that one day, but she and Rich kept warning me that it was a lot harder than it looked. A dropped tray was the worst disaster for a server because when it crashed to the ground, everyone turned around to stare, and also someone's dinner just bit the dust and the chef had to start over. No one was ever happy about a dropped tray.

I brought a huge stack of napkins to the table. "Just in case!" I said to Mrs. Sherer, who smiled and thanked me.

"Is that good?" I asked six-year-old Christopher Sherer, who was eating his grilled cheese at record speed.

He nodded. "So good!" he said. Then he pointed to the picture he'd drawn of a giant cookie. "And if I eat my grilled cheese, you'll bring me this?"

"Yes, sir," I said, watching him, half-horrified and half-impressed, as he stuffed the rest of the sandwich into his mouth.

"Christopher!" his mother said, exasperated. "Manners count!"

"Okay, should we see if your brothers make the dessert challenge too?" I asked.

"That would be a good idea," said Mrs. Sherer. "Because if only one of them gets a cookie, the rest of the table is going to crumble."

Christopher's two brothers, Bradley and Greg, immediately started drawing their favorite dessert.

But Christopher looked like he was going to cry.

"I have to waaaaait?" he wailed. "But I want my cookie now!"

I peeked around and saw Lily sitting at the host's podium. The host greeted guests, then showed them to their tables and gave out menus. The first rush was over, so she was just hanging out and nobody was waiting.

"Christopher, who's your favorite babysitter?" I asked quickly.

"Lily!" he said.

Lily babysat for the Sherer kids a lot. I have no idea how she did it.

"How would you like to go say hello to Lily while your brothers finish dinner?" I suggested.

"Oh, you don't have to—" began Mrs. Sherer.

"YES!" yelled Christopher, and he climbed out of the booth.

"It's totally fine," I told Mrs. Sherer as I took Christopher's hand and led him toward the podium.

"Christopher!" Lily squealed as he ran to her and gave her a big hug. "You came to visit me!"

"Christopher finished his dinner first and he's patiently waiting for his brothers to finish before he gets dessert," I explained. "He said he wanted to visit his favorite babysitter, Lily."

Christopher was still clinging to Lily. I felt a little jealous. "Even though I was also his babysitter at the lake this summer," I added.

"I'm sure we're both his favorites. Right, Christopher?" asked Lily.

"No," said Christopher. "I like you better."

Lily tried not to laugh. "Oh, Christopher, that's not nice."

"Mom says if it's not nice, then don't say it," said Christopher. "Why was that not nice?"

"It wasn't nice because you don't tell some people you like them better than others," Lily explained.

"Oh," said Christopher, thinking about that.

"Okay, Christopher, I have to help my sister with the table. Stay here with Lily, okay?" I said.

"Who's your sister?" Christopher asked.

"Jenna," I said. "And Kelsey. And Lily is my cousin."

"But you don't look like them!" said Christopher.

I sighed. Suddenly the fact that I was adopted was becoming a big deal everywhere.

"I'm adopted, Christopher," I said.

"Oh," said Christopher. "Do you help your sister with dessert?"

I smiled, grateful that there was no follow-up about being adopted. "I sure do."

"Then you're my favorite sister right now!" said Christopher.

When Jenna and I brought dessert to the Sherer kids, I waved Christopher back over from Lily's station. We put the plates down with a big flourish.

"Ta-da!" I sang. "It's dessert time!"

Mrs. Sherer smiled. "You girls are the best. Thank you so much for your help. We were just talking about making this a ritual for when Mr. Sherer is at the firehouse on Tuesday nights."

I must have looked a little worried, because suddenly Jenna pinched my arm, hard. "That's a tradition we can get on board with, Mrs. Sherer," said Jenna. "We're always happy to see you at the Park."

I nodded and waved at the kids. I looked at the clock on the wall . . . six thirty. Things had really slowed down, so I went over to Grandpa.

"Grandpa, do you need me until seven?" I asked.

He did a scan of the room. "Things look under control here," he said. "Plus your mom, Kelsey, and

Family Recipe

Lindsay are all itching to go home, so take off. The old man can pitch in if things get crazy again." He laughed. "Nice job tonight with those kids, honey. You are now going to be assigned to every table with kids. You're a natural!"

"Every table?" I shrieked.

"Hard work is good for you! Melissa," he called to Mom. "I'm discharging Molly. Round those girls up and get them home!"

I noticed he was holding a box. "What's in the box?" I asked.

"Oh! I almost forgot," Grandpa said. "This," he said to me, putting a pie box in my hands, "is from Nans. She said you're helping her make her perfect apple pie more perfect."

"Well, if you insist we taste pie, then we'll just have to eat pie," said Mom. "C'mon, girls. The 'get-out-of-work taxi' is leaving the parking lot!"

"Thank goodness," said Kelsey. "I am *so* tired."

Grandpa rolled his eyes. "Your sister Molly was running all over creation tonight. She's got to be tired, but she isn't complaining!"

"I wasn't complaining," Kelsey said. "I was stating a fact."

DONUT DREAMS

She gave Grandpa a hug. Only Kelsey could be sassy with Grandpa without annoying him.

※ ※ ※ ※ ※

We trailed Mom out to the car and headed home. When we dropped Lindsay off, Sky came to the door with Nans and waved. Then we drove toward our house, which was on a winding road closer to the lake.

It was still light out at this time of year, although the days were definitely getting shorter. Mom and Kelsey were talking in the front of the car, but I zoned out. The pie was still a little warm on my lap, and I breathed in deeply. The smell made me happy.

It had been a long day, and I still had homework to do. I tried to figure out my strategy. I could bang out my math problems in a half hour. Then I had to write an essay for English lit that might take a while. Then I thought about Ms. Blueski's assignment, and my stomach began to twist a little bit. What was my strategy going to be for that? For the first time in my life, I was going to push one bit of homework off for another night. Tonight was Happy Pie Night.

Chapter Six
No Puppies

Since Dad teaches at the high school, which starts earlier than the middle school, he leaves the house early during the school year. We have Mom to do the morning routine with us and Dad after school. Mom is always on time for everything, so we never really worry about running late. Dad is really laid-back when we get home and doesn't bombard us with questions like Mom does. It's the perfect balance.

Mom was already dressed for work and sipping coffee in the kitchen when I came downstairs the next morning.

"The usual?" she asked, and I nodded, yawning.

My usual was fruit and a bowl of yogurt. I got the yogurt and Mom sliced me some cantaloupe.

"I feel like we're seeing the last of the good melons until next summer," she said. "And I can't believe it's already apple season. Hey, so what did you do to change up Nans's pie recipe?"

"Nothing," I said. "Her pie is delicious as is."

"Well, she seems to think she can make it more perfect," said Mom. "You, my love, must be pretty special to mess with that. And the first apple batch of the season, too!"

Mom is always talking about what seasons certain fruits and vegetables peak, as she says, which means they are best. Despite not being able to cook, Mom is kind of a foodie, and she's always harping about eating fresh fruits and veggies.

Dad built her a really cool vegetable garden one summer, but she killed everything growing in it. I think she worried too much and ended up overwatering the plants every day.

Mom also is in tune with seasonal foods because if a food is "in season"—like, say, watermelon during the summer—when it grows locally, it costs less. As the accountant for the restaurant, Mom cares about things costing less, since they have a really strict budget for how much they can spend on the groceries and food for the restaurant each week. If they splurge on things, or prices go up, they have to adjust the prices on the menu, and people get annoyed if the price of their meal goes up. So you won't see blueberry cake on the menu in February, but you might see pear cake.

Jenna is always saying that when she moves to California, which is her dream, she won't have to worry about that anymore. Fruit is in season all year long there, because it's warm enough to plant and grow crops in all seasons. It sounds really cool to be able to have strawberries in January, but California is pretty far away.

"Kelsey!" Mom called upstairs. "Get going, sweetie! We have to roll in twenty!"

I heard the hair dryer upstairs, which meant Kelsey had not heard a word of what Mom just said. Not that it would matter anyway, since Kelsey did not exactly rush in the morning, no matter how late we were running.

Once Mom made me get into the car to prove to Kelsey that we'd leave without her. A full ten minutes later, when Mom was fuming, Kelsey wandered out of the house, casually peeling a banana, which I guess was appropriate, since Mom went bananas.

Mom checked the calendar and her phone. "Okay, you have soccer after school, so Dad can take you to that. Jenna has a piano lesson, and Kelsey has hockey. Whew, full boat today. Jenna can drop Kelsey at hockey, and then Dad can pick her up and swing back and get you. Are you okay with that?"

I was kind of half listening. "Uh-huh," I said.

"Who's taking me where?" asked Kelsey, strolling into the kitchen.

Mom looked at the clock and sighed. "Jenna will drive you to hockey. And you now have ten minutes to eat your breakfast."

"Okay," said Kelsey, taking out her laptop.

"What are you doing?" I asked.

"Finishing my homework," said Kelsey softly.

"Kelsey Jane!" said Mom. "You didn't finish last night? What were you doing up so late if you weren't doing homework?"

"I wasn't up that late, Mom," said Kelsey. "Besides, my biology homework took forever. I just have to finish some Spanish." She looked over at me.

"I can't help you," I said. "I'm taking French."

She sighed. "Great, you're no help to me."

Family Recipe

"Gracias!" I said, grinning. "That means 'thank you' in Spanish."

She glared at me. Kelsey and I mostly get along, but sometimes she really gets under my skin.

"Family helps family," she said. "Isn't that, like, our motto?"

"Yes," said Mom. "It is our motto, it's not 'like' our motto. But everyone does their part. That means you have to do your own homework."

"Mom, can we adopt a dog?" I blurted out. I couldn't stop thinking about that puppy. "Mrs. Rose has the most adorable puppy who really needs a home!"

"No puppies," said Mom, grabbing her keys from the hook by the door. "And clear your plates and wrap up the leftovers, please."

"But why?" I said, rinsing out my bowl before I put it in the dishwasher.

Mom handed us each our lunch bags from the counter. "Don't forget these. And no puppies because they're a lot of work and a lot of responsibility. And with all of us running in five different directions every day, no one is home to give enough attention to a puppy."

"But there are a lot of dogs that stay home all day!" I said as we got into the car. "And Mrs. Rose was at the Park yesterday, and she was telling me that she's in a rescue group for dogs. Do you know what that is?"

"A rescue group?" said Kelsey. "Where do they rescue them from?"

"They take puppies and dogs that are homeless and would go to shelters and they keep them in their houses until they can be adopted. This way the dogs don't have to live in cages in the shelters."

"Poor puppies," said Kelsey.

"Mrs. Rose does great things with those dogs," said Mom. "And it's a lovely thing to be able to take care of them like that. But would you really be okay leaving a young puppy by itself all day, with no one to play with?"

"Well, puppies sleep a lot," I said.

"Not for seven hours," said Mom. "If we leave at eight o'clock and Dad is home at three o'clock, that's a heck of a lot of time to leave a dog alone."

"We could get a dog walker," said Kelsey. "That's what Casey has, because her parents work and are at school all day."

"Sorry, girls, but it's not happening. We're just not

Family Recipe

at the point where it's a good situation for the dog or for us," Mom said.

"Okay," I said, pouting a little. "But the next time you see Mrs. Rose, ask if you can see a picture of this puppy. She was the cutest, sweetest thing I've ever seen. Jenna saw the picture too."

"I'm sure Mrs. Rose will help find her a very good home. And now," said Mom, putting on her blinker and pulling into the school parking lot. "I hope you girls have a very good day. I love you!"

"Thanks," said Kelsey, as we walked into school.

"For what?" I asked.

"For distracting Mom so much with the puppy talk that she forgot to ask if I finished my Spanish homework." Kelsey grinned.

I rolled my eyes, and we went to morning meeting.

Ugh, Eric Sellers was the first person we saw when we walked in. "Good morning, ladies!" he said.

I mumbled, "Hi," and Kelsey said cheerily, "Oh, hi, Eric," and kept walking.

"What's wrong?" she asked.

"Nothing," I said. "He's just really annoying."

"He's always annoying, but he's harmless," said Kelsey.

I wasn't so sure. My stomach was doing the flip-flop thing again. Luckily, we didn't have history today.

In middle school we did what they call an A/B schedule, so on A days I had history, French, English lit, and phys ed. On B days I had study hall, math, earth science, and media (my elective this year.)

We went over to our usual tables, and Kelsey gave me a slight wave as she left to go sit with her friends. I usually sat with Madeline at a separate table.

"Give me a G!" said Madeline, giving me a hug. "Aren't you so excited for the game this weekend?"

"To be honest, I haven't really thought about it," I said.

"You haven't?" she asked, shocked. "And here I was thinking you already had a strategy to win it in the second half!"

I laughed. "Well, you won't know the full strategy until we see the team we're dealing with, right?"

"True," said Madeline. "The first game is always hard because you're getting to know your team and the others."

"That's what I was telling Dad!" I said.

"Yeah, Grayson said the same thing." Grayson was

Family Recipe

Madeline's older brother. He played soccer for the high school team.

Principal Clarke tapped the microphone, which made an awful, loud sound. "Good morning!" she said. "May I have your attention, please? Let's get started with the announcements today!"

No one really ever listened to announcements. After morning meeting, your phone had to be in your locker for the whole day. If you were caught with it, you'd be in big, big trouble. Because we couldn't talk during morning meeting but it was our last chance to have our phones, we all just texted each other instead.

It was really quiet, and it wasn't long before I got a text from Lindsay, who was sitting with her BFF, Casey.

> Hey just checking in to see how ur family tree assignment is going?

I texted back,

> Haven't started!

Lindsay's reply came back a few seconds later.

> **I figured u'd have it done by now! LOL**

I didn't know what to text back. If I just sat down and did it, I could probably have it done pretty fast. I mean, it's not like I didn't know who was in my family. There were a couple third cousins whose names I'd need to double-check, maybe, but overall, I could spit out everyone who was at our last Fourth of July family barbecue . . . and there were more than fifty people there.

A minute went by. Then Lindsay texted again.

> **R u upset by what Eric said? Bc he's just a moron.**

Sometimes I can be more honest when I'm texting than when I talk.

> **Yeah, a little. But I don't know why.**

Lindsay's response came instantly.

> **Do u want to talk about it?**

Family Recipe

I could see her looking at me, so I shook my head before texting back,

> No. Not yet. But thanks.

Lindsey's response made me feel a little better.

> Luv u, cousin. And I AM ur real cousin.

I smiled.

> You are? Who is this?

> Hahahahaha

After that the day went pretty fast. Last year we stayed in one classroom for most of the day, but in middle school we move classrooms for each period, so I kind of feel like once I settle into a class, it's time to get up and move again. It does make the day zoom by.

Kelsey and I usually walk home from school together, unless it's raining or really cold, and then Dad comes and picks us up. We usually walk with

Sophia and her sister and sometimes Casey and Riley, too, since we all live right near each other.

When my last class was over, I went to meet Kelsey, who was waiting for me in front of school, texting away.

"Ready?" she asked, without even looking up.

"Yeah," I said. "Let's go."

It's less than a ten-minute walk for us, and on a really crisp day like today, I was very happy to have some fresh air. Being outside always made me feel better. Even though it's such a short walk, Mom usually drives us because it's just easier for her to take us in the mornings.

"I totally got in trouble in Spanish class today," Kelsey said, blowing her bangs off her forehead.

"Why?" I asked.

"Because I didn't do my homework, and when Señora Diaz called on me, I had no idea what she was saying. She kept telling me I was messing up the pronouns and calling her a him."

I giggled.

"It wasn't funny," Kelsey said. Then she giggled too. "Señor, Señora, I mean, come on. There are more important things in life to worry about!"

Family Recipe

"Well, if you can't speak the language properly, that is sort of an issue, Kels," I said. "The whole point of Spanish class is to learn to speak Spanish."

"If you were taking Spanish, it would be so much easier."

"I'm not doing your homework for you," I said.

"I'm not asking you to do my homework. I'd be asking you to help with my homework. There's a difference. In this family we help each other out. Mom always says that!" Kelsey protested.

I sighed and said nothing because I didn't want to start arguing with her, especially since we had just gotten home. I opened the screen door and stepped inside.

"Hi, Dad!" called Kelsey.

"Hello, my girls!" said Dad. "Good days?"

"It was okay," said Kelsey, eyeing me. "Mostly good."

"Mine too," I said.

"Hey, I heard you had a bad day yesterday," said Kelsey.

"Who did you hear that from?" I asked.

"Lindsay," said Kelsey. "She said Eric Sellers was a real jerk to you in history class."

"What happened?" asked Dad, looking worried.

"He's just a pest," I said. "It was just that he was annoying me. He also kept asking to go to the bathroom and kept interrupting Ms. Blueski. It was annoying all around."

Dad looked at me for a moment, then said, "Oh well, if that's all, that's not too bad. Unless he was annoying you specifically. Or on purpose."

I shrugged.

Kelsey was looking at me in a way that I could tell Lindsay had told her what happened. But unless she wanted me to spill on her episode in Spanish class, I knew she'd keep it to herself for now.

"Can we have a snack?" I asked.

"Right here," said Dad.

He had sliced some bananas in half the long way, and spread peanut butter on top. He had a cup of raisins we could sprinkle over them, which we used to call "ants on a log" because the raisins looked like ants on the banana log. But the idea of ants freaked Kelsey out, so he always put them on the side.

I flung some ants/raisins on top of the banana as Dad put down a plate of graham crackers.

"Yum," I said, making a sandwich.

Family Recipe

"Today's practices start early," said Dad. "So I'm afraid you'll have to have your snack, then turn it right around."

"I hate rushing!" Kelsey whined.

"We're aware of that," said Dad. "Nobody likes to rush. That's why I'm telling you that there's still a half hour before we have to be anywhere. Jenna is already home, and she's taking you to field hockey practice."

Kelsey sighed and jumped off her chair, headed over to her knapsack, and took out a folder.

"What are you doing?" I asked.

"My Spanish homework," said Kelsey, giving me a scowl.

"Well, Kelsey, I am impressed," said Dad. "It will feel so good to get it out of the way early!"

If he only knew.

Chapter Seven
Ruby and Rusty

We had only a few practices before the first game, and I think everyone was a little anxious about it. Coach Wendy kept telling us that it didn't matter if we won, but the thing is, it feels much better to win than to lose. There's no denying that.

Coach Wendy likes us to stretch before we do drills, so I put my leg on the bench and leaned over to touch my toes.

"Hiya," Madeline said, her head upside down next to me. She was doing toe touches too, and was literally bent in half.

"Well, fancy seeing you down here!" I said, laughing. We both stood up.

"Ugh, I feel like my muscles are all tight," she said.

"Probably from sitting in class all day!"

Just then we heard barking, so we looked over. Mrs. Rose was walking three dogs around the track, and she waved.

"Ooh, puppies!" cried Isabella, and she went running over.

Madeline and I jogged behind her. By the time we caught up, Isabella was on her knees shrieking, and one of the cutest dogs I have ever seen was licking her face.

"Ruby, Ruby!" said Mrs. Rose, stroking the dog on the head. "She gets a little excited when she meets new people."

"Hi, Mrs. Rose!" I said. "Oh my goodness, that's her!"

It was the dog Mrs. Rose had shown me on her phone!

I dropped to my knees, and Ruby jumped over her leash to come lick my face too.

"I saw a picture of you," I said. "And I haven't stopped thinking about you!"

Ruby rolled over on her back.

"Do you want your tummy rubbed?" I asked her.

"She loves that," said Mrs. Rose, smiling. "And

yes, this is the adorable puppy you saw on my phone. She has a lot of energy. Don't you, Ruby?"

"Who is this?" asked Isabella, petting a dog that had climbed onto her lap.

"That's my Lucky," said Mrs. Rose. "And this . . . c'mon, sweetie. This one is shy." The third dog was behind Mrs. Rose. He almost looked like he was hiding. "This is Rusty."

"Rusty?" asked Madeline.

"Yes," said Mrs. Rose. "Most of the time we don't know the names of the dogs when they come to us, so we have to name them. This little guy was rescued from under some rocks, where a hiker found him, and we all admired his reddish brown fur, so we named him Rusty."

"Does he belong to anyone?" asked Isabella.

"Well, he probably did," said Mrs. Rose. "He's old enough that he wouldn't have been on his own this whole time."

"So someone just dropped him off somewhere?" I asked.

"Unfortunately, it does seem like that's what happened," said Mrs. Rose. "Sometimes people get overwhelmed if an animal doesn't fit into their

Family Recipe

family or they can't properly train it not to go to the bathroom in the house. And feeding an animal and paying for checkups definitely adds up."

"Well, what if he's just lost?" I asked.

"We definitely always hope we find the animal's home," said Mrs. Rose. "We put up posters and send e-mails and alert all the shelters and veterinarians' offices in the area. When the animal is truly lost, we usually are able to get them home within one or two days. We sent out a lot of alerts for Rusty, but it's been weeks and no one has claimed him."

"Poor Rusty!" said Madeline.

We were fussing over the dogs so much that we didn't hear Coach Wendy blowing her whistle.

"Girls!" she said, exasperated. "Practice is starting!"

We all said goodbye to the dogs, and I gave Ruby a kiss on the head. "You," I whispered. "I'm going to make you mine!"

I was paying attention during practice, but out of the corner of my eye I was also watching Mrs. Rose walk around the track. The three dogs listened to her and were all walking at about the same pace. Ruby was running ahead.

I didn't know how old Mrs. Rose was exactly,

but she could really power walk. And she must have walked a few miles during our practice.

After practice we were all panting, including the dogs. Ruby was tugging at her leash a little bit.

"Oh my," said Mrs. Rose. "This dog could walk all day and not tire out!"

"Can I take her around once?" I asked eagerly.

I saw Dad and Kelsey approaching the soccer field from the parking lot, but I figured I could get one quick lap in before we had to head home.

"You know, if you could run her once, that'd be great," said Mrs. Rose. "I don't really run, and this puppy seems to need a little bit more that I can do."

"No problem!" I grinned. I had never walked a dog before, so I took the leash but wasn't sure if I should pull it or not. I looked at Mrs. Rose.

"You don't want to pull or tug too hard," said Mrs. Rose. "Think of the leash more as a guide, so you show her what direction you want her to go."

I nodded and started to run. In half a second Ruby was at my ankles, running with me. But soon the leash was getting tangled around my legs, and she kept running in front of me, then behind me.

She was yapping so much that I almost didn't hear

Family Recipe

Mrs. Rose calling, "Rusty! Rusty!" behind me.

I turned my head and Rusty, the shy dog, was bolting toward me, his leash trailing behind him. Mrs. Rose was half running, half power walking to try to catch up to him.

Just then Dad sprinted down to the track. Rusty saw him following and really took off. That dog was fast. But so was Dad. Dad and Rusty were running together around the track, and if you didn't know that Dad was trying to catch him, it looked like they were actually playing a game. Rusty kept looking at Dad, then pulling ahead a little bit. Dad would catch up and Rusty would take off again, like a big game of chase. But Rusty didn't take off so far ahead of Dad. He seemed to want to stay with him.

Finally, Dad and Rusty went all the way around the track. Rusty saw Mrs. Rose waiting for him and slowed down, and Dad was able to grab his leash. Ruby and I finished our lap, Ruby yapping all the way. Kelsey was standing next to Mrs. Rose.

"Oh my goodness," said Mrs. Rose, panting. "Well, that was a workout I didn't expect!"

"This dog can run," said Dad admiringly, petting Rusty's head.

DONUT DREAMS

"Who knew?" said Mrs. Rose. "He's been so quiet and timid. That's the first time I think we've seen a little bit of his personality come out."

Rusty looked up at Dad and closed his eyes. "Runners can always find each other," said Dad, scratching Rusty under the chin.

"Ohhhhh," said Kelsey, patting Ruby. "Dad, Molly was right. This dog is the cutest!"

"She's pretty cute," said Dad, still petting Rusty.

"Molly has always wanted a dog," said Kelsey. "So, you know, this one . . ."

"First of all, we've talked about this," said Dad. "A dog is a huge responsibility and a lot of work."

"It is a big responsibility," said Mrs. Rose. "And it's important to think through. Not thinking it through leads to situations like poor Rusty."

Rusty didn't look sad exactly, but he did sort of look like he was worried. "You have just the right touch with him, Chris," said Mrs. Rose.

"Molly and I both love dogs," said Dad.

"Well, now that I see how he can run, I wish I could run with him more regularly," said Mrs. Rose. "I may reach out and see if anyone in the rescue group runs, so I can pair him up with someone."

Family Recipe

Dad looked like he was mulling something over.

"Well," he said, then stopped.

We all looked at him.

"Molly has been telling me to get my runs in while she has soccer practice. I think it's her way of trying to distract her embarrassing dad."

I rolled my eyes.

"But if I could bring Rusty to practices, then I can get my workout in, and we'd be able to get Rusty a run in too."

Rusty perked up his ears and stood up.

"Ah, you like to run!" said Dad to Rusty in a mushy baby voice. Kelsey and I started laughing.

"Well, that would be super," said Mrs. Rose. "If you can manage it, I'd love to take you up on that offer!"

As Dad and Mrs. Rose looked at their schedules on their phones and coordinated Rusty's runs, Kelsey and I took turns petting Ruby.

"Isn't she the sweetest?" I said, sighing.

"She's super cute," said Kelsey.

"Wouldn't you love to come live with us?" I said to Ruby, pulling her onto my lap. She settled in, then jumped up again and went chasing after a squirrel.

DONUT DREAMS

Kelsey and I ran after her, and then I ran ahead, blocking her, and Kelsey scooped her up. "You are a handful!" she said breathlessly.

"She's totally going to be ours," I said to Kelsey.

Kelsey said, "Mom will never say yes."

"We'll see," I said, already dreaming of Ruby snuggling next to me in bed at night.

Chapter Eight
Family Love

We got home a few minutes later than planned, and Jenna and Mom were already getting dinner on the table.

"I got dinner started!" said Mom, and the four of us looked at each other. "It seemed like a good fall night to start with soup, so I brought some of Nans's squash soup home from the restaurant."

We all looked relieved.

"And I stopped and picked up a loaf of bread and a salad," Mom said.

"That sounds like a perfect fall dinner," said Dad.

"And Nans sent home more apple pie for taste testing. Since Molly told her it was perfect, she's obsessed with making it absolutely perfect," Mom said. "She made about five pies today and told me to bring this one home to see if 'perfect can get more perfect.' Oh, and she said to put ice cream on top of it. Vanilla, if possible."

"Well if she said to add ice cream, I guess we'll have to add ice cream," said Kelsey.

We sat down and Mom said, "Let's do best and worst."

Best and worst is a thing Mom and Dad do at dinner: each person has to tell the best and worst thing that happened that day. We do the worst part because as Mom always says, sometimes bad comes with the good, but that's okay.

"I'll go first," said Jenna. "Best is that I'll be doing a piano solo in the fall recital. Worst is that now I have tennis, tutoring, work, and a solo to study for."

"Jenna, that's wonderful!" said Mom. "A solo is a big mark of excellence and confidence from your teacher."

"Well, my best thing today was playing with an adorable dog that Molly says we're going to adopt," said Kelsey.

"What?" said Mom, looking at Dad.

"Oh, no, no, no," said Dad. "I said it was not a

good time for us to adopt a pet. And I meant it."

"Well, then I guess the worst part is that we aren't getting a dog," said Kelsey, looking at me.

"It's not fair!" I said. Suddenly I was just really frustrated. "I can take care of a dog. I'll need help buying food and taking her to the vet, but otherwise I don't need anyone's help!"

"Sweetie," said Dad. "I love you, but I saw you today and you could barely walk that dog yourself, let alone take care of it yourself."

"Where were you walking a dog?" asked Jenna.

"Mrs. Rose was walking her three dogs around the track while she had soccer practice," Dad said.

"What's your best thing?" Mom asked me.

I sulked a little and didn't answer. I knew getting a dog was a lot of work, and I knew Mom had already said no, but I'd had a bad week, and it was getting worse. "Nothing," I said. "Nothing was good today."

"Find one good thing," said Dad.

I dug in. I knew I was kind of acting like a baby, but tonight I was just not in the mood to play this game. "Nope."

"So your day was so terrible that not even one little good thing happened?" said Dad.

DONUT DREAMS

They all looked at me.

"Are you upset because of the Eric thing?" asked Kelsey.

I glared at her.

"Okay, now this is the second time I've heard 'the Eric thing' come up today. What is going on?" Dad said. He and Mom were looking at me.

"You brought it up, Kelsey," I said. "So you tell them."

I was mad at Kelsey, but honestly, I was a teeny-tiny bit grateful. I didn't know how to tell them about what was going on with the family tree. So I let Kelsey do it.

Kelsey sighed. "Lindsay told me. She was worried about Molly."

"What is it?" asked Mom, her voice getting a little high.

"In history class we have to do a project with a family tree," said Kelsey. "It's supposed to be a lesson where we learn more about our family history and how it shaped us. Ms. Blueski said history can be about wars and stuff, but it can also be personal."

"And?" said Dad.

"Eric Sellers told Molly that her tree wasn't real.

Family Recipe

He said that because she was adopted, she had a real family and us, who I guess aren't her real family. Molly got upset and ran out of class," Kelsey finished.

It is not usually quiet in our house. Jenna is loud, Kelsey is always talking or singing, and Dad often hums or has music playing. Mom is always moving around doing something.

But just then it was silent, and we all sat there staring at our food. I could hear the *tick tick tick* of the grandfather clock in the front hall.

Then Dad said, "Oh, Molly!" and burst into tears.

"This is not about you, Mr. Goo," said Mom.

"It's about my daughter!" said Dad, sniffing into his napkin.

"Okay," said Mom. "Kelsey heard this from Lindsay. I don't like playing the telephone game with things like this. Molly, can you please tell us exactly what happened?"

I didn't want to talk about it, but I knew if I didn't, they'd never let it go. And also I had no idea how to handle Eric. Or the feeling I had in my stomach, all tight and queasy.

"Eric Sellers asked me if I was adding my 'real mom' to my family tree, because Mom wasn't my real mom. Lindsay turned around and told him that Mom was real and not fake, but he kind of wouldn't let it go. I didn't run out of class. I just left quickly when it was over."

"All right," said Dad, blowing his nose. "Let's break this down. First of all, you are our real daughter, and Mom and I are your real parents."

"I know that," I said.

"Good," said Dad. "You are adopted, but you know that, too."

"I do recall being told that, yes," I said.

Dad stifled a laugh. "You do have biological parents, and a mother who gave birth to you."

"I know that, too," I said.

"Okay," said Dad. "Now, sometimes people say stupid things, but not because they're trying to be awful. It's because they have questions, but they don't know how to sensitively ask them. Do you think that might be the case with Eric? That maybe he's just curious about your family tree?"

I thought about that a second.

"Maybe," said Kelsey. "He's not a bad person; he's just, like, the most annoying kid in the class."

"Molly?" asked Dad.

Family Recipe

"I don't know," I said. "But he upset me."

"Are you upset because he was rude, or are you upset because you didn't know how to answer him?" asked Mom.

Bingo. The thing about Mom is that somehow she always knows what I'm feeling.

I looked at her. "Yes," I whispered. "Both."

"Okay. The simple answer is that, yes, you are adopted. And technically you have a biological mother, who gave birth to you, and me, the person you call Mom, who actually is your mother."

I nodded.

Mom continued. "What's important on this tree isn't just the facts of it, although there are, of course, facts. The tree is about your family. The family tree can represent your history in whatever way you feel is best."

"Isn't history based on facts?" Kelsey asked.

"Well, yes, but the fact is that Mom and I are Molly's parents," said Dad. "So if she lists that, then it's factually correct. If Molly also lists her biological mother, that's factually correct too. But she can also leave her out if she's not comfortable discussing that."

"But how factual is it if she leaves out some facts?"

asked Jenna. "I mean, she should put everything she knows in the tree."

I felt like everyone was talking about me, but nobody was talking to me. Suddenly I felt the same way I had in class, like I just had to get out of there. I pushed my chair away and ran out the front door.

Chapter Nine
Nature Vs. Nurture

I sat down on the front step, not sure what to do next. A few minutes later the door opened. Dad threw my sneakers on the step.

"C'mon," he said. He was already wearing his running shoes and was carrying more gear.

I put my sneakers on. "Where are we going?" I asked.

Dad jogged down the front walk. He put on his reflective jacket and headlamp and handed me one of each too. I guess they were Mom's.

"Sometimes when you feel like running, the best thing to do is actually run," said Dad. "Let's go."

I followed him down the path, out into the quiet street, and the two of us took off. We just ran, side by side, a nice slow pace, not saying anything for a long while.

"Look at those stars," said Dad.

I looked up and he was right. There were a ton of stars. It was crisp and cool, and it felt good breathing in the night air.

We jogged around the neighborhood. I followed Dad as we ran past Casey's house. I could see her sitting at her desk in her bedroom. I wondered if she was texting Lindsay. The two of them were best friends.

There's one road in our neighborhood that leads to a dead end. If you go on the trail, it leads to the lake. We reached the dead end and Dad turned around. Someone had their windows open, and you could hear music and people's voices.

I heard a kid shout, "Nooooo," and I wondered if it was one of the Sherer kids since they lived in our neighborhood.

I was waiting for Dad to try to talk about things. I kept looking at him, but he was just looking straight ahead. Maybe he was waiting for me to start talking. But there was something really nice about being together in silence. We were both breathing hard,

… and all I could hear was the *slap slap* of our sneakers hitting the pavement. I felt my body begin to relax.

When we finally came back up our street, I was tired. We reached our driveway, and Dad turned off his headlamp.

He smiled. "You have the running bug!" he said. "I'm sorry to say there's no cure. But running regularly definitely helps."

I laughed. "It must be genetic!" Then I stopped. "Dad, how can I tell what's genetic and what I just pick up from you and Mom?"

Dad went up the front walk, and I followed him.

"Well," he said, sitting down on the step. "There's something called nature versus nurture. Nature means what you are genetically predetermined to do or have, like brown eyes or a tall frame. Nurture is more about what affects you growing up, like what language is spoken at home, if you live in a city or a small town, or what your family does on the weekends. If, say, you grow up in a family who cooks a lot, you might be more likely to cook."

"Well, nature or nurture, I'm not getting any cooking skills from Mom," I said, sitting down next to him.

"No," said Dad. "But you might get her love of eating together as a family, or the importance she puts on fresh foods."

I nodded. "Which matters more?"

"There's a lot of debate about that," said Dad. "There's no definitive answer, but they both affect you."

"So maybe my biological father was a runner?"

"Possibly," said Dad. "Or your biological mother. But Mom and I are also runners, so it's unclear whether that's nature or nurture."

I sighed.

"I'm sorry this week was hard for you," said Dad. "Mom and I are always worried that you might have questions, but we don't always think about the questions other people might have about you."

"Yeah," I said. I tightened my fists, just like my stomach was tightening.

"What is it?" Dad asked.

"It's just weird to think there's this other family out there. I never really thought about it like that. Like, is there a person walking around wondering about me?"

"Maybe," Dad said. "In terms of your adoption, we

Family Recipe

don't have a lot of details. We know your biological mother's name but not your biological father's name. And your bio mom's name is a very common name in South Korea. We tried to find out more information so we'd have it for you, but we've come up short. We have her medical history that she gave the adoption agency, but that doesn't say anything about, like, what her favorite food was, or if she liked to play soccer."

We'd gone through my story many times before. My biological mother put me up for adoption when I was a few weeks old. We don't know exactly why, but she was very young, and Mom and Dad thought maybe she wasn't ready or prepared to become a mother.

I was also born with an eye condition that required me to have surgery when I was about a year old. It went fine, but I still wear glasses now to see a movie or to see the whiteboard in class. It wasn't major surgery, but hearing that a baby needs surgery can be scary. Maybe that had something to do with my birth mother's decision too.

I lived in a house run by an adoption agency for a few months until Mom and Dad flew to South Korea to bring me home. We have the picture on the mantel of Jenna holding me at the airport, wearing a BIG SISTER T-shirt. Nans and Grandpa were there, and Grandma, my dad's mother, and PopPop, my dad's father, too.

Everyone looked happy except for me. I was really red in the face and crying.

Mom opened the door and peeked out. "Oh, you're back!" she said. She came out and sat on the step next to me. "I do not like you running at night," she said.

"Who, me?" said Dad.

"Well, you, too, but mainly Molly. Cars speed on these streets."

"We stayed in the neighborhood," I said. "And we wore our headlamps so people could see us."

"I'm your mom," Mom said. "I worry."

"Do you think my biological mother worries?" I asked.

Mom thought for a second. "I don't know if 'worry' is the right word," she said. "But she probably thinks about you. I hope she knows that you are safe and loved and that you're mostly happy. Or at least that's what we tell her when we write her."

Every year Mom and Dad wrote a letter to my

biological mother with details about what I was learning or doing or interested in and a picture of me. They sent it to the adoption agency, who had them translated into Korean and said they would keep the letters in case my bio mom reached out and wanted to know more about me.

"Maybe I can help write the one this year," I said.

"That'd be great," Mom said. "In your own voice."

"Always in your own voice," said Dad. "That's the best way to be."

"So my voice and version over facts?"

"No," said Dad, knowing I was thinking about the family tree project. "Facts are facts. You have a biological mother and father, and that's part of your history. But how you define your family is really up to you. We have friends you call aunt and uncle, for instance, who aren't your 'real' aunt and uncle."

That was true. Aunt Miranda and Uncle Albert were Mom and Dad's best friends from college. We weren't related to them, but they acted like our aunt and uncle. They were at holidays and birthday parties, they had pictures of us on their refrigerator. And sometimes when Mom and Dad had to work, Aunt Miranda stayed with me if I was sick. This whole family thing was getting more complicated.

"You have a family that you are born into and you have a family that you create throughout your life," said Mom. "When I married Dad, I got this whole other part of a family that I hadn't even known before."

I nodded. "So your family keeps growing?"

"Yes," said Dad. "Your mom and dad stay the same, and your siblings, but outside that, your family really expands."

"But no matter what," said Mom, "you will always have Dad and me, and Kelsey and Jenna."

"Speaking of which," Dad said, motioning behind him. Kelsey and Jenna were looking out the window at us.

"I'm guessing Kelsey is worried that you're telling me she got in trouble in her Spanish class today," said Mom, smirking.

"She told you?" I said.

"She felt bad that she told us about Eric, so she spilled when you and Dad went out for a run."

"What?" said Dad.

"Kelsey didn't do her Spanish homework and got in trouble in class," I said. "She also mixed up the

Family Recipe

pronouns and called Señora Diaz a man."

Dad laughed. He motioned to Kelsey and Jenna, who came out and sat on the bottom step, right in front of us.

"You know what the best part of my day was?" Dad asked.

"This!" said Mom.

"Yes!" said Dad. "Sitting here on a beautiful night under the stars with everyone I love most in the world."

"And you know the best thing about the best part coming later at night?" Mom asked.

"What?" asked Jenna.

"The worst parts of our days are behind us."

"Let's end it on a high note, gang," said Dad. "It's getting late, and we have school and work tomorrow. Tomorrow is another day."

Tomorrow was another day indeed.

Chapter Ten
Eric Is Still Annoying!

I felt better the next morning after talking to Mom and Dad the night before, but I was still dreading going to history class. I took a deep breath as I entered the classroom.

"Okay, everyone," said Ms. Blueski. "Let's take out the trees. You should all have the basic information filled in. At this stage you should be talking to your family members to find out stories that you may not know."

Everyone took out their trees. I laid mine on my desk and stared at it. So far I had only Kelsey and Jenna on it.

Eric leaned over. "So how many moms and dads did you put on there?" he asked.

Family Recipe

Lindsay whipped around. "Eric, mind your own business!" she said.

"Hey, I asked Molly, not you!" said Eric.

"Mind your own business, Eric," I said.

He looked surprised. "But I just wanted to know where you were putting your real mom!"

"My real mom is right here," I said, writing Mom's name. "And here is my real dad." I wrote his name too.

"But what about your other mother?" said Eric.

"I don't have another mother, Eric!" I yelled.

"What's going on over there?" called Ms. Blueski.

"Molly is very sensitive," said Eric in a high voice.

The whole class turned around. I could feel my eyes get really teary, but I didn't want to cry. I swallowed hard.

Ms. Blueski came and stood in front of my desk. "You okay, Molly?" she asked softly.

I nodded.

"Ms. Blueski, Eric is pestering Molly about her tree," said Lindsay.

"Because she's adopted, so her tree is complicated!" said Eric.

Ms. Blueski closed her eyes for a second. "Okay,"

she said. "I hadn't thought about that coming up." She bit her lip and looked at me, then knelt down. "If you are uncomfortable with this project, we can think of another one for you to do."

I was aware that everyone was looking at me. I shook my head. "I'm fine with it. I know who my family is."

Ms. Blueski nodded. "Good. But you let me know if I can help." Then she turned around. "You, Eric, need to make sure you get your tree done before you start worrying about everyone else's. Please leave Molly to her own tree."

Ms. Blueski walked back up to the front of the class again, and everyone went back to their project. I just sat there.

Lindsay turned around. "Everything all right?" she asked.

I wanted to crawl under my desk, and I must have looked like it.

"Molly, it's okay," Lindsay said firmly. "It's going to be okay."

I hoped she was right.

Family Recipe

After school we had our last soccer practice before the game, and everyone was a little nervous.

Dad had been meeting Mrs. Rose, as they'd discussed. After dropping me off at practice, he'd take Rusty to do laps. Rusty seemed to be listening when Dad slowed down or told him to stop. Dad seemed to be having a lot of fun.

Coach Wendy was making us do running drills. You had to run down the field, stop, then come back through a lane of orange cones. It seemed easy, but running around the cones meant you had to pull your body in tight or you'd trip.

"That's it, that's it!" said Coach. "Be aware, be aware!"

Riley was running behind me. I heard "ooof" and turned around to see her sprawled out on the grass.

I held out my hand and helped her up. "Um," I said. "You have some grass in your hair."

"Oh, boy," she said. "I don't know whether to laugh or cry."

I giggled. "Laugh?" I said.

She shook her head and the grass sprayed all around.

"It happens," I said.

"Well, I hope it doesn't happen at the game tomorrow," said Riley. "I just get so nervous! When I just play, I'm fine. When I think about it, I fall!"

"If you fall," I said, "you get back up. We've all fallen during a game."

"Thanks," said Riley. "Maybe Kelsey was right and I should have done field hockey instead."

"Kelsey told you what sport to do?" I said, surprised.

"No," said Riley. "We were all planning on trying out for field hockey, but then I decided to do soccer with Isabella instead, and I think she was disappointed."

This is when it gets weird to have your sister in your grade. I knew Kelsey wasn't just disappointed; she was really angry at Riley, and I knew she was hurt that Riley had decided to play soccer. She had been moping and stomping around the house for a week about how middle school changed everything.

"Well," I said, "the thing is that Kelsey gets over things quickly."

This was true, so it was easy to smile reassuringly at Riley.

"She'll be at the game on Saturday cheering you

Family Recipe

on. Friends root for each other," I added.

"I know," said Riley. "She's a good friend." Then she turned to me. "You know, everyone says you say the craziest things sometimes, but I think you always say exactly the right thing."

I smiled again, and we jogged back for the team huddle.

Coach Wendy went over a few things, like playing our zone and being aware on the field. "It's not just you running down to make a goal," she said. "This is a team sport. So let's all be aware of our teammates and where they are, so we can pass properly, and line up our offense or defense."

As we were packing up our bags, I saw Dad talking to Mrs. Rose, who held Lucky's leash. Dad had Rusty on a leash, and Ruby was running around him in circles.

I shoved my cleats in my bag, because Mom freaks out if I wear them in the house and track in clumps of grass. I quickly tore off my socks, slipped my flip-flops on and ran to Ruby.

"Ruby!" I called, and she came bounding over.

"Ruby is ready," said Mrs. Rose, and I noticed she was carrying a large tote bag.

DONUT DREAMS

Mrs. Rose looked at Dad.

He grinned. "Ruby is coming for a sleepover!"

"Ruby is coming to live with us!" I shrieked.

"No, no, no!" said Dad. "She's coming for a sleepover while Mrs. Rose does an overnight shift at the hospital."

"I have to do a few overnight shifts each month," said Mrs. Rose. "Usually another person in my group takes the dogs, but your dad volunteered!"

"So both dogs?" I said, eyeing Rusty, who was patiently sitting at Dad's feet.

"Yep," said Dad. "Lucky stays with his dog walker."

"That's what the old dog is used to," said Mrs. Rose, rubbing his head.

"This way we can have some company over the weekend, and you can see exactly what having a dog entails," said Dad.

"So if it goes well, we get to keep Ruby?" I said excitedly.

"No," said Dad. "We've been pretty clear on that, Molly."

We'll see, I thought. *If this goes really well, then maybe they'll see that we are a dog family after all.*

Chapter Eleven
From No Dogs to Two!

"Let's load them up!" said Dad.

I took Ruby's leash and she ran off, streaking ahead of me. I had to pull on her leash, and I guess I pulled a little hard, because she yelped.

"Oh, I'm sorry!" I said.

"Here," said Dad, giving me Rusty's leash. He bent down and scooped up Ruby, who started licking his face. "This one is literally a handful!"

We got into the car and Rusty sat in the back seat, looking out the window. Ruby was running from the front seat to the back seat, barking.

Mrs. Rose was waving good-bye as she got into her car with Lucky.

"Ruby's excited!" I said.

DONUT DREAMS

"She's nuts," sighed Dad.

Ruby jumped behind the back seat and wedged herself up against the back window.

"Can you see?" I asked Dad.

"Yeah," said Dad. "I just hope I don't have to stop short."

"Does Mom know this is happening?" I asked, a little nervously.

"Of course!" said Dad. "We discuss everything."

When we got home, I took Ruby off her leash and she bolted through the back door and into the kitchen.

I heard Kelsey scream, and then I heard a crash.

"This dog just ran under my feet and tripped me!" yelled Kelsey.

The plate was broken and there were cheese cubes all over the floor.

"Okay, let me help," I said. I wanted everything to go just right for this visit.

I got the dustpan out of the closet and swept up the pieces of the plate and the cheese, except a cube that Ruby was batting around like a ball.

"You'd better get that," said Jenna. "She can choke on that if she tries to eat it."

Family Recipe

Choke? Oh no.

I hurriedly reached down, but Ruby thought we were playing a game and snapped up the cheese.

"Drop that, Ruby!" I said.

I swear she smiled at me as she ran into the family room. I chased her from the family room to the living room to the dining room, where I cornered her, picked her up, and grabbed the cheese out of her mouth.

She was either a little miffed about that or she thought we were playing, because then she nipped my fingers.

"Ouch!" I squealed.

It didn't hurt, but I was surprised. Unfortunately, because I was surprised, I also dropped Ruby, who whimpered.

"Oh, Ruby!" I said, feeling immediately awful. "Are you okay?"

Jenna came in and looked at her. "Can you walk to me, Ruby?" she asked.

Ruby whimpered more, and I started to panic, my heart beating fast.

"Come here, pretty baby," said Jenna in a soothing voice.

Ruby got up and skittered over to her.

"Okay, she's walking. I think you just startled her," Jenna said.

"Well she startled me by biting me!" I said.

"She bit you?" said Dad, who must have come in during the commotion.

"She just nipped," I said quickly, immediately feeling a little defensive. "I think she thought we were playing. She didn't do it on purpose."

"This one is a wild one," said Jenna.

"You seem to have a way with her," said Dad.

As Jenna held Ruby, she calmed down.

"This is a new place for both dogs, so they're probably a little nervous. Let's try to make them comfortable," Dad said.

"Where's Rusty?" I asked.

"By the door," Dad said. "I could barely nudge him out of the car, and now he won't come into the house."

Rusty was standing right in the doorway. I never knew a dog could look worried, but boy, he did.

I bent down and whispered into his ear, "It's okay, Rusty. This is your home for this weekend, and we'll take care of you!"

Family Recipe

He looked at me, and I think he was a little reassured, because he sat down.

"Okay," said Dad, running his hands through his hair. "This is going to be hard work and require some team effort. Let's get the dogs fed, since it's almost dinnertime."

Dad peered into the bag Mrs. Rose had given him and took out four stacked dog bowls. He opened two cans of dog food and spooned them into two bowls.

"Ah, Mrs. Rose thought of everything," he said, and he pulled out what looked like a place mat and put it on the floor. "Okay, Kels, fill the other bowls with some cold water and put them on the mat too."

Ruby and Rusty watched us. When Dad put the dog bowls down with the food, Ruby started wiggling and yelping in Jenna's arms.

"Are you hungry, baby?" Jenna asked, and placed Ruby in front of her dinner.

Ruby ran around the mat a few times, then hungrily started eating.

Rusty seemed a little wary. He didn't move and instead watched Ruby gulp down her food.

"C'mon, Rusty," I said, holding up the bowl. "This one's for you."

DONUT DREAMS

Rusty looked at me and then the bowl. Slowly he walked over to the bowl, lowered his head, and took a little bite. Then he looked up. We were all looking at him.

"You have an audience, Rusty," said Dad, laughing.

I guess Rusty realized he was hungry too, because then he started eating faster and faster, licking the bowl when the food was gone.

"Okay, now the humans," said Dad. He opened the refrigerator and took out a bunch of stuff to make a salad. "Jenna, can you boil a pot of water for pasta?"

Jenna filled the pasta pot and Dad started sautéing tomatoes for the sauce.

As soon as Ruby finished, she kicked her bowl over, and the gravy from her food splattered everywhere.

"Eeeuuuww!" yelled Kelsey. "Dog food is on the wall!"

"Well, you'll have to clean that up," said Dad, chopping away.

I got a wet towel and wiped down the wall and the floor.

Ruby was running around the kitchen table.

"In a way I guess it's good that Mom isn't home yet to see this mess," I said, looking around.

Family Recipe

"You want to race?" teased Kelsey, who playfully started chasing Ruby.

I guess Ruby got a little wound up, because the next thing we knew, she peed all over the floor.

"Gross!" Kelsey screamed, jumping up on a chair. "It's all over the floor!"

Dad sighed and put down the knife. "Okay, girls, we need a bucket and some paper towels. I'll get the cleaner."

Kelsey didn't move. I went to the closet and pulled out the mop and bucket. Dad squirted the floor with the cleaning fluid, and I squatted down to help wipe it up. It was pretty easy.

Ruby was yelping and trying to jump up to the chair Kelsey was still standing on.

"Ruby, Ruby," said Dad. "Shhhhh . . . and Kelsey, come down from there!"

Kelsey came down and Ruby stopped yelping.

Rusty had finished his dinner and was sitting next to his bowl.

"What now?" I said to Dad.

"What?" he said, a little flustered. "Why don't you and Kelsey take the dogs out to the yard and play while Jenna helps me with dinner?"

DONUT DREAMS

"C'mon, boy," I said to Rusty, who slowly followed me outside.

Kelsey was right behind me, with Ruby racing to beat us. We went down the back steps into the yard.

Other than having catches with Mom and Dad, I hadn't really played in the backyard in a long time. We still had a tire swing and a fort that Dad had built us, but neither seemed quite right for dogs.

Kelsey picked up a tennis ball that was lying in the grass. "Hey, maybe they'll like this," she said.

She tossed the ball to Ruby, who tried to pick it up in her mouth. It was too big for her, so she was kind of wrestling with it, and she totally fell over it.

"Grrrrrr," she growled.

"Hey, Rusty, do you want to play?" I asked.

Rusty was watching Ruby curiously. I ran to the shed and got the bucket of tennis balls we had in there from Jenna's tennis lessons.

"Here, Rusty!" I said, tossing a ball to him.

He was about to go chase it, but Ruby beat him to it, growling and batting the ball around with her paws.

"Hey, that was for Rusty!" Kelsey said. "You are a piggy puppy!"

Family Recipe

Every ball I threw to Rusty, Ruby went after, leaving a bunch of balls lying in the grass around us.

Finally, I picked one up and went over to Rusty. "Here, boy," I said. "This one is for you."

He nudged it out of my hand. I threw it up in the air and he jumped for it, going up on his hind legs. I caught it, then tossed it a little farther. He ran for it and caught it in his mouth.

"Good catch, Rusty!" I said.

I guess that made Ruby a little jealous, because she came bounding over, nipping at Rusty.

"Kelsey, throw her a ball of her own!" I said.

"Look at this!" I heard Mom say over the fence.

I guess we hadn't heard her pull up in the driveway, but she opened the gate and Ruby went running over to her.

As Mom leaned down, Ruby licked her face.

"Oh, so you know exactly who to butter up!" said Mom, laughing.

Rusty sat next to me, watching.

"Is this Rusty?" asked Mom. She patted him on the head. "I hear you're going to run with us tomorrow!"

Rusty barked, which must have been his version of "yes."

We made our way back into the house for dinner. With all the excitement, I hadn't realized it was a little later than usual, and I was hungry.

As soon as we sat down, Ruby began to yelp, putting her paws on my lap.

"What do you want?" I asked.

"She wants your dinner," said Dad. "Some dogs are fed scraps from the table, which is not something we're going to do. Plus, Mrs. Rose said she was trying to cure Ruby of this habit."

"Want to do best and worst?" Mom said.

But every time we started to talk, Ruby would yelp and run around. It was kind of a chaotic dinner after a long day.

I cleared my place and was looking forward to going upstairs and chilling out when Dad said, "Okay, let's go."

"Go where?" I asked.

"Dogs need to be walked a lot," Dad said. "And …," he said, handing Kelsey and me each a plastic bag. "Dogs mean you have to go on poop patrol!"

"What are these for?" asked Kelsey.

Dad grinned. "When the dogs poop, we have to clean up after them."

Family Recipe

Kelsey shrieked. "You mean we have to pick it up? That is so, so gross!"

"It's not gross," said Dad. "It's part of having a dog. You have to take care of them and clean up after them!"

We got the dogs on their leashes and started off down the street. Of course Ruby pooped in about five minutes.

Dad looked at me. "Well, you wanted a dog...."

I sighed and got out the baggie. Dad showed me how to turn it inside out to hold the poop through the bag so I wouldn't have to touch it. I kind of held my nose and did it quick. I dropped the baggie into the bigger bag Dad had brought. It wasn't great, but it wasn't terrible.

I can do this, I thought.

Three poops later I was beginning to wonder if having a dog was worth it. Ruby kept pulling at my leash, and I was starting to get chilly.

"C'mon," I said. "Let's go home."

"Rusty hasn't gone yet," said Dad. "One more block."

I sighed.

"Hey, at least it's autumn," said Dad. "Just think

about doing this three times a day in the middle of winter when it's sleeting outside."

Kelsey put her arm around me and squeezed. Dad walked on the other side and put his arm around me too. Rusty finally pooped and the three of us walked the dogs home.

"Molly," Kelsey said as we turned onto our street. "I love you and I'm glad you're my sister. And if we ever get a dog, I won't fight you on it. I won't ask you to share it."

"Okay . . . ," I said.

"Because," she said, "cleaning up poop has to be one of the grossest things ever, and I promise you I'm never doing it. That dog will be all yours."

"Thanks, sis," I said, squeezing her back. "Or should I say *gracias*?"

"Ugh," Kelsey said, giving me an annoyed look. "Let's pick up the pace. I still have Spanish homework to do."

Chapter Twelve
Teamwork—at Home and on the Field

We all woke up really tired, and that's because Ruby kept the whole house up most of the night.

Dad had thought it would be best for Ruby and Rusty to sleep in the laundry room, even though I tried to convince him that Ruby should sleep with me. Rusty lay down and went to sleep quickly. But Ruby yelped, whined, and scratched the door.

Finally, Dad went down and tried to pet her and soothe her to get her to sleep in her dog bed that Mrs. Rose had sent. But Ruby would not sleep.

After midnight, Mom went downstairs and brought Ruby up to my room. She put Ruby on the bed, where she happily curled up.

"Good night, girls," whispered Mom.

DONUT DREAMS

I put my head down on the pillow, happy with Ruby sleeping on my feet.

But an hour later Ruby was up again. She was chewing on an old stuffed animal in my room and was running around with it.

This went on until Dad came in and took Ruby downstairs again.

Jenna opened her door and yelled, "That dog is keeping me up!"

Mom and Dad took turns all night. Dad even texted Mrs. Rose, who told them that Ruby was frequently up a lot in the night

We were all bleary-eyed at breakfast.

"It's like having a baby that's been up all night," moaned Mom. She poured some more coffee.

Dad yawned. "Molly, are you ready for your soccer game today?"

I nodded. "All set except for my cleats," I said, standing up.

I had already put on my uniform, even my shin guards and socks. I wanted to be ready.

"Thatta girl," said Dad. "Bring on the soccer game!" Then he yawned again.

"Have another cup of coffee, Chris," said Mom.

Family Recipe

Kelsey came stomping down the stairs. "I. Am. So. Tired! I don't care how cute that dog is," she said, glaring. "She kept me up all night!"

"It was not a great night," said Mom. "But you girls are seeing firsthand how much getting a dog affects the whole family in many different ways."

"Well, maybe we could just get a dog who sleeps," said Jenna, putting her head on her arms.

"When do they go back to Mrs. Rose?" asked Kelsey.

"Tomorrow afternoon," said Dad.

"We have another night with them?" Kelsey yelped. "Can I sleep over at Sophia's house?"

"Maybe it will be easier now that the dogs are more used to the house," said Mom.

We all looked at her doubtfully.

"We should get going soon," said Dad. "Molly, you have warm-up in half an hour."

I went into the laundry room to get my cleats. I rummaged around. Finally, I lifted up Ruby's dog bed and then let out a huge yell. "RUBY!"

Everyone came running.

I held up my cleats, which were both chewed all the way through. The laces were in tatters, and there were teeth marks and little holes all over them.

"Uh-oh," said Kelsey.

"Oh boy," said Mom.

I stormed out of the room into the family room, where Ruby was blissfully sleeping on Mom's favorite chair.

"Whatever you do," said Jenna, "I beg you not to wake her up."

"But it's the first game of the season!" I wailed. "These were broken in just right! And the rules say I need to wear cleats for the game. What am I going to do?"

Kelsey's feet were a least a size smaller than mine, so I couldn't wear hers.

Mom grabbed her phone. "I'm texting around to see if anyone has a spare pair," she said. "The sporting goods store doesn't open until ten, and the game starts at nine thirty."

"Agggghhhh," I said, sitting down on the floor. "Why is everything so hard right now?" I felt like I was going to cry.

A few minutes later, Elizabeth Ellis's mom texted back that she had an extra pair in my size. They were brand-new and all mine.

Family Recipe

"Brand-new!" Dad said. "That's lucky!"

I looked at him. "Like brand-new running shoes?"

Cleats, like running shoes, sometimes hurt when they were new and stiff. They felt a lot better once you'd worn them a few times and they kind of molded to your feet.

"Well, you'll have to break them in," said Dad, picking up my destroyed cleats. "It's better than wearing these. We can pick Elizabeth's up on the way to the game."

It took us forever to get into the car, because the whole family was coming for the first game and because Mom and Dad thought it was better to bring Rusty and Ruby with us. I think they were afraid of what Ruby would do to the house if we left her there alone.

Rusty got in the back with us, but Ruby decided to hop around the car. Finally, Dad kind of tackled her and got into the front passenger seat.

"GO!" he said to Mom, and we finally pulled out of the driveway.

We stopped to pick up the new cleats, and by the time we got to the field I was running a few minutes late, which always drives me crazy.

DONUT DREAMS

I raced out of the car as Mom yelled, "Have a great game, baby!"

I joined the team on the field. "How is having a dog?" Riley asked.

I rolled my eyes. "Not easy," I said.

Coach Wendy called us in for a huddle. "Remember, girls," she said. "This is the first game, and we have a whole season ahead of us. Let's perform as a team. That's the goal today, not making goals."

I overheard the other coach yell in their huddle, "Do what you have to do to win!" I was really grateful right then for Coach Wendy.

The whistle blew and we were on. Isabella had a few really great runs, and Madeline and I passed down the field, but we couldn't seem to score. I noticed Riley was lagging behind.

"C'mon, Riley!" I said.

She looked really nervous.

Coach Wendy had taught us during drills to call out as we were about to pass. I got the ball and called to Madeline, who ran right next to me. We managed to get the ball down the field, but I was blocked. In practice we had a drill that we ran again and again where it was Madeline, then me, then Riley. I looked up and saw Riley was open, and I kicked to her.

Her face was surprised and she jumped a little, then kicked right over the ball and fell. The other team snatched the ball and went back up and scored

"It's okay, Riley!" I heard Coach Wendy call. "Get your game back on!"

"Sorry," Riley mumbled as she jogged past me.

We set up the same play again. Madeline, who just seemed to appear next to me, passed to me. Then I passed to Riley. She tripped again. I felt bad, but I was also getting a little frustrated.

"Time-out!" called Coach Wendy, and we ran to the huddle.

Riley looked down, not wanting to meet eyes with any of us.

Madeline threw her arm around her. "Riley, you can do this," she said. "This is just nerves!"

"Yes!" said Coach Wendy. "I need you to relax and trust yourself, Riley. You have a whole team behind you."

That didn't seem to help. On the next play Isabella passed to Riley, and she slipped.

I saw Coach run down the sidelines. "Riley!" she called. "You have this!!"

But at that point I wasn't taking any chances. I passed back to Madeline instead, and we took the ball down the field. Madeline passed back to me, and instead of passing to Riley, I ran down and sank it in the net.

Finally!

Madeline and I jumped up and down, giving each other high fives.

"Molly!" Coach called, and pointed.

I figured she was rotating Samantha in for me to give me a break. Instead she sat down next to me on the bench.

"I'm taking you out so you can get a little perspective," she said. "You left Riley out of that play, and that's not how we do things as a team. We work with each other, not around each other. Okay?"

The whistle blew and she jumped back up.

I was so surprised. I mean, I scored. I know we were supposed to work on teamwork, but I didn't just break away and score. Madeline worked the ball with me. Plus, I scored!

Ten minutes later Coach Wendy put me back in.

"What was that about?" asked Madeline.

"Teamwork," I said.

Family Recipe

She looked puzzled, but the ball was in play again.

I passed to Madeline, who passed back to me. I looked up and saw Riley hovering and passed to her. She got the ball, but the other team snatched it and ran back up the field to score again.

I kept my head down and kept passing. Finally, on the fourth play Riley got the ball and ran with it. I was so surprised I kind of stood there for a second, then ran down behind her.

"You've got it, Riley!" called Madeline.

Sure enough, Riley scored. She let out this big whoop, and I gave her a high five. I was happy, but it was too late. We lost 8–2.

"Okay, girls," said Coach Wendy in the final huddle. "We didn't win in scoring, but we won in teamwork. Riley, I know you had a tough game, but your teammates didn't give up on you. Molly and Madeline kept running the play that we practiced so much. They did it again and again until you broke through and scored. That is true teamwork, and I am so proud of you girls!"

As we were shaking hands, I thought about what Coach Wendy had said. I kept passing because she told me to, but I didn't really think about Riley. She really did hang in there and kept trying. I felt bad for thinking about winning instead of thinking about how she felt.

I was disappointed about losing, but mostly I was disappointed with myself. Mom, Dad, Jenna, and Kelsey came down to the field, with Ruby barking and nipping at Jenna's heels. Rusty followed Dad.

"Are you keeping her?" asked Madeline, bending down to pet Ruby, who was chasing a leaf.

"No," said Mom. "We're just taking care of her until tomorrow."

"She is just too cute," said Isabella, making baby sounds at her.

Ruby ignored all of us and continued to chase the leaf.

I felt something wet on my hand and looked down to find Rusty's nose nuzzling it.

"Hi, boy," I said. He rubbed his head on my leg, kind of resting it there.

Dad had to chase Ruby down the field, which annoyed me. My feet hurt from the new cleats, and I just wanted to go home.

Finally, we got Ruby in the car. Rusty followed us into the back, and he sat down at my feet, looking up

Family Recipe

at me. I softly scratched him behind his ears.

I looked at him and he cocked his head, watching me, maybe realizing that I was a little unhappy. Then he put his head on my lap. Rusty wouldn't get mad if I missed a ball. He was a loyal friend.

We drove home like that, with him resting on me and me leaning on him a little. It hadn't been a great day, but I felt so much better that my new friend was looking out for me.

Chapter Thirteen
Mom Saves the Day

The next day I had to get up and work four hours at the Park, which was not good. I didn't mind working, but we'd had another sleepless night. Ruby was up for most of it howling at the moon, which was really bright that night.

"Harvest moon," Dad groaned as he and Mom ran around the house, trying to pull all the shades and curtains shut.

I think even Rusty was stressed out, because he had his paw over his eyes. I brought him up to my room, and he got all the way under the covers with me. It was nice to sleep with a soft dog. Especially one who actually slept and cuddled.

We all had to be at the restaurant at six thirty in

Family Recipe

the morning. I was usually up early, but we had to drag Kelsey out of bed, and she was grumpy.

"At least you just need to stand behind the counter," Jenna told her. "If you were a waitress, you'd need to be running around. And Sunday mornings are the busiest."

"Busy is good for business," said Mom, almost automatically.

We all tumbled in at 6:25 and scrambled to get to our stations. Lindsay was waiting for Kelsey at Donut Dreams, and Lily and Rich were prepping the coffee trays. I jumped in.

To prep the coffee trays, you made sure all the sugar bowls were full, that the little milk and cream pitchers were full, and that you had extra spoons ready. People liked their coffee right away in the morning, so we were all working fast to make sure the waitstaff could just grab a tray and go.

Nans called us in to go over breakfast specials. The omelet of the day was a western omelet, which had peppers and ham. The pancake special was banana.

"And for dessert," said Nans, "our special of the day is a new donut, Molly's Apple Pie donut. It's a new recipe and one that I'm sure will be a hit."

I perked up.

"Molly gets a donut named after her?" asked Kelsey.

"She does," said Nans. "Because she came up with the idea."

"Hmmph! I'm jealous!" Jenna said jokingly and stomped out of the kitchen, pretending to be mad.

Everyone got a taste, and as Nans handed me mine, she winked. "The pie is perfect now," she whispered. "And I think these are almost there!"

I was still grumpy from losing the game and from not sleeping. I bit into the donut. I felt a little better immediately.

"Wow," I said to Nans. "I think I have a new favorite!"

"Coffee on table four, please," said Jenna, and I shoved the rest of the donut in my mouth, grabbed the pot, and headed over . . . right to Eric Sellers, his mom, and his older sister.

I could not believe my bad luck lately.

"Hi, Molly," Eric said.

"Hi, Eric," I mumbled, and poured coffee into his mom's cup.

As soon as it was full, I rushed straight back into the kitchen.

Family Recipe

"What's wrong?" asked Jenna, passing me with a tray. "You look a little freaked out."

"Nothing," I said, and took a deep breath. I tried to avoid Eric's table after that.

Rich and Jenna didn't seem to notice, because it was really busy. But Kelsey did. She saw me from across the room and pointed to Eric's table, then made a face.

I shrugged and went back into the kitchen to hide.

"Hey, I need help," said Rich. "Syrup on four, please, Molly. Okay?"

"Got it," I said.

I grabbed a syrup pitcher and went to drop it at table four. You had to wipe down all the syrup pitchers after the breakfast rush because they got so gross and sticky.

As I turned from table four, I saw someone waving a hand at me. It was Eric's mom.

I could pretend I didn't see her and rush by, but I knew Grandpa would have a fit. I groaned inwardly and went over.

"Can I get you something?" I asked, trying to look only at her.

"Sweetie, I know you're busy, but I need some more milk for my coffee, please."

Eric was doodling on his place mat and didn't look up. His sister was watching me.

"Hey, aren't you Jenna's little sister?" she asked.

"I am," I said, starting to turn away.

"You're in Eric's class, right?"

"I am," I said.

I felt my stomach flip around again. I looked down and realized that Eric wasn't doodling on his place mat. He had his family tree sheet out, and he was writing on it.

"Let me get that milk for you!" I said, and turned and fled into the kitchen.

Mom had been working in the office after she brought us to the Park, and she came into the kitchen for another cup of coffee.

"Did you go through a whole pot already?" Grandpa joked. Mom drank a lot of coffee.

"We were up all night again with Ruby," Mom groaned.

I filled up the pitcher with milk but was just standing there. I really, really didn't want to deal with Eric Sellers.

Family Recipe

"What's wrong?" asked Mom, narrowing her eyes.

I sighed. You just could not get anything past her.

"Eric Sellers is at table four," I said. I held up the pitcher. "His mom needs more milk."

Mom looked at me for a second. "You know, Jenny Sellers and I grew up together. Give me the pitcher."

I handed her the pitcher. Grandpa looked like he was going to say something, but Mom shook her head and gave him a look.

"I've got this. It's been a while since my waitress days, but it's like riding a bike. Come on, Molly," she said, and strode out of the kitchen.

"At least put on an apron if you're going to serve!" yelped Grandpa.

Mom went right over to table four. "Jenny!" she said. "I haven't seen you in ages! How are you?"

"Melissa, it's so good to see you!" said Mrs. Sellers, standing up to give Mom a hug. "How have you been?"

"Can't complain," said Mom. "Are you still teaching at the community center?"

"Sure am," said Mrs. Sellers. "You know, I'll be stuck in preschool for the rest of my life!" She laughed heartily, and Eric looked a little embarrassed.

"I hear Eric is in Molly's history class," said Mrs. Sellers.

Eric looked startled.

"I hear that too," said Mom, putting her hand on my shoulder.

"Well, I don't know how you feel about this family tree project," said Mrs. Sellers. "But it's causing a lot of drama in our house."

"How so?" asked Mom.

"Well," said Mrs. Sellers, "you know Jeff and I divorced years ago."

"Yes, I did hear that, and I'm sorry," said Mom.

"Oh, no, no," said Mrs. Sellers. "It actually all worked out. I'm married now to Dan Ostfield. You remember him?"

"I do," said Mom. "He was a nice guy!"

"Yep, and he still is," said Mrs. Sellers. "I suppose at some point I may change my last name to Ostfield," Mrs. Sellers continued. "But Eric didn't like the idea of me having a different name than his, so I kept Sellers. For now anyway."

"I can understand that," Mom said.

"And Jeff is now married to Laura Farmer."

Family Recipe

"Oh, Justin Farmer's sister!" said Mom.

"Right," said Mrs. Sellers. "We're all very happy and the kids are happy. But this family tree is a problem. Eric seems to think there's just a straight line in every family and the tree has an even number of branches, like Ms. Blueski drew on the worksheet. But our family has a few more branches."

"But that's not what the worksheet has on it," said Eric.

"Eric really wants to include Laura and Dan in our tree, because they're like a second mom and dad to him," said Mrs. Sellers. "And he has stepbrothers and stepsisters. But he's not sure how to do it, and he's embarrassed to have a tree that looks different from everyone else's."

"I see," said Mom, giving me a look.

"I told him to ask around, because I'm quite sure there are many kids in the class who have branches that weave around, but he claims no one does."

Ohhhh. So that's why Eric kept asking me about my "moms."

"Well," said Mom, looking at me.

"I have a couple different branches," I said.

Eric looked up.

"I was trying to figure out how to put my biological mother on there but have my mom in the main spot," I said. "Because, you know, Mom is my mom."

Eric nodded. "Yeah," he said. "I mean, Dan isn't my dad—my dad is my dad. But it doesn't feel right not to have Dan on the tree too."

"He's been putting off this project," said Mrs. Sellers, pointing to his worksheet.

"Me too," I said.

"I have an idea," said Mom. "Eric, can I see that sheet?"

Eric handed it to her.

"I can make a copy of this in the office. I don't know how much time you have, but Molly can take a break soon. Maybe we put you guys at a table with some donuts and you can help each other?"

Eric smiled, and I grinned back at him.

"That would be awesome," Eric said.

Mrs. Sellers beamed too. "Thank you, Melissa," she said. "That would be terrific. See, Eric?" she added, turning to her son. "I told you that if you asked, other people could help!"

"Okay," said Mom. "Molly, you can take a break

Family Recipe

in twenty, which gives you, Eric, time to eat the rest of that breakfast!"

Eric picked up his fork and started hungrily eating his pancakes.

"Good, right?" asked Mom, and he nodded.

"Best in town!" said Mom. "See you around, Jenny!"

"Thanks again, Melissa!" said Mrs. Sellers. "You have no idea how relieved I am."

I smiled. She wasn't the only one.

Chapter Fourteen
It's Dog Day!

I was feeling so much better about things after we spoke to the Sellerses that I didn't mind that we were so busy. Sundays are always busy, but it seemed even more so today.

I cleared table five and noticed that the Sherers were seated at table two, the big round top.

"Warning," Jenna whispered, passing by. "Tornado on two! Can you make sure there are extra napkins?"

I breezed over with a stack of napkins.

Christopher jumped up. "Hi, Molly!" he said. "I get to have chocolate chip pancakes today because it's a Special Occasion!"

"Is it your birthday?" I asked.

He shook his head, but his face had a wide grin.

Family Recipe

"No, it's Dog Day. Today, we're getting a doggy!"

"Oh, Christopher!" I said. "I am so jealous. I've wanted a dog my whole life!"

"You should ask your mommy and daddy for one," said Christopher.

"I have," I said. "And they keep saying no!"

"Were you bad?" Christopher asked in a whisper. "Because my brothers and I had to do chores and clean up to show our mom and dad that we can help take care of a dog."

"I have definitely done my chores and listened to my parents," I said, trying not to crack up. "But they say it's just too much work for us."

"It *is* a lot of work," said Mr. Sherer. "We are totally nuts for having three kids and getting a dog!"

"But we love dogs," said Mrs. Sherer. "And with the kids so young, we're home all the time. Plus, the dog will have three active children to keep her busy."

"And we're nuts," added Mr. Sherer.

I saw Jenna coming out of the kitchen with a full tray. I could tell she needed help.

"Hang on," I said, and grabbed the tray rest, which is this foldout thing that holds the tray while you unload all the plates.

DONUT DREAMS

"Thanks," said Jenna, putting the tray down and then setting the pancakes in front of the boys and eggs in front of Mr. and Mrs. Sherer. "Can I get you guys anything else?"

"Syrup!" yelled Christopher.

Mrs. Sherer gave him a look.

"Syrup, please," said Christopher.

I smiled. "Syrup coming right up!" I said.

"Molly is adopted," said Christopher.

"Christopher!" said Mrs. Sherer sharply. "Oh dear, Molly. I am so sorry."

"It's okay," I said. "I *am* adopted."

"Her mommy and daddy adopted her like we're going to adopt the puppy today."

"No, Christopher, not like a puppy!" said Mr. Sherer loudly. "For goodness' sake!"

"No, it's not the same," said Mrs. Sherer. "But let's try to help Christopher understand. When you adopt something or someone into your family, they or it becomes a part of your family. A sister is not the same as a puppy, but they're both members of your family and you love them very much."

"I'd like a puppy way more than a sister," said Christopher.

Family Recipe

"Well, you are definitely not getting a sister," said Mrs. Sherer.

"Sisters are pretty awesome, though," said Jenna.

"I have enough brothers," said Christopher.

"Yes, you do," said Mr. and Mrs. Sherer together.

"Okay, Christopher, you enjoy those pancakes!" said Jenna. "Molly, I need you in the kitchen."

I got the syrup for the Sherers, dropped it off, and went to the kitchen.

"What?" Grandpa asked, looking up from where we stacked the tickets. He was watching to see what people were ordering and how long the orders were taking.

"Nothing," said Jenna. "Just some talk between girls."

She started filling up some glasses with orange juice at the counter on the other side of the kitchen, and I followed her. Nans was at the counter too, rolling out dough for the donuts.

"Are you okay?" Jenna asked me in a whisper. "I mean, Christopher is just a kid and all, but still . . ."

"Yeah," I said. "It just seems like suddenly the fact that I'm adopted is . . . I don't know."

"What happened?" asked Nans gently.

DONUT DREAMS

"Christopher asked if adopting Molly was like adopting a puppy," said Jenna. "Plus, there's been some stuff going on at school."

"Well, Melissa told me about the school stuff," said Nans, cutting round circles out of the dough.

I wasn't surprised. In our family we really do tell each other everything.

"I mean, I am adopted," I said. "It's a fact. That's how I got here. But it's not really a big issue."

"I understand that," said Nans. "And it isn't anything you should have to explain if you don't want to."

"Christopher's just a kid," said Jenna. "He doesn't know any better."

"That's right," said Nans. "He's curious and asking questions, which is natural. But it's still not okay if it makes you uncomfortable, Molly."

I thought for a second. "I'm not uncomfortable with it," I said. "That's the thing. But it seems like everyone else is uncomfortable with it and no one knows how to deal with it *but* me."

"Order up for table three!" came a voice from the kitchen.

"I have to pick this up," said Jenna. "I'll be back."

Family Recipe

She looked at Nans, and Nans waved her off. Nans was taking donuts out of the fryer with a slotted spoon, and getting ready to put the next batch in. The donuts looked perfect when they came out, but once she put them on the rack to cool, the inside oozed out a little bit.

"That filling won't stay in," I said.

"I know," said Nans. "And it was driving me crazy not to have it perfect, just like my pies. But you know what?"

"What?" I asked, wondering if she was going to let us all eat the donuts that weren't perfect.

"It tastes good anyway. And this is a family recipe," said Nans. "Family is sometimes messy. And sometimes it's not so bad if what's inside comes out."

"Like our feelings?" I asked.

"Yes, feelings," said Nans. "Especially all the love we have on the inside."

She finished the batch and had about two dozen donuts on the rack. Most of them were kind of drippy.

"I think these are going to be a hit, Molly," said Nans. "And I think they're just perfect."

"I'm pretty sure I have a table with kids who would love these," I said.

DONUT DREAMS

"The Sherer kids?" laughed Nans. "They love anything with sugar!"

"You know," I said, "maybe on Sundays for the next month we can pass out donuts to all the tables for dessert, on the house. That way we can introduce people to new flavors they might not buy at first."

Nans smiled. "Hey, Jack!" she called to Grandpa. "Your granddaughter over here has your business sense. Just listen to this plan she has!"

I explained to Grandpa, who did a little excited hop and gave me a huge hug.

"That's brilliant!" he said. "Let me round up the Donut Dreams team to help!"

"It runs in the family!" said Nans, and then she threw a few more donuts into the fryer.

I skittered out to the floor because I realized I had been missing for a while. The Sherer table was a mess, and Jenna was trying to collect all the sticky napkins.

"I've got it," I said, coming up behind her.

She gave me a grateful look, then moved on to do coffee refills at her other tables.

The rest of the shift was pretty busy but not terrible. Grandpa handed Lindsay, Kelsey, and me each a big platter of the apple pie donuts with a set of

Family Recipe

tongs. We went from table to table offering them—and let me tell you, it went over extremely well.

People were so excited. We heard a lot of "Oh, I shouldn't have a donut, but ...," and then they ate the whole thing in three bites.

Chapter Fifteen
A New Member of the Family

After we were on donut duty, as Grandpa called it, Lindsay and Kelsey went back to the Donut Dreams counter, because Sunday was not only the busiest day for the Park, it was the busiest day for donuts.

Mom had made a space for us in her office so that Eric and I could tackle the family tree. I had the copy of Eric's tree Mom made for me. I tore a page out of my notebook and put a fresh piece of paper in front of me. Eric had his page with a tree template on it.

"Okay, so how are we going to do this?" I said, staring at my blank piece of paper.

"I've been thinking," said Eric. "Maybe we just

Family Recipe

have to be a little creative. Think outside the lines..."

I watched as he drew in more branches on his sheet, some that were long, and some that were short.

"Now there are more spaces," he said.

I nodded. "You could also"—I grabbed a pencil and started drawing—"do this..." I drew more of a forest, with a bunch of trees.

"That might work better," said Eric.

"Right?" I said. "Because this way you can see how all the trees around you make up the forest where you live." I shrugged. "You can do your family tree however you like. This is just a suggestion."

"That's really smart, Molly," said Eric. "This way you can see that no tree really stands alone. It's... what's that word we learned in English lit where an image or an idea stands for something else?"

"Metaphor," I said. "It's a metaphor for the fact that no family is really alone, that it takes a lot of trees...a whole forest, really."

Eric nodded and continued sketching, and so did I. I filled in our family, then added a tree next to us with Aunt Miranda and Uncle Adam.

I sighed.

"What?" asked Eric. "Are you stuck?"

"Yeah," I said. "I mean, I guess my biological mom should be on here, but I don't know how to add her."

"How about a leaf, then?"

"A leaf?" I asked.

"Yeah, just a leaf. I mean, your biological mom doesn't play into your family, but she is a part of you, or I guess you're a part of her. So just one leaf on the big branch."

I thought about that. "Actually, that seems about right," I said.

I sketched in a leaf off to the side. Mom and Dad still sat on the big wide branch, and Jenna, Kelsey, and I were smaller branches off their big one.

"Hey, I think we figured it out!" I said, and I looked over at Eric's page. "Wow."

I had never realized he could really draw. There were all sorts of trees and bushes, and some of them touched or the branches crossed. Some had flowers. It was really beautiful.

He laughed. "I'm going to present this as My Tangled Tree Family Forest."

"But tangled is good here," I said.

"It works for me," said Eric. "I'm sorry that I was pestering you about your tree in class."

Family Recipe

"It's okay," I said. "But you should have told me why."

"Yeah, I realize that now," he said. "My mom says that sometimes I don't think before I speak. My sister says I'm just annoying."

I stifled a giggle.

"I'm sorry if it came out the wrong way and I upset you," said Eric.

"Apology accepted," I said. "And thanks for that."

"Your mom ordered these for you two," said Nans, putting down a plate of apple pie donuts.

Eric's eyes got big.

"The perks of being in the family business," I said.

"These are called Molly's Apple Pie donuts," said Nans. She winked. "It's a special family recipe."

Eric inhaled the donut and said, with his mouth full, "I'd like to be a part of your family!"

I nodded and bit into mine. "Sweet, delicious, and a little messy," I said, wiping my fingers on a napkin and smiling at Nans. "Our family is perfect."

※ ※ ※ ※ ※

I was really glad to have the family tree project done, but I was still dreading the next thing we had to do:

give Ruby back to Mrs. Rose.

Jenna, Kelsey, and I all left the restaurant with Mom and drove to the park. Mrs. Rose had found a family who wanted to adopt Ruby, and they were meeting her at the park for the exchange.

We were meeting Dad, who was bringing the dogs from home. Our meeting spot was the gazebo near the baseball field, and we all quietly walked over.

"I know you're sad, Molly," said Mom. "But I'm not so sure it's a great time to have a puppy in the house."

"I know," I said. Even I had to admit this weekend proved she was right. Between being kept up all night and having Ruby demand constant attention and make messes, not to mention eat my cleats, it had been exhausting. "But I'll still miss her."

"We'll all miss Ruby," said Mom.

"No, we won't," said Kelsey. Mom gave her a look.

"What?" said Kelsey. "That dog is a pain. But I like Rusty."

So did I. I hoped Mrs. Rose would find a good home for Rusty, too.

We sat on the bench in the gazebo and watched for Dad, who was planning to run to the park with the dogs. He thought it would be a good idea for them to get some energy out before they went to a new home.

Then we saw Dad and Rusty come running up the path. Dad seemed to be holding Ruby.

"What happened?" asked Mom as he jogged up.

"Well, turns out the run was a little much for the puppy," said Dad, panting a little. "But Rusty here handled it like a champ." Rusty sat down next to Dad and looked up at him. "Good boy, Rusty!"

We all sat there, waiting. Rusty put his head on Dad's lap.

"Awww, such a sweet pup," said Jenna.

Ruby barked and barked. After a while I saw Mrs. Rose walking down the path, and Ruby went berserk barking and running around.

"Hello, dear," said Mrs. Rose, bending down to pet her. "You ready to meet your new family?"

Just then Christopher Sherer and his two brothers came tearing down the path, screaming, "Doggy Day! Doggy Day!"

Wait, Ruby was being adopted by . . . the Sherers? I remembered what Christopher had said at the Park, but I hadn't really put it together.

Mr. and Mrs. Sherer were trotting after the boys.

"Okay," said Mrs. Sherer. "Now, boys, we talked about this, right?"

The three boys stopped screaming. They sat down on the ground, crisscross applesauce style, and watched the dogs.

"Remember, a new puppy can get excited," said Mr. Sherer. "So we have to be very calm."

The boys nodded, not taking their eyes off Ruby.

"Ruby," said Mrs. Rose, squatting down, "meet your new family."

It was almost like Ruby understood, because she looked at the boys and went running over, wagging her tail. One by one she licked each boy's face as they laughed and tried to pet her. Then she stopped barking and curled up in Christopher's lap, resting her head on his knee.

"Well, will you look at that," said Dad.

"That looks like it was meant to be," said Mom, smiling.

Christopher was beaming. "This is my new puppy, Ruby!" he said proudly. "She's adopted."

Everyone looked at me.

"But it doesn't matter," said Christopher. "Because Mom says that it doesn't matter how you get your

Family Recipe

family. It just matters that you're a part of it."

I smiled. "That's exactly right, Christopher."

The boys were quietly taking turns petting Ruby, and she seemed to bask in the attention. It felt a little weird that she'd been such a handful for us but seemed right at home with the Sherers. But I couldn't be upset that she'd found the perfect family for her.

"Okay, slowly, gently," said Mr. Sherer.

The boys slowly got up. Ruby stood next to Christopher and looked up at him.

"Ready, Ruby?" asked Christopher.

Ruby barked, and Christopher looked delighted.

"Okay, gang," said Mrs. Sherer. "We are homeward bound!"

We all said goodbye to Ruby, even Kelsey, who petted her head and said, "I'm glad you will be loved. Just not by us."

We watched as the Sherers walked out of the park, with Ruby trotting calmly next to Christopher.

"Well, she didn't even look back, did she?" Mrs. Rose chuckled.

"That was a great match," said Dad.

"I have an eye for these things," said Mrs. Rose. "Okay, now for the next one."

DONUT DREAMS

We all looked at Rusty.

"Goodbye, Rusty," I said.

Jenna bent down and nuzzled him, and Kelsey stroked his back.

"If we ever get a dog, I hope it's one like you," said Kelsey.

"Welllll . . . ," said Dad. He looked at Mom.

"Getting a puppy isn't right for us," said Mom. "But an older dog like this is a good fit for our family. Rusty is about six, which isn't a puppy, but he still should have quite a few good years left in him."

"So," said Dad, "if you girls are willing, we can take Rusty home."

The three of us looked up.

"He's ours?" screeched Jenna.

"He's yours," said Mrs. Rose.

"We got a dog! We got a dog!" Kelsey was jumping up and down. Then she stopped. "Wait, do I have to clean up his poop?"

"You all have to take turns," said Dad. "That's part of the deal."

Kelsey grimaced but said, "Okay, good with the bad. I can do that."

"C'mon, boy," said Dad. "Let's go home."

Family Recipe

We thanked Mrs. Rose and walked toward the car. I heard Mrs. Rose say she'd bring over the paperwork for Mom and Dad to sign next week. Mom and Dad were holding hands. Jenna was holding Rusty's leash, and he was walking in between us. Our family had just gone from the five of us to the six of us, and it felt just right.

"I think I know what the best part of everyone's day is going to be!" said Mom.

"I know what the worst part is going to be if I have to walk Rusty tonight," said Kelsey. Rusty looked at her. "You know I love you anyway," she said.

I thought about our family and the fact that it had just grown a bit. Our family was a little crazy, a little loud, and a little messy. But it was also filled with a lot of love, and it usually dripped out in the best way. You could say it was perfect.

A Donut for Your Thoughts

Chapter One
The Dream Team

"Casey Peters to the rescue! Yasss!"

I hung up the phone and tossed it onto the bed, pumped the music up loud, and danced around my room.

It was Monday after school and I had nothing planned, so I was excited to get called in to work with my BFF, Lindsay Cooper, at her family's restaurant, which also happens to sell the most delicious donuts ever made.

Back in the day, Lindsay's grandparents, Grandpa and Nans Cooper, opened the Park View Table, which is now a booming family business in Bellgrove, Missouri. True to its name, it sits right across the street from and has a dashing view of, you guessed it, the park!

DONUT DREAMS

Between Nans's finesse in the kitchen and Grandpa's tight ship on the floor, the Park is the only restaurant in town worth talking about, with its legit menu and flawless service.

Nans initially started the Donut Dreams counter in the Park to stack enough dough (so to speak!) to send Lindsay's dad, their oldest child, to the university of his dreams. Unlike his brother and sister, who stayed close to home, Mike Cooper ended up going away to school in Chicago.

There, he fell in love with Lindsay's mom, Amy, and traveled to Europe with her. Amazingly, out of all the places they could have chosen to live in this whole wide world, they came right back to Bellgrove to put down roots and have kids—Lindsay and her younger brother, Skylar, aka. Sky.

Lindsay's dad took over Donut Dreams, and Lindsay's mom became an art teacher at Bellgrove Middle School until she passed away a few years ago.

My mom says it was Amy Cooper's choice to settle here instead of some big city or foreign land. Mom knows this because my mom and Lindsay's mom were the original BFFs! They even ended up having Lindsay and me at the same time, literally. Lindsay

A Donut for Your Thoughts

and I first mingled cries in the hospital, since we were born one day apart. Our oldest photo together is with our moms in the hospital nursery. And the rest is history.

My mom loves to tell me how Lindsay and I used to stare at each other in the hospital and smile and coo to each other. She just assumed we were just friendly babies, but we never did that with anyone else.

Then a few weeks after we both were home with our families, my mom brought me over to Lindsay's house for a visit. She says the minute we saw each other again, we reached out for each other and cooed and giggled and laughed. True BFFs from the start!

I guess Lindsay's mom actually preferred the charmed small-town life that Lindsay and others hope to escape. I totally understand why Lindsay wants out—going to school with the same kids since kindergarten, everyone is always in your business, that sort of thing.

But small-town life also has its perks. Not only delectable donuts, but also this feeling of safety and being known by everyone you see.

The truth is, Donut Dreams is more than just a pretty name for a donut spot. People patiently wait in line here just to sink their teeth into the pillowy sweetness of a banana cream or elderberry jelly donut.

Without Nans's bright idea, Lindsay's parents would never have met in Chicago, which means my best friend wouldn't be my best friend, because Lindsay wouldn't even be a thing in my life.

And where, oh where, would I be without Lindsay Cooper?

I feel honored to be the only non-family member who works at the Park on days like today, when one of Lindsay's cousins has a cold or a big exam.

All of Lindsay's aunts, uncles, and cousins are employees at the restaurant. The only family member of hers who isn't recruited to work at the restaurant is her brother Skylar, aka. Sky, who's nine.

I pranced over to my dresser and pulled out my yellow Donut Dreams T-shirt, the back of which read THE DREAM TEAM. Thankfully, I keep my room pretty neat—except for the closet and under the bed, that is—so I wasn't tripping over stuff looking for my stretchy jeans when my mom popped into my room carrying a load of clean laundry.

My mom is the assistant principal of Bellgrove Middle School, where I just started going this year.

A Donut for Your Thoughts

Ever since she got her back-to-school hairdo, I admired how her reddish-brown ringlets framed her perfect round face.

"Casey, it sounds like New Year's Eve in here!" she was shouting. "What's going on?"

I lowered the music. "They need my help at Donut Dreams today," I said. "Is it okay if I work for a few hours, Mom? Pleeeease?"

I already knew what the answer would be. As long as I ace my schoolwork and keep my room somewhat tidy, any opportunity I have to be responsible is all right with Laurie Peters.

"I hope you'll always be this enthusiastic about work," Mom said with a laugh. "Go ahead and make some dollars . . . not eat empty calories!"

Mom knows me to a T. Lindsay and I always manage to sneak in a donut or two when no one's looking.

"Yes!" I cheered, my mouth already watering.

Mom left my room, and I went back to zipping around in search of my comfiest jeans to wear (why is it that even though my room is pretty neat, I can never find what I want to wear when I want to wear it?).

DONUT DREAMS

I finally found them and paired them with the bright Donut Dreams shirt that makes me feel like a superhero whenever I slip it over my head.

Even though I see Lindsay all the time, it was still exciting to work with my BFF. Plus, every time I was at Donut Dreams, I felt inspired.

Let's just say, there's something dreamy about spending time in a place so creative and colorful!

Chapter Two
First Crush?

"Casey, are you ready?" Mom called from downstairs minutes later.

The car keys jingled as she lifted them from the hook by the front door.

I hurriedly swept up my hair into a messy bun, slipped my phone into my back pocket, and galloped down the stairs, grinning from ear to ear.

On the way to the Park, my thoughts drifted to Matt Machado. Matt is a friend I made at sleepaway camp this summer. Ever since I came home from camp, he's never been too far from my mind.

Before meeting him, I can't say I was really into boys. I'm still not, but Matt's different. He isn't lame like the other boys at camp or the Bellgrove boys I've been ignoring since kindergarten. We actually have real stuff in common, not just liking the same candy or music or whatever.

For instance, we're both biracial, except his mom's black and his dad's white, and my parents are the opposite. Before meeting Matt, the only other biracial person I knew was my older sister, Gabby, but she doesn't count.

I have friends at camp that I've known from years of going there, but Matt was new this summer and didn't know anybody until we met at orientation on the first day, during one of those corny icebreaker activities.

We became camp BFFs, which made some of my other camp friends jealous, because just like with Lindsay, once we clicked, I wanted to spend every spare moment with Matt.

We would find each other during breakfast and eat together before jetting off to our different activities. Then we'd loop back in for lunch before kayaking together on the lake and then we'd have dinner. Sometimes we'd end our days at the campfire. At camp we were each other's worlds.

After being two peas in a pod all summer, it was

A Donut for Your Thoughts

strange not being in each other's business all day, every day.

We've texted back and forth a few times, but there's no rhythm to it. And whenever he does text back, sometimes days later, it's usually a one-word response.

Ugh. Back to reality, I guess. Whatever.

Since I was in such a good mood and everything, I thought about texting him something funny to help him remember the jokes we shared . . . in case he forgot.

Matt thought I was hilarious and got 95 percent of my jokes. I hadn't realized I could have such a wicked sense of humor with anyone else besides Lindsay.

I stared into my phone and thought about what to text.

I must say, it's harder to plan on being funny than to just be funny naturally, in the moment. I couldn't think of anything to say and lost track of time.

I must have been staring into the distance, not saying anything, for too long because Mom took notice.

"With Lindsay hard at work, I wonder who else could have you so deep thought," Mom said.

DONUT DREAMS

She peeled her eyes from the road for an instant to glance down at the blinking cursor on my phone.

Mom never misses a beat, especially when it comes to me. She knows Lindsay is the only person that I text 24/7, and there's a no-texting rule for all workers at the Park.

I hadn't breathed Matt's name to anyone besides Lindsay. The only reason Mom would know that Matt existed was if she noticed his picture in my room on the bulletin board, but she never asked me anything about him.

"Nobody special," I answered, my face warming.

I fired off some silly cat meme to Matt and put my phone away.

But oh, Matt was special. He was funny, smart, mysterious, and certifiable eye candy.

I never had a reason to talk to my mom about a boy before, and even now, I wasn't sure if there was anything to talk about besides our kayaking and campfire coziness.

And that wasn't something to bring up to your assistant principal mom . . . or was it?

Thankfully, we arrived at the restaurant before Mom could dig any deeper.

A Donut for Your Thoughts

"Have a good afternoon working hard," Mom said, beaming with pride.

"Thanks, Mom. And I'll try to save room for dinner after I've sampled every kind of donut in the case!"

I let out a wicked laugh, leaped out of the car, and shut the door before she could open her mouth to protest.

Chapter Three
Picture Perfect

"There she is!" said Lindsay's grandfather when he spotted me breezing through the doors of the Park.

I made a beeline for the podium near the entrance, where Grandpa Coop greets his hungry customers and oversees the floor to make sure everything is sanitary and moves smoothly. When I got to him, I gave him a big hug.

"How's my honorary grandchild?" he asked.

I adore everything about Lindsay's grandfather, like he's my own. I love how he makes such intense eye contact with every person he speaks to, and how he makes it a point to greet everyone who enters the restaurant. He has this way of making everyone feel special and seen. I also love his crinkly eyes and how

A Donut for Your Thoughts

the lines in his face tell a story of who he is—someone who likes to laugh as hard as he likes to work.

I even love how he manages the Park with his "iron fist, sunny glove" style. Along with the delicious food, the restaurant's level of friendly professionalism is key to its success. Grandpa Coop is strict about certain things—okay, well, everything. Counter crumbs and sauce smears make him cranky, and his radar for fake smiles from his staff is crazy accurate.

He's no-nonsense about the rules, but never unpleasant. I don't know how he does it. Even when he throws us his signature side-eye for having our phone in hand at work, or reminds us to wipe a teeny smudge we missed off the glass display, no one ever feels like they're being bossed around.

"Thank you for coming on such short notice to save the day," he cheered.

Grandpa Coop always has this way of making me feel like a vital part of the restaurant.

"Now go rescue your other half behind the donut counter!" he said.

Clearly, my BFF needed some rescuing, because she was swamped.

After going into the back to wash my hands,

DONUT DREAMS

clock in, put on an apron, and glance at the inventory, I raced over to the Donut Dreams counter.

Lindsay looked a bit overwhelmed as she struggled to serve the first wave of the elementary school crowd, three squealing Girl Scouts. Her gloved hand hovered over a different donut each time the girls changed their minds. By the look on Lindsay's face, this had been going on for some time.

"The pink one with sprinkles . . . no, wait. The chocolate one. No, wait! Maybe the glazed. Ooh, I don't know which one I want!" said one of the girls.

Lindsay stood there silently, but knowing her, especially after a full day at school, she was probably cranky and losing her patience.

I put on my best smile and swooped in to join her behind the counter.

"Can I make a suggestion?" I asked. "How about lemon cream? It's like eating two kinds of donuts with every bite. It's so yummy—sweet and tangy at the same time."

"Ooh, that sounds . . . dreamy!" one girl said, making the others giggle. "Give me that one!"

"Make it two! Make it three!" the others chimed in, raising their hands.

A Donut for Your Thoughts

Lindsay smiled at me gratefully as she put the donuts in the bag I opened for her and rang up their order. After the girls left with their bag of donuts, she high-fived me.

"You're a lifesaver!" Lindsay said. "What made you suggest the lemon cream?"

I shrugged.

"I looked at the inventory and noticed we had a lot of lemon donuts. Those girls obviously didn't know what they wanted, so I just gave them a push in the lemon donut direction," I said.

"Genius!" Lindsay said. "They were cute, but a couple more minutes and I would have paid for their donuts and pushed them in the 'get out now' direction!"

I laughed at the thought of Lindsay doing such a thing and tried to imagine Grandpa Coop's stern expression lasting for more than ten seconds. It made me wonder if he would ever fire one of his grandchildren for getting cranky with a customer.

I almost jumped when my phone buzzed in my back pocket, which, oops, was actually supposed to be stowed under the counter during my shift. It was just a text alert, but my heart was racing.

I looked around to make sure that Grandpa Coop's

eagle eyes weren't focused in my direction and took a quick peek.

Sigh. My heart slowed in its tracks. It was just my mom, trying to be funny.

> You'll want to keep your stomach empty for what's cooking. Now put your phone under that counter and get back to work!

That's my mom, all right. She always has to have the last word.

I sighed again, but a little part of me wondered what yummy thing Mom was making for dinner as I put my phone away.

"Don't worry, he didn't see you," Lindsay told me, eyeing Grandpa Coop.

One thing I love about our friendship is how we always have each other's backs.

"Thanks," I said.

I put my phone next to hers. When I looked up again, Lindsay was studying me.

"Whoever you're texting with must be mighty

A Donut for Your Thoughts

important to risk a scolding from Grandpa," she said with a giggle. "And I'm right here! Who could be more important than me?"

"No one is more important than you," I assured her. "It's just ... well ..."

"Come on ... spit it out," Lindsay said.

She stared at me while I busied myself wiping the already spotless display glass.

Lindsay knows all too well how embarrassed I get by my own feelings—big or small—and I can't stand to be embarrassed.

Maybe that's why it's so difficult for me to say how I really feel. Something I like about Lindsay's family is how open and messy they are with each other sometimes, but it's clear that the love is always there.

"Before I got here I sent my friend Matt a text, and I was kind of hoping this was him texting back. But it wasn't," I explained.

Okay, that wasn't so bad.

"Ohhhh, I see," Lindsay said.

She continued to look at me carefully. "So what's the deal with you guys?"

"There is no 'deal,'" I said.

DONUT DREAMS

I could feel the temperature of my cheeks shoot up a few degrees.

"Uh-huh," she said, clearly not convinced.

"We're just good friends, and I sent him something I thought he'd think was funny, and I'm just . . ." I trailed off.

"Wondering if he thought it was funny?" Lindsay finished my sentence for me.

"Yes," I said. "That's all."

But what I didn't say was that every time I get a text, my heart starts pounding fast until I see who sent it. And when it's not him, I start to feel really sad and I'm not even sure why, because he's not even my boyfriend.

Why I couldn't say this to Lindsay, I wasn't sure. Something felt different with us ever since I got back from sleepaway camp.

I couldn't figure out what it was just yet. We were usually so in sync with each other. But I guess spending some time apart over the summer and going to middle school might have changed things a bit.

It's true that I had no phone or Internet access and so couldn't contact Lindsay all summer, but we're used to that now. We've been out of communication

A Donut for Your Thoughts

for the past few years when I started going away to camp.

This time I felt different, more than ever before. Even though Lindsay got her first job this summer at Donut Dreams, she was the same old Lindsay that I've always adored. I wasn't sure if she could say the same for me, however.

"So how are you liking middle school so far?" Lindsay asked, changing the subject.

I breathed a sigh of relief, though something in Lindsay's face told me this conversation was far from over.

My best friend always knew when I needed a change of subject, but she never forgot what we'd be talking about.

"Can't say yet," I said slowly. "But it's been okay so far, I guess."

This was our first year at Bellgrove, where Lindsay's mom taught art for years until she died. To be honest, I wasn't all that enthused about attending the school where my mom is the assistant principal.

Okay, I was mortified! I didn't want to be insensitive though and talk about the extent of this with Lindsay, who I'm sure would give anything to see her mom in the halls on the regular.

Now the most visible trace of her mom is a colorful and kind of chaotic mural in the hallway that her students painted in her memory. Basically, the students painted what came to their minds, so the mural was a hodgepodge of storms, rainbows, and wildflowers.

I don't know what the storms and rainbows were about, but Lindsay's mom was a lover of all flowers. Mrs. Cooper was an amazing artist, mostly known for her paintings. She's the reason I fell in love with art.

At Lindsay's house, on one wall of her art studio are paintings of the flowers that she so loved. On the opposite wall are my favorites, these black-and-white sketches of her family. There are some sketches of Lindsay and Sky, and there are also a couple of sketches of Lindsay's dad, too, with a grin as wide as the horizon, as wide as Grandpa Coop's.

I always thought it was so cool that Lindsay had a mom who could draw so beautifully, and how she could take a simple pencil and create such a realistic portrayal of someone she loved. She made it look so simple; with just a few strokes of her hand, she'd make a blank sheet of paper come to life.

A Donut for Your Thoughts

Until I was about six, I was convinced it was magic. Sometimes her drawings looked so real I imagined that they could start talking or walking off pages. Lindsay's amazing mom had a way of making someone's personality and color lift off the page, without using a single drop of paint.

I would watch her make sketches, wishing I could do that one day. It's a wish that has never quite faded like many things do over time.

There was a lull in traffic at the Donut Dreams counter. Grandpa Coop always wanted us to look busy so I straightened the already perfectly straight donuts.

"Who are your favorite teachers so far?" Lindsay asked, wiping invisible crumbs and sprinkles off the spotless counter.

"Ms. Reyes actually makes math fun," I answered. "And our art teacher, Mr. Franklin, was really encouraging when I asked him about doing sketches from my photographs."

"Wait. What sketches? What photographs?" Lindsay asked.

"Oh! I took a lot of photos while I was at summer camp. It was really beautiful there. The trees, the lake, the campfire at night." *Matt's smile!* "Then I started making sketches of the photographs. Now I'm trying to—"

"Oh. I didn't realize you liked making art so much," Lindsay said, cutting me off.

Her voice carried this strange tone that I'd never heard from her before.

"Well, I'm no Amy Cooper," I said. "But your mom definitely inspired me to take up sketching. Then at camp I took a still-life class that taught me so much."

I continued, "So when Mr. Franklin asked us what we'd like to sketch for our first assignment, I showed him my photos and asked if I could do a sketch based on one of my pictures, and he said definitely! He said my photography showed talent."

"Hmm," Lindsay said.

She looked genuinely confused. "I didn't know it took talent to snap a photo. I just click and send."

I wanted to say, *Um, hello. Photography is a legit career. It takes knowledge, talent, and practice to become successful.*

"Well, it's more than snapping a photo, at least for me," I said instead. "It takes creativity and attention to detail. You need to make sure the lighting is good, that your subject is in focus, that it's visually appealing—"

A Donut for Your Thoughts

"Visually appealing?" Lindsay repeated.

She rolled her eyes. "You're starting to sound like Mr. Franklin!"

It made me uneasy being compared to our art teacher in such a mean way.

I mean, I wasn't trying to sound like an expert or anything, I was just sharing what little I knew.

Besides with Lindsay being the daughter of an artist, I wasn't sure why she was acting so clueless all of a sudden.

"You know . . . um, you need to make sure that your photo isn't too busy—like, remember that time I took a photo of you in your new dress? You were standing in your room, and there were some books and clothes on the floor, and I pushed them out of the way? I just wanted the focus to be on you—so I simplified the photo," I explained.

"Simplified the photo, wow. I never knew you were so . . . artsy," Lindsay said.

She looked at me with a look I'd never seen before, like she felt betrayed or something, like she hardly knew me at all.

Then she shrugged. "Well, like I said, I just click and send."

DONUT DREAMS

I didn't have anything nice to say, so I bit my lip and quietly went on wiping the glass of the donut case. I forced down the lump that had formed in my throat. It actually made me sad that my best friend in the world wasn't really relating to this new and exciting part of my life.

I was glad for the next wave of donut lovers flowing in, since chatting it up with Lindsay at the workplace was not turning out to be as fun as I'd hoped.

Chapter Four
Let Go, Let Flow

That night at the dinner table, my dad was in a super good mood.

As the town doctor, he often comes home from the clinic with deep creases in his forehead that not even an iron could smooth out. Here was a man with the weight of our town's health and well-being on his shoulders.

But tonight he looked years younger. He beamed at Mom as she placed a large bowl of homemade pasta with marinara sauce and a bowl of shredded parm on the table.

I loved the way he looked in that moment, smiling like a boy with no cares in the world.

"Remember my John Doe?" Dad asked as he

spooned out a mountain of pasta into his bowl to satisfy his huge appetite from skipping lunches.

He was talking about one of his recent patients, who'd been hit by a car. Dad's been talking about this poor guy for days.

"We were able to save his leg after all," he told us.

Dad took a confidentiality oath, so he can't tell us who his patients actually are.

But between the vividness of his stories and the smallness of our town, it's easy to put two and two together. Because inevitably, a week from now, "John Doe No Mo" will come hobbling up at the Park or the supermarket with a brand-spanking-new leg cast. A lot of these mystery patients actually come up to me and gush about how much my dad helped them.

I was starting to feel squeamish just thinking about lost limbs and tried to change the subject.

"Mom, this marinara sauce is on point," I said.

"That's great news!" Mom said. She wasn't talking to me, though, but to our dad. "I know you've been worried sick."

"Completely." Dad sighed and then his eyes lit up. "But get this ... the artery wasn't completely severed, so we were able to connect the healthy tissue to—"

A Donut for Your Thoughts

"DAD!" Gabby and I shrieked.

"What?" Dad asked, like he genuinely had no clue what our problem was.

"We're eating pasta—" I started.

"With red sauce—" Gabby added.

"And you're talking about severed arteries," I said.

"It's über-interesting, Pops, but not dinnertime conversation!" Gabby scolded.

Gabby and I are seven years apart and nothing alike, but we have definitely formed a united front when it comes to not hearing about Dad's surgical adventures at the dinner table. Personally, the stories make me queasy, even when I'm not sending food down the hatch.

Gabby, an aspiring doctor, loves talking shop; she just doesn't think that the table is the correct place for it. Gabby has this thing for polite dinnertime conversation.

As for the extremely gruesome tales of Dad's emergency-room experiences, Mom loves his stories, all day, every day. Why they don't just save the gore for when they are alone is a mystery to me.

"I find your surgeries fascinating," Mom said to him. "And I'm so glad Mr. McKin—I mean, um, John

Doe will be strutting out of the hospital on both legs. That's the most important thing, that he's getting a renewed lease on his life and limb. Bravo, Dr. Peters!"

By the look on Mom's face, she wanted to kiss him, I could tell. Instead she took in another forkful of penne pasta.

But just before her face changed, I grinned at my assistant principal mom smiling like a high school girl crushing on my brainiac dad. I imagined it's how she must have looked when they met at a party all those years ago.

Soon enough, she slipped back into assistant principal mom mode and changed subjects almost as smoothly as Lindsay.

"Gabby, how was your day?" she asked.

"It was okay," Gabby said, jumping right in. "I don't think I stretched enough before dance. I trained hard today too. My legs feel kind of sore."

I don't know how Gabby balances her passion for dance with the demands of college. She was a straight A student all through high school.

On every report card, I usually get a B or two, but she gets mostly As.

Really and truly, my grades are still higher than

most of my friends, but Gabby already set the bar in our household, so I always catch shade from Mom on report card day.

"Ice packs and a warm salt bath for sore muscles," Dad suggested, between bites.

"I've told you a million times you need to warm up before class. You could strain something or pull a muscle—" Mom started.

"Don't I know it," Gabby agreed, cutting her off.

She's a master at shutting Mom down before she can go too far.

It would probably take me another few years to develop that superpower.

"I just get so impatient with stretching. It's like I can't wait to get out there on the dance floor. But I've learned my lesson . . . again. Okay, enough about me! How was your day, Casey?"

"It was decent," I said. "My highlight was getting to work at Donut Dreams after school, which means I made more money to put toward a new camera lens and some art supplies."

"What happened to the lens that came with the camera?" Dad asked.

"It didn't break, did it?" asked Mom.

"Nothing happened to the stock lens," I assured them. "Most photographers have several. Some lenses are better for shooting up close, and others, like the wide-angle, are great for capturing more scenic pictures."

Dad nodded, looking sort of impressed.

Mom narrowed her eyes.

"Ooh, big-shot photographer!" Gabby cheered.

I shushed her and kicked her foot under the table, trying not to smile through chews.

When it comes to art, I guess I'm what you would call a perfectionist, which is not a characteristic of mine in other areas of my life.

For years, I've been pretty private with my artwork because I didn't think it was really good enough to show anyone. But since we've grown up in the same house and everything, Gabby has caught more glimpses of my failed artwork than anyone.

Over the years, she would come visit my room randomly and see one of my clumsy drawings, which I would later feed to the paper shredder in Mom's office downstairs.

I wasn't one for leaving a paper trail of my failures. The only ones I kept were the ones that didn't make

A Donut for Your Thoughts

me cringe, but even some of those weren't very good.

I guess I could see why Lindsay was surprised by my passion for art.

My camp's art class was life-changing. I mean, don't get me wrong, it wasn't like I turned into Claude Monet overnight or anything like that (he was Lindsay's mom's fave), but that class made me see how good I already was with no formal training.

With a few weeks of practicing every day, my sketches began to take on a whole new life.

Okay, I don't want to brag, but they went through the roof! Since then, I've been focused on getting better and better.

Even though Dad and Gabby were concentrating on their food, I could tell that Mom hadn't had her full say yet.

Until I started getting straight As like Gabby, she would not be satisfied with a single one of my report cards.

"I've never heard you sound this knowledgeable about your core subjects," Mom said.

Core subjects. Gosh.

These days, Lindsay and my mom were starting to have more in common than I ever thought possible, with these jabs at my inner artist. Couldn't they just be happy that I was finding myself?

"I'm doing good in all my classes, Mom," I assured her, keeping my tone light.

"But I'm sure you already know that."

Seriously. Surely Mom was behind the scenes, checking in with my teachers on the regular. Not in an overbearing way like she was here at home, but in brief exchanges by the coffee machine in the staff lounge, casually asking about me between sips.

"Well, I just want to make sure you're doing well in what you're supposed to be studying, that is, your academics, and not just . . . recreational subjects." Mom stressed this with a casual brush of her hand.

"I heard that!" said Dad, who never goes against Mom.

"Low blow, Mom," murmured Gabby.

When Mom shot her a look, she zipped her lips, but not her innocent grin.

Leave it to Gabby to tell it like it is, and somehow make it out intact without a five-point lecture from our mom. Meanwhile, Mom and I always managed to lock horns, especially these days. And I was struggling to fix a problem of mine. It had to do with

A Donut for Your Thoughts

my emotions, which tend to overheat and cause me to either blow up or shut down.

When someone gets me heated—usually Mom, who lives under my skin—I don't say anything at first, and I let my feelings pile up until one day they all topple out of my mouth in one irreversible mess.

Up until the last year or so, I was much worse off because there was no buildup; I would just turn weepy or go defensive. I was like a time bomb that went off before it even started ticking.

Good thing "ugly-cry-face Casey" hardly shows up, thanks in part to Gabby's coaching. Gabby's helped me get to this point where I can sometimes respond to our mother by just keeping quiet, rather than fighting with her about everything.

Now Gabby's "cope with Mom" techniques are starting to become a little more second nature to me. Like in this case, where Mom ruffled my feathers during polite dinner conversation, the best tool was to focus on my breathing and nothing else.

I took a deep breath and counted to four on the inhale, four on the exhale. It really did kind of help. I let Mom have the last word and just concentrated on breathing and digging into my pasta, which now unfortunately was cold and tasted like cardboard, by the way.

I glanced at Gabby, who was beaming at me like a proud parent as she mouthed, *Woo-sah.*

If I wasn't so annoyed at Mom, I would have had a laugh attack just remembering how Gabby liked to sit on her bed, cross-legged and eyes closed, pinching together her thumbs and index fingers on each hand in a "calm yogi" stance as she exhaled, "Woo-sah!"

I repeated Gabby's mantra in my head, *Let go, let flow.* I was still heated, but I guess you could call it taming my dragon.

Next, Gabby is going to teach me techniques for expressing my hurt or sadness or whatever without getting all tongue-tied and emotional. Like Gabby says, I could be saying something completely valid, but if I'm ugly crying then all the other person will hear is my sadness instead of what I'm actually saying. She has a point there.

I loved watching Gabby, Ms. "It's Not What You Say, But How You Say It" play our parents. She was always showing me that you can say basically anything with the right tone and word choice and actually come out on top!

A Donut for Your Thoughts

I told Gabby she needed to write a book with her expertise. Whether she ends up becoming a bestselling author, a prima ballerina, a doctor, or all three, the world is Gabby's oyster. Whatever she decides to do with her life, our parents will be proud.

I was secretly hoping to make art my career, but maybe it was best to keep that on the hush for just a while longer.

Ugh. First Lindsay and now Mom doesn't understand or appreciate what I want to do with my life.

Chapter Five
Boundaries

The next day at school, I hustled into the cafeteria and plopped down into my usual space at the lunch table next to Lindsay. I was a little late after talking with Mr. Franklin after art class.

Our friend Michelle sat across from us in her wheelchair. I waved at Lindsay's cousin Kelsey, who sat at the next table over with her field hockey and soccer friends.

I glanced over at Michelle's food. She was already scarfing down her ever mysterious vegan lunch.

Lindsay waited for me as usual to unveil hers in our game of lunch telepathy.

"What took you so long?" Lindsay said when I sat down.

A Donut for Your Thoughts

I shrugged.

"Fine. You guess first," she said.

"Fine," I said, looking at her wrapped meal and then deeply into her eyes. "Turkey and dijonnaise mustard on whole wheat?"

Lindsay unwrapped her sandwich to reveal . . . turkey dijonnaise on whole wheat!

"Yes!" I air-guitared. "Your turn."

"Hmm . . . it's a Tuesday, so, let's say . . . your mom's amazing chicken salad on rye?" she guessed.

"Ding ding ding!"

We giggled like dorks as I unwrapped my lunch and we swapped sandwich halves.

I could see Kelsey grinning and rolling her eyes at this pastime we've managed to keep up since kindergarten.

"So did you ever hear back from Matt?" Lindsay asked.

I nodded. "LOL," I said.

"LOL?" Lindsay repeated, confused.

"Yep. 'LOL'—that's all he texted back," I said.

Lindsay shrugged and took a bite of her turkey sandwich. She always liked to save my mom's chicken salad sandwich for last.

"What?" I asked.

"Well, you said you sent him a funny text. So . . . LOL is a perfectly legit response."

"I guess," I said, a little dejected.

Then why did I feel rejected? Lindsay didn't know Matt, so I didn't expect her to get it.

But after getting to be such good friends with this cool boy at camp, I just wished he texted more than three letters at a time. Not that I was expecting a whole paragraph or anything, but I wanted at least some tiny window into his life.

Instead I hadn't been able to inspire a full sentence out of him since we left camp. He wasn't exactly ignoring me; he was just being so super casual. Almost like I meant nothing to him, even though I knew that wasn't true.

Or did I? A familiar lump started rising in my throat, the same lump I've learned to swallow for years.

I turned to Michelle. "Hey, Michelle, are you going to the field hockey game this Saturday?"

Michelle nodded happily. "I need to take some photos for the school website."

"Maybe I'll join you," I said. "I think it would be

A Donut for Your Thoughts

fun to sketch some of the players in action."

"Hold up," Lindsay said. "I thought you were on still objects. When did you graduate to sketching people... in motion?"

I could tell there was a little shade in her tone, like she didn't think I could do it.

"You don't learn unless you try," I said, leaving it at that.

Lindsay gave me a long look, then opened her mouth a bit like she was going to say something else. But she stopped herself and instead shrugged and took another bite of her sandwich.

I didn't get into the deep conversation I'd had with Matt at our last campfire night before camp ended. Or the countless hours I've started to spend lately in my room obsessing over every feature of my photography subjects, studying anatomy and sketching different body parts over and over, eyes, legs, collarbones.

At first, my subjects looked like aliens with gangly arms and oversize heads. Now my human sketches were finally starting to look amazingly... human.

I was just about to bite into Lindsay's turkey sandwich when I heard a familiar voice behind me.

"So what do we have here?"

I didn't have to turn around to know whose voice that was. My face went hot.

"Hi, girls. Hey, honey," my mom said.

"Hi, Assistant Principal Peters," said Michelle.

"Hiya, Mrs. Peters!" Lindsay called out.

"Hi . . . uh," I said, still not sure what to call her.

"I see you girls are still sharing your lunches. I'm sorry to rain on your parade, but your pastime of swapping food is not permitted at Bellgrove Middle School. With so many food allergies going around these days, school administrators decided it's better to be safe than sorry. As you may remember, this was discussed at orientation."

"Oh, I forgot all about that," said Lindsay.

"But we aren't allergic to anything!" I protested, surprising myself with my own loudness.

One . . . two . . . three . . . four . . . inhale. One . . . two . . . three . . . four . . . exhale.

"It's in the school handbook, Casey. There are no exceptions," Mom said with one of her sharp looks that let me know she meant business.

With that, Lindsay took my half of her sandwich from me, gave me back my half, and continued eating.

A Donut for Your Thoughts

But I was furious.

"But Mom!" I wailed.

Some boys at a nearby table turned and laughed.

"Rules are rules," Mom said, before walking away.

"It's okay, Case," said Lindsay.

She patted my shoulder and struck up a conversation with Michelle when she saw I wasn't saying anything.

Fuming, I ate in silence for the rest of lunch period.

When lunchtime was over and I stood up, the boys at the next table mimicked, "But Mom! Mom!"

I ignored them, wondering how I was going to draw some boundaries at school between me and my assistant principal mom. Because this wasn't going to work.

Ugh. This sort of thing was everything I'd ever feared. I couldn't wait for this day to be over.

Chapter Six
Boys Are Clueless!

Later that night, after I finished all my homework, I was alone in my room, staring at my cell phone like all the answers to my questions were locked inside.

Mostly, I was thinking about Matt.

What's he doing right now?

Is his home life crazy or what?

Is there something or someone new taking up all his time?

Another girl, maybe?

Doesn't he miss me ... even a little bit?

I had sent him a sketch of the campfire at camp that afternoon, hoping that it would warm his heart and maybe jog his memory of the long talk we had in front of it.

A Donut for Your Thoughts

Even though I hardly heard from Matt, I was constantly being reminded of him. I mean, I couldn't even walk past a pack of marshmallows in the grocery aisle without some memory awakening. Like the night he toasted marshmallows for me by the bonfire. He didn't even like marshmallows, but he knew I loved them.

"I'll cook, you eat," he said, roasting each one to crispy perfection before handing off the stick to me.

I also remembered the night he inspired this fire drawing of mine. The first thing I noticed about him at orientation was a black notebook he was carrying around. It reminded me of my own trusty sketchbook. In fact, almost every time I saw him, he was holding that black notebook.

After weeks of friendship, I finally had the courage to ask him what was inside it. The bonfire was blazing that night. It was mesmerizing, how the flames licked the night sky.

"Oh, this?" he said. "I'm just writing the story of my life."

I didn't know what I'd been expecting, but not that. I laughed, and his face changed into a defensive mask.

Matt had a bit of a chip on his shoulder, and I kind of liked this about him, because I did too.

"What's so funny about writing down some of the details of what happens in my life?" he asked.

"Sorry, I didn't mean to laugh at your hobby. I think it's actually kinda cool," I said, and I meant it.

"First of all, it's not a hobby, and I'm not doing it to be cool. I'm doing it to stay sane," he said. Then he looked at my sketchbook. "So…what you got going on over there?" he asked.

"I hear you," I said. "Meet my therapist, Ms. Sketchbook."

Matt laughed and flashed a sly grin.

"Can I get a peek? Come on! Let's swap notebooks," he suggested.

That stopped me in my tracks. I'd never shown anyone my notebook before, not even Lindsay.

"Okay, but seriously just for a minute!" I said.

It was going to feel like showing someone my heart and soul, but at the same time I was dying to get a peek into this boy's world.

"Okay, bet," said Matt. "Book swap, go."

Opening Matt's writing notebook felt like falling into a Netflix series. His handwriting was really hard

A Donut for Your Thoughts

to read, so I had to squint a lot, and I didn't always know who or what he was talking about, but in that endless minute I was shocked to learn that a boy my age could go through so much and have so many feelings.

I was amazed by how many pages he filled with up with life stuff. My life was nowhere near as interesting. I wondered if I would ever be added to his pages, if I would ever be a supporting character.

After a minute we traded books again.

"So what did you learn about me?" he asked.

His face looked almost . . . nervous.

"That I'll need a magnifying glass to decode that chicken scratch of yours!" I blurted.

He laughed, looking relieved.

"You know," he said, watching me in a new light, "I'd secretly guessed that you were really good at something. I was right."

"Oh, you're just saying that," I said.

"Hey, if your drawings weren't amazing, I wouldn't say anything. But they are just that good," he said. "What inspires you?"

"Photographs," I said. "I draw off photographs that I take of everyday things."

"That's cool," he said. "Hey. Have you ever frozen a memory in your mind? When I write, I paint the memories with words. Sometimes I want to explain a scene exactly as I remember it, like how crooked someone's smile looked, or how wild the sunset was the day my uncle died. Description is not my strong point, but I'm getting better at it.

"I bet you could do something similar for your drawings. Then you wouldn't need photographs as inspiration."

"How do you . . . freeze a memory?" I asked.

"Well, what I've had to learn to do is basically pay attention to everything!" Matt said with a laugh. "And every now and again an image will come my way and I just know it's something that I'll want to remember for the rest of my life.

"That's when I take a mental picture. I look at it with my full concentration, tuning out everything else around me. I just focus and snap the picture. Then I keep remembering it over and over again. That's how it begins to freeze."

"Wow" was all I could say.

This sounded complicated, but I wanted to give it a try.

A Donut for Your Thoughts

"Okay, let's make that our homework from camp. Let's choose something from this scene to take a mental picture of to draw or write about. Deal?"

"Deal," I said.

So for the rest of our time by the fire, I tuned out everyone else around us, since some of the remaining campers were still milling about in groups and clusters, roasting marshmallows and the like.

My eyes kept going back and forth between the fire and Matt, the fire and Matt, wondering which mental picture would come out the clearest.

Fast-forward to this afternoon, weeks later, back in Bellgrove, in the grocery store with Mom. I came across a bag of marshmallows and of course thought of him.

I sent Matt a sketch of the campfire when I got home and texted him.

> Remember this? You cook, I'll eat.

It took him hours to respond.

> Coolio.

He's truly the king of one-word responses.

What irked me the most was that I knew Matt could write. When I looked at his notebook, I could tell he noticed details most people didn't.

So how could a boy who knows how to capture a moment so perfectly with his words, not have anything perfect to write back to me?

I couldn't help but feel that there was some kind of miscommunication happening. Just like with everyone else in my life.

I was scrolling through our old texts when Gabby breezed into my room, holding up two dresses. She had just come home from dance practice, looking so carefree and happy. I took a mental picture.

As a dancer, Gabby's bun game was always on point, and her long neck didn't hurt that elegant dancer image. Since our white mom had curly hair and our black dad had straight hair, our hair texture was destined to have an identity crisis. Most days, I couldn't put my hair into a neat bun to save my life, so I resigned myself to making the messy bun work for me.

"Okay, which one?" she asked, holding up the dresses. "For the party this weekend."

A Donut for Your Thoughts

One dress was a deep sapphire blue with an empire waist, and the other one was classic black with an asymmetrical hem.

Something I appreciate about my older sister is how much she appreciates my fashion sense! My mood lightened as I envisioned my sister at the party in each dress.

Though Gabby can never go wrong with black, I preferred the way the sapphire blue brought out the deep brown tones in her skin. I decided not to tell her this, because Gabby feels some kind of way about being the darkest girl in every classroom and at every party. I actually admire Gabby's mocha skin, and she just happens to be the most beautiful girl anywhere she goes. Some guys get it, and some don't.

"I'd say go with the blue," I said. "I like them both, but unless you wear a lot of funky accessories with the black, it might seem a little too dressy, like you're trying too hard."

Gabby studied both dresses for a moment, then nodded at me.

"You're right—as usual. Blue it is! Thanks."

She was about to leave when she took another look at my face.

DONUT DREAMS

"You okay?" she asked.

I glanced at my phone again and sighed.

Gabby was no stranger to the universe of boys. They've been giving her grief for a long time. This made her super easy to talk to about this stuff.

"Are all boys clueless?" I asked.

Gabby laughed.

"Pretty much," she said. "Why do you ask? Is there one actual boy making your life miserable?"

I nodded. "My friend Matt from camp. When we were together, everything was so great. He's cool and funny and we shared things. But since I've been home, I've gotten exactly three texts from him in response to my reach-outs. And they were exactly one word each. If you consider LOL a word."

"Please tell me you didn't torture him with any cat memes," Gabby said.

I lowered my eyes.

"I couldn't help it, it's a reflex."

"You and your BFF are the only people on this side of the planet who think those are actually funny," Gabby pointed out.

"Hey!" I said. "I got an LOL, okay?"

"Ha!" Gabby laughed, and sat on the bed.

A Donut for Your Thoughts

"Anyway, as I was saying . . . that's the thing about camp: you're far from everything and everyone that's comfortable and familiar. So any real connection you make there is going to be super intense. You two shared stuff in common, right?" she asked.

I nodded and gestured to a picture of Matt, tacked to my bulletin board.

"He was new to camp this year, a scholarship kid. So that was different. But get this, he's biracial too, except his dad left when he was two, so he doesn't really know him," I said.

"There you go! I'm sure that being so alike and also so different made your connection extra intense," Gabby said, examining the picture. "He's cute. And you both have the same skin tone, too."

I nodded.

Matt and I both share that in-between skin color that some biracial kids have, somewhere between beige and brown.

"But since you mention it, I think it was our differences that made us tick. I'd never met anyone like him before, and he'd never met anyone like me . . . that's what he said."

"Yes, but now it's back to reality," Gabby said,

"and he's home with people and things that are really important in his everyday life. Like his friends, his family, heck, maybe even video games—"

"Video games?!"

Was she serious?

I didn't remember Matt mentioning anything about video games being a passion of his.

Gabby laughed.

"Yeah, girl. Haven't you ever met anyone who was a gamer? I made a pact with my heart to never get involved. Those guys can sit in front of a screen and it's over—until the next meal or bathroom break. They are obsessed," she said.

"Well . . . Matt did ask me once if I played Minecraft," I said.

Gabby nodded.

"There you go. Your boy is probably glued to a video screen as we speak," she replied.

I groaned.

"Well, if that's true, and I'm not a hundred percent certain that it is, why doesn't he just text me and say he's busy doing that?" I asked.

"Says the world's best communicator," Gabby said.

She winked and I shut my mouth.

A Donut for Your Thoughts

"I'm just teasing, but not really. Look, the bottom line is . . . he's a boy. And boys are clueless," Gabby continued.

And with that, Gabby hopped away to her room, leaving me to ruminate over what she had just said.

Was Matt really as clueless as the other boys in my grade?

Or was it me?

Chapter Seven
Heart-to-Heart Talk With Dad

That Saturday my parents made their delicious hot honey shrimp and waffles to jump-start the weekend. I came downstairs to find them cooking up a storm.

Gabby sometimes joked that if Mom and Dad ever decided to ditch their careers to open up a restaurant, they would put the Park out of business. With Donut Dreams in the equation, I wasn't so sure about that.

At the stove, Mom was sautéing shrimp in a skillet, and Dad stood at her side, in front of his old-fashioned waffle griddle.

I stopped in the kitchen archway, and before I knew what I was doing, I was taking a mental picture.

A Donut for Your Thoughts

It was a rear view of Mom and Dad standing hip to hip at the stove, laughing together at one of their many inside jokes. Watching them so in love reminded me of something Matt said to me at camp after listening to me complain about my parents for over half an hour.

He shrugged and said, "Well they sound like angels to me. I haven't heard you say a rotten thing about them yet. You just have no idea how good you have it, that's all."

I now understood what he meant, and it made me see my parents in a different light, a lucky light. I watched them work around each other in our homey kitchen like it was a dance they'd been practicing for a lifetime.

The way Mom could sense that Dad was going to reach around her for a dishcloth and leaned forward at just the right moment. How he opened the fridge to take out the fresh strawberries and left it, knowing she was going to close it with her heel. They each had their job and helped each other out without stepping on each other's toes.

Hashtag cooking goals.

"Morning, Case. I'm on driving duty this

afternoon, so you know what that means," Dad called over his shoulder.

YES! That meant he was taking me to the field hockey game on his day off.

This was great. Mom and I could use a break from each other anyway. After weeks of being together on the way to and from school, only to see each other in school, and at home . . . well, as they say, absence makes the heart grow fonder.

I laughed.

"What it means is, you won't have driving duty later, so Mom will be the one taking Gabby to that party," I said.

Gabby, who was still upstairs getting her beauty rest, is always going to some lake outing or party. That's because she basically gets anything she wants from our parents.

Her secret is no secret at all. Gabby is so amazing at everything she does—dance, academics, her ballet bun—that our parents would feel bad for denying her anything.

Mom turned around and grinned at me.

"True story, Casey. Your dad made sure to negotiate that one first thing this morning!"

A Donut for Your Thoughts

Mom and I laughed. We all knew Dad absolutely dreaded driving his gorgeous daughter to parties where boys were present. His overprotective dad side always kicked in and he always said he had to fight the urge to turn the car around and take Gabby home.

After family brunch, Gabby and I washed the dishes and cleaned up. Then it was time for me and Dad to go to the game.

That afternoon was a beautiful Saturday for field hockey. It was perfect fall weather—the air cool and still, sun high, not a cloud in the sky.

As we settled into Dad's SUV and buckled our belts, he glanced down at my sketchbook and seemed like he was about to say something, then decided against it.

I side-eyed him. I knew why he wasn't going to go there. If he was even slightly interested in the fact that I was bringing a sketch pad to a school sporting event, well, there was no way he was going against Mom who said I should be spending more time on "academics."

After all these years, Gabby and I have never been able to come between our parents on any front, and Gabby's a pro. They are so united on every possible thing, it's like they possess this weird parental telepathy. They're such different people in the world, but when it comes to me and Gabby, it's like our two parents merge into one. I personally found it super annoying, but then Matt came along and showed me another perspective.

Back at camp, I thought Matt and I had some sort of telepathy going. By the last week, we were finishing each other's sentences and saying the same expressions. Then camp ended, and poof, he fell off the face of the earth, like the imaginary friend you suddenly outgrow.

After his last one-word text, I didn't really know what else to say without coming off as too "in my feelings"—even though I was! So I remained silent.

And then there was Lindsay, who I've had a telepathic friendship with since kindergarten, until just lately. I didn't know what was happening with us, but we weren't so in sync these days either. It was like we'd lost our radio signal and there was all this static between us, interfering with our connection.

I was losing my grip on two people I cared about, and I wanted to know my parents' secret recipe for relationship success once and for all. Despite their

A Donut for Your Thoughts

busy lives with competing responsibilities, how did they manage to stay so . . . in sync all the time?

I was just about to ask my dad about this when he interrupted my thoughts.

"So what are we filling our ears with this morning, Miss DJ?" Dad asked, fiddling with the Bluetooth on his phone.

I was so lost in thought I almost didn't answer. Usually, I decided what we listened to when Dad drove me, but music was the last thing on my mind today.

"I dunno. Whatever you pick, I'm game," I mumbled absentmindedly.

"Well, that's a first," Dad said, before choosing his favorite Otis Redding playlist.

He started the car and backed out of the driveway.

"Dad . . . do you and Mom agree on everything?" I asked, once we were well on our way.

"Heck no, we don't always agree," he answered with a laugh.

"For real?" I asked, disbelieving.

"Well, you and best buddy Lindsay are practically married. Do you two always see eye to eye?"

"Definitely not," I grumbled.

Especially not lately.

"Well, same goes with your mom and I. We're not always of the same mind on things and have to talk it out behind the scenes. Thankfully, our home is spacious enough, or else you'd hear us."

He paused before adding, "Especially when it comes to you and Gabby. As the parents, we must find common ground, or else you two queens of schemes will walk all over us!"

Dad and I laughed hard at this for a good minute because it was so true.

Gabby alone would debate our Mom and Dad all day and all night if necessary to get her point across.

Dad continued, "But what I'm saying is, we don't always agree on issues that bubble up concerning politics, religion, and the two of you, but when it comes to our children, we have to land on a position. Through the process of doing this since you were babies, essentially, your mom and I merged into our own organism."

Ha. After blowing my mind with his honesty, leave it to Dad to put his scientific spin on everything.

"Can you two read each other's minds?" I asked.

Dad laughed loud and looked away from the road

A Donut for Your Thoughts

for a half second to throw me a glance.

"Sorry to disappoint, but we have no such abilities. Your mother is one of the greatest mysteries of my life, next to science. I don't think I'll ever understand her completely.

"Yet, over time, we've learned to accept each other for exactly who we are. Years of disagreeing to find our middle has made it easy in our later years to predict what the other's response will be to any question or situation you two come at us with."

"Now this is one real-talk Saturday," I said.

I still didn't get it all, but I couldn't wait to tell my sister the good news, that Mom and Dad didn't have telepathy after all.

※ ※ ※ ※ ※

The field hockey girls were doing warm-up drills when we arrived. I scanned the first row of bleachers for Michelle. When I spotted her, she was already waving me over from her wheelchair at the far end.

I sat in the front row with Michelle, and Dad sat a row behind me to cheer on our team. He's really into sports and gets really loud at games, so I never let him sit next to me.

DONUT DREAMS

"I've already gotten some great shots. Check these out," Michelle said excitedly.

She handed me her camera to take a look.

"Michelle, these are amazing," I said.

There were some wide shots of the girls stretching, and more close-ups of them talking with their coaches. Michelle had zoomed in on their faces so you could see how intently they were listening to every word their coach said.

I felt especially inspired by photos of the girls laughing and fooling around. I wondered how well I would be able to capture all that personality with the mental pictures I was planning to take, plus my pencils.

My favorite was a photo of Kelsey that was really incredible. She was holding her hockey stick laughing, lots of blue sky above her and a look of pure joy on her face.

"You can see how much she loves to play," I said. "This could be the cover of a sports magazine!"

Michelle grinned.

"Thanks. That's my dream, actually! I want to one day see a photo of mine on the cover of a magazine," she said.

A Donut for Your Thoughts

"Keep taking photos like this and you'll be well on your way," I assured her.

With a smile, Michelle looked through her camera lens and started snapping away again.

The game started. We became quiet for a while, each of us deep in thought.

I turned to a blank page in my sketchbook and glanced at the players. Sophia caught my eye. She was small, swift, and dark-haired, and played with a fierce intensity. That made her a great subject to draw, but also a challenging one. She moved like a minnow on the field, making it harder for me to pin down a mental picture. It took me a while to latch onto something, but once I did, it was exhilarating to capture her energy on the page.

After a few minutes, Michelle leaned over to peer at my sketch.

"Now that's amazing," she said, then laughed. "Sophia looks so serious, doesn't she? You almost want to give her a hug and tell her to lighten up."

I beamed, silently overjoyed that Michelle knew exactly who I was sketching, and that I'd done Sophia justice.

"That's why I thought she'd be great to sketch.

I loved the expression on her face." I turned to Michelle. "Since I got back from camp, you're the first person to be interested in my artwork, so thank you for saying that. Sometimes I struggle with whether I'm even any good. But I've been working really hard to hone my craft. I guess it just feels good to have my work . . . seen."

I surprised myself, saying this much to Michelle. She was more Kelsey and Lindsay's friend than mine. I guess I was feeling more comfortable talking about this with someone who shared an eye and appreciation for life's beautiful moments.

"Yeah, I could tell you weren't feeling it at lunch the other day when Lindsay was just not getting it," Michelle said.

"Oh, you noticed, huh?" I asked, laughing.

Michelle smiled.

"I have an eye, remember?" she said, holding up her camera. "Casey, you're not great at keeping your feelings hidden. Even if you don't say what you feel, you're saying it anyway."

"Good to know," I said.

"Look at it this way," Michelle said, lowering her camera and turning to look at me. "Sometimes,

A Donut for Your Thoughts

people don't get things they're not interested in. My cousin Joanne wants to be a physics teacher. Physics! I break out into hives just thinking about math. So you know, to each her own."

She raised her camera again and took a few more photos. Then she added, "And you know what else? I think Lindsay might be a little jealous."

"Jealous? Why?"

"Her mom was a great artist. I'm sure Lindsay would love to have a little of talent herself. But you have talent."

"Hmm." I was silent for a moment, considering this. Lindsay and I have never had problems with jealousy in all our years of friendship. She didn't ever seem to be jealous about me going to sleepaway camp every summer, and Lindsay wanted nothing more than to leave our small town, where anybody's business is everybody's business.

Michelle continued, "Don't get me wrong—she's not crazy jealous. It's not like she hates you or anything like that! I'm just saying I think she feels a little uncomfortable when you get excited about your artwork. It probably reminds her of her mom or something."

DONUT DREAMS

I sighed, because she had a point.

"You know, you might be right. I never thought about it that way," I said.

"You should talk to her about it," Michelle said. "It's never good to keep things bottled up. She's your best friend, after all."

I nodded. "Maybe I will."

I know Lindsay's my best friend, but still, why do I feel so uncomfortable?

Chapter Eight
Cute With a Capital C

The following Monday at lunchtime, the girls' field hockey team huddled around Michelle at our lunch table. From the outside, it could have looked like they were strategizing their next play. But really, they were gazing at Michelle's photographs from their game on Saturday.

"Shelly, you always make me look *sooo* good!" Kelsey squealed. "I want a copy of this picture."

It was the photo I loved too, with Kelsey gripping the hockey stick and laughing with the blue sky.

"If you think these are good, you should see Casey's sketches. They're even more amazing," Michelle said.

Before I knew it, the girls were grabbing at my sketchbook.

DONUT DREAMS

Now with the spotlight suddenly on me, my face went hot with embarassment, which then turned to pride. Since the art exhibit at the close of summer camp, I haven't had a chance to show my artwork to anybody. I've been pretty secretive about it.

"Wait, wait! Hold up!" I said, laughing.

I was kind of happy that people were actually interested in my work for a change. I opened my sketchbook and flipped some pages, looking for the field hockey sketches.

A sketch that I had torn out of the book fluttered to the floor. It was meant to be private, but it was already too late.

"Now *you* hold up—who is this?" Kelsey said, picking up my sketch of Matt.

I hadn't planned to show it to anyone. Actually, I had torn it out to put it someplace private but got sidetracked.

I hadn't drawn it from a photograph like the others before it, but from a mental picture of my campfire memory of Matt. I had to close my eyes for a long time until every feature of his face froze into place and made sense. I had tried to remember him on paper, but it didn't come out exactly as I saw it in

A Donut for Your Thoughts

my mind. No matter how good or bad the drawing was, it could never capture Matt in living color.

But even my drawing of his dark hair, sparkling eyes, killer smile, and deep dimples had a table of girls captivated for a few moments.

I guess that meant I'd done something right.

Matt had that effect on all the girls at camp too, but he was only interested in spending his kayaking and campfire hours with me. Maybe it was because I was biracial like him, or the only girl who wasn't fawning over him.

It felt kind of awesome seeing people so mesmerized by my sketches but I also felt super exposed, as if everyone, just by staring at the picture, could overhear our campfire conversations and taste the marshmallows Matt roasted just for me. It was like everyone was reading from a ripped-out page of my private journal.

"CUTE, with a capital C!" squealed Sophia. "Is that your boyfriend?"

I sighed inwardly.

I wish! Or do I?

"I'm not even allowed to have a boyfriend, Sophia. We're just friends," I said.

"What's his name?" Michelle asked.

"Matt."

"Ooh, Maaaaatt," said Sophia, drawing out the sound of his name and making the rest of the girls giggle.

Kelsey put the sketch down on the cafeteria table, and Lindsay leaned in to take a look.

"So this is Matt-who-never-texts-back, huh? He's cute, I guess," she said.

My face was burning up.

"He texts back. Just not . . . a lot."

Kelsey sighed.

"He's dreamy, Case," she said. "Why aren't there any guys who look like this around here?"

"We need to get them imported," Michelle joked.

The rest of the girls exchanged high-fives and laughed.

"Hi, girls. What's so funny over here?" asked an all-too-familiar voice.

I froze.

How long has she been spying?

"Hi, Assistant Principal Peters," some of the girls said in unison.

"Hi, Mrs. Peters!" Lindsay perked up.

A Donut for Your Thoughts

Funny, Lindsay hardly ever looked this excited to see me anymore.

"Casey, I was just sitting in my office, thinking that it's been a while since we invited Lindsay over for my famous lasagna," Mom said, looking at her with a smile.

Don't assistant principals have other things to think about? I thought.

Mom waved a manicured hand.

"What do you say, Linds, would you like to come over for dinner tonight?"

"Ooh, that's so nice," said Sophia.

"Jealous!" Michelle half joked.

"I have to ask, of course, but I'd love to!" Lindsay said enthusiastically.

In a sudden movement of excitement, she knocked over a container of juice ... all over my Matt drawing. The bottom half of my sketch got soaked.

All of the girls gasped in horror.

"Matt!" Kelsey cried out dramatically, as if he were really drowning.

"Wait? What?" Lindsay said, clearly embarrassed.

Thinking quickly, Michelle grabbed her camera and snapped a photo of the sketch.

"I'll send this to you and you can print it out," she told me. "Just lighten the part that's darker because it got wet. Good as new."

I didn't say anything, just took a napkin and gently blotted the wet part of the sketch. I realized then that how much the sketch meant to me.

Kelsey looked at Lindsay. "Gosh, Lindsay. Can't you at least say you're sorry?"

Lindsay shot me a look, but I noticed she couldn't hold my gaze for more than two seconds.

"She knows I'm sorry . . . don't you, Case? Like Michelle said, you can print out a new copy. Or you can just whip up a new sketch."

I fumed.

Whip up? This is not a kitchen and I'm no Betty Crocker!

"What do we have here?" Mom asked.

With all the commotion, I had forgotten that she was even there. She leaned down to look at the half-wet sketch and then looked at me with a raised eyebrow.

"Clearly this is your handiwork. Who's the boy, Case?" she asked.

"Nobody, Assistant Principal Peters! It's just a

A Donut for Your Thoughts

stupid drawing I whipped up . . . right, Lindsay?" I shouted.

Tears stung my eyes, threatening to fall.

I quickly scooped up my sketch and sketchbook and rushed out of the cafeteria, leaving my lunch, and probably a lot of confused faces, behind.

Chapter Nine
That's the Tea

After school, I sat outside the closed door of Assistant Principal Peters's office, as usual, waiting for a ride home.

If a stranger were to walk into our school at that moment, I would probably look like some troublemaker waiting to get detention. But the truth is, I've never gotten in trouble at school a day in my life, and there are no strangers in Bellgrove.

My science teacher, Mr. Sanders, smiled as he strolled to the school exit.

"Put on your game face, Casey," he said, laughing at my frown. "She'll be out any minute."

I forced a smile until he disappeared out the door, not taking a mental picture, but making a mental note

A Donut for Your Thoughts

to find another place to wait for Mom.

How could I possibly cheer up after the most embarrassing day of my middle school existence? It was bad enough having the field hockey team gawking at my top secret drawing of Matt, but to have my assistant principal mom popping up whenever she felt like it? I sent up a silent prayer to please make it stop.

A few minutes later, the office door opened and a few teachers streamed out. They all greeted me before heading for the exit.

Assistant Principal Peters drifted out, looking pleased until her eyes fell on me. Maybe my stormy expression made her smile shrink just a tad.

"Ready, honey?" she asked.

"Ready," I said, standing.

Mom grabbed her jacket and car keys.

"Okay, let's jet," she said.

On the slow drive home, the air inside Mom's car was so thick you could cut it with a butter knife. Mom tried to make small talk, about the beautiful fall weather, and the upcoming games, but like Matt, I could only manage one-word responses.

There was definitely an elephant in the car with

us, something that was obviously important to talk about, but difficult to bring up. If I were Mom, I'd be trying to figure out the best way to bring up something uncomfortable, without getting the usual defensive response from me. She knew she was treading on thin ice as it was.

Talking things out without erupting, or without my emotions spilling all over the place, was such a chore. It made us both uncomfortable, and we knew that too. I just wanted to run from it all and be left alone to sort out my tangled mess of feelings with the help of my therapeutic sketchbook.

My phone buzzed. I had a new text. I glanced down at it, my heart pounding.

It was Michelle.

> U ok?

I sighed and texted back.

> Yes. Thanks for asking. TTYL

I was happy Michelle had texted me, but where was Lindsay? Did she not even care that she had

A Donut for Your Thoughts

ruined my sketch? As if this day couldn't get any worse, my BFF was not even texting me.

Halfway home, we had to stop at a railroad crossing. This freight train was moving at the pace of a sloth. Leave it to the most awkward car ride of the year to become the most epic.

I looked out my window, even though there was nothing interesting to see. Even though I couldn't see her, I could feel Mom staring at me.

She sighed.

"So are you going to tell me what that outburst at lunch was all about?" she asked.

Here it comes. Mom wasn't one for beating around the bush like Dad.

My head got blank and my lips refused to move.

But Mom didn't let up.

"Casey? Are you upset with me for some reason?"

Fair question, I had to admit. When I really thought about it, Mom technically didn't do anything wrong as a parent. Okay, she didn't appreciate my love of art, and that stung. And I definitely wasn't cool with her rolling up on me at school whenever she felt like it.

However, when I thought of her reason for today's lunch-table visit, she actually meant well.

I usually loved having Lindsay over for dinner, almost as much as I loved my mom's lasagna. But after what happened at lunch, I actually would have appreciated a little space from Lindsay. Which felt kind of icky, because I've been totally crazy about Lindsay for as long as I can remember.

So, tangled up inside, I became tongue-tied.

The sloth train continued to crawl past, and I started fidgeting with my almost-curls.

"What's going on in that beautiful head of yours?" Mom asked.

She hesitated when I didn't answer, and then continued, "Sometimes it's like pulling teeth trying to get you to tell me how you feel. Just remember that no feeling is too big or too small because all feelings are important and deserve a voice. Especially when someone is showing their willingness to really hear you."

Mom sure knew how to get me thinking.

These days I can't tell big feelings and small feelings apart. I don't even know how much space any of my feelings should take up.

Is it big or small that the people closest to me don't give a hoot about my passion in life?

A Donut for Your Thoughts

That my BFF might possibly be jealous of me?

Is it big or small that Matt ditched our friendship to play Minecraft or maybe for another cool girl?

That my mom is my assistant principal and I feel like I can't sneeze without her showing up out of nowhere with a box of tissues?

I guess the point my mom was making was that the size of my feelings doesn't matter. The important thing is that I have them and can share them with a welcome ear if I want to. It isn't easy to open myself up to my mom, because I feel she always expects perfection from me.

As for Lindsay, who used to be my walking diary? Since her mom died and especially since I came home from camp this year, much less.

My dad? Maybe if I got to spend more alone time with him.

Truth be told, my sister Gabby is the only one who knows me fully and totally accepts me. I don't want to run to my big sis for every little thing, but knowing that I can if I want to means plenty.

It would've been nice to have that level of comfort with my mom, but she sometimes makes it hard, with her own strong opinions on things having to do with me. While some kids say their moms are bulldogs, mine's a bulldozer.

Sometimes I feel like she's trying to demolish my own opinion of myself, to build it back the way she wants.

Clearly this sloth train isn't going to let me off the hook either, so . . .

Suddenly, I turned my head to lock eyes with my mom. I never noticed that we were the same height sitting down.

I looked at her and saw her, us, and, well, everything so differently. It was like this invisible veil between us fell away. We looked at each other as if we were seeing each other for the first time. I had to take a mental picture because never had my mom looked so beautiful.

Is my bulldozer mom . . . emotional?

Her eyes were a little wet, and I could see in them her love for me. I saw warmth, worry, regret, confusion, fear.

Whoa. My mom was actually, officially, certifiably in her feelings! Maybe in our private universes, most of us are.

I took a breath and went for it.

A Donut for Your Thoughts

"Ever since I came home from camp this summer, I feel like nobody gets me anymore," I said.

Mom zipped her lips and studied me.

"I also feel like I've changed . . . like, a lot. I think I grew up at camp this summer more than usual. I was excited to come home as this changed girl. But at home, nobody seemed interested in all the cool things I learned there. Everybody was on their back-to-school grind, and then pretty soon, there was this feeling that I never went anywhere at all this summer. Except I felt so much different, so much clearer about who I am because of what I'm passionate about.

"I want to talk about art to every person I meet. I like to take photographs of interesting things and capture precious moments in my mind and develop my photographic memory. I love to draw people and study their faces and bodies and how they move.

"I feel like people who've known me forever understand me the least, and people I hardly know see me clearly. It's confusing to be afraid to tell the people that I love most that I want to be an artist and nothing else. I think I'm already an artist, and I want more than anything for you, Dad, and Lindsay to see that. I want you to be proud of me for being me, not some mini version of you.

"Artists do all kinds of interesting things with their lives. I want to do art with my life! I don't know what that means exactly, because I'm still figuring that out, but I believe that whatever I decide to do, I can do! I used to doubt myself so much, and for the first time I actually believe in myself! And it's all because of art!"

I took a deep breath and looked at my mom. She was still looking at me, expecting me to continue, so I did.

"I used to say that I would follow Lindsay out of this town to the ends of the earth just so we could keep swapping lunches for the rest of our lives. I came back from camp not feeling that way anymore. Don't get me wrong, she's still my best friend. But I don't really know if I want to go away and live in a big city like her.

"After art school I feel fine about staying close to home, but I would like to make an interesting life for myself as an artist wherever I end up! I want to scream out this window, 'I am an artist!'—even if no one hears. I want this to be a hashtag fact in our family from now on."

A Donut for Your Thoughts

"Hashtag fact?" Mom asked.

By then, the train had passed and the light turned green. We were finally moving forward.

"Oh, just some social media lingo, learned it at camp." I waved it off.

After saying my piece, I already felt better and was even breathing easier.

"Hashtag, oh, okay, gotcha." Mom nodded, filing that one away in her brain.

She was a middle school assistant principal, after all, and needed to stay in the know.

"Wow. I'm listening to you, Casey. Go on," she said encouragingly.

"That's really about it." I shrugged.

I didn't know what else I wanted to say. I was amazed that I'd said that much without blubbering all over the place. I was just happy to know that lightning didn't strike or that waterworks didn't come just because I shared my feelings.

"How's that for pulling teeth, Mom?" I asked.

Mom couldn't help but laugh. "I mean, phew, Casey." She smiled before she said, "You sure put me in my place with that soliloquy. I knew you had it in you, not to tell me about myself, but to tell me about yourself. Thank you so much for telling me how you feel. You really do have a lot going on in that big brain of yours."

"I know!" I laughed. "And so much more."

"I bet," Mom said.

I could actually hear with those two words that she'd heard me, everything I'd said.

She took a deep breath and let it out.

"Okay, my daughter the aspiring artist. I'm sorry I didn't take you seriously in the beginning. I guess a large part of me saw art as a passing phase in someone's life until reality hits. One day you'll have bills to pay and a family to support. I think it's difficult for artists to pull that off, especially in a small-town setting like ours. But then, I always have to remember that the world is changing.

"I also have to remember my friend Amy Cooper, the beautiful, important artist," Mom said. Her voice filled with emotion then.

We shared a few moments of silence, misty-eyed as we remembered Lindsay's mom, whom everyone had cherished and loved.

"I miss her," I said.

My lip quivered as I pictured her angular face and

A Donut for Your Thoughts

soft features in my mind. She was beautiful, inside and out. I could see her so clearly in my mind's eye that I could almost smell the lavender and see the shade of blue she always painted with and wore. That and her wind-chime voice always filled me with this safe, calm feeling.

I never told Lindsay that it still made me endlessly sad that her mom was no longer here. I couldn't imagine how Lindsay must feel to wake up every day without her own mother.

I looked at my mom's profile as she drove us home, and something about the way the afternoon light was hitting her round face and her curls reminded me that she was not just a bulldozer, but a beautiful bulldozer, more beautiful than words could say.

As much as she got on my nerves, I couldn't imagine life without my assistant principal mom. I could do without the assistant principal part, but that would be the same as her saying that she could do without the artist part in me.

I knew what I had to say to her next.

"Casey, I love you," my mom was saying. "Your life is your show. As your coproducer, I want you to be who you are meant to be, but you better work your butt off to be successful at it. Don't let me or anyone get in the way of your dreams. As long as you continue to maintain your grades, I will support you one hundred percent in your artistic pursuits. If your grades begin to slip, you will be hearing from me. Fair?"

I breathed a large sigh of relief.

"Fair. Thanks for hearing me out . . . this time. There's something else."

Mom sat up a little straighter in her seat and nodded, keeping her eyes on the road.

"I want to apologize for being such a sourpuss about you being the assistant principal of my school. I came into middle school with a bad attitude that created my responses to certain things. I should be more grateful and proud to say you're my mom. I can't speak for kids in the older grades, but my friends at school admire and respect you. A friend from camp this summer has helped me see how ungrateful I've been. Sorry, Mom," I finished.

"This means a lot to hear. I accept your apology," Mom said.

Her eyes scanned the road as she navigated the more congested part of town, close to the Park. She

A Donut for Your Thoughts

wiped away a tear with the side of her hand.

"I now understand why you combusted on me at the lunch table," she said.

"I mean, in the middle of having friend drama—" I started.

"Here comes your assistant principal, inviting your friend home for lasagna," she finished.

"Without even asking me first!" I added. "How rude. What if Lindsay and I were in a fight or something? What if I had a ton of homework?"

"Valid points." She nodded. "I'll make sure to check in with you first before inviting your friends over. Deal?"

"Deal," I said. "Well, at least you didn't invite Lindsay over for fish sticks. You had all the jocks so hungry for your lasagna, no one was paying attention to just how lame I felt!"

We laughed long and hard.

"I guess we do need to set up some boundaries at school," Mom said, after catching her breath.

She then fell quiet as she thought for a moment.

"How's this?" she suggested. "No chatting on school grounds unless it's something important and school-related. From now on, when I see you anywhere at school, I'll just wave unless you stop to talk to me first. How does that sound?"

I considered this with a smile.

"Do you have to wave? Can't we just work on our mother-daughter telepathy?" I asked, half joking.

Telepathy with me would be impossible!

"Casey! You're my daughter! I'm not going to ignore you if I see you! That would draw even more attention."

I sighed. "Yeah, that's even weirder. Okay to wave."

"Deal," Mom said, turning onto our tree-lined street.

She parked the car in our driveway and turned to me.

"Are there any other feelings you want to share, about anything at all?"

"My mug isn't empty, but I think I've spilled enough tea for one day," I said.

I hugged her.

"Thanks, Mom," I said.

"Thank you for being so vulnerable with me just now," Mom said. "You taught me something today."

"It wasn't easy to speak up at first, but once I started, it felt really good," I said.

A Donut for Your Thoughts

Next up, Lindsay.

Just then my phone signaled that I'd gotten a text message. This time my heart didn't speed up, hoping, wondering if it was you-know-who as I pulled out my phone to check.

"It's Lindsay," I said. "Turns out she can't come over for dinner tonight."

Phew! Because I feel like I've just run a marathon!

Chapter Ten
The Big Surprise

That week, instead of going to lunch, I stayed in art class a few days to work on a new drawing that had me quite obsessed. I was starting to like spending more time in the most vibrant and inspiring classroom in school.

Our art teacher, Mr. Franklin, had an open-door policy during lunch hour for student artists. Anyone working on independent art projects could go to his room during lunch period, and Mr. Franklin pretty much left you alone to do your thing.

He didn't helicopter the room like in his regular art class. Instead he just sat with his feet up at his desk, chomping away at his lunch and jamming out on his cushiony headphones.

A Donut for Your Thoughts

That Wednesday, I texted Lindsay to let her know I wasn't coming to lunch . . . again.

> Finishing something up in Franklin's room today. Lemme guess . . . pastrami & swiss on pumpernickel?

> Yup.

Sheesh.

If Matt was the king of one-word responses, Lindsay was joining him on the throne.

Things weren't the same with us these days, and it was my fault. We both knew we were long overdue for a heart-to-heart, but I wanted the moment to be just right.

Mr. Franklin was my favorite teacher for a number of reasons, one of which was that he had turned Mrs. Cooper's old room, now his room, into a constantly changing art exhibit.

Actually, if you really think about it, you can spot examples of art almost everywhere in school, thanks to the art department that Lindsay's mom directed for years: from the self-portraits that line the long wall on the way to the library to a ceramic octopus sculpture at the main office sign-in desk. And of course there's the funky mural in the main hallway that's dedicated to Amy Cooper.

My favorite is the painter's palette that she always used, which Mr. Franklin suspended from the ceiling of his classroom with fishing wire. At least once a week, usually before class starts, I stand still in front of the hovering palette, spotted with paint colors.

I gaze up at it for a few seconds, I don't know why exactly, just to send up a prayer. My way of remembering her, I guess.

Something about the palette being in midair makes me imagine her on the other side wearing angel's wings, floating above us as we make art in what used to be her classroom.

I also feel close to Lindsay's mom every time I talk to Mr. Franklin.

He can sketch and paint, too, but he's more into collage work and bookmaking. He's mostly known for these awesome, one-of-a-kind handmade books with collages on the cover, which he sells online.

What I didn't know until I started talking to

A Donut for Your Thoughts

Mr. Franklin was that Amy Cooper had been his mentor for many years. Actually, he says she's the only reason he is an artist at all.

We definitely have that in common, because I feel the same way about her.

"Hey, Casey, I want to talk to you about something," said Mr. Franklin.

The door was wide open to welcome any other lunchtime artists, but for now, the room was empty.

Once I reached the front of the room, Mr. Franklin picked up Twin Flames, my first sketch from memory of the campfire, which I'd recently turned in.

"Casey, this is wonderful work," Mr. Franklin said, smiling at me.

He pointed to the campfire flames and continued, "I'm halfway convinced that I can warm my hands over this drawing, it's that good."

I laughed, a little embarrassed. But I was touched by the compliment, especially since I really admired Mr. Franklin as an artist.

"I'm so glad you like it! Most people might look at it as a stupid fire, but I actually spent a lot of time on it," I admitted.

"Well, I am not 'most people' and can see your

potential a mile away in just one of these flames," Mr. Franklin replied.

He waved a hand over my sketch and said, "Your eye for detail is incredible. It actually inspired an idea I have for the school website."

"What idea?" I asked.

"Well, how would you like to submit sketches for the site? We could call it 'A View from Bellgrove,' or whatever better thing you can suggest. You can sketch friends in everyday scenes like lunch in the cafeteria, competing in sports, or chilling in the hallway.

"Of course, you'd need permission from anyone you decided to sketch—especially with the realism of your sketches.

"But I think it would be fun and interesting to show a student's view of the school, and maybe we could expand it to include photographs as well— from you and from other students. But I'd like you to head up this visual component of the website and be in charge of it. It might mean staying after school a few days a week to do it justice."

I was floored by Mr. Franklin's offer, which was a perfect solution to a number of problems.

Seeing that I only got called into the Park as a

A Donut for Your Thoughts

flyer every once in a while, I had been wanting to do something after school that was more productive than sitting around waiting for some clueless boy to get back to me. Besides, I was waiting around aimlessly after school for Mom for up to an hour these days anyhow.

Now I would be able to fill that time doing something worthwhile.

"Mr. Franklin, I would love that!" I said.

I thought about it some more, and then suddenly, I had a great idea.

"My friend Michelle is a really great photographer. She also would have a lot to contribute," I told him.

"Yes! I'm familiar with her work," Mr. Franklin said, smiling.

I beamed back.

"Let's loop her in, and you can curate this together with her, if you want," he continued. "Let me talk to our website designer, and we can start moving on this right away. I think this will be a very nice endeavor for you, Casey."

He paused before adding, "And it's never too early to start thinking about college. I'm sure people will be impressed when they see you had your artwork featured on a website at such an early age."

DONUT DREAMS

I might not have been jumping up and down, but I was so thrilled, like, surprise-birthday-party thrilled.

This would be a great way to show everyone that art was around us, all the time. That artwork was important and should be appreciated.

I couldn't wait to tell everyone the great news.

Chapter Eleven
In Our Feelings

That evening Dad and Gabby teamed up on the cooking, which always led to a delightful meal.

Sometimes Dad came home a little later from work than usual, so he would ask someone here at home to start the process of preparing dinner, like chopping up vegetables.

That was fine by me. I was happy to contribute in a small way because I can't cook to save my life. My dad teases me that I can't even boil water for a cup of tea. I find it hard to concentrate on measuring ingredients, or timing a recipe.

But Gabby was no sous chef. Whenever she started dinner, she would end up putting her own spin on Dad's original idea.

DONUT DREAMS

Dad's Southern roots make him a hopeless BBQ romantic, and Gabby loves Asian cuisine, so... steamed shrimp wontons and Hunan barbecue chicken were on tonight's menu.

I mean, with a whole house smelling this good, no one had to call me downstairs for dinner. I was already in the kitchen hovering over wontons by the time dinner was served.

"Another patient came into the emergency room last night after being hit by a car." Dad sighed.

He shook his head as he carefully spooned some coconut-baked candied yams onto his plate.

The creases in his forehead were way pronounced. From being on call at the emergency room for so many years, Dad's seen it all, but he never stops caring about each and every patient.

"Another one?" Gabby said. "Why are so many people being hit by cars these days?"

"There are more geniuses on the road who think it's a good idea to drive while texting," Dad answered.

Mom added, "Girls, take this as a reminder to never cross a street right after the walk signal comes on. Always wait a few seconds and look both ways before crossing."

A Donut for Your Thoughts

"It happens all the time. A split second could cost you a leg or your life," Dad said. "Last night's Jane Doe came to us in such a state of shock she didn't realize how badly the car had damaged her until she looked down at her leg and saw that her bone was exposed—"

"Dad!" Gabby shouted, looking down at her drumstick.

Usually, I was right there along with Gabby shutting Dad down, but this time I kept quiet.

Something was different this time. I was different. Instead, I was creating a mental picture of my dad in this moment that happened so often at our dinner table, and I noticed something new.

A crumpled expression that I'd never seen before rippled over my dad's face. In that millisecond, Dad looked similar to how I felt after being totally misunderstood by the people closest to me. My mind started racing.

What if my dad, the town doctor, also felt like a total reject . . . at his own dinner table (which he built, by the way)?

What if coming home from work, for him, was like coming home from summer camp for me?

DONUT DREAMS

How did it feel to be the town hero coming home to your kids, who didn't want to hear the gory details of your lifesaving days in the ER?

I guess I hadn't been fair to my father, either.

"Excuse me?" Dad said coolly. "What happens during my day should also have a seat at this table."

Gabby and I looked at each other with wide eyes and closed mouths.

Whoa. I'm now convinced that we are all in our feelings!

I spoke up.

"Dad's right. Five minutes of Dad's day is way more important and exciting than both of our school weeks combined," I said, reasoning with Gabby. "I should be able to forget my silly sensitive stomach for a few minutes of dirty details at dinner."

With that, I popped a wonton into my mouth and started chewing.

Gabby nodded, agreeing.

"So what did you do with the exposed fracture?" she asked Dad.

I tried to compose myself as Dad went on to unfold the whole gory scene in great detail.

"So how was your day, Casey?" Gabby asked,

A Donut for Your Thoughts

smoothly changing the subject the instant Dad seemed to have gotten it out of his system.

"Mine was great!"

I told them about my exciting conversation with Mr. Franklin.

"That sounds wonderful, Casey," Dad said, glancing at Mom and tossing her a wink.

"Congratulations!" Mom added. "Soon you'll be making a name for yourself at Bellgrove. Get ready, because people are going to start commissioning you with candy bars to feature them in your drawings!"

We all laughed.

"They better come with more than just candy bars," I joked. "My services aren't cheap."

We laughed some more.

"Look who's feeling herself . . . Ms. Artsy," Gabby teased me, with a slight shove.

"Casey, would you like to show us some of your artwork sometime?" Mom asked.

"Woo-hoo! Art showing!" said Gabby.

"I'd love to."

I beamed. I couldn't wait to show them my newest sketches, all created from memory.

"I don't mean to put a damper on things, but

your story could explain why Lindsay was looking so glum in the lunchroom today," Mom said. "Have you two gotten a chance to talk since last Monday's BFF drama?"

That grabbed Gabby's attention, and her eyes went wide.

"Who has drama? Lindsay and Casey?" she asked Mom. She shot me a curious look and waited for an answer.

I sighed, pushing the food around on my plate before I said, "We haven't talked yet." I felt a bit ashamed to admit it.

Mom did have a point, though. No wonder I was getting only one-word answers from Lindsay. I'd gotten so involved with my latest drawing that I totally fell off the map with little explanation. Lindsay must have been feeling confused.

I would definitely be salty if she did the same thing, especially with how different our friendship was feeling since middle school started. Heck, we couldn't even swap sandwiches anymore thanks to the school rules!

"Sounds like you might want to remedy that soon," Dad suggested.

A Donut for Your Thoughts

"Well, can I hang out with Lindsay after school tomorrow, please?" I asked.

My parents shot each other that telepathic glance Gabby and I knew all too well.

"Sounds like a terrific plan," Mom said.

Chapter Twelve
The Two Artists

That night after dinner, I texted Lindsay.

> BFF hang after school tmrw?

My heart was beating quickly . . . like every time I ever texted Matt.

What if she was already too mad and totally rejected me?

A minute later, Lindsay texted back.

> Sure.

I smiled. Finally, a one-word response that was music to my ears.

A Donut for Your Thoughts

The next day I asked Lindsay to meet up with me after school in the art room before walking over to my mom's office together.

Mr. Franklin agreed to make himself disappear, so we had the room to ourselves for at least half an hour.

Even though this had been Mrs. Cooper's room for so long, Mr. Franklin had done a good job of making the classroom his own universe. Just the vintage Woodstock posters alone are enough to transport you into a different decade each time you walk in here.

Everywhere else you look is student art galore. Mr. Franklin is a total enthusiast about displaying student art in the freshest ways possible, even hanging pieces from the ceiling to catch the eye.

Mrs. Cooper's palette would be there forever, but it was cool to see the art constantly changing.

We entered the room and stopped just short of Lindsay's mom's floating paint palette and stared up at it.

"You know what will be the hardest part about leaving Bellgrove?" Lindsay asked.

It's no secret that she feels stifled by small-town life and has always had her sights set on bigger, faster places where no one would know her life story. Where she could just melt into any crowd.

"You'll feel like you're leaving her behind?" I guessed.

"That's why you're my BFF," said Lindsay.

She squeezed my hand.

It was good to know that even after weeks of weirdness, there were some things Lindsay didn't have to explain to me.

Now I had some explaining to do. I could feel the usual traffic jam of words in my throat begin to form, so I took some deep breaths and felt the congestion clear.

"Listen, I know I haven't been the best BFF lately," I said.

Lindsay's eyes widened.

"OMG. I haven't been the best BFF either!" she exclaimed.

"Okay, who wants to go first?" I chuckled.

Clearly we both had some explaining to do.

Lindsay raised her hand.

"This summer, I was actually secretly jealous for the first time when you went to sleepaway camp and I had to stay in Bellgrove," she said. "Then you came

A Donut for Your Thoughts

back like this whole new person, with lip gloss and a boyfriend and talking differently and acting more like my own mom than . . . well . . . me! I was also surprised by how good your drawing was. I didn't even know you liked to draw!"

"That's my fault," I said. "Your mom's been my inspiration for as long as I can remember. When we were little, I used to watch her sketch you and Sky. I think she even made a sketch of me once. It was mesmerizing to watch her blank sketchbook fill with captured moments in just a few pencil strokes. I used to leave your house wishing my mom had a superpower like yours did.

"The older I got, the more I wanted to be just like her. I was seven when I started drawing, but I thought my sketches were too horrible to show. I didn't show my sketchbook to anyone until summer camp this year."

"Lemme guess . . . Matt?" Lindsay said.

"Like I said, I haven't been the greatest BFF." I smiled sadly.

I then explained to Lindsay how Matt and I ended up swapping notebooks for a whole minute just because we were curious about each other.

"For being such a cutie, he had sort of ugly handwriting." I laughed.

"I'm sure he wasn't ready for how amazing your drawings are," Lindsay said softly.

"Thanks for saying that. He kinda wasn't!" I agreed.

"Well, he sounds as dreamy as he looks," Lindsay said. "I'm happy for you."

She smiled.

"It was fun while it lasted. He completely fell off the map. Oh well." I shrugged before I added, "I was really sad at first, but now I'm just a little sad. Hopefully soon, I won't be sad about it at all. It's good to be busy with other things, anyhow."

"I've noticed," said Lindsay, looking around Mr. Franklin's room. "You sure have been spending a lot of time in here. What have you been up to?"

I told her about Mr. Franklin's idea to curate "A View from Bellgrove" using my drawings and photographs from other students.

"Casey, that's fantastic!"

Lindsay's eyes lit up, and I could tell that she was genuinely happy for me.

"This gives me an actual reason to visit the school

A Donut for Your Thoughts

website. You might need to give it a cooler title than that, though," she said.

"You might be right about that," I said thoughtfully, wondering what other title would be more ear-catching.

I told Lindsay that I'd been busy working on the first sketch for the series.

"I'd like to publish my first piece with your permission," I said.

"My permission?" Lindsay was clearly surprised.

She followed me to the annex room, where Mr. Franklin stored student works.

I found my large folder and pulled out a finished portrait, the one I've been obsessing over for the past week. I put it in Lindsay's hands.

She gasped, and her hand flew to her mouth.

"I know I've been MIA lately, but I wanted this drawing to be just perfect, to come out exactly as I saw it in my mind," I said. "It's not perfect, but I hope it's good enough. Do you like it?"

I was a little nervous while I waited for her answer.

Lindsay's eyes welled up as she stared at my sketch of her mom, who was smiling directly at us from the other side of life, wearing angel's wings.

DONUT DREAMS

"Casey, it's . . ." Lindsay was choked up. "My favorite drawing ever. It looks realer than any photograph I've ever seen of her. I love it. My family would love to have Mom honored in this way. I'm officially obsessed with your talent!"

"I've been practicing drawing from memory, and this is how I see her . . . behind my eyes," I explained.

"Is this what I think it is?" Lindsay said.

She grinned as she ran her finger over the halo I'd sketched above her mom's head.

"A donut halo, Case?"

We laughed our butts off.

"Sorry, I was hungry and couldn't resist," I giggled. "Now the title should make sense."

"'A Donut for Your Thoughts,'" Lindsay read the title at the bottom of the sketch.

We laughed a heap more.

"Perfect," she said.

"I try," I said, grinning from ear to ear.

"Now I feel stupid for being so jealous," Lindsay said. "It's just that I wished my mom's artiness had rubbed off on me, too. She taught me to appreciate art, but I'm pretty sure I'm not an artist. I'll never be as good as my mom."

A Donut for Your Thoughts

"I don't think anyone's expecting you to be," I said, trying to comfort her.

"Wrong about that!" Lindsay said. "Since I started drawing stick figures, people have asked me if I'm going to be an artist like her. Whenever I say my last name, people assume I'm going to be a great artist. Then . . . they quickly see how wrong they are. I feel like I'm letting everyone down when I don't churn out some amazing drawing . . . including my mom."

"Wow, Lindsay, I had no idea."

Now it was my turn to be surprised. I guess that goes to show that even though we've been BFFs since day one, literally, there were always things to learn about each other.

Maybe this was what my dad meant when he said that he would never understand my mom completely, even after all their years of marriage.

Mr. Franklin strolled into the art room.

"How are you two doing?" he asked, with a wink.

"Good," Lindsay and I said at the same time.

We looked at each other and started cracking up. Because we were.

"I'm glad I have you here, Lindsay, because I want to ask you something," Mr. Franklin said.

He joined us in the annex room, pulled some work out of one of the large student folders, and came over.

When she saw what he was holding, Lindsay covered her eyes and her face turned bright red.

"Your continuous line drawing this week was one of the best in your class," Mr. Franklin said, holding up a drawing she'd made of her art partner. "Look at how smooth and effortless your line is. Excellent eye-hand coordination."

Continuous line drawings are not my favorite; I have serious problems drawing someone's face in one continuous line without being able to pick up my pencil. Mine come out all shaky.

But Lindsay had done a great job. I could recognize our friend Michelle's face in her drawing, clear as day.

"Thanks, Mr. Franklin." Lindsay beamed with pride.

"I wanted to ask you if I can hang this up. I already have an idea for what kind of frame I want to use to make it pop," said Mr. Franklin. "Do I have your permission to do so?"

"Well, I'll have to think about it," Lindsay said, twirling a lock of her hair and looking up. "Okay! Yes!"

A Donut for Your Thoughts

We all laughed at her terrible acting skills.

I nudged her with my elbow. "So, as you were saying?"

Grinning, Lindsay turned and hugged me.

"Okay, I guess it's still possible that I can be an artist."

Chapter Thirteen
Two of a Kind

Later, Mom dropped us off at the Park to continue our BFF date. Everything was arranged for me to get a ride home from the Coopers after dinner.

At the podium, Grandpa Coop greeted us as he did everyone, like we were special.

"Now here's my favorite pair in town," said Grandpa Coop. He always chuckled, for some reason, at the sight of us.

"I know I'm doing something right when my employees show up to work on their day off."

Uh-oh.

Did Grandpa Coop mean work as in place of business, or work as in grab an apron and get cracking?!

A Donut for Your Thoughts

Maybe he thought we were coming in to save the day instead of to hang out like regular customers. What is he actually saying?

I glanced at Lindsay to see what she thought.

She looked back at me with confused eyes that said, *I don't know.*

Her eyes angled toward the Donut Dreams counter behind her, which she'd have to turn her head to see.

From where I was standing, I only had to look straight past her head to see what was going on there.

Lindsay's older cousin Lily was behind the Donut Dreams counter, and that was a sight to see.

Lily was my favorite of Lindsay's high school cousins. She had such a genuine smile and a beautiful nature that made her really good with kids. When she spoke to them, her voice was like a bottle of honey, warmed in sunshine.

If the Park View Table hadn't snatched her up at birth, she would be the town babysitter or something.

Lily also happens to be the clumsiest waitress as well as the most anxious driver I've ever seen. After many broken dishes, she retired from being a server.

Thankfully, everyone in town knows Lily's car

DONUT DREAMS

and can look out for her on the big bad roads of Bellgrove.

With the Donut Dreams customers, Lily was keeping the conversation moving, all smiles, but as a worker it was clear that she was super overwhelmed. She almost dropped a fresh tray of donuts, but the queen of close calls played it off with her million-dollar smile.

I gave Lindsay a *sorry* look.

She turned to Grandpa Coop and said, "We are here to rescue Donut Dreams if need be."

It might not be Mom and Dad's, but our BFF telepathy wasn't so bad.

"Thank you, girls, but it's not my call," Grandpa said, glancing at Lily and looking a little relieved. "You know where to find the Donut Dreams powers that be. Why don't you go back there and see what they have to say about the fate of Donut Dreams this afternoon."

Lindsay and I headed to the back to the kitchen, where all the magic happened.

Nans and Lindsay's dad were having a friendly disagreement about something. They looked relieved when they saw us.

A Donut for Your Thoughts

"We're here!" said Lindsay.

"Do you need help with anything?" I asked.

"I need someone to tell Nans here that her taste buds are aging faster than she is," said Mr. Cooper.

"I don't know what you're talking about, Mom. This lavender lemon cake donut is my best creation yet!"

Lindsay's dad gestured to his newest donut flavor like he was some game show host unveiling the grand prize. The donut sure looked dreamy, with yellow sprinkles and true blue icing, his wife's favorite color.

Lindsay and I glanced at each other and smiled. I was pretty sure we were both thinking the same thing, that this would be the perfect donut for her mom's halo.

"Not so fast," said Nans.

She was a tough critic when it came to the dream status of new donut flavors.

"The lemon is too loud. I can't taste the lavender. That's false advertising!"

"Well, we have two more judges," Mr. Cooper said, offering us a donut each.

He was looking mighty confident.

"Tell us what you think, girls," he said.

Now here was a donut for your thoughts. I must

say, when you bite into one of Mr. Cooper's freshly made cake or yeast donuts of any flavor, it's hard to be a real critic. The consistency of the lemony cake was perfectly soft and dissolved in my mouth like a dream.

In a minute flat, Lindsay and I were licking our fingers.

"Dad, this is amazing," Lindsay said. "But Nans is right. I don't know if I'm tasting the lavender."

"Neither am I, but I've never tasted lavender before!" I said.

"Same here!" said Lindsay. "Maybe we need one more donut each just to make sure!"

"Hah! Nice try," Mr. Cooper said. "But I think I got the answer I needed. Back to the drawing board I go. Have fun with your BFF on your day off, Linds."

Funny thing: donut making sounded very similar to art making, after all. Maybe Lindsay had more art in her genes than she realized.

When we returned to the floor, Lily had the Donut Dreams counter under control. Streams of happy kids and their parents were flowing out of the Park with bags and boxes of pure sweetness.

Lindsay grabbed our favorite booth by the window,

with a lush view of the park. Minutes later, her older cousin Jenna automatically brought us cream sodas, our favorites.

"Hey, I never got to say how sorry I was for ruining your sketch of Matt," Lindsay said. "I was way too embarrassed to think about how it must have made you feel. And the way everyone was looking at me like I was the worst person on the planet . . . I wanted to disappear!"

"I know the feeling," I groaned. "Especially when my mom showed up."

"Yeah, that must have been pretty mortifying," Lindsay agreed. She gave me a sympathetic look before taking a sip of her soda. "She was all up in your business."

"Who's the boy, Case?" I imitated in my best Assistant Principal Peters voice.

We laughed so hard at my impression that tears started to form a bit in my eyes.

"So what did you do with the portrait?" Lindsay asked. "I hope that it isn't too ruined. Do you still have it in your sketchbook? Can I see?"

I quickly finished the last of my soda before I opened my sketchbook. I flipped through it until I came across the sketch. It wasn't too bad once the OJ dried.

"It was just going to sit around and become yellow on its own anyway," I said.

"You mean, you weren't going to show it to him?!" Lindsay's eyes got huge.

"No way!" I almost shouted. "Why would I do that?"

"Because it's amazing!" Lindsay insisted. "If that doesn't get you more than a one-word response from him, I don't know what will."

Lindsay got me thinking.

Matt was really turning out to be one of those out-of-sight, out-of-mind friends. I was just starting to put our friendship behind me, and I wasn't so sure that I wanted to put myself out there again, and risk feeling rejected . . . all over again.

Matt also lived far away. Our camp is five hours away from where I live and Matt lives five hours away too…but in a different direction. If he didn't land a scholarship, then most likely he wouldn't be at camp next summer and I would never see him again.

Was it even worth it to reach out one more time? What if he didn't even like the drawing?

A Donut for Your Thoughts

"Let me see something," Lindsay said.

Before I knew it she was picking up my phone and carefully positioning it over Matt's sketch to take a picture.

"The damage doesn't show up that much."

She handed me the phone.

The sketch did look pretty legit.

Funny how I'd started out making sketches from photographs. Now I was making photographs of my sketches, and I had Matt to thank for it all.

I supposed sending him the picture of him that I'd drawn was the least I could do.

I thought of that night at the campfire when we promised to create mental pictures from memories. Little did he know that it was not only the campfire burning its way into my mind. His face had snuck its way into the fabric of my thoughts. If it weren't for his encouragement, I'd still be in my comfort zone, sketching from photographs.

Now my memory was becoming sharp, like my dad's old-fashioned razor. If it weren't for Matt, I would never have had the bravery to start sketching from memory, at least not now. In a huge way, Matt played a big part in the artist I am today.

DONUT DREAMS

Maybe some thanks were in order.

"Atta girl," Lindsay said, as I went ahead and sent him the picture.

But it felt different this time.

The difference was, I sent it to him without hoping for a response. It was like a wordless thank-you for believing in me when I didn't even believe in myself.

"So what else are you working on?" Lindsay said, eyeing my sketchbook.

Now I was actually excited to show her my newest project, "Two of a Kind."

It was a sketch I was working on of my parents, a back view of them standing hip to hip at the sink. Dad is washing dishes with his eyes on Mom, grinning like a boy, and Mom is drying dishes and watching him, too, all in her feelings.

"Ooh, Case, this is so romantic," Lindsay said. "This is going to make them fall in love with each other all over again!"

As if my mom and dad needed any help in that department.

Lindsay and I looked through more of my sketches and ordered some delicious food to eat.

It felt nice to get back into the groove of our

A Donut for Your Thoughts

friendship. I could see what Mom had meant about talking things out. It definitely felt good to clear the air, even though it had been hard.

I could see now that even Lindsay and I were two of a kind.

Chapter Fourteen
Close to Perfect

Later that night, alone in bed, I was putting the finishing touches on "Two of a Kind." I was planning on unveiling it to my family the next morning at our Saturday brunch. I had dragonflies in my stomach just thinking about coming out of my artsy closet to my family once and for all, but I was ready.

My phone buzzed. I guessed it was Lindsay, but no, it was Matt's name flashing across my screen.

He definitely had more than one word this time.

> Hey C. Ur sketch was sooo good I didn't know what 2 say @ 1st. I will never 4get it or u! Thank u!

A Donut for Your Thoughts

By the way my heart was flopping around in my chest, you would have thought Matt had just walked in my bedroom door.

What was up with me?

I thought I was close to forgetting this clueless boy, but also the most mature boy I've ever known. Now all our memories were rushing back, our nicknames and jokes and life talks over blackening marshmallows. If I'm being totally honest, his more-than-one-word response was way more than I'd expected, but why was I sitting there wishing he'd said . . . more?

I guess it was good to know that he'd remember me at least, that he remembered our private joke about our skin deserving its own Crayola color, biracial beige.

Still, I wanted more of a window into his world.

Was he writing as much as I was drawing?

And was school kicking his butt this year or what?

And did he ever think of me before he fell asleep?

If only I could get another peek into his notebook, squinting at his chicken scratch, just to get a clue. Too bad he was so far away.

I stared into my phone for a while, thinking of how to respond. I got up to go visit Gabby's room

DONUT DREAMS

for boy advice, but I quickly sat back down instead. It wasn't like this was a crisis. I had this.

I belly-flopped back onto my bed and picked up my phone.

> Um . . . never forget me? Are you going on a secret mission to Mars or something?

LOL I dunno. Just didn't want 2 assume.

> Assume what? That I'm your friend and want to know what's up with you?

Sorry, Case. Been crazy busy w/ school + Mom's giving me lots 2 write about. Think of u daily, tho.

> Been thinking of you too and busy with new drawings. Just finished one for my parents.

A Donut for Your Thoughts

> They'll love it. Still can't get over how much better u got after camp.

> Thanks! Tomorrow morning will be their first time seeing a drawing of mine!

> I love ur parents + I don't even know them. Can I come + meet them?

> Are you for real? They don't know you exist!

> LOL! That hurts, ice queen. I told my mom bout u. She loved ur cat meme btw!

> ...

> U there?

> Sorry, wasn't expecting that. Are you serious??

DONUT DREAMS

> Yeah we talk bout u all the time. Is that weird?

> Um... yeah! You talk about me but not TO me??

> My bad 4 not telling u sooner. Mom takes my phone 4 no reason! I nvr have time on here. I just got it back 2day after she had it all week!

> ...

> Hello?

> Crazy, I thought you were forgetting about me.

> I couldn't do that if I tried, girl.

> Well I tried.

> LOL. Fo sho. How'd that work out?

A Donut for Your Thoughts

I was feeling all warm and sleepy by the time I put down my phone. For minutes on end, I stared at the ceiling with a silly grin, all those familiar summer feelings coursing through my body like my own blood.

Matt and I had had such a great conversation. It felt just like the summer had—no pressure and no issues. After weeks of worrying over the state of our friendship, I now felt the opposite, that Matt and I were friends for life.

Life suddenly got totally cool and super weird.

Had Matt just invited himself over for a visit? To meet my family?!

And I couldn't believe his mom saw my cat meme!

I was feeling mighty guilty. While Matt and his mom were chatting it up about me, he's been the elephant in my house.

What was my problem, anyway?

Aside from the fact that he was a boy, and a cute boy at that, Matt was hands down the closest friend I'd ever made at sleepaway camp.

Even worse, when my mom spotted his portrait

and asked me about him in front of the field hockey team, I actually called him a nobody.

A nobody!

Maybe I was the weird one. Ugh.

I picked up my phone and texted Lindsay.

> Brilliant BFF for making me send that photo!

> I just got waaaay more than a one-word response and I am not mad at it! 😉 Stay tuned for more Casey tea tomorrow! Love ya!

> LOL! Groan. Ur such a tease. Love YOU!

I couldn't wait to tell Gabby in the morning that her video-game theory was way off.

Back at camp, Matt didn't talk about his mom a whole lot, but I got the impression that they were really close, even though she was super strict and no-nonsense.

A Donut for Your Thoughts

One story he told me stood out in particular. One morning he said something disrespectful to his mom on the drive to school, and she pulled over and made him walk the rest of the way.

He was ten!

I couldn't imagine my mom doing something so hardcore, but with my snotty attitude these days, I'm sure she's thought about it at least once.

As for his dad, well, he didn't make sense to me at all, because he left when Matt was two. Matt didn't sound sad about it, though; he was very matter-of-fact about it all.

I picked up the sketch of my parents and studied it, cocking my head to the side like Lindsay's mom used to do when she came close to finishing a painting.

I resisted the urge to pick up my pencil once again and mess with it some more. I was learning that in art there were always things that I could change, or wished I could change. But there comes a point when it's time to let it go.

And while sharing my portrait of her mom with Lindsay was nerve-racking, even though I might not have shown it, the true test was my parents. I felt kind of jittery inside just thinking about presenting this to

DONUT DREAMS

them tomorrow at brunch. The more I looked at the picture to spot something wrong with it to fix, the more I realized that I didn't want to change a single thing.

In a world where there was no such thing as perfect, this was close enough.

Chapter Fifteen
Matt Meets the Family (Sort Of!)

Whatever goodness they were cooking up that special Saturday lifted me out of a dream and out of bed and pushed me into the bathroom to brush my teeth.

I trudged into the hallway, and I could hear my family downstairs chatting and laughing—Gabby's laugh drowning out everyone else's, of course. Just listening to them filled me up with that warm, lucky feeling I had only started feeling lately.

It was inevitable that Mom would end up working some nerve of mine, but I wanted to hold on to this feeling for as long as I could.

I tossed some water on my face and looked at myself in the mirror. For once I didn't start fussing with my combination hair. I didn't care that it hadn't yet decided if it was going to lie down straight or levitate, or that today it looked sort of blah.

Today's mirror showed me so much more than myself. It was my mom's round eyes staring back at me, hovering over my dad's nose, the way our nostrils flared when we breathed. When I lifted my chin, I almost had Gabby's swan neck. Almost.

Before going downstairs, I scooped up "Two of a Kind" and gave it a final once-over.

And you know what? The dragonflies in my belly weren't even there anymore.

Of course I still hoped everyone would swoon over my newest work, but that mattered less now, for some reason. But it felt more important that I loved the outcome almost as much as I'd loved making it!

I was also itching to figure out what my next project would be.

"Casey!" Gabby called from downstairs. "Food's ready!"

"Coming!" I called, and galloped downstairs.

Three pairs of eyes smiled my way when I entered the room. Mom, Dad, and Gabby were patiently sitting in front of untouched plates of shrimp and grits.

A Donut for Your Thoughts

"Morning, fam," I said, plopping into my chair.

"What you got there, Case?" Gabby asked, nodding with her chin at my sketch.

Leave it to her to move this thing right along.

This is it.

"Mom, thank you for asking to see my artwork. It meant a lot to me. So I've been working on something all week to show you . . . during my recreational hours, of course, ahem," I said, giving Mom a totally unnecessary, petty sideswipe that made her laugh with surprise.

And that, my friends, is what you call the Gabby effect.

"Shots fired!" Gabby said, looking like a proud mama, giggling at the low-key shade of it all.

"Well let's see this A-plus artwork," Mom responded haughtily, but with a big grin that got us laughing all over again.

When I turned over the page to show off my newest creation, I admit my heart must've stopped for at least an instant.

Mom's hand drifted to her mouth.

"Oh my," she said.

Her eyes were welling up when she looked at my

dad, who was getting a little misty-eyed too.

I considered it a slam dunk, getting both my parents in their feelings at the same time.

"This is us," was all my dad could manage.

"My two and only," I answered, beaming.

"Casey, I must say, this is incredible work," Mom said, snapping back into assistant principal mode.

It made me wonder if I had imagined the whole teary-eyed thing.

"I thought you were holed up in that room of yours doing some cartoon drawings, what do you call those . . . man . . . ?"

"Manga, Mom!" said Gabby.

"Yes, that," Mom said, waving away the matter. "But this is really realistic stuff, Case, and it's amazing. Extraordinary. So meticulous! This must have taken forever—"

"Just every spare moment I could squeeze out of this past week," I said.

"Well done. It's a real level up for you, Case," Gabby said, nodding her head sincerely.

That meant a lot coming from the only person who has seen my drawings grow from stick figures.

"I see a bright future ahead for you and your art,"

A Donut for Your Thoughts

Dad said. "It's actually inspired an idea that I hope you'll say yes to, as long as it doesn't take too much away from your schoolwork, of course. You would also earn some dollars to keep up with your art supply bill."

Well, that got my attention.

"I'm listening," I said.

"I've wanted to do something to make people more aware of the perils of texting while driving, sort of like a PSA. And after seeing the realism of your drawings, this came to me. With their permission, of course, can I commission you to do portraits of survivors of text-related accidents? I would like to feature their portraits in and around my office to humanize the PSA. What do you say?" Dad asked.

My turn to be in all my feelings. I was speechless.

Without saying anything, I got up to hug my dad.

Then Gabby got up for a three-way hug.

Mom must have been feeling a little left out, so she wrapped her arms around all of us.

"End scene!" Gabby called out, making us explode into giggles as we took our seats.

She picked up "Two of a Kind" and placed it on the counter to protect it from shrimp grease.

"Let's dig in!" she said.

"So, Case, do you have any more work that you'd like to share with us?" Mom asked, heaping shrimp and grits onto her fork. "I'm hooked!"

If I could raise an eyebrow like a movie star, I would've, because I definitely wasn't expecting that from my mom!

"I do have another thing," I replied, beaming, and whipped out my phone.

Oops.

Lindsay had sent me a text two hours ago dying to know what went down last night.

I flipped to my photos and showed them the sketch of Matt. They approved of the picture, but would they approve of the boy?

"This is Matt Machado, a boy I met at camp," I said.

"A boy?" my dad said slowly, as if it was just dawning on him that I hadn't been attending an all-girls sleepaway camp for the past five summers.

He clearly hadn't gotten the memo, but Mom wasn't surprised. I knew she remembered this picture from the cafeteria.

"Handsome young man," Mom said, nodding.

A Donut for Your Thoughts

"Looks interesting, too. When will we have the pleasure of meeting him?"

"OMG, he said the same thing in a text message last night, but I thought he was mainly joking," I said. "Truth is, he lives pretty far away. And he is interesting, since he's a writer and all."

"Ooh, a writer and an artist! What an interesting pair you must've been at that boring ol' sleepaway camp!" said Gabby, totally rubbing it in.

"Text . . . last night?" Dad repeated in a sort of daze.

"Earth to Dad!" said Gabby, waving her hand in front of his face. "No worries. He's just her camp friend. Right, Casey?"

"He's not just my camp friend," I said.

The room went quiet.

"He's my camp BFF!" I finished.

"Hmm. I wonder what the Bellgrove BFF would have to say about that," said Gabby.

"Nice try, Lindsay already knows," I said.

Gabby was always finding ways to make me and Lindsay argue, mostly because she thought our best friend drama was hilariously cute, even cuter than cat memes.

DONUT DREAMS

"If you say he's your BFF, then we're going to have to meet him eventually," Mom said and looked at Dad. "Right, hon?"

"Well, I don't see why that's even necessary," Dad huffed. "And doesn't he live far away?"

Gabby and I looked at each other. Had Dad just disagreed with Mom openly?

"Um, there's something called video chat," said sweet and sarcastic Gabby. "We can beam him in right now if we wanted."

And as if by magic, my phone lit up in my hand and sounded.

"Speak of the devil," I said.

It was Matt texting.

> Hey C, wanna say hi 2 my mom?

> Yeah, but only if you say hi to mine too.

> Ha! Mom swap! I'm game if u r. Let's go!

A Donut for Your Thoughts

"Is everyone ready to meet Matt and his mom?" I asked.

I took an extra-long look at Dad, and he nodded.

"Beam him in," he sighed, quickly wiping his grease-lined mouth with a napkin.

I answered Matt's request to video-chat, and just like that—Matt and his mom were at our table.

"Hey, everyone, hey, Case, meet my twin!" he said.

He put the camera on his mom and we all laughed, waved, and said hello. His mom really was just a darker and more beautiful version of him, with short, dyed locks.

And before we could say anything else, our moms hit it off, just like that. Somehow, they started talking about everything under the sun all at the same time! They talked so much that my hand was starting to ache from holding up the phone for so long.

The last time I saw Mom speak so candidly with someone outside of our family was, well, with Lindsay's mom. Clearly, they needed to exchange digits and talk on their own time.

Before we all hung up the phone, Matt's mom said to me, "Matt told me he met an artist at camp, and boy, he was right. He showed me your drawing of him, and I must admit, I got a little teary-eyed."

"Well, yes, we're now just learning Casey's art does have that effect," Mom said. "We've been unaware."

"Speak for yourself and your husband," Gabby laughed. "I've always known my little sister had crazy talent!"

Matt's mom laughed and rumpled his hair. "Talking about talent, my twin here shared the story he wrote about you two, Case, and it brought tears to my eyes."

"Mom!" Matt groaned.

And I thought my cafeteria scene on Monday was the height of embarrassment!

"Story about *moi*?" I said.

Then I remembered the night at the bonfire when we talked about mental images, and the deal we made to re-create a campfire moment using our photographic memories, no cameras.

Matt's mom said that when I sent Matt my campfire drawing, he got to work on re-creating our scene for the book of his life.

Matt promised to read it to me later on.

"So does that mean I'm officially a character in your book?" I asked.

A Donut for Your Thoughts

I couldn't hide my blushing any more than Dad could hide his dismay.

"That's entirely up to you, Casey, because in my son, you've got a fan," Matt's mom said.

I glanced at Gabby, who just about melted.

After we said our goodbyes, I couldn't wait to put down the phone and dig into the rest of the delicious meal my parents had made. Even though I was packing on hundreds of calories, I felt a thousand pounds lighter.

And I couldn't wait to call Lindsay. It seemed like everything had finally fallen into place.

As I ate and laughed with my family, I couldn't help but smile at everything that had happened these past few weeks. Who knew so many changes could be like, so totally rewarding!

Now I was an official artist, I had learned to appreciate my awesome family, and I had not one, but TWO BFFs!

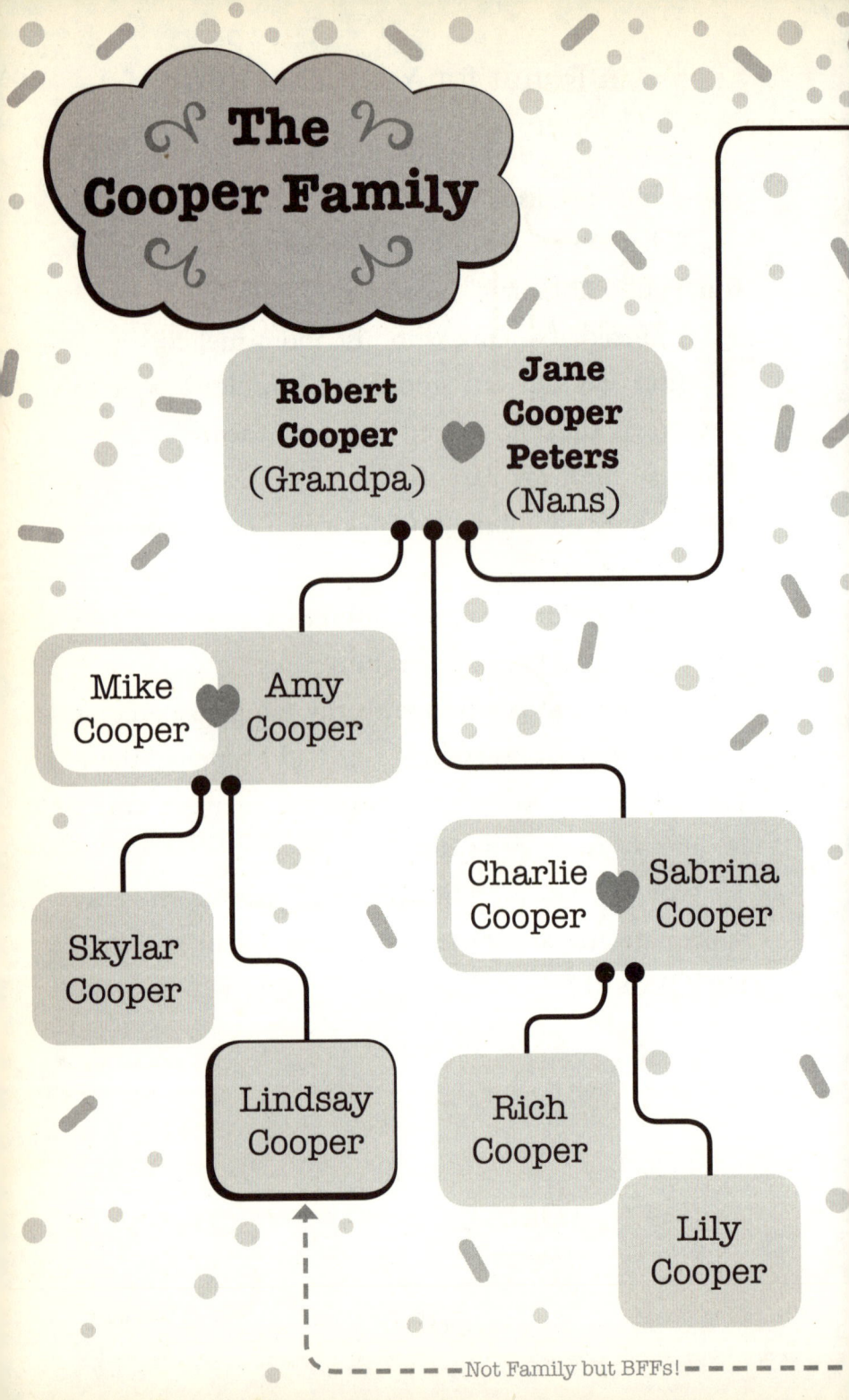

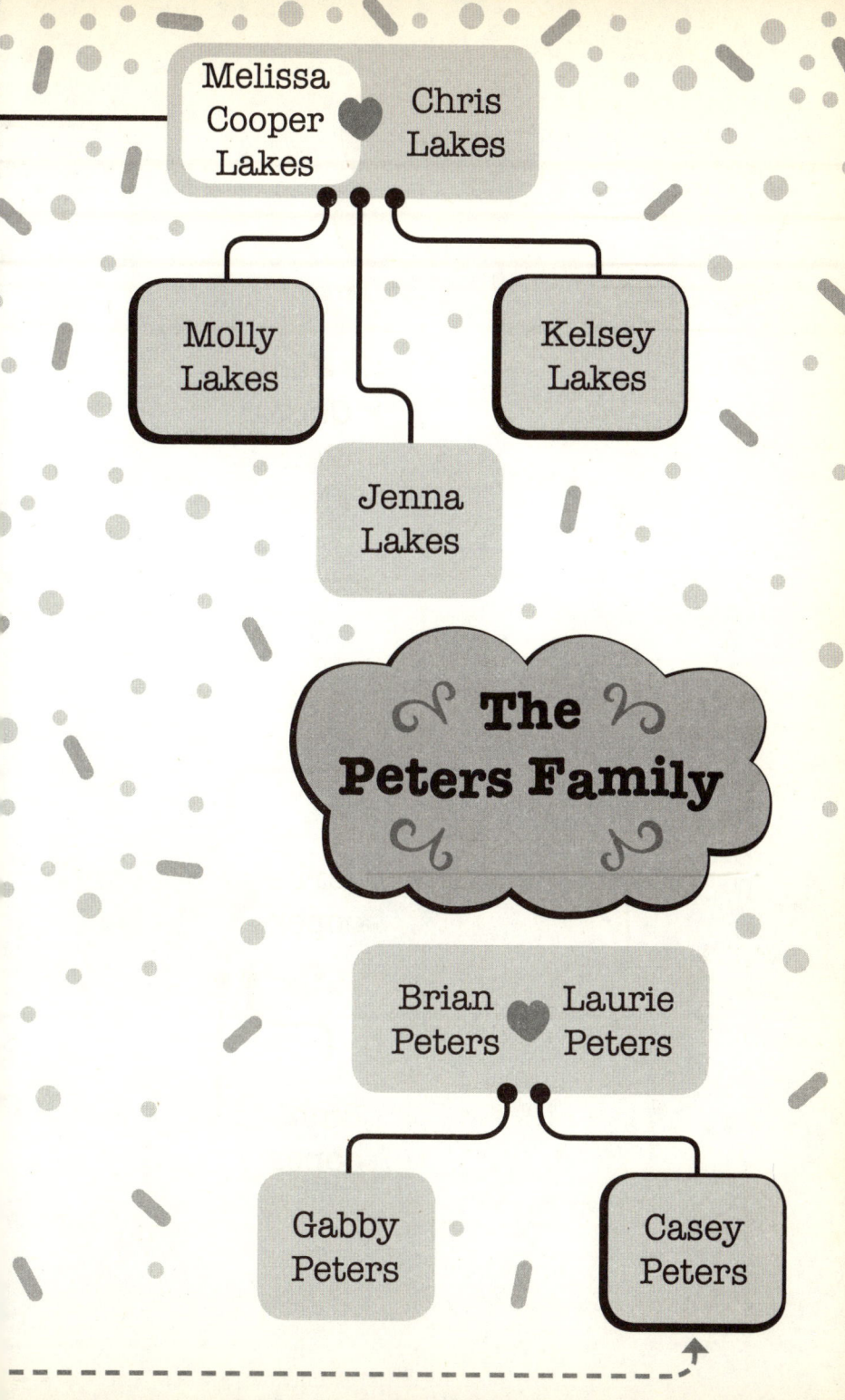

Still Hungry?
Here's a taste of the fifth book in the

series, Ready, Set, Bake!

Chapter One
The New Normal

I woke up this morning feeling totally at peace, even though it was a Monday.

Crazy, right?

But after a few weeks of middle school, I finally felt like I had the hang of things: I knew exactly how long I had to get to each class, where I could hide and take a phone break, and the best locker to grab when I had to change for PE.

One thing I didn't like, though, was that our seats weren't fixed in all of our classes. In elementary school, my BFF Casey and I would pick our seats right next to each other on the first day of school, and those would be our seats for the year. We could relax.

Now, I'm scrambling to try to get a seat next to Casey at least half the time. And if we don't time it right, we're way far apart. I wish I had the hang of that.

Still, I've kind of been loving the routine of middle school. It's funny, because all of my life I've dreamed about getting out of Bellgrove, my tiny hometown where everyone knows everyone else's business and routines.

But lately, I've been kind of liking it. I've felt happy knowing exactly where I had to be, what I had to do, and who would be with me every day. For the first time, it actually felt good knowing everyone in town and having all of them know me. It felt like things were under control.

Speaking of control, my grandmother's kind (but bossy) voice floated up the stairs and curled under my door. "Lindsay? Sweetheart? Are you up yet? Rise and shine!"

Nans comes over every weekday morning to get me and my brother, Skylar, to school. Ever since our mom died a few years ago, our whole extended family has pitched in to help fill the giant Mom-sized hole in our lives.

My mom's mom, my grandmother Mimi, is our only relative on her side of the family. Mimi lives in Chicago, which is two hours away by car, but she visits a lot and we go see her there often. It's really hard on her that my mom is gone, so we comfort each other in both directions.

My dad's family is from Bellgrove and they all settled here. Our family owns a restaurant called the Park View Table that's like the hub of our town. It's centrally located and overlooks our beautiful town park, and inside it is a small donut shop called Donut Dreams.

Almost everyone in my family has a job at the restaurant: there's my dad, Mike (he runs Donut Dreams); me (donut counter); my grandpa (manager); Nans (chef); my dad's sister, my aunt Melissa (finances); her girls Kelsey (donut counter with me), Molly (a "runner" or bus girl), and Jenna (waitress); my dad's brother, my uncle Charlie (ordering and inventory); and Charlie's son Rich (waiter) and daughter Lily (hostess).

My aunt Sabrina is a nurse and my uncle Chris is a carpenter who also teaches shop at our town high school, but even they help out at the Park from time to time. We all pitch in together and take care of each other, though lately it's mostly been all of them taking care of me and my family.

All of this has been great for me and Sky and my dad, and I know that. It's just that I really wish my mom were still here. I wish I could have her back, even for a minute, even just to talk about some boring thing in school, or what was going on in her garden.

My mom was an artist, but she was crazy about flowers. She had a beautiful garden out behind our house (it's gotten a little wild, I hate to admit) and she loved planning it and tending it and cutting and arranging its flowers.

My mom often said she could have been a florist almost as happily as an artist and art teacher. "It's the same skill set—shapes and colors!" she used to say.

At the very end of my mom's illness, she told me to remember that after she died, whenever I saw a flower, it would be her saying, "Hi."

And whenever I saw a blue flower (her favorite color was cornflower blue, or "true blue," as she called it), it would be her sending me a huge hug. It's made me notice flowers a lot more, which I guess was her point.

"Flowers bring joy," she would always say. "Seek out joy!"

But now that fall was settling in, there weren't too many flowers around, and certainly not any blue ones. All I'd been seeing were those tubs with ginormous balls of Halloween-colored mums in them, orange and yellow and rusty red.

Yuck.

I missed my mom.

"Lindsay!" Nans called again.

"Coming, Nans!" I whipped off my comforter and scrambled to get ready.

※ ※ ※ ※ ※

Downstairs, Skylar was already at the table, eating his bottomless bowl of Coco Snacks, or whatever the flavor of the week was. The kid is always starving, and Nans lets him have junky cereal for breakfast because it makes it easier to get him out of bed that way.

"Some call it bribery," Nans would sigh when asked. "I call it time management."

My morning job was to get our lunches ready while Nans fixed breakfast. Since our family owns and runs the Park, we're all pretty comfortable in the kitchen.

Nans was making me a quick omelet, just the way I like it with cheddar and chives, while I made ham and cheese sandwiches on whole grain pita pockets with mustard and baby spinach for me and Sky.

I wrapped them in our new reusable Bee's Wrap waxed cloth (my dad's gone environmental lately as part of some research he's doing for the Park) and filled two small Tupperware tubs with corn chips. Then an apple each and our Yeti bottles filled from the water cooler; it all went into our soft, reusable lunch coolers.

I set the coolers by the back door and sat down just as Nans was putting the piping hot omelet at my place.

"Perfect timing!" she said, kissing me on the head. "Toast?"

"No, thanks," I said as I dug in. The omelet was delicious—the perfect start to a Monday morning. "Mmmm. tastes just like fancy restaurant cooking!" I said.

That's a family joke of ours, since we all pitch in at the Park and Nans actually does do a lot of the cooking there. We all say it anytime a family member cooks anything.

Nans swatted at me playfully with a dishtowel and turned back to the counter to clean up.

"Nans," said Skylar though a mouthful of Cocoa Snacks. He was already on his third bowl.

"Yes, my love?" said Nans, scrubbing the frying pan.

"When's it my turn to bring donuts to school for my class? All the kids are asking."

Nans turned off the water and looked at Sky with a smile. "Have you checked the chart?"

Sky shook his head.

Since so many people in the family and in town ask for free donuts all the time, Nans and Grandpa finally had to make a giveaway chart to hang at the Park to keep track of donations.

My aunt Melissa is the accountant at the restaurant and Donut Dreams, and she said we'd fall into financial ruin if we didn't keep better track of our donuts.

"You can't keep giving away all of your product for free to every bingo night in town! Here's the rule:

Twice a month. Four dozen at a time. That's all we can afford. Tell people to sign up early," she said.

So that was the rule. Each of the seven grandkids got a turn to bring donuts to school once a year, and we tried to time it to our birthdays. Some families bring cupcakes to school but we bring donuts. People love it.

The best part is that when it's your turn, you get to go into the restaurant really early in the morning and fill the four boxes with the four dozen donuts in the flavors of your choice.

My BFF, Casey, is totally down with this tradition and starts reminding me the week leading up to my birthday how much she *loooooves* our cinnamon donuts.

As if I didn't know that by now. As if I wasn't already slotting a dozen cinnamon donuts into my birthday assortment way in advance!

Nans continued, "Okay, I'll check the donation calendar for you when I get to work and I'll let you know this afternoon. Your birthday is next month, Sky-baby, so it's coming up!"

Sky grinned and some gluey chocolate mush oozed through his teeth.

"Ugh!" I groaned and went to clean up my dishes and get my things for school.

Minutes later, we were in the car and on our way.

☀ ☀ ☀ ☀ ☀

As soon as I walked into school, I saw Casey.

"Hey!" I said, coming up behind her and pulling on one of her long, dark curls.

"Hey, girl!" Casey said, twirling me around and grabbing me in a hug.

"Long time no talk," I joked, since we try to always text right before we go to sleep and right when we wake up.

We're on a Snapstreak right now—haven't missed a day in two weeks—and we're trying to keep it that way. We like setting silly goals like that for ourselves.

"I have a big scoop!" said Casey, her dark eyes wide and her eyebrows scrunched way high in excitement.

But before she could fill me in, we were interrupted.

"What's up, chicas?" asked my cousin Kelsey, popping open her locker.

She's in my grade, as is her sister, my cousin Molly. They aren't twins, which is confusing since they're almost the exact same age.

My aunt and uncle adopted Molly from Korea and then my aunt had a surprise baby, Kelsey. I liked having them both in my grade—they were so different that they each added a lot in different ways—but we all had our own small friend groups.

"Hey, Kels," I said.

I wanted to hear Casey's news, but I wasn't sure if it was for public consumption. I glanced at her and she looked ready to burst.

"Guess what?" Casey said, looking all around the busy hallway. She lowered her voice to a throaty whisper and Kelsey and I leaned in. "We're getting a new student today!"

"A new student? Now?" blurted Kelsey loudly, swiveling her head and generally making a Kelsey-like scene. Kelsey doesn't do anything in a small way.

"Shhh!" said Casey. "My mom will kill me if she thinks I'm spilling news."

Chapter Two
The New Girl

All the buzzing was definitely about the bakery boxes.

I wondered whose birthday it was. I'd been with the same kids all my life, so I had a good idea when birthday treats were coming up, and I didn't think we were due for one for another few weeks.

I glanced at the birthday chart at the far side of the whiteboard and saw that no one was scheduled until next month.

Huh. And where was there even a bakery near here? Someone must've imported them from Linkstown, about half an hour away.

"Linds! Over here!" called Casey.

She'd snagged two seats side by side. The seat ahead of her was empty but had someone's bag on it.

I crossed the room quickly and rejoined Casey.

As I stowed my bag under my seat, Ms. Ogden turned to face the class, and I could suddenly see there was a new girl with her.

She was petite and had glossy jet-black hair, olive skin, and dark eyes that flashed like she'd just heard a joke. Her ears were pierced and she had little gold earrings that dangled as she looked this way and that, as she smiled broadly at us all. She wore dark-washed skinny jeans with perfectly frayed hems, a floaty, pleated white blouse with lace insets down the arms, and a pair of sleek pink flats on her feet.

"Wow. I bet she didn't buy *that* outfit at the Denim Doll," said Casey under her breath.

The Denim Doll was our local cheap fast-fashion place, with clothes that looked trendy but fell apart after, like, two washes.

I nodded, studying the girl. She didn't seem shy or nervous at all!

If I'd had to stand up in front of a room of new people, my mouth would get totally dry and I wouldn't be able to say a word.

"Class, could I have your attention, please?" Ms. Ogden began with a smile.

The room quieted.

"I'd like to introduce you all to Maria Salas, who has just moved to Bellgrove and will be joining our class. Please join me in welcoming Maria and be sure to be your most helpful Bellgrove selves. Being new is hard!"

Maria laughed, revealing little dimples in her cheeks, and she waved at the class.

"Thanks, Ms. Ogden. It's nice to be here. I've brought some treats to share so please help yourselves. I'm looking forward to meeting everyone."

Treats to share? When it wasn't even her birthday? What was Maria trying to do, bribe us all to like her?

As the class began to buzz again, I watched as Maria made her way through the aisles of desks, returning people's greetings with a smile, and plopped into the seat right in front of Casey.

Casey leaned forward and patted Maria on the shoulder, and Maria turned to her with a grin. Casey whispered something and Maria laughed and whispered something back.

I strained to hear what they were saying, but I couldn't make it out among all the chatter of our class. Casey and Maria said a couple more things to each other, and then Ms. Ogden called us all to order again.

I caught one last thing Maria said to Casey before she turned away: "Thanks for the lunch offer. I'll see you there!"

If I were an emoji right then, I would have been that red-faced mad one. My morning's fears had been confirmed: someone new had entered our class and now things were changing, just when I'd gotten the hang of everything.

Worst of all, what was changing were things between me and Casey, just when we'd finally gotten them sorted out after a couple of weeks of awkwardness.

Casey and I had been a little rocky a few weeks ago, and it was mostly because I was annoyed she'd become this so-called great artist, like, living and breathing her "art," which seemed to kind of come out of nowhere.

Suddenly, she was the expert on photography and sketching and drawing and she was being asked to contribute work to the school website, and I was left in the dust.

And it was my mom who'd been the art teacher

at our school and I was supposed to be the one who was good at art. Only I wasn't that good at it and Casey actually was. This all drove me nuts.

Also, Casey had come home from camp at the end of the summer all stirred up about some boy she'd met there named Matt, and I just didn't get it.

I mean, boys are fine, but who wants to be all lovey-dovey with one? That's just gross to me. Sure, someday I'll probably like one, but right now ... ugh. No *thanks!*

But Casey was alternating between being all gooey and obsessed with him and then all stormy and not wanting to talk about him, and it was just putting a little rockiness in our otherwise calm friendship.

Finally, my annoyance had grown to the point where we'd had to have a heart-to-heart, and I admitted that her artiness and her boy obsession were pushing me away.

Casey had explained everything then, which made me feel a little better.

The talk made me see that she was still the same old Casey and that her art skills wouldn't make me feel less close to my mom, and her interest in a boy wouldn't make her less close to me.

We cemented our making-up with milkshakes at the Park and a good Snapchat streak.

It had been about two weeks since we'd gotten back to normal, but now Casey was annoying me again with her buddying up to the new girl.

I just didn't think our delicate new balance would be able to stand the weight of someone new joining us at lunch and crashing our friendship. Especially someone who liked bringing yummy baked goods to school.

That was kind of *my* department!

※ ※ ※ ※ ※

Mr. Franklin is the art teacher who replaced my mom, and he's extra nice to me. I think he probably feels bad that he got this job because my mom passed away, which makes sense.

A few weeks ago he hung up my line drawing—the kind you create without lifting your pencil—which was an honor. Mine was of my friend Michelle, and it did vaguely look like her.

It was one of my better pieces, but it wasn't exactly good. I felt that maybe he was just looking for any work of mine that was slightly above bad that he could celebrate. Like I said, he's kind, and this makes art class bearable for me, even though I'm missing my mom hard the whole time I'm in his classroom—also known as her old studio.

Today, as we worked on our perspective drawings, which use a vanishing point to make something look far away, I gazed up at my perfectly okay framed line drawing.

Right next to it was a drawing by Casey of our classmate, Riley, running across a playing field. It was pretty awesome, even though it was just a line drawing. It had action and good composition and realistic detail.

It was plain to see: Casey was a much better artist than I was, and she enjoyed it more than I did too.

I looked back at my sketch pad on the table and sighed.

"Come on, Lindsay!" I said out loud, but no one heard me over the din.

Unlike other teachers, Mr. Franklin lets us all talk once he's taught us the lesson for the day. If it gets really loud while we're doing our own work, he'll say, "People, volume, please!" and everyone pipes down.

Anyway, today's chatter was all about Maria Salas,

who was off at some other class right now, probably with Casey, since Casey isn't in my art section either. They were probably already passing notes and playing with each other's hair and making plans for sleepovers.

I was not looking forward to lunch, when I'd have to share Casey with her.

"She's from Chicago!" I heard someone say.

I looked up and it was Melanie Fox, across the table from me.

"The new girl's from Chicago?" I asked, sitting up straight. "For real?"

I adored Chicago, especially because my mom was from there, and I planned to move there one day.

Maybe this Maria and I had more in common than I had expected.

"Yeah! Who'd ever want to move to Bellgrove from Chicago?" said Melanie incredulously.

"Seriously!" I agreed, though inwardly cringing as I realized that was just what my mom had done.

"I would!" said my cousin Kelsey, eavesdropping from another table.

I laughed, since it was so typical of her. Kelsey loves Bellgrove so much that she's barely interested in going away for college.

"We know, Kels!" I called over to her.

"Volume, people!" said Mr. Franklin, without even looking over from the easel where he was working.

"Why did she move here?" I whispered to Melanie.

She shrugged. "I barely had a chance to speak to her. I can't wait for lunch to thank her for those treats. Did you have any of them?"

I shook my head.

Melanie rolled her eyes and said, "OMG, they all looked amazing. Like, cream puffs and little coconut chewies. I had a shortbread cookie with sprinkles, but there were also cookies with frosting . . ."

My mouth watered despite my irritation.

"Wow," I said.

"I wanted to try them all!" said Melanie.

"Not too shabby, Linds," said a voice over my shoulder.

Instinctively, I shielded my paper, but it was only Kelsey.

"Hmm. That's not really a compliment, Kels. Let me see yours," I said.

Kelsey and I can be a little competitive, but we're so different that none of it really matters.

"No way!" laughed Kelsey, darting away from me.

"I'm not part of the artistic dynasty. That's your side of the family!"

I looked up at the other three people at my table, but everyone was suddenly quiet and very, very focused on their work. I knew it was because they were feeling bad for me about my mom right then. Like I said, one of the things that bugs me about Bellgrove is that everyone knows your business. But that can be comforting sometimes too.

Like, I don't mind Kelsey mentioning my mom. It's not like I'm not thinking about my mom all the time anyway. And when people who knew her remember things out loud about her, it kind of comforts me.

Sometimes Kelsey can be insensitive, and that bugs me. But for the most part, I'd always rather have people say things about my mom than not. And the last thing I'd want is for people to forget her.

A quiet voice next to me said, "My mom has one of your mom's flower bouquet cards on our fridge."

It was Jamie Enders, a kid I'd been in school with for my whole life but hadn't spoken to much since the third grade, when we had a weird playdate where he tried to make me eat ants in his sandbox and I had refused to play with him ever again.

"Oh yeah?" I said. "She used to love doing those."

"It's really good," he added. "It looks almost real, and my mom says it cheers her up on rainy days."

He smiled apologetically at me, as if he felt bad mentioning his own, alive mom.

This was one part of grieving I hadn't expected: you end up comforting other people all the time. Whether they're sad about your person who died or they feel awkward not knowing what to say to you, or they worry they should have said something, or shouldn't have said something, it's all just a lot.

My dad reminds me sometimes when I get tired of it that everyone means well, and death makes people awkward. It's good to try to remember that, and like I said, I always appreciate people saying stuff about my mom rather than not.

I smiled back at Jamie. "Thanks. I have one in my room, and there are still a bunch in my mom's studio at home that I like to go look at sometimes."

"Class! Hand in your work and take the last five minutes for free drawing!" Mr. Franklin's voice boomed across the room.

"Want me to bring yours up?" asked Jamie.

"Sure. Thanks."

I tore the sheet out of my sketch pad, wrote my name on the bottom, and handed it to him. It wasn't great, but it wasn't horrible.

I turned back to my sketch pad and began drawing flowers, thinking of my mom's bouquet cards. The Party Shoppe in town had sold them in a spinner rack with a HAND-PAINTED BY LOCAL ARTIST sign on top. After a while, the sign was kind of unnecessary, because everyone knew the bouquet cards were by my mom.

I sketched in a vase under the flowers, and some tendrils and leaves.

Jamie rejoined me and said, "Yeah! Like that, but with lots of color!"

Then he sat back down and we drew quietly, side by side, for the remaining minutes of class.

When the bell rang I said, "See ya, Jamie," and he smiled widely at me.

I guessed we were friends again, ants or no ants.

Now I had to go see if this new Maria girl had taken over my best friend, Casey.

Chapter Three
Friend or Foe?

When the bell rang for lunch, I headed to my locker, stashed my backpack, grabbed my lunch cooler, then looked around for Casey, figuring she'd already be with Maria.

But lo and behold, when Casey arrived at her locker, she was solo.

I looked around her and over her shoulder, but Maria wasn't there.

Had I dodged a bullet? Had Maria found other new friends? I didn't want to mention her for fear of jinxing it.

"Ready?" I asked.

"Yup!" said Casey cheerfully, kicking her locker shut with her foot.

There was a pause as we set off down the hall, and I began to relax.

But then Casey said, "Ria said she'd meet me at lunch."

Not "us," mind you. "Me." *Hmm*. Was Casey planning on ditching me to sit with "Ria" when we got there?

"Ria?" I asked.

Casey nodded. "That's what Maria's friends call her," she explained.

"Oh," I said.

I was quiet while Casey babbled on about long division word problems all the way to the cafeteria.

"I mean, seriously, what do I care when a train leaves Chicago and how fast it's going? I mean, I know *you* probably care, what with your plans to move there and all." Casey laughed. "And Ria probably cares because all her friends are still there."

"Right," I said. I wished I had lots of friends in Chicago.

We entered the cafeteria and I spied our usual table, which was only half-full. Phew. Nothing worse than coming into the cafeteria and having to rethink your plan because your usual spot is unavailable.

I began to cross the room when Casey suddenly said, "Linds. Hold up!"

I turned back and she was waving across the room in the other direction. The person on the other side of her wave was, of course, Ria. She was sitting with a group of girls from study hall.

"Oh, she's all set. Okay, then," I said in relief, turning back toward our table, which had just gained two more people.

There were now only two empty seats left: just perfect for me and Casey. I began to hustle.

"Wait, Lindsay. Ria's waving us over there. Come on!" said Casey.

"But what about our seats?" I protested. "They'll be gone if I don't snag them now. Why don't you go say hi and I'll save the two seats for us?"

"No, we've got to be nice to the new girl. I promised my mom. Plus, she's cool. I want to get to know her! Come on." Casey grabbed my elbow and began pulling me along behind her.

"Casey, okay. Enough. I'm coming! You don't have to drag me!" I shook my arm free and Casey gave me a look.

"What?" I said huffily. "I just don't want to be

dragged like a little kid!" I also didn't want it to look like Casey was making me go say hi to this Ria person, even if that was the truth. It would just look bad.

"Whatevs," said Casey with a shrug, turning away.

I sighed and followed her, feeling like kind of a loser now. As we got closer to Ria, I could see there was a large group of girls surrounding her, and she was showing them images on her phone.

No one seemed to be eating, and I glanced around for the lunch monitor. We weren't supposed to be on our phones at lunch. The school wanted to make sure people ate but also that we didn't turn our brains to mush or do any, like, cyberbullying in the cafeteria.

"Hey, Ria," Casey called.

"Hey, you!" said Ria. She looked back down at her phone. "Oh, here's a good one!" she said, then she handed her phone over to Riley and the rest of the girls leaned in, oohing and aahing.

"What's up, Casey?" said Ria, grinning.

"You all set for lunch?" asked Casey, all smiley and upbeat.

"Yeah! I've got my lunch bag right here," Ria said. "Is it okay if we all sit here together? These girls also asked me to sit with them." She laughed. "My papí was right! Bellgrove *is* the friendliest town in America!"

"We aim to please!" said Casey, swinging her lunch bag onto the table.

Ria was smiling at me. We hadn't actually met yet.

"Hey there!" she said. "I'm Maria. Ria for short."

"Hi, I'm Lindsay," I said quietly.

Ria was so outgoing, it kind of intimidated me, made me quieter.

"Hi, Lindsay. I saw you in study hall. It's nice to finally meet you!"

"Ria, tell us about this one!" said Michelle, interrupting with Ria's phone.

"Are we staying here?" I asked Casey quietly so that everyone else wouldn't hear.

"Yeah?" replied Casey, like, *duh?*

"Okay," I said.

I put my bag on the table and sat down. I had expected Casey to sit next to me, but instead she chose to sit across from me and next to Ria.

I fought back the twinge of annoyance; it was easier for me and Casey to talk if she were across from me anyway.

I unpacked the food I had made for myself this

morning and began to eat while Casey engaged in all the conversation around us.

"Ria, wow! Your family is so talented!" Riley was saying.

"Thanks!" said Ria. "I didn't get any of the talent, though. I'm all thumbs."

I wondered what the talent was that they were talking about.

"Wow! Look at this one!" sighed Michelle. "It's dreamy!"

Ria glanced back at the phone and nodded. "Oh yeah. I loved that one."

I was watching them all while I ate, but I'd be darned if I was going to ask Ria what it was that her family did. But of course, Casey didn't hold back.

"What is everyone staring at?" she said, unwrapping what I knew would be a tuna fish sandwich and taking a bite.

Casey's mom stuck to a strict weekly lunch menu. Would Ria be able to predict what Casey would have in her lunch cooler on any given day? I think not! But I could!

"My family's Instagram for their business," Ria explained.

She hoisted a Japanese lunch box onto the table. It was a small tower of adorable assorted mini food containers in pretty pastel colors, all held together with a wide, hot-pink rubber band.

"Cool lunch box!" Casey squealed, before either of us could ask what Ria's family's business was.

"Thanks," said Ria. "I got it at Rotofugi, this cool Japanese collectible store back in Chicago."

She began to open the compartments and wonderful aromas started drifting across the table.

Everyone turned at the delicious smells and began chattering at once. "Ria! What's in that?! What's this one? What's that one?" they asked.

"My mamí is a really good cook," she answered with a laugh. "This is *arroz con habichuelas*, and these are *empanadillas*. They are all Puerto Rican specialties! I'm originally from Puerto Rico!" she said.

"Wow! You're from another country. That's so glamorous!" sighed Riley.

Ria chuckled. "Actually, Puerto Rico is part of the United States. We're a territory. I bet it becomes an official state soon though."

I had thought the same thing as Riley, and now I was glad I hadn't opened my mouth.

I watched as Ria dug into her food and was super friendly with everyone. She was so confident and breezy, it made me feel like *I* was the new kid and *she* was the queen bee of Bellgrove. This was not a great feeling.

Most of the other girls had to dash off to a yearbook meeting, and soon Ria, Casey, and I were the only ones left at the table.

There were still five minutes left in our lunch period, and while normally lunch felt way too short, today it somehow seemed way too long.

"So tell us about where you're from! Like, how long did you live in Puerto Rico and how long in Chicago?" asked Casey. Her voice was full of excitement.

That annoyed me because Ria was new and exciting. I'm just the same-old, same-old Lindsay, her BFF since the week we were born in the same hospital.

Ria gave us a quick overview, filling us in on her first two years of life in Puerto Rico, then her family's move to Chicago.

"Lindsay has family from Chicago too! And she's always dreamed of living there! Her mom was from there and her grandma still lives there," Casey interjected.

She was only trying to include me in the conversation, I knew, but it annoyed me. Like, I could speak for myself. Plus, I didn't want this new girl knowing all my hopes and dreams on day one.

Ria smiled brightly at me, hinting for me to share more about myself, but I took another bite of apple and fake-smiled through the crunch.

"Does your mom go back all the time? Please tell me yes, since I left behind so many people and things I love!" said Ria.

My heart sank and Casey looked aghast. I usually didn't have to tell people my mom was dead. Everyone in Bellgrove already knew.

Casey put her hand on top of mine and spoke for me. Earlier today, this would have really gotten on my nerves, but suddenly I was grateful for Casey's outgoingness.

"Lindsay's mom passed away a couple of years ago. She was awesome. She was actually the art teacher here."

Ria's eyebrows knit together in sorrow and her brown eyes were warm and sympathetic.

"Oh, no! I'm so sorry, Lindsay. That's terrible. I saw the mural in the hall. Was that for your mom? It's beautiful. She must have been really special."

I nodded and waited for the familiar lump in my throat to appear. I can be fine 90 percent of the time and then one random comment can make me want to bawl my eyes out. But thankfully, today with Ria, it didn't happen.

Casey kept talking, covering for me even though she didn't actually need to. It was nice but a tad annoying all of a sudden.

"Yes, her mom was the best. And she was an amazing artist. Lindsay's also a great artist," she babbled.

"Not really. You're the great artist around here!" I said modestly.

Really?" Ria asked, turning to Casey. "What do you do? Draw? Paint?"

Casey began to chatter on about sketching and photography; she even showed Ria a photo of the portrait she'd recently done of my mom.

"Wow! You're so talented!' said Ria admiringly. "I've got to tell my papí. He's looking for someone local to photograph my parents' work—maybe it could be you!"

"Oh, wow. That would be so cool! What is their work?" asked Casey.

Ria smiled. "It's a cake shop, called the Rich Port Cakery. My parents are kind of cake artists. They make spectacular, arty, themed cakes for special occasions. They're opening a new branch here; that's why we moved. They baked all the things I brought in this morning."

"Is Rich your dad's name?" I asked.

Ria giggled. "No, it's a play on Puerto Rico, which means 'rich port' in Spanish."

"Oh. Right," I said, my face aflame.

Casey covered for me. "A cake shop in Bellgrove! How awesome!" she crowed. Then she looked at me, her eyes shining. "You two have a lot in common!" she added.

I was still embarrassed. "We do?" I asked.

Brilliant, Linds, I thought sarcastically.

Ria smiled at me. "Great! Like what?"

Casey took over again. "Lindsay's family owns the Park View Table restaurant—our number one place to eat in town. And inside, they have the Donut Dreams counter, where they make the most incredible, mouthwatering donuts you've ever tried. You should see the lines in the morning. Right, Linds?" Casey said, giving me a huge smile.

"Right," I agreed.

Her compliments helped me recover from my embarrassment.

But Ria was smacking her forehead now. "Duh! The Park? Donut Dreams? Our families are friends! I think your family is part of why we're here!"

"What?" I asked.

Ria was nodding. "I forget the details, but I'm gonna find out. Our families are friends. That much I know. So now we're friends too! Yay!"

Ria and Casey beamed at me.

I squeaked out a smile and nodded. "Yeah. Friends," I agreed.

But in my heart, what I felt was another story. How could my family possibly be friends with this glamorous stranger who was trying to steal my best friend? One thing was for sure: I would not be fawning over the Rich Port Cakery Instagram like everyone else in my grade. And I needed to get to the bottom of this supposed family friendship.